A touch sparked against the skin of her ankle like a live electrical wire. She struggled and tried to scream, but every movement met an avalanche of warm tar, stifling, smothering.

Hauling in a lungful of air, she now tried to scream herself awake, to burst through the curtain of sleep into the clear air of reality. But she could only croak and whimper.

Sleep was an enemy now, falling upon her like black snow. Throughout her adult life, she'd suffered dreams about the outrages she'd suffered at his hands, about the things she knew he'd done to other girls . . . The dreams had always featured bolts of bright light reflected off the blade of his knife, and spatters of red blood—somebody's blood, maybe her own. *God, how many years had she fought those dreams?*

Blood dries faster than tears . . .

His breath hit her flat in the face and nearly made her retch, for it was the breath of a meat eater, rich with the stink of the slaughterhouse. . . .

MA	MB	MC
MD	ME	MF
MG	MH	MM
MN	MO	MP
MS	MT	MW

CARNAGE

Andrew Billings

JOVE BOOKS, NEW YORK

CARNAGE

A Jove Book / published by arrangement with
the author

PRINTING HISTORY
Jove edition / September 1999

The Penguin Putnam Inc. World Wide Web site address is
http://www.penguinputnam.com

ISBN: 0-515-12564-4

A JOVE BOOK®
Jove Books are published by The Berkley Publishing Group,
a division of Penguin Putnam Inc.,
375 Hudson Street, New York, New York 10014.
JOVE and the "J" design
are trademarks belonging to Penguin Putnam Inc.

PRINTED IN THE UNITED STATES OF AMERICA

10 9 8 7 6 5 4 3 2 1

Prologue

Blood dries faster than tears.

The girl heard the words in her head as the first hint of dawn crept into the sky above northeast Portland—her grandmother's hushed murmur, like a whisper through a curtain. *Blood dries faster* . . . a lament for the fallen boys of some long-ago war, she thought, but who could say for sure? Her memory of the old woman was as faint as the morning mist.

She hurried across the athletic field of MacArthur High School, clutching the bundle to her chest. The baby was dead weight, but she couldn't think of him as dead—not yet. Less than an hour earlier his life had passed out of her with a pain that still lingered, his few strangling cries breaking her heart before fading away. In the candlelight of the cellar she'd held him in her bloody hands and tried to imagine what he might have become if she could have saved him. A doctor, maybe, or an artist. Or a cancer researcher or a teacher, someone who could have made the world a better place. But then again, he could have turned out like the one who'd fathered him. The thought made her flesh crawl.

For an excruciating moment she'd doubted whether she was strong enough to cut the cord—she feared knives and sharp blades like some people fear snakes or spiders. But eventually she'd managed, her hands moving like a robot's, and then the knife had clattered to the floor with a spattering of red.

Blood dries faster . . .

She hurried on, her heart aching, until coming to the area where MacArthur High's offensive line practiced blocking and the girls' gym classes played soccer. She quickly found what she was looking for, a cement square lying flush against the ground, with a steel plate in its center. She'd noticed it several times during gym class and had wondered what was under the plate, but had never dreamed that one day she would have occasion to look. Squatting, she rested the bundle on her knees and used both hands to pry the plate out of its cement frame. Looking down into the oblong hole, she saw a water pressure gauge, and next to it, a valve wheel that presumably controlled the sprinkler system in this section of the athletic field. Plenty of room here for a small bundle, just as she'd hoped.

She laid the baby in the hole and lingered over him a moment, a sob squeaking out of her throat. She knew that sooner or later a groundskeeper would remove the plate in order to turn on the sprinklers, reach down to twist the valve handle and discover the bundle. Then he would peel away the stained doll's blanket, find the moldering lump. And, of course, he would notify the authorities. The newspapers would publish grim stories with lurid headlines, and the cops would investigate. But the girl would be far away by then, beyond the reach of the horror that had engulfed her life, beyond shame and vengeance. Someone, she dared to hope, would arrange to give the child a decent burial.

Crouching over the open grave, she said her silent good-byes—to the world she'd known, this school, her friends. To her mother, who would scream a prayer heavenward, beseeching God to bring her only daughter back. And to this little one whose existence she'd concealed under bulky, baggy clothes, ever smiling over the anguish and pretending that life was simpler than it was.

Blood dries . . .

She bolted upright. She felt the eyes of someone watching, a familiar feeling. *His* eyes, probing her, invading her. She tried to swallow, but couldn't work up any spit, tried to make herself believe that her imagination had gone wild. He was here, he'd followed her—it was as certain as the rising sun. No way to know if he'd seen her bury the child.

She shoved the steel plate back into place, lurched to her feet and fled toward the wood line at the south end of the field, where kids gathered during lunch hour to smoke dope and drink beer.

Now the woods lay dark and dead-still. She wriggled through a rip in the chain-link fence that ran along the campus boundary and hid herself in the nest of shadows.

She felt safe for the moment, deep within that nest. Staring out through the mist, she saw no sign of the one she'd loved, loathed, feared. Would he kill her, she wondered, if he discovered what she'd done, if he found his baby? Would he cut her throat as he'd done to Mandrake, her beloved old calico cat, just to prove he could kill in the service of his peculiar, twisted notion of justice? The image of his knife flashed in her mind, razor-bright and lethal, and her pulse thudded in her temples like a fist against a pillow.

Hours later, on a bus bound for Seattle, she rested her forehead against the window glass and tried to imagine what lay ahead. She felt woefully unprepared—a sixteen-year-old girl without money or high school diploma, no skills, no prospects. More than once she asked herself why she bothered to run, whether her life was worth all this trouble. Even if she managed to find her father in Seattle, she couldn't be sure that he would help her, for he hadn't set eyes on her since she was a toddler. And without this man who had abandoned her long ago, she had no one.

Blood dries faster than tears. An innocent old lie, she now knew. At her tender age the girl had already discovered that some tears never dry at all.

One

A Lincoln limousine glided to a halt at an address on B Street N.E. in Washington, D.C., where a brick town house stood behind a rank of steel pikes. The U.S. Capitol was only a few blocks away, the Supreme Court even closer. On this street some of the most powerful people in the world cast their shadows, a street where houses stood like brick fortresses—dignified and gated, the homes of congressmen and senior congressional staffers, the offices of lobbyists and interest groups.

Six passengers piled out of the car and trooped to the gate, on which hung a simple brass plaque: INTERACTS, INC. They waited a moment in the January chill, their hands thrust deep into the pockets of their mohair overcoats, their breath rising in hoary puffs. Their designated spokesman muttered something into the intercom, and a security attendant buzzed them in. They walked to the entryway, passing directly beneath a second-floor window, where a man waited, watching through the naked branches of a cherry tree.

He knew them, knew their names. They were executives of three major industrial interest groups—the North American Association of Meat Processors, the National Association of Fur Producers, and the International Council of Cosmetics Manufacturers. They represented the power of international brand names, and they weren't people to trifle with. They all sported hundred-dollar haircuts and two-hundred-dollar ties. They were his clients.

Richardson Zanto was tall and still hard-muscled at fifty, his graying hair clipped to a military bristle. Glancing into a mirror on the wall of his office, he straightened his tie, squared his shoulders and whispered something to the reflected image—"gravity, simplicity, piety," the ancient Latin values that had guided his life. It was a private mantra that he never uttered aloud, an old habit that he supposed made him something of an anachronism in 1997, in an age when nothing was simple anymore, when hardly anyone was truly pious, when gravity showed up only on the faces of news anchors. A lifelong student of classical Rome, he'd emulated the great figures of that era, the men who had enacted laws still in use and had created architecture still copied today, whose poetry still moved people after two thousand years. Sometimes Richardson Zanto believed that he'd been born two millennia too late, for he felt closer to those long-dead Roman knights than to anyone now living.

He'd once considered himself a soldier, a patriot, back when his only client was his country. He'd worked in the CIA's Special Operations Division during the Cold War, and he'd done things that still gave him bad dreams. In those days Uncle Whiskers had needed men willing to get their hands wet, and Zanto had answered the bell for twenty-one years, because this was his duty, his calling. In 1990, however, he'd read the writing on the crumbling Berlin Wall: World communism was collapsing under its own dead weight, the Cold War was ending, and the CIA was about to lose its principal opponent. The corridors of Langley had crackled with whispers about cutbacks and layoffs. Insiders had expected a disaster on the scale of the Stansfield Turner purge in 1974 and the Jimmy Carter purge in 1977, when thousands of veteran CIA officers ended up on the street, cashiered for their lack of enthusiasm over détente. So, Zanto had gotten out in order to spare himself the ignominy of being handed his walking papers.

He'd joined InterActs, Inc., a private espionage boutique that specialized in commercial spying and subversion. Its operatives were former intelligence officers who had left the service of Uncle Whiskers, some under their own steam, others with the Uncle's shoe print on their asses. As a veteran of the Special Operations Division, Richardson Zanto had fit right in.

He locked the door of his small private office and went down to the elegant main conference room, where the newly arrived

clients were munching croissants and schmoozing with InterActs'
aged founder, Brenton Bryson, himself a CIA legend and a casualty of the Turner purge in '74. The old man grinned when he
saw Zanto, waved him to the head of the table, then stood up
slowly and cleared his throat to signal the start of the proceedings.

"You've all met Rick Zanto, our lead man on your project.
He's just flown in from the field in order to brief you personally.
Insofar as your time is valuable, I'll ask him to begin. Rick . . ."

Zanto forced a smile and made eye contact with each of the
six clients. All were younger than he, all smug and cocksure. Not
a woman among them, or a black or a Hispanic. Political cor-
rectness went only so far in the New World Order. He opened
his laptop computer, plugged it into a jack on the edge of the
table and snapped it on. Donned his half-lenses, took a sip of
water.

"Good morning, gentlemen, it's a pleasure to see you again.
My purpose today is to report on the first quarter's activity with
respect to your project . . ."

He tapped a key on the computer, and a video screen opened
behind him, on which appeared the mug shots of a couple in their
mid-thirties, Vera Kemmis and Ian Prather, both English subjects,
according to the captions. Kemmis, a full-faced woman with auburn hair and defiant green eyes, stared level into the camera, her
upper lip twisted into a convict's smirk. Prather looked like a
movie star with his craggy grin and layered hair, his perfect teeth
and regular features.

The pair were key figures in the ultramilitant Front for Animal
Freedom, the most violent arm of the international animal rights
movement. They'd entered the U.S. illegally six months earlier,
having waged a two-year terror campaign against meat-packing
plants and fur producers throughout western Canada. Each had a
long record of violent activities against the meat industry, the
cosmetics industry, fur producers, and the medical research community.

The assembled representatives of industry had hired InterActs
to track Kemmis and Prather, to find out what they were up to in
America, and then to determine how best to neutralize them without creating a stir. The clients were less worried about the material
damage the pair might do than the public's reaction to their antics.
Widespread soul-searching among consumers over things done
to animals in the production of meat, clothing, and cosmetics

couldn't be good for business. Such soul-searching might change buying habits or militate for restrictive laws and regulations, neither of which the industry wanted.

"We've confirmed," Zanto announced, "that Prather and Kemmis have established close contact with the animal rights community here in the U.S. They've settled in Seattle, where they've gotten close to the power structure of the League Opposed to Cruelty to Animals. We've confirmed what many in your industries have suspected for years, that LOCA provides direct support to terrorist activities by the Front for Animal Freedom and other such groups, a fact that may have some propaganda value—"

"Let's not call it propaganda," the clients' designated spokesman deadpanned, interrupting. "Let's call it public relations, okay?"

Zanto smiled, ground his teeth, soldiered on. "They live in a safe house in the Ballard district of the city, courtesy of none other than Lauren Bowman, who—as you know—happens to be LOCA's national treasurer and chief fund-raiser. They've also begun preparations to 'liberate' animals and call public attention to the killing of animals for profit."

The video screen now showed a prosperous-looking woman in her mid-to-late thirties, dark-haired and slender, getting into a Range Rover. She had sharp, intelligent eyes and a look of nervous energy about her. Subsequent shots showed her in gesticulating conversation with Kemmis and Prather, the three of them hunkered over a table in some swank-looking restaurant.

"We have reason to believe," Zanto continued, "that Kemmis and Prather are preparing a major escalation of their program, taking it to a new level. We know that they're getting direct help from LOCA and other mainstream organizations, from people like Ms. Bowman here. If we play our cards right, we think we can prevent a significant act of terrorism."

The clients' designated spokesman thrummed his manicured fingers on the table and stared at Zanto. "A *significant* act of terrorism. What does that mean, exactly?"

"We're expecting something on the order of the demolition of a major laboratory facility or a meat-processing facility, based on the information we've gathered. Chances are they'll run several smaller operations to get tuned up for the big one."

"You're absolutely sure about all this?"

Old Man Bryson spoke up. "We've developed an inside source who's very reliable, someone close to Lauren Bowman herself. Naturally, we must keep this person's identity a secret, at least for the time being. Suffice it to say that this individual has agreed to keep us apprised of Kemmis and Prather's activities."

Zanto winced, wished that the old man hadn't revealed this much. LOCA was a formidable interest group that raised ten million dollars a year from animal lovers nationwide, not all of which it spent on lobbying legislators. Zanto assumed that LOCA possessed the wherewithal to do what his own clients had done— hire spies. LOCA could have planted someone in the offices of the North American Association of Meat Processors or either of the other clients, someone who might overhear a whispered conversation in the executive suite about an "inside source" close to Lauren Bowman. Vera Kemmis and Ian Prather might thus learn of the informer in their midst, and months of hard, expensive work would go down the drain.

A brief discussion ensued over risks, costs, and benefits of several different scenarios, among them the option of simply alerting the FBI to Kemmis' and Prather's whereabouts and hoping for an arrest on immigration charges, followed by extradition to Canada. But Bryson warned that federal enforcement agencies were unlikely to give a high priority to a matter like this one, inasmuch as the world was full of honest-to-goodness terrorists who blew up airliners and machine-gunned busloads of tourists— people more deserving of government attention, in other words. He convinced the clients that continued private surveillance of Prather and Kemmis offered the greatest potential benefit with minimal risk. InterActs would move forcefully when necessary to prevent any major damage, he assured them.

"We'll forge ahead, then," said the clients' spokesman, glancing around the table for his colleagues' acquiescence, "even though this project is getting expensive. There's a limit, you know, as to how long we can support this level of activity."

"Understood," Zanto replied. "We don't know all the particulars yet, but we believe that Kemmis and Prather will make their move before spring. We'll notify you the minute we learn anything substantial."

An hour later, Richardson Zanto was en route back to Seattle aboard a commercial jet. At thirty thousand feet above the Minnesota lake country, he closed the book in his lap, a commentary on Ammianus Marcellinus, the great historian of Rome in its decline. The book contained numerous passages in classical Latin, a language that sometimes gave him a headache, beautiful though it was.

He made a decision and placed a call to a telephone in downtown Seattle. A male voice answered, merely repeating the number—an answering machine, with no invitation to leave a message. Zanto waited for the beep.

"We're still a go," he said, without preamble. "What you and I talked about before, the flies on the wall and the mice in the corners—let's do it. We'll use our fish. Go ahead and make the arrangements. I'll be landing in two hours."

Fish was InterActs' code for "informer."

Two

At 2:55 A.M. on Thursday, May 29, a midnight-blue Econoline van swung into a wooded lane near Seattle's Volunteer Park and halted, its lights off. Crouching in the cargo bed of the van, Lauren Bowman thought, *I'm crossing the Rubicon. I'm about to commit a crime, become a criminal . . .*

A young woman huddled next to her, a comrade in the Front for Animal Freedom. Even in this poor light Lauren could see that the girl's eyes were wide with apprehension, for never before had the local FAF cell launched an operation against a target with this high level of security. In the front seat of the van a man listened for a moment to a portable police scanner, then turned to face those in the rear. His voice was cold, yet reassuring. He'd trained them, drilled them for this moment. They were his soldiers.

"Once we're inside, remember not to say anyone's name out loud, in case of audio recorders," he said. "Keep calm, stay together, and take your cues from me. We do this right, we score big for the movement, and nobody gets hurt. Let's go, then."

They pulled on ski masks, rubber gloves, and rucksacks. They scrambled out of the van, having earlier taped down the buttons that would have turned on the dome lights when the doors opened.

This cell of the FAF was an unlikely mix. Lauren Bowman was a prominent businesswoman whose face had appeared frequently on the business and society pages of the *Seattle Times*. Megan Reiner, the girl who'd crouched next to her in the van, was a philosophy graduate student at the University of Washington. Rod Welton, the driver, was a juvenile probation officer in his late forties, a Vietnam vet who wore his silvering hair in a short ponytail.

Their leader, Ian Prather, was a rangy Englishman whose accent resembled Michael Caine's. A fifth team member, Vera Kemmis, had arrived at the target an hour earlier in order to prepare the way.

The raiders unloaded the van and trotted toward the ornate wrought-iron gate that guarded their target, each lugging an armful of empty pet carriers suitable for cats and small dogs. Their rucksacks contained pliers, wire cutters, flashlights, spray paint, and pepper mace. Rod Welton carried a ten-pound sledgehammer, and Lauren had a Sony camcorder on a strap over her shoulder. She would soon learn that Ian Prather carried another tool under his dark sweat gear: a nine-millimeter Glock pistol.

The Pacific Northwest BioCenter stood at the end of the lane, a grand old Queen Anne built of gray and white brick, surrounded by hardwoods and cedars. Twenty years earlier a wealthy Seattle family had gifted the house to the Pacific Northwest Biomedical Research Foundation, which had converted it to a laboratory facility and made it the foundation headquarters. The *Seattle Times* had recently reported on a study taking place here, directed by the renowned Dr. Gregory Kirsch, into the growth of connective tissue in the spinal nerves of mammals. Dr. Kirsch's goal was to restore function to the paralyzed limbs of humans who had suffered spinal trauma. His project, like the others under way at the BioCenter, made extensive use of laboratory animals, mostly rats and rhesus monkeys.

Lauren saw the security camera mounted on the brick gatepost, its tiny red light having gone black. A sign on the gatepost read:

WARNING!
These premises are guarded by ProGuard Inc.
Intrusion will bring Armed Response.

Earlier scouting had revealed that ProGuard normally posted no on-site patrolmen at the BioCenter, but relied instead on passive infrared motion detectors, acoustic sensors, and a computer link with the security firm's headquarters in downtown Seattle. Prather and Kemmis had driven past the mansion a dozen times in daylight to take photographs, study the comings and goings of employees, and record the regular rounds of mobile ProGuard patrols. They'd analyzed the photos in order to determine the likely locations of terminal boxes, sensors, and data lines. They'd even tailed the ProGuard patrols in order to learn how far they ranged both by day and by night, thus to gauge their reaction time to an intrusion at the BioCenter.

Vera Kemmis had scaled the fence exactly thirty minutes before "zero hour." She'd found the power and data lines that ran from the terminal boxes to the sensors and camera at the gate. A school-trained technician, she'd known exactly what to look for, and had cut the links at precisely the appointed moment. Seconds later Lauren and the others gained entry courtesy of Rod Welton and his sledgehammer.

For now, the computer at ProGuard's downtown headquarters behaved as if nothing was amiss, but the raiders couldn't afford to dawdle: After three minutes the computer would discover it had lost the coded signal from the sensors at the front gate of the BioCenter, an interval that allowed for innocent glitches and routine power interruptions. Following that interval an alarm would sound, and armed responders would head for the scene. An alert would also go to the Seattle Police Department. Based on their reconnaissance, Prather and Kemmis had estimated that the civilian responders wouldn't arrive for five to seven minutes after the alarm sounded, which meant that the raiders had eight to ten minutes to get in, do their thing, and get out.

Lauren Bowman and her comrades jogged toward the mansion, a black hulk against the night sky. Stars peered through rips in the cloud cover, and a chill breeze sliced through Lauren's windbreaker—too cold for May. An hour earlier rain had fallen, leaving the paving stones of the drive glistening and slippery. Lauren lost her footing once, dropped a pet carrier, and caused a clatter.

"There," Prather whispered, shining a flashlight through the latticed panes next to the front door. "Passive infrared motion detector on the ceiling of the foyer. They've probably got long-range acoustics in the labs." He pulled a walkie-talkie from a holster and called Kemmis, who'd embarked on a hunt for the main security terminal. "Snoop, this is Creep. I'm at the front entrance. I've got a PIR on the ceiling inside the door, and it's still blinking red. I'd say there's at least one LRA in each work area, probably cameras, too. What're you gonna do about it, love?''

Lauren heard the radio break squelch, heard Vera Kemmis' rough whisper. ''I've just now located the main data line, but it's thirty feet off the bloody ground—tucked under the eaves of the south wall. I can't get to it without mountain-climbing gear.''

''You can't kill the indoor sensors—is that it, then?''

''Look, you've only got another minute and a half till the main computer sounds an alarm. I say bull your way in, do what you can, and get the fuck out, never mind the ruddy PIRs and LRAs.''

''Got it. Go back to the van and bring it round to the front door, like we planned. We're going in.''

Lauren's heart pounded as Rod Welton demolished the glossy hardwood doors with his sledgehammer—a half-dozen noisy blows. No Klaxon sounded, no sirens. Lauren knew, however, that silent alarms had already raced to ProGuard's computer, that armed responders were now leaving their regular patrol routes to head for the BioCenter.

Ian Prather led the way into the foyer, followed by Welton, their flashlight beams roaming over the walls. Megan Reiner looked back at Lauren and hesitated for a heartbeat or two, her eyes huge inside the holes of the ski mask. Lauren herself experienced a fresh attack of old misgivings. What was she doing here, for the love of God? Getting caught would mean humiliation, long and ugly legal proceedings, even jail time. She stood to lose all she'd worked so hard to achieve—her fortune, her standing in the community, everything.

She'd struggled through it long before now, of course, fought down the fear. A time comes when you can't play it safe any longer, when you need to put your butt on the line alongside the real soldiers. For Lauren Bowman, that time was now. Writing letters to congressmen, hosting fund-raisers, and giving speeches weren't enough anymore. She needed to do something tangible, something direct. Nothing less than the fate of the earth depended on the willingness of people like herself to make a stand against the madness. She believed that with all her heart.

She scrambled into the foyer after her comrades, chasing their flashlight beams. Then she heard something—footfalls, a soft thump. She glanced back toward the entryway and saw . . . it—a man-shape darting through the shattered door, swimming into the shadow along one wall. Lauren's gut roiled.

Kemmis, she thought, letting her breath out. But no—Ian had sent Vera to fetch the van. Who, then? A security guard? She remembered that ProGuard hadn't posted on-site security guards at this facility. She beamed her flashlight into the shadows where the thing had gone, and saw . . . a potted palm, a Greek statue, and a padded settee for visitors. No sign of a security guard or anyone else.

Half-convinced her imagination had played a nasty trick, Lauren clambered after the others, the pet carriers bouncing against her hips. Ian Prather halted the team at a door marked NERVE TRAUMA LABORATORY. He tried the knob, found it locked, and motioned to Rod Welton, who stepped forward and opened it with the sledgehammer.

"Crude, but effective," Welton whispered to Lauren, chuckling. She started to tell him about the movement she'd seen in the foyer, but before she could get the first word out Welton lunged into the lab behind the others. Lauren followed, not wanting to spend even a few seconds alone in the corridor.

A security light over the door imbued the room with a reddish glow. Glassed-in cabinets lined the walls, holding a vast array of laboratory equipment—beakers, tubing, jars of chemicals, and specimens. Long countertops stood in rows, each with a pair of sinks. Everywhere were computer terminals, microscopes, and centrifuges. A surgical table occupied one corner, together with anesthesiology gear—a veterinary OR.

Decades ago this room had been a library or a parlor, a place of innocent fun and laughter, but now it was a torture chamber, a place where blameless animals died hideous deaths. Anger welled up inside Lauren, dousing all traces of the misgivings she'd suffered moments earlier.

Again Prather motioned to Welton, who went to work with the sledgehammer, smashing computer monitors, racks of test tubes and beakers and centrifuges, his gray ponytail swinging wildly. Prather then led Lauren and Megan through a door marked LIVE TEST SUBJECTS and into a room that had a cement floor with a screened drain in the center. Cages of wire mesh stood in stacks, row upon row, to a height of six feet. The air stank of antiseptic and urine.

Lauren instantly became aware of a low rustling, the consternation of rodents. Pinprick eyes reflected the beams of their flashlights, and at the far end of the room a monkey screamed. Lauren saw twitching, whiskered noses and an occasional tail whipping through metal mesh. An old image flashed through her mind, that of a ragged calico cat she'd befriended as a kid. *Mandrake* . . .

"Look at this," Megan said, shining her light into a cage at eye-level. A tag identified the resident as "Pepe: Subject 6704," who'd received "surgical alteration" for an experimental attempt to regenerate a severed spinal nerve. Pepe was a large white rat with a pink nose and tail; he could only pull himself around with his front legs, because his rear legs hung limp and useless. A bare patch of shaved skin on his back bore witness to surgical maiming in the name of science.

"Let's not waste time!" Ian Prather barked. "Get as many into the carriers as will fit. Start over here. I'll handle the monkeys . . ."

Lauren saw two large cages against the far wall, each of which held a rhesus monkey. One of them, "Simon," according to the tag affixed to his cage, wore a plaster cast that covered much of his torso. He cowered in a corner of the cage, his small, sweet face twitching with panic. Clearly, his lower body was paralyzed, his keepers having performed an operation to make him a cripple. Now they were trying to "cure" him. Lauren assumed that they had similar plans for his neighbor, a slightly smaller female whose tag identified her as "Nora."

Lauren dropped the pet carriers and switched on her camcorder, tried to focus the viewfinder through a blur of hot tears. She starting shooting footage of the monkeys and crippled rats. This was part of her mission—to get pictures for use in underground publications and the Internet, to show the barbarity that occurred in the name of research. LOCA's national magazine, *Animal Realm*, would publish the best of the pictures, claiming that anonymous raiders had sent them.

She packed away the camcorder, helped with the evacuation, and the minutes flew by. Tragically, the raiders lacked both the time and wherewithal to evacuate all the animals. They'd managed to transfer the monkeys and nearly fifty rats from the cages to the carriers to the van before Prather called a halt to the operation. Fifty or more rats remained in the lab, all chittering and scrabbling at the wire walls of their cages, as if pleading not to be left behind.

"All right, open up the other cages, and we're off!" Prather commanded, waving his flashlight. "Those who're left will have to take their chances in the wild."

"We can't just *leave* them," Megan Reiner protested. "They're domestic animals. They won't know how to survive out there."

"They're *rats*, love. They'll head for the storm drains, like all rats do. We've been over this before, haven't we? They'll be fine down there, believe me."

"We can't do this!" Megan insisted, sounding like an angry teenager. "They'll starve. . . ."

Lauren went to Megan's side. "He's right," she whispered. "They're better off in the sewers than here. We talked about it, and this is what we decided, remember? At least they'll have a chance down there, but *here* . . ."

"Goddamn it, it's cruel to just turn them loose to fend for themselves."

Lauren glanced at her watch and saw that they'd used up their allotted time and then some. ProGuard and the cops would arrive any second. "We've got to go," she said, steering Megan toward the door. But the girl pulled away and started throwing open the cages, apparently having concluded that this was indeed the best she could do under the circumstances. After opening each door, she spanked the wire mesh to roust the inmates out. "Go!" she shouted. "Get out! Go!"

Lauren ran back into the main lab, then outside to the corridor. Welton had just finished spraying a crude FAF on a wood-paneled wall with a red paint can, the signature of the Front for Animal Freedom. Lauren dug into her rucksack for her spray paint, but Prather waved her off—no time.

Then it happened. The overhead lights came on, and a man stepped around a corner of the corridor, a pistol in one hand, a huge flashlight in the other. He wore a uniform that covered his potbelly like a sausage skin. He leveled the pistol at them and shouted, "Freeze! Armed security!"

Lauren's heart tried to climb into her mouth, and she knew that the shadow she'd seen earlier had been no mind-trick. During the next few seconds a bleak scenario played out in her head—police hauling her away, steel doors slamming behind her, investigators bombarding her with questions, lurid headlines over her picture in the paper. Worse still was a crushing sense of failure, knowing that the animals she'd tried to rescue would go back to the lab, where the torture and killing would continue as if nothing had happened, as if no one had cared enough to act.

A shout came from the foyer, an obscenity, Vera Kemmis' unmistakable voice. The uniformed man whirled around to face her, and Ian Prather went down on one knee, a pistol in his fist. The uniformed man whirled back again, saw Prather's gun and fired wildly. Blinded by the muzzle flashes, Lauren *felt* the bullets hiss past her cheek and slam into the wall behind her. Prather's weapon roared, spat flame, and the uniformed man's head exploded.

Lauren screamed as the man went hard to the carpeted floor, where he flailed and quivered and went still as stone. Horror washed over her as she ran to him, bent over him, tried to cradle him in her arms—the horror of killing any living thing, not to mention a human being. Ian Prather had lied to her, she now understood. She'd forced him to promise that no one would carry any deadly weapon on this raid, a condition that she'd imposed in return for furnishing a safe house and a sizable sum of money to support the operation. Ian Prather had *lied*, this man who she'd let touch her, whom she herself had touched. ·

Prather grabbed her arm and pulled her toward the foyer, Rod Welton following close on her heels. Lauren remembered Megan, still with the rats. She fought Prather's grip on her arm, shouted the girl's name, shouted it again.

"I'm here!" Megan answered, but she seemed too far back, too far away. A siren whooped in the distance. Rats were everywhere, newly freed, scurrying in files of white puffs along the edges of the corridor.

Into the van now, Ian pushing Lauren, shoving her through the rear door into the cargo area. The air was alive with the chittering of rodents, the screams of monkeys. Lauren huddled against the plastic pet carriers and felt something on her face, the swipe of a rat's tail through an air hole. Her clothes were sticky with the dead man's blood, and the darkness was like a blanket over her head. Vera Kemmis shouted, *"Go!"* and the cargo doors slammed home.

"Wait!" Welton shouted. "Megan's not here!"

"Jesus Christ!" Vera Kemmis swore, sliding out of the passenger's seat. "Where the bloody hell is she?" Kemmis darted away, and Lauren imagined her dashing through the corridor of the BioCenter, her ropy legs pumping like pistons. But mere seconds later Kemmis returned, much too soon.

"Hit it!" Ian Prather shouted, for the sirens were coming nearer with every heartbeat.

Lauren scrambled to her feet in the rear of the van. "Megan's still in there!" she shouted. "Christ, we can't just leave her! Ian . . . !" Welton gunned the engine, and the van swung away from the BioCenter, heading down the curved drive, its tires thumping over the brick paving. Centrifugal force threw Lauren against the cages, and the monkeys shrieked in panic. "My God, what are you doing? Ian, tell him to stop!"

Prather wrapped an arm around her waist, steadying her, as the van careened through the front gate. Welton made a sharp right turn and headed for Volunteer Park in accordance with the escape plan. The van jounced over a curb and hurtled into the blackness, kicking up knots of turf as the night erupted with red and blue light.

Three

At 4:55 A.M. on May 29, Matthew Burgess rolled out of bed, shrugged into his sweat gear, and did his pre-run stretch in the living room of his tiny apartment above Shorty's Tavern in Ballard. From his window he could see the marina at Shorty's Landing, a thicket of booms and spars poking above a morning mist. The marina handled working boats, mostly—fishing trawlers, tugs, and cargo barges—though here or there sprouted the mast of a sleek cutter or sloop, craft built purely for fun. Beyond the marina lay Salmon Bay, which constituted the western section of the busy Lake Washington Ship Canal, its surface mirroring the lights of Magnolia, one of Seattle's nicer neighborhoods.

At Shorty's Landing the workday started early. Already Matt could hear gears grinding and diesels grumbling as crews prepared their boats to head west through the Chittenden Locks into Puget Sound. He liked getting up early and starting work, liked having a good share of the afternoon to himself after putting in his eight hours.

Before leaving his apartment, he went to the medicine cabinet and popped his daily dosage of Wellbutrin, a prescription antidepressant. He'd begun suffering clinical depression seven years ago, and for the past several years had held it at bay with a combination of medication and therapy.

He put in his daily five-mile run, a routine he'd fallen into sixteen years ago at the police academy. As usual, he jogged east on Canal Street through Ballard's maritime industrial quarter and took a breather at Gas Works Park on the north shore of Lake Union. Before heading back he gazed a moment at a Seattle skyline shrouded in mist, still glittering in the thin light of predawn—gems on gray felt, it seemed. He promised himself that someday he would capture the sight in a watercolor, or at least try.

Matt Burgess was thirty-eight and lean like a swimmer. He had rusty hair just long enough to lie down when he combed it straight back, and a red mustache that he'd started growing three years ago, on the very day he quit the Seattle Police Department. His eyes were steady and gray, his eyebrows ample and unruly, like those of all the Scotsmen on his mother's side of the family.

He did his post-run stretch at the rear of the tavern, next to an exterior stairway that led to the back door of his apartment. Rain started to fall, and a breeze kicked up from the Sound, tart with the smells of salt and diesel oil. The weather was unseasonably wet and raw. Matt headed for the stairs, eager for a hot shower and the sensation of heat soaking into his bones.

"You want some coffee or what?" someone growled behind him.

Royal Bowman, his landlord and boss, stood in the doorway of the tavern's back room, scowling against the rain. Scrawny and wind-brown at sixty-eight, Royal had wavy white hair, rheumy eyes, and a nose that someone had broken long ago in a California prison called Pelican Bay—at least this was the story he'd given out for as long as Matt had known him. He owned both the tavern and the marina, and lived in the apartment next to Matt's.

"Do I have a choice?" Matt asked.

"I need company, and you're the best I can do this early in the day. Cleo won't roll out of the fart sack for another two hours." Cleo Castillo was Royal's lover of twenty-some years—the brains of the operation, he called her.

Matt had worked for Royal since leaving the PD, doing light repair on marine diesels, sailboat maintenance and general cleanup. He appreciated the straightforward simplicity of the job, the satisfaction of toiling with his hands. He loved the marina, the bar, and the cramped apartment where he'd taken refuge after failing at his marriage and career. Royal and Cleo had become his family.

"Make it strong," he told the old man. "This is Seattle."

They sat at a table in the dusky kitchen of the tavern, drinking a pot of U-Ban that Royal had brewed potent enough to grow hair in the bottom of a mug—a far cry from the high-end espresso for which Seattle was renowned. The rain of May thrummed against a metal chimney over the grill, like a constant roll on a snare drum. The place smelled of fried food and cigarettes.

"Hear the morning news yet?" Royal asked.

"I never listen to the news. You know that. I don't even know what day it is."

"It's Thursday, the twenty-ninth. Somebody tossed a big scientific laboratory up in Capitol Hill in the wee hours. Animal-rights people, they say. Went in and tore the place up, let loose a bunch of rats and monkeys. Fella got himself killed, security guard or some such."

"Christ. They catch anybody?"

"Nah. Security guard was an older guy—had a couple of grandkids, they say. Something like three hundred Gs in damage. Makes you wonder, doesn't it? People killin' a man in order to save animals. Seems to me somebody's got his priorities mixed up." Royal sipped his coffee and lit a Camel. The bags under his eyes had purpled like bruises. He kept quiet a long while, the smoke of his cigarette ribboning around his thin face. "I've got a bad feeling about this thing, Matt," he said finally.

"Oh?"

"I think I might know someone who's involved."

Matthew Burgess and Royal Bowman went back more than twenty years, back to when Matt's own father wore the uniform of a Seattle cop and patrolled this stretch of the canal. Officer Chuck Burgess and Royal had become friends. On his days off, Chuck had often brought Matt to Shorty's for fish and chips. In later years the two of them had regularly tipped brewskies here together, listening to Royal's stories of his younger days, his adventures on the seas and in ports throughout the world. Never in those twenty-odd years had Matt heard Royal say anything about animal rights, good or bad, until just now.

"You know somebody in the movement, is that what you're telling me?" Matt asked.

"What I'm trying to say is, I think maybe . . . I think my daughter might be mixed up in this."

"Your daughter? Skipper, I never knew you had a daughter."

"Yeah, well—there's a lot about me you don't know."

This was true, Matt realized suddenly. He'd known Royal as a storyteller, a weaver of tall tales, a drinking buddy. He'd come to love the old man's generous spirit and crusty commentary on everything from foreign affairs to sailboat maintenance. But about Royal's *life*—his youth, his early career, his failed love affairs—Matt knew next to nothing.

Royal got slowly to his feet and went to the cooler to fetch a pan of fish scraps. He tossed the scraps out the back door, where the usual gang of bedraggled cats had rendezvoused in the lee of the building for their morning handout. Sitting down again, Royal looked decrepit and old. Lately his pained appearance had begun to worry Matt.

"I never told you this, but years ago I had a wife down in Portland, before I went to the joint. Her name was Marlene, met her in an amusement park, standing in line for corn dogs. Sweet thing, pretty as a flower in those days. We got married in a lather and nine months later had ourselves a baby . . ."

A little girl, Royal explained. Born in the summer of 1960, named Lauren, big-eyed and dark, like her mother. He'd supported them by driving a delivery truck, but the job was a no-brainer, a dead end. He'd longed for better. And because he'd had more guts than brains back in those days . . .

Matt knew the story of how Royal had ended up in prison, having heard it from his father. An old pal from the merchant marine had lured Royal into a scheme that involved cracking a safe in a mob-owned warehouse in L.A. They'd gotten caught and each had drawn fifteen-year sentences in Pelican Bay. While he was in prison, Royal's mother had died, leaving him a life insurance policy worth a quarter of a million, only a little less than he and his pal had tried to steal from the mob.

Ten years into his term, Royal had gained parole and gone to Seattle, where he'd discovered Shorty's Landing, met Cleo and fallen in love with both. He'd bought the marina and tavern with his mother's life insurance money, and had asked Cleo to move in with him. He'd vowed to live the honest life, and had done so for more than two decades to this very day, if you didn't count habitual philandering. He hadn't gotten rich, but he'd survived nicely, thanks to Cleo's business sense and a killer recipe for fish and chips.

A *daughter*. Matt could hardly believe it.

"I wrote to Lauren now and then while I was in the joint, but never heard back," Royal went on. "Her mother finally sent me a letter telling me not to contact her anymore. Wanted me out of their lives, which ain't too hard to figure, I guess. She'd gotten religion, okay? Aimed to live for the Lord, and wanted our kid to do the same.''

Another long silence. Royal rubbed his crooked nose, and Matt stared into his mug. The wind rattled at the windows. The old man drummed his fingers on the table—a *hard* sound, as if he wore metal thimbles on his fingers.

''Lauren ran away from home when she was sixteen,'' Royal continued finally. ''Had some kind of big crisis in her life—I don't know what it was, but she couldn't go to her mother with it. Came to Seattle, intending to find me. I'd written to Marlene just before I got out of Pelican Bay, saying this is where I'd be. Lauren must've seen the letter or overheard Marlene talking to somebody—who the hell knows? Anyhow, when she got here, she lost her nerve. Maybe she was worried that I wouldn't want a daughter hanging around my neck, crampin' my style. She had no way of knowing how bad I wanted to see her. Shit, I would've given her everything I had . . .''

She'd ended up on the street, he explained, panhandling down in Pike Place, sleeping in doorways with a gaggle of other young runaways. Fortunately she had sense enough to stay off drugs, to seek help from one of the local relief agencies, the People's Resource Center in Seattle's Belltown. She'd met a volunteer named Elise Lekander.

''*The* Elise Lekander?'' Matt wanted to know. Elise Lekander was old-Seattle money, an A-list socialite. Her late husband had owned half the city.

''That's her, the rich lady. In fact, she ties up a boat here— s'pose I never mentioned it to you. The big Grand Banks trawler in number twenty-eight is hers.''

''Your daughter got to be buds with Elise Lekander?'' Matt was incredulous.

''More than buds. Elise saw potential in her, saw how smart she was. Took Lauren under her wing, you might say . . .'' Treated her like a daughter, gave her a home. Encouraged her to finish high school, helped her qualify for a scholarship to the University of Washington. In 1983, Lauren graduated with high honors and a degree in business administration. Two years later she earned her MBA. Armed with a substantial grubstake from the Lekander family, she burst upon the world of real estate with no intention of taking any prisoners.

Something clicked in Matthew Burgess' mind—the name *Lauren Bowman*. He remembered seeing it in the business pages way back when. The woman had gained a reputation as the "green developer," professing a strong sense of environmental values in the design and siting of residential properties. Houses should lie easy on the land, she'd said. Seattle's yuppie home-buyers had flocked to her like roaches to spilled jam. Matt had never dreamed that she and Royal were from the same Bowman family.

". . . and my little girl turns out to have a nose for the business. Went to work for a small outfit right out of school, and two years later she owned the goddamn place. It was right around then when she got in touch with me—felt a need to make contact with her own flesh and blood, and I was all she had, seeing as Marlene died of a stroke in eighty-five. Lauren had known for some time where I was, but never looked me up—scared of what she might find, I guess." The old man grinned feebly. "I almost shit a brick when she showed up here one day, drivin' a damn Mercedes, wearin' a grand-worth of clothes. It seems she met this guy, Gabe Granger, ten or twelve years older than her . . ."

Royal's grin dissolved into a scowl as Granger's name crossed his teeth, and Matt's mind clicked again. Gabriel Granger was one of the city's mandarins of commercial real estate, an owner of shopping malls and skyscrapers, a racer of hydrofoils. A few years ago he'd almost swung a deal to buy the Seattle Seahawks.

". . . and they got married. They merged their companies and moved into a mansion on the water over in Magnolia, not ten minutes from here. Lauren wanted me to give her away at the wedding, but I wouldn't do it. I figured I'd be bad for her image, being an ex-con and all, so I kind of hung in the background and tried not to get stepped on by any of Gabe's big-shot friends."

"See much of Lauren now?"

"We've been gettin' together two, three times a month. We go to restaurants, as long as they serve vegetarian food, 'cause that's all she'll eat. Or we go drivin', or sometimes we take in a movie, a ball game. Sometimes she has me over to the mansion in Magnolia, and we just sit and talk. She keeps trying to give me money, but I won't take any."

And neither would Royal let himself become a visible, day-to-day feature of his daughter's life. He didn't feel entitled, he confessed to Matt. And he didn't want any of his tarnish to rub off on her.

"Get back to the animal-rights thing," Matt said. "What makes you think Lauren had anything to do with the raid on that laboratory?"

Royal drummed his fingers on the table again, making the hard sound—metal against wood. "She's been involved with the movement for the last four, five years. Raising money, mostly. Goes around making speeches, organizing protests, pounding on politicians' desks, I don't know what all. Got herself appointed to the board of some big outfit, the League of Something or Other, and now she's the national treasurer."

"You're talking about LOCA, right? The League Opposed to Cruelty to Animals. My ex-wife sends money to them."

"That's the one."

"From what I've read, they're pretty mainstream. They don't bust up research labs or burn down butcher shops."

"Not officially, but they're connected to the guys who do the rough stuff. It's all on the sly, Lauren says. The League funnels in money to support the *real* soldiers, she says, pays their expenses and fines, hires lawyers to defend them whenever they get caught. She's been drifting over to the radical side herself these last few years, feels like she needs to get directly involved in rescuing animals and shutting down the people who kill them for profit."

"Maybe that's the way she feels. It doesn't mean she actually did anything violent or illegal."

"She *told* me about it, Matt. About three weeks back, she told me she and some other soldiers were planning to hit that lab. That's what they call themselves—soldiers." Royal stubbed out his cigarette and rested his forehead against a fist. "Swore me to secrecy, of course. Knew she could trust me."

"Right."

"And now some fella's dead, some poor fuckin' security guard with grandkids. You know what that means, don't you?"

Indeed Matt knew, being an ex-cop. If Lauren Bowman had taken part in that raid, she was an accessory to murder. "Have you heard from her yet?"

The old man shook his head. The rain grew louder. A seagull screamed outside. "It's just a matter of time, though. What the hell am I gonna tell her?"

"I don't know, skipper. I'm not good at stuff like this." He patted Royal's arm and stood. "Let me know if . . . if you need me." Matt climbed the stairs to his apartment and took a long, hot shower.

Four

It was one minute before midnight on the following night, but Megan Reiner had lost all sense of time. The pain fused with the music, the ache in her upper body twining with the guitar riffs and the bluesy lyrics . . .

> *Don't matter if you got money, woman,*
> *'Cause money ain't what makes me go.*
> *I said, It don't matter if you got more money than Oprah*
>   *Winfrey, girl,*
> *'Cause money don't make the sun shine or the wind*
>   *blow . . .*

Megan lay on a plank that rested at a forty-five-degree angle from the floor, her legs tied spread-eagle, her wrists strapped above her head. She was naked and cold. The straps had cut off the circulation in her fingers. She'd lain this way for nearly forty-eight hours.

> *. . . and no matter how far you run in this big, wide world,*
> *The day's gonna come, yes it is,*
> *When you gotta pay what you owe.*

The room was dank and musty. Underlying the stink of Megan's body wastes were the smells of a basement—damp cement and mildew. And something else, something *worse*—a coppery tang that filled her with sick dread. She knew that she wasn't the first to end up here. Someone had come before her, and that someone had *bled*.

During breaks in the blasting music, she heard the sounds of plumbing, a flushing toilet, and water flowing through pipes overhead. From somewhere far away came the occasional honk of a horn, the *whoop* of a siren. The only sources of light were the controls on the preamp against the wall on her right, red dots and back-lit displays on a graphic equalizer, showing the gradations of bass, mid-range and treble. The light was just enough to reveal *his* shape whenever *he* came around, a bulky shadow that moved as silently as a highlight on dark satin.

Sometimes he came to change the reel on the tape deck. Sometimes he came to jab a hypodermic needle into her arm, causing all pain and terror to dissolve into giddy warmth. And sometimes he came only to *breathe* on her.

> *Yeah, you gotta pay what you owe, little woman,*
> *You gotta pay what you owe . . .*

During the long hours of aloneness, Megan Reiner forced herself to relive the opening moments of the nightmare again and again, hoping that by doing so she could somehow *will* the outcome to change. Not a rational hope, but it was the only one she had.

Megan sees herself throw open the cages to free the remaining rats, slapping the sides with her hand to frighten them out. Lauren, her fellow soldier, has darted out to the corridor, and someone else has come in, maybe Rod Welton—the light isn't good. Megan sees him slip behind a rack of cages, as though intent on some chore that needed doing. Suddenly she hears gunshots, three or maybe four, and the distant wail of sirens. She hears shouting, shrieking—something has gone horribly wrong. Someone screams her name. . . .

"I'm here!" She jogs toward the exit, knowing that time is short. "We've got to get out of here!" she shouts, glancing toward the cages, expecting to see Rod. But it's someone else, someone darker, more powerful, a man who moves like a highlight on dark satin. Too late she remembers the pepper mace in her rucksack, a last-resort weapon to be used only in dire emergencies . . .

That was the point at which Megan Reiner wanted to change things. She wanted to insert new details and thus escape the blow to her head and the drug-soaked rag pressed to her face. She wanted to amend the part about someone dragging her through a rear corridor to the service entrance of the building, stuffing her into the trunk of a car . . .

But she *couldn't* change things. Reality had hardened like cement, and she had no choice but to endure it.

> . . . *the day's gonna come, yes it is,*
> *When you gotta pay what you owe.*

A door opened, and Megan knew that *he* had returned. Another needle probably, another reel of blues. Possibly a squirt of water from a squeeze bottle and a marshmallow to chew on, as before— a feast for the condemned. She wondered how much longer she could last like this. She wouldn't wonder long.

Five

At 11:19 A.M. on the Saturday after the catastrophe at the Bio-Center, Lauren Bowman stared level into Ian Prather's eyes and said, "Ian, I want you to go." She and Ian Prather had quarreled savagely over who was to blame for the killing of the guard, the disappearance and probable arrest of Megan Reiner, and whether or not Lauren could ever again trust him. "I don't think we should see each other for a while. God only knows what Megan has told the police. It's just a matter of time before they come sniffing around here. You're better off somewhere else."

She retreated onto the deck of the guest house, needing distance between herself and this man, who only days ago she'd loved as much or more than any other man she'd ever met. But he followed her and stayed close, leaned against the railing next to her. A stiff breeze blew in from Elliott Bay and invaded Lauren's simple cotton shirt, chilling her to the bone.

"Let me make sure I understand this," Ian said. "You're dismissing me after I saved your bloody life?" The breeze fanned his chestnut-colored hair, and Lauren thought, *He's a beautiful man. On the outside.*

"You can use the house in Ballard as long as you need it," she told him. "You and Vera should probably lie low until . . ."

"You can't stand the sight of me, can you, love?"

"You broke your promise. You carried a deadly weapon, and you used it. You killed a man, and you abandoned one of our own."

"Must we go through that again? The guard was *shooting* at us, Lauren. The police were about to arrive."

"He wouldn't have shot at us if you hadn't pulled a gun."

"Good Lord." Ian strode back toward the living room, but halted and turned to her again, as if following stage direction. Out on Elliott Bay a Washington State ferry plowed through the white-capping water toward the towers of Seattle, honking its arrival. "I don't plan to simply give you up, you know. What we've had together—it means too much to me. If I've broken a promise to you, I've also broken one that I made to myself a long time ago—never to get involved with a comrade. I'd kept that promise until I came here and met you. I love you, damn it, so you'd better get used to having me around, all right?"

It *wasn't* all right. Ian Prather was a swashbuckler, Lauren now realized. Like the motorcycle-riding thugs whom she'd found irresistible when she was a teenager. Like Gabe Granger, the man she'd married, who raced speedboats and climbed mountains. Like a dozen other such square-jawed specimens who'd sauntered into her life and ducked out again, both before and after Gabe. She'd learned through bitter experience that most swashbucklers were selfish men with dark rooms in their souls, men who could hurt you in a heartbeat.

"Ian, we don't have anything anymore."

"And why's that? Because I had the temerity to carry a gun? Well, here's a flash for you, love. This movement that you fancy yourself a part of—it's more than a mere movement now. It's a *revolution*, which means that we're revolutionaries, you and I. It's what we do. And sometimes it's distasteful, dangerous, even brutal. You begged me to let you in, to make you a soldier, remember? That's what we have, you and I—our revolution."

"I didn't ask to become an accessory to murder."

"But you bloody well knew from the outset that we're not pouring sugar into hunters' petrol tanks anymore, or carrying placards outside fur shops. We're sending letter bombs these days, and demolishing research laboratories. We're burning down slaughter-factories. We're doing violence against the Establishment, Lauren, and surprise-surprise. The Establishment is shooting back. Don't you get it? I carry a pistol to defend myself and those I care about. If I hadn't done so, you'd either be dead or in jail."

He stomped off, trailing a cloud of anger that was almost palpable. Lauren heard the engine of his car roar as he sped out of the drive, through the front gate, perhaps out of her life forever.

She'd wanted to become a revolutionary, yes, but not *his* kind. Before throwing in with the FAF, she'd prepared herself to break and enter, commit theft and vandalism, to destroy property in order to save animals' lives—but not to kill. She'd believed that controlled violence could generate an awareness that all species have equal rights, that this awareness would eventually elevate the human spirit, change beliefs and behavior, even save the world. Ian Prather, legend of the animal-rights underground, had personified that cause, or so she'd thought.

"You'd better come in before you catch a cold," Elise Lekander called from the doorway. She'd waited in the study while Lauren and Ian raged at each other, and now that Ian had left, she'd finally ventured out. Lauren went back into the living room, sank into an overstuffed chair and rubbed her eyes. A headache gnawed the base of her skull.

"Did you hear any of that?"

"Of course. The man's voice carries," Elise replied. She handed Lauren a snifter of brandy. "Take this. You look as if you could use it."

"You must think I'm a fool."

"I think no such thing."

"But you warned me, didn't you? About his kind. You saw through him right from the start."

"I've always admired those who have the nerve to risk everything for principal—it's what Socrates called the 'highest morality.' I admire Ian Prather, if you want to know the truth, just as I admire you. Of course, that doesn't mean I endorse his methods. Neither does it mean that I *like* him. To begin with, he's far too theatrical for my taste."

Elise Lekander was a slender woman in her mid-fifties who'd kept her physical tautness through the services of a personal trainer and a cosmetic surgeon. She had a strong patrician face, sharp blue eyes and honey-blond hair swept back from her face.

Though she herself was a longtime animal-rights activist, Elise Lekander believed in incremental change, not revolution. She believed in lobbying for new laws and regulations. She preferred a well-coordinated op-ed campaign to breaking and entering, paid ads and political contributions over letter bombs. Even so, she'd remained Lauren's strongest and closest personal ally.

"You pointed out that he has beady eyes," Lauren reminded her. "You've always told me to stay away from beady-eyed people because they all have secret agendas."

"Yes, well—perhaps I did say that." Which was as close as Elise would come to saying *I told you so*.

The intercom chimed, and a female voice called for "the boss," which meant Lauren.

"What is it, Jandee?"

Jandee Vernon was Lauren's live-in personal assistant, a petite blond dynamo with an advanced degree in art history. "A police car has just driven through the front gate, and there's a couple of cop-looking types walking this way, one of whom doesn't look old enough to shave." Like Lauren, Jandee was a card-carrying believer in the cause of animal rights. Her job was to handle the clerical duties attendant to Lauren's high position in LOCA, as well as the myriad other chores that needed doing for a rich woman who'd set out to change the world. "Do I let them in, or do we shoot our way out and hole up in the Andes?"

Lauren suffered an attack of low-grade panic. "Just answer the door. And for God's sake, Jandee, no stand-up comedy while they're here, okay?" She threw a pleading look at Elise, the woman who'd been more a mother to her than the one whose genes she carried. "Ian was here not five minutes ago. Those cops probably passed him on the road." She drew her arms over her chest, hugged herself. "God, I don't know if I can do this."

"Nonsense, darling. We've worked out what we'll say. Stick to the script, and you'll be fine."

"Would you *listen* to us? Elise, we're talking about lying to the police. A man is dead, we know how it happened, and we're about to lie—"

Elise grabbed Lauren's shoulders, shook her gently as a mother might do. "Lauren, listen to me. The next few minutes could be the most important ones of your life. You must think about what you say, and you must believe what you say. If *you* believe, so will *they*."

Lauren pressed her palms to her face, fearing that she might start screaming. "It's catching up to me. Megan's missing, and I'm an accessory to murder. How in the hell could things have gone so wrong?"

"Someone you trusted lied to you, broke his word. If he hadn't carried a gun, that poor security officer would still be alive. You may be guilty of trespassing, breaking and entering, and God knows what other minor infraction, but you're *not* guilty of murder. You did everything in your power to prevent anyone from getting hurt. Hold on to that, Lauren. *Use* it.''

"I'll try."

"Of course you will. Be your usual charming self. Pretend you're talking to a beady-eyed banker. Beady-eyed bankers are scarier than police officers, wouldn't you say?"

Doorbell, footfalls, voices from the foyer. Jandee Vernon ushered in two detectives, one a squat, red-haired woman who looked like a high school principal, the other a slender, olive-skinned man who looked like the president of the student council. They introduced themselves as Detective Sergeant Connie Henness and Detective Aaron Cosentino, homicide. They asked to speak with Lauren alone, upon which Elise and Jandee retired to the study.

Lauren offered refreshments, tea or coffee, but the cops were all-business. She seated them in the living room before an expansive view of Elliott Bay and the Seattle skyline.

"Ms. Bowman, we talked to a maid up at the main house a minute ago," Sergeant Henness said, taking out a small spiral notebook, "and she told us that this is a *guest* house. Yet, you actually live here, is that right?—not in the mansion next door with your husband?"

"That's right. You see, Mr. Granger and I have had some, uh, disagreements over decorating, and some other issues . . .''

"You're separated, is that it?" asked Detective Cosentino.

Lauren wondered if this was any of their fucking business, then decided that she'd better make nice. "Not officially. The fact is, I'm a vegan, and . . .''

"A what?"

"A *vegan*, someone who doesn't eat meat or any animal products—no milk, no eggs, no butter, no cheese. True vegans don't allow themselves to use or come into contact with any substance or material that's derived from harming animals. I don't wear leather, for example. I don't use cosmetics manufactured with animal oils, and I don't buy from companies who use animals in testing. If you'll look around, you'll notice that we don't have leather furniture and anything else that might've cost a creature its life or caused it to be oppressed."

"And your husband, Mr. Bowman—er, I'm sorry—Mr. *Granger*—''

"I kept my name when I married him."

"He doesn't share your taste in food or decorating, so you moved into the guest house?"

"It runs deeper than that, Detective," Lauren replied with her most blinding smile, the one that had sealed many a lucrative real-estate deal. "Let's just say that he and I live apart for the time being, even though we're still business partners." The cops just stared back at her, as if they didn't know what to say. "Now, how can I help you?" she pressed.

"Ms. Bowman, can you tell us where you were and what you were doing during the early morning hours of Thursday, May 29th?" Sergeant Henness asked.

To her own amazement, Lauren was able to lie smoothly and forcefully. No stammering, no fluttering eyelids. Her palms didn't sweat and her nose didn't grow. Two nights ago she'd stayed at the Lekander house up in The Highlands, she said. She and Elise had worked on plans for a summer fund-raising gala, and it had gotten late. Rather than drive back here, she'd used one of Elise's guest rooms.

"Elise Lekander—that's the lady we met a minute ago."

"Yes."

"And you didn't leave the Lekander house between midnight and three?"

"No, I didn't. We stopped working about eleven, had a glass of wine and turned in."

"I assume that Mrs. Lekander can confirm what you've just told us," Cosentino said. His voice was much older than his face.

"I can't imagine why not. Why don't you ask her? Oh, her son was there, too—that's Marc Lekander, 'Marc' with a C. I'm expecting him shortly for lunch, so you can check with him, as well. In fact, you're welcome to have lunch with us, if you're hungry. My cook is out shopping even as we speak. We're having portobella mushroom patties on baguettes with a Thai mustard sauce—all organically grown. Taste one, and you'll never go back to meat."

The detectives traded glances. "This fund-raising gala you were working on," said Henness. "Something for charity, is it?"

Lauren explained that she and Elise Lekander planned to host a summer event for the League Opposed to Cruelty to Animals, an A-list affair with attendance by nationally known celebs. They'd slated it for mid-August and had gotten together Wednesday evening to look at bids from caterers, florists, and stringed quartets.

"You're an officer of LOCA, aren't you?" Henness asked, as if the thought had just hit her.

"I'm the national treasurer, as I'm sure you know. You're here about the raid on the Northwest BioCenter, aren't you?"

Sergeant Henness nodded. "You're a prominent figure in the animal-rights movement. Which puts you on our interview list. I'm sure you understand."

"Yes."

"Are you aware that a man was killed, a security guard?"

"I saw it on the news. I should tell you, Detectives, that LOCA is four-square committed to nonviolence. We don't believe in putting people in physical danger. We believe in the sanctity of life, and that includes human life, first and foremost."

"With all due respect, Ms. Bowman, I've read articles that put a slightly different spin on it," Cosentino replied. "Some say that LOCA secretly channels money to support violent activities by the Front for Animal Freedom and similar outfits."

"To my knowledge, that's simply not true, and I'm in a position to know. You see, the FAF doesn't have a formal organization, and it puts out no single statement of beliefs. From what I gather, it's a rather disjointed assortment of local cells who operate without any central guidance. Its members are all over the map philosophically, and many of them are interested in much more than animal rights. Quite a large percentage are militant anarchists who hate corporations, banks, governments, and anything else that resembles an institution. I doubt they would want help from people like me."

"People who've gotten rich by using the system?" the young cop asked.

"People who believe in using the system for change," Lauren clarified, smiling.

Though she was outwardly calm, her insides were a tumult, a nasty thought having just hit her. Perhaps the cops had already taken Megan Reiner into custody. Perhaps the girl had cracked under questioning, and the purpose of this interview was to mire Lauren Bowman in a tar pit of her own lies.

"Do you live here alone?" Henness asked. "I mean, does anyone else occupy the guest house?"

"My personal assistant lives here. You've already met Jandee Vernon."

"Anyone else?"

"Occasionally my cook stays over—her name is Rainy Hales. Actually her first name is Adrienne, but no one calls her that. She should be here soon, if you'd like to talk to her." *Don't overdo the helpfulness bit,* Lauren told herself.

"That won't be necessary, at least not for now."

The interview ended as suddenly as a summer squall on the Sound. The detectives spoke briefly with Elise Lekander and Jandee Vernon, scribbled things in their notebooks, distributed business cards. They requested that Elise instruct her son to call them at their earliest convenience, presumably to provide additional corroboration of Lauren's alibi. Then they were gone.

Lauren collapsed onto a sofa and swallowed the rest of her brandy in one gulp. Jandee let Lauren's two dogs into the living room, a pair of large, black Belgian Tervurens named Desi and Lucy. They bounded over to Lauren, jumped up on her and licked her face, overjoyed to be let out of a rear bedroom where Jandee had confined them since Ian Prather's arrival earlier in the morning. Prather didn't believe that anyone had a right to keep animals as pets, so Lauren kept them out of sight whenever he was around.

"Confession time," Jandee said. "We eavesdropped, heard every word, and I say it's time to breathe easy. Who else needs a drink?"

"I do," Lauren said, pushing Lucy off her lap.

"By the way, you were absolutely magnificent—wasn't she, Elise?"

"You handled them beautifully," Elise confirmed. "And it's a relief to know that Megan didn't get caught."

"We can't be sure of that," Lauren cautioned.

"Don't you think the police would've mentioned her? Surely they would've asked whether you knew her, if you'd seen her lately, that sort of thing."

"Or," Jandee added, "they would've tried to make you believe that she's given you up, get you talking about your part in the crime in order to set the record straight. That's what cops do—they lie. Don't you ever watch *Homicide* or *NYPD Blue?*"

"If Megan isn't sitting in a jail cell, she's missing," Lauren reminded them. "Her boyfriend has called three times since Thursday afternoon, looking for her. She hasn't contacted any of her friends, and she's AWOL from the philosophy department at U-Dub. If she doesn't turn up soon, he plans to file a missing-person's report."

"Would he have any reason to connect her disappearance with the raid?" Elise asked. "And would he pass his suspicions on to the police?"

"Good questions," Lauren answered. "I don't think Megan would have broken security by telling him about the operation, but I wouldn't swear to it. I wasn't supposed to tell anyone, either, but both of *you* know about it." As did her father, Royal, but Lauren made no mention of this.

"Jesus Christ, we're part of the movement," Jandee protested, "and have been for years. If you can't trust us, who *can* you trust?"

The front door opened, setting off an explosion of barking by Desi and Lucy. A slight man with thinning blond hair walked into the room, and said, "It's only me, folks." It was Marc Lekander. Desi and Lucy went to him and licked his hands, begging to be petted. Marc obliged them. "I'm happy to announce," he said, raising his arms as if to acknowledge cheers, "that the rats and monkeys have been taken care of. By this time tomorrow, they'll all be headed to humane homes all over the West Coast and British Columbia."

He referred to the animals that Lauren, Ian, and the others had rescued from the BioCenter. For the past several years he'd handled the disposition of animals that local activists removed from inhumane circumstances. He'd cultivated relationships with like-minded people around the country who could place infant minks stolen from fur ranches, chickens and turkeys freed from factory farms, even a male adult chimpanzee rescued from a display cage in a shopping mall. He was good at this, and Lauren valued his services and his commitment to the cause. She thought of him as a brother, though some of her friends had warned her that Marc's feelings toward *her* were far from brotherly.

Lauren went to him, hugged him, told him thanks. The disposition of the animals was a load off her mind. Then she told him about the visit from the homicide detectives, and his face paled. She recounted her conversation with them, the fact that they hadn't mentioned Megan Reiner.

"Which means that Megan wasn't caught after all," Marc said, sitting down.

"Possibly. But if she's not in jail, where the hell is she?"

"Maybe hiding out somewhere, holed up with a friend until the heat dies down."

This made no sense to Lauren, and she said so. The raiders had planned to go on with their everyday lives in order not to arouse suspicion, and Megan had bought into the plan. Besides, she was a teaching assistant at UW, with responsibilities that she took seriously. She had a boyfriend who loved her. She wouldn't have abandoned her life of her own free will.

Marc picked up a package from the carpet next to his chair and looked at it. "What's this?" He handed it to Lauren. "Must be yours—those are your initials."

The parcel was about the size of a videocassette, wrapped in plain brown paper. Someone had jotted L. B. on one side with a blue ballpoint pen. "No postage, not even an address," Lauren said, puzzled. "So it obviously didn't come in the mail. I wonder why no one noticed it before now."

"It was lying out of sight beside this chair," Marc said. "No telling how long it's been here."

"Maybe one of the cops brought it," Jandee suggested.

"Neither of them was carrying anything, as I recall. It's clearly intended for me, wouldn't you say?" Lauren tore the paper away, revealing a plain black videocassette. No label, no markings. "I guess the next step is to see what's on it."

"Hope it's a comedy," Jandee said. "I could use one. Anything but Pauley Shore."

Marc took the cassette from Lauren and pushed it into the VCR. The tape leader played out on a blank screen, and the audio kicked in abruptly, filling the room with the gravelly voice of a male blues singer, accompanied by an electric guitar and a bass.

> Don't matter if you got money, woman,
> 'Cause money ain't what makes me go . . .

Lauren went rigid when Megan Reiner's face appeared on the screen, pale and chalky, a dark bruise covering her right temple. Tears glittered in the girl's eyes. Pain twisted her face.

"Jesus . . . !" breathed Marc Lekander, stepping back from the TV.

The shot was so tight that the tracks of Megan's tears showed clearly against her bloodless cheeks. Her breath came in sharp bursts.

"My God, I think she's being raped!" Jandee whispered.

> ... I said, It don't matter if you got more money than
>   Oprah Winfrey, girl,
> 'Cause money don't make the sun shine or the wind
>   blow ...

Lauren was on her feet now, moving toward the screen, her hand extended as if she meant to reach into the television set and put a halt to the outrage. She became aware of sounds underlying the music, guttural grunts and gasps, the noise of a man's sexual frenzy. Something writhed deep inside her, an old terror set loose by the sight and sounds of Megan's torture, and by the music itself.

> ... and no matter how far you run in this big, wide world,
> The day's gonna come, yes it is,
> When you gotta pay what you owe.

For a few seconds the rapist's shoulder came into view at the edge of the screen, a dark boulder ramming against Megan's chin. The rhythm of the act quickened, and the grunts became louder, sharper, as the rapist started to climax. Megan squealed with revulsion through clenched teeth, cutting Lauren to the quick.

Lauren tried to tear her eyes away from the screen, but couldn't, even though her flesh was trying to crawl off her bones. The others in the room—Elise, Jandee, and Marc—watched with the same excruciating fascination, as if frozen in tableau, no one breathing or moving.

A knife appeared, blinding the camera for a split second with a shard of strobe light reflected from a fat, curving blade. Panic clawed at Lauren's heart, for she feared knives so intensely that she couldn't allow even a butter knife next to her plate. The rapist pressed the blade against Megan's throat.

"No!" Lauren screamed, her knees buckling. The dogs rushed her and nuzzled her, thinking this was some kind of game. Jandee shrieked as the knife slid into Megan Reiner's flesh and blood oozed around the cut. A useless plea escaped the girl's lips ...

You take what you take,
Your lovers come and go,
But when it comes right down to it, woman,
You gotta pay what you owe . . .

Six

The sun warmed his naked shoulders as the Blues Beast grilled a tenderloin on the back deck of his house in West Seattle. Summer had invaded Puget Sound overnight, bringing a breeze as warm as a baby's breath and a sky so blue that it hurt his eyes. He felt almost real again, almost alive.

Almost.

Life without Lauren could only get so good and no better. Life without Lauren was unreal, a dead region where little mattered except playing the blues, which the Blues Beast did like some people shoot heroin.

His real name was Tyler Brownlee. He was a powerfully built man of twenty-one, broad-shouldered and slim-waisted, with muscles sculpted in his own private weight room. He worked out at least three hours a day, sometimes four, because working out was a good way to eat up time, which was drudgery without Lauren at his side. He wore no jewelry except for a gold stud in his left earlobe and a costly Audemars Piguet watch that showed the phases of the moon.

He had a long, oddly handsome face that seemed a bit too sharp-featured at first glance, a nose excessively pointed, discomfiting hazel eyes. On his right cheek lay a faint scar, which he considered a badge of manhood, the beauty mark of a natural fighter. He had artificially blond hair that flowed to his shoulders, kept just the right shade by a stylist who owned a shop on Alki Beach a few doors away. The stylist had advised him that his

Mediterranean complexion contradicted the color, but this didn't bother the Blues Beast—he'd wanted long, blond hair and that was that.

The hair hid a pair of ears that folded forward along the top edges, a congenital defect that had caused laughter among his peers when he was a kid. "Dog Ears," they'd called him, until he had grown big and strong enough that no one in his right mind any longer dared to piss him off. On his chest he had a tattoo of a lion's head, while an eagle spread its wings around one forearm and a cobra coiled around the other—all meat eaters like himself, beautifully rendered by an expert tattoo artist. A few years earlier a dermatologist had removed his crude juvey-hall tats, leaving only a few rough patches on his otherwise flawless skin.

He carried Lauren Bowman's photograph in his billfold, a tattered class picture that his father had snipped from the 1979 yearbook of MacArthur High School in Portland, Oregon. Tyler had made enlargements of the picture and had hung them on the walls of his weight room and bedroom, together with blowups of more recent photos that he himself had shot through a telephoto lens. He never tired of staring at Lauren's face and body, but he craved seeing her up close and in the flesh, not through a camera or a pair of binoculars. He craved putting his hands on her, but in the *real* world, not in a daydream.

His housemate and business partner, Arnie Cashmore, sat in his boxer shorts at a rattan table a few feet away, absorbed in the chore of cutting loaves of heroin into *half-pieces* and *dealer's pieces*, twelve and twenty-four grams each. A high cedar fence enclosed the tight backyard, ensuring privacy. It was Sunday morning, the first day of June.

Wearing a green sun visor and Coke-bottle glasses, Arnie weighed each piece on a set of pharmaceutical scales, then wrapped it in waxed paper and sealed it with a rubber band. Street dealers would further divide the wares into eighth-of-a-gram hits for sale to junkies at twenty dollars each. Those in the trade called these *twenty-pieces*.

"Sure you don't want some breakfast?" Tyler asked Arnie, who was a scrawny man in his early forties. "You're getting skinnier every day, man. You look like some kind of big insect, with your spindly arms and legs, and your huge fuckin' eyes."

"I'll eat later," Arnie said, not looking up. "And fuck you very much, by the way."

Tyler gave him a crooked half-grin. He never grinned all the way, or frowned all the way. His face never fully committed itself.

His cell phone bleeped, and he snatched it out of a hip pocket. "Enlighten me," he said by way of greeting. He pressed a spatula against the steak, causing the meat to sizzle and snarl. The man on the other end spoke without identifying himself, following the security rule that Arnie Cashmore had laid down to everyone they did business with: no names on the phone. But the caller's German accent told Tyler instantly who he was—Horst Stumpf-nagel, with whom Tyler and Arnie had done business for years.

"We have something important for you," Horst said. "How soon can you come?"

"It's Sunday, man. Can't it wait till tomorrow?"

"You have said that you wish to be notified the very moment we discover anything—*interesting*. This is indeed interesting."

"Give me a couple of hours, okay? I'm just sitting down to breakfast."

"A couple of hours, good. We will be waiting."

Tyler switched off the phone, sat down at the rattan table across from Arnie and proceeded to devour his rare steak.

"I talked to the Fat Woman last night," Arnie said, finally looking up. "She had some disturbing news." The Fat Woman was the operator of a major pipeline of Mexican black tar heroin into the Pacific Northwest. She was also Arnie and Tyler's supplier. A longtime player in Seattle's dark world of drugs, she had ways of knowing things.

"Is this going to upset me? I'm having my first half-assed decent mood in weeks."

"Our little buddy up on Capitol Hill is a lop."

"You're talking about Kevin Hilldahl?"

Arnie nodded, his green sun visor barely dipping.

"I guess that's why he's so hot to get into the trade, right?" Tyler said, chewing his meat.

"Let's say it has nothing to do with scoring a means of paying for his own dope, as he's fond of telling people."

Kevin Hilldahl was a street kid who aspired to become a dealer, who'd made his aspirations known through the heroin net-work on the Hill. For the past several months he'd pestered local dealers with offers to round up new "clients," do them favors, run errands.

"You know, I pegged that lame-o for bogus the minute I laid

eyes on him," Tyler replied. "Remember? I said, Arnie, this guy
is B-O-G-U-S. Can I pick 'em, or what?"

"Somebody wants to put him next to us. I don't need to tell
you why."

"This all comes from the Fat Woman?"

Arnie's visor dipped again. "One of her people saw Hilldahl
talking to a known narc, someone named Cage, even saw Cage
give him some money—not once, but twice. Like, I don't need a
piano to fall on me to figure out what's going on."

Tyler shook his head, clicked his tongue. "The fucking kids
these days."

Arnie handed over a folded slip of paper, on which he'd scribbled an address. "We've got to nip it in the bud, send a message
to all concerned. We can't afford to let some junked-out lop bust
one of our dealers."

"I'm on it, *compadre*."

"Be careful this time. Nothing fancy-schmancy. Just do the
magic that you do so well and get the hell out. If things get goofy,
bail. There's always tomorrow."

Tyler grinned in his crooked, noncommittal way and pushed
back from the table. "I probably won't be back until after the
show tonight—gonna do some jammin' with the Ranger to get
ready. You ought to come by, listen to my licks. I'm getting damn
good, if I do say so myself."

He'd recently picked up a regular Sunday gig with an amateur
group at the Blue Lion Club downtown, playing guitar. His dream
was to get good enough to go pro, quit the tar business, become
a real person—something he couldn't remember ever feeling like.
He envisioned himself touring with a decent band, with a front
man like the great Curtis Salgado, playing respectable venues
where no one sold dope out the back door. Lauren would come
with him, of course, for she would insist on being at his side
during every waking minute. That's how it would be, for this was
what the Ranger had promised, and the Ranger had never broken
a promise.

"Yeah, maybe," Arnie said, going back to his work. "We'll
see."

The Blues Beast rode his 1979 Harley Davidson, an immaculate eighty-cubic-inch Shovelhead, a spectacle of purple paint
and blinding chrome. Wearing a black leather jacket and snakeskin cowboy boots, his guitar case slung across his back, he knew

that he cut a cool image on the road. Babes stared from the side-walks he thundered past, the wind tussling his blond hair. Some-times he flipped a little wave with a forefinger, not taking his hand off the handlebars, and the babes almost always grinned and waved back.

He motored east on Alki Avenue to Duwamish Head, then took the West Seattle Freeway across the Duwamish Waterway into Seattle proper, past the King Dome and the downtown busi-ness center. Traffic was heavy, both pedestrian and vehicular, the sunshine having lured rain-weary Seattlites out of their burrows. He rode up Broadway into Capitol Hill, an old neighborhood between Lake Washington and Lake Union. Here the currency was newness, and cutting-edge fads were on nonstop display. At all hours of the day and night Broadway teemed with Seattle's youth in full strut—slackers, punkers and post-punkers, achingly slim junkies with pierced ears, noses, nipples, and eyebrows. Among them browsed boomers and yuppies in gear from Nord-strom or Land's End, lured by hip restaurants and chichi bou-tiques that sold everything from Turkish-made cymbals to designer condoms.

Tyler turned right on East Mercer, swung into an alley over-hung with oaks, and parked at the rear of a dilapidated Victorian apartment house. Carrying his guitar, he walked in through the unlocked back door and climbed the creaking rear stairs to Num-ber 24, the address Arnie had written on the slip of paper. Grunge rock thumped within the apartment, a song from Hole's second album, a cacophony of skronking guitars and tuneless screeching. Unlike most of his generation, the Blues Beast loathed such noise, didn't consider it music.

He picked the lock, which was an old Corbin disk-tumbler, using a rake pick and a tension wrench that he carried in a cloth pouch under his shirt. In the movies, picking a lock almost never took more than a few seconds, but this wasn't a movie, and in real life it wasn't that easy, not even for an expert like himself. The job took five minutes, but only because the lock was old and worn—it could have taken much longer. He tucked away his tools and pulled a Smith & Wesson .357 Magnum from its shoulder holster, flicked the safety off and slipped into the apartment.

The stink hit him immediately, nearly knocked him over. The place was a landfill—empty pizza boxes, beer cans, liquor bottles, used tampons and rubbers, wadded cigarette packs. Half a dozen filthy sleeping bags littered a distressed sofa. No telling how many called this pit home, for street junkies routinely couch-surfed among their friends who had apartments.

Tyler peeked into the bathroom and saw that the john was clogged, that the junkies had used the bathtub for shitting and pissing. He fought to keep his breakfast down. The Hole song ended, and he heard the sounds of sex in the bedroom, low moans and mews. He braced his guitar case in a corner, then eased the door open a crack, peered inside and saw a couple on the bed, the girl straddling the boy, her head thrown back in ecstasy. They were emaciated kids, pale as summer clouds and liberally tattooed, their limbs scarred with needle tracks. The girl had scabs on her neck that looked like vampire bites, meaning that she was a veteran junkie. The veins in her arms and legs had collapsed from overuse, so her neck was the only remaining spot on her body where she could inject heroin and still get high.

Unreal, Tyler thought. *None of this is real, thank God. I couldn't take it.*

He recognized the boy, Kevin Hilldahl, a typical Capitol Hill skell, his skin as white as the belly of a fish. He had rings through his eyebrows, teardrops tattooed in the corners of his eyes. A lingering smell of burnt vinegar signified that the pair had cooked tar and shot up only minutes ago. They fucked with junkies' languid rhythm, oblivious to everything but each other.

The next song started on the Hole album, rattling the window with its bass line, and Tyler walked into the room, the revolver out in front of him. The junkies didn't notice, didn't open their eyes. He stood at the foot of the bed and thought a moment about what he was about to do, about the fact that the girl had done nothing to deserve this. Her only sin was getting mixed up with a lop like Hilldahl—hardly a capital offense. But the Blues Beast wasn't in a position to forgive sins, capital or otherwise, and he sure as hell couldn't leave any witnesses.

He holstered the gun and reached for the knife in his right boot, a custom-made Redstone folding knife from Australia. Taking hold of the girl's hair, he drew her head toward him, which caused her to open her eyes and stare up at him with dilated pupils, unblinking, disbelieving. Before she could scream, he pulled the blade across her throat, severing her trachea and carotid arteries. Blood geysered out and cascaded over her skimpy breasts onto her lover's torso, sprayed the wall and the bed. Tyler stood behind her and held her at arm's length by the hair, in order to avoid ruining his clothes. *You can't get bloodstains out of leather*, he'd learned from bitter experience.

The girl thrashed and trembled, finally went limp, apparently misleading her heroin-fogged lover to conclude that he'd just given her the orgasm of her life. Tyler released her hair, and she flopped forward.

That's when Kevin Hilldahl opened his eyes, saw the riot of red and his lover's slack face, saw Tyler Brownlee hunkering over him. He didn't scream, didn't struggle. His mouth yawned as he tried to talk, but only a moan came out.

"It's cool," Tyler said, pressing the blade against the boy's neck. "None of this is real, Kevin. You understand me, dude? Someday we're all going to wake up and find out that this life has been nothing more than a nasty dream. You're lucky, know that? Because your wake-up time is *now*."

The boy's eyes welled with real tears that spilled over the blue-teardrop tats. "Just do it," he gagged, sounding not quite like a Nike ad. "Do it and get it over with."

So Tyler did it, leaping back to dodge the fountain of blood, and he felt almost real again, like he felt when playing the blues. Like he knew he would feel with Lauren on top of him. *Almost*.

His next stop was Stump's Quality Appliances, which occupied a tatty building on Republican Street, near the southern tip of Lake Union. Carrying his guitar, he walked through the front door and rubbernecked like a customer in search of a new refrigerator. A banner strung across the ceiling cried, 90 DAYS SAME AS CASH!

A worn-looking salesman with yesterday's beard motioned him to the rear, where he found Horst Stumpfnagel, all three hundred pounds of him, dressed in a flowered Hawaiian shirt and white Bermuda shorts. Stumpfnagel had slick hair, eyes that twinkled like bits of Arctic ice, and fingers like Bavarian sausages. He and his brother, Rudi, had emigrated from Munich two decades ago and had opened an appliance store, which was merely a front for their main business—fencing stolen goods, mostly high-end consumer electronics. They called themselves the Stump brothers, because they'd never met anyone in America who could pronounce "Stumpfnagel" properly.

Horst and Rudi were experts in electronics, particularly surveillance and security systems, which made them useful to people like Tyler Brownlee and Arnie Cashmore. As purveyors of Mexican tar, Tyler and Arnie sometimes needed someone to sweep their house in Alki for bugs, or to tap the phone of a street dealer to confirm that he wasn't getting friendly with the wrong people. The Stump brothers had answered those needs. For the past year, though, Tyler had needed to know everything that went on in the house of Lauren Bowman, and the Stump brothers had answered that need as well. Tyler had paid them handsomely.

Horst welcomed him with warm Bavarian *Gemütlichkeit*, offered a Bismarck and coffee, which Tyler declined. "To tell you the truth, Horse Man, I've got a heavy day lined up, and I'm in a semi-hurry. What's so important that you've got to call me down here on a Sunday?"

"We must go upstairs—come."

They climbed the rear stairs to a room where another man sat before an elaborate audio console on which spools of tape spun. He wore earphones and jotted notes on a spiral pad, so absorbed in his work that he didn't hear Horst and Tyler arrive. This was Rudi, who weighed less than half as much as Horst and looked as if he belonged in a cornfield with a pole up his ass. He wore a Planet Hollywood T-shirt and a backward Mariners' baseball cap—a forty-five-year-old butthead with purpling needle tracks on his arms.

"I think you will find this to be quite interesting, my young friend," Horst said, indicating a chair for Tyler. "Rudi, *steig ab*! Mr. Brownlee is here!"

Rudi Stumpfnagel laid aside the earphones and spoke to Tyler in mildly accented English. "This is what I know," he said, not bothering with pleasantries. "I drove by the Bowman-Granger house this morning to test our low-band receiver, make sure all the equipment was working. As you know, we keep the receiver in a car parked on the street near the estate. We move it regularly in order to keep the neighbors from getting suspicious . . ."

"I understand all that. So, what've you got for me?"

"I accidentally started testing on the wrong frequency, but I was still picking up stuff inside the house. I heard conversations taking place, plain as day. I even listened in on a phone conversation between your girl, Lauren Bowman, and that English dude who schemed the attack on that laboratory a few nights ago. All on the *wrong* frequency."

"Okay—so what does this tell me, exactly?"

"I wasn't listening on our frequency. Don't you get it?"

"Rudi, *hello*! If I got it, would I be sitting here like a lame-o, asking you to explain it to me?" Tyler was still in high color, having cut a pair of throats less than twenty minutes ago. He wouldn't come down to earth for hours yet.

"It means there's another set of bugs in Lauren Bowman's house. It was only dumb luck that I even found out about them, because I happened to start testing on the wrong frequency, which was actually the *right* frequency, if you know what I mean."

"Another set of bugs? This still isn't registering. Why would there be another set of bugs?"

Horst muscled his brother aside and leaned into Tyler's face. "What he's telling you, Mr. Brownlee, is that someone else has bugged the place, too—planted equipment like ours, VHF low-band transmitters, very similar to our own."

"And drop-in telephone transmitters, I think," Rudi added. "All broadcasting to a portable receiver. It sounded like they were using voice-actuators, just as we do."

Tyler put a hand on his head, dug his fingers into his blond hair. "This is getting *sooooo* fucking weird. Someone *else*? Who?"

"We have no way of knowing," Horst answered apologetically. "But we decided that we must notify you immediately. Naturally, I considered the matter too sensitive to discuss on the phone, telecommunications being what they are."

Tyler stared a moment at the array of electronics on the console, thinking, wondering. He took deep, easy breaths to slow his pulse, blinked his eyes. "You did right, Horst. You've made me proud. Both of you. Anything else I should know about?"

"Oh, there's more, Mr. Brownlee," Rudi said. "The police came to the Bowman house yesterday, asking questions about the raid on the laboratory. We got good audio of the interview—you'll find it fascinating, I'm sure. But then, after they left, your girl discovered a videocassette. She watched it with some of her friends. It must've showed something extremely nasty, judging from the sounds Lauren and her friends made—lots of crying and screaming. I think it had something to do with the one called Megan. Perhaps it will make some sense to you."

"How soon can you get all this on cassettes for me?" Tyler asked, his face flushing.

"A few hours, I suppose. But there's one thing more." Rudi

paused, dropped his stare to the floor. He pushed a finger under his cap to pick a scab on his balding crown. "Mr. Brownlee, I really could use . . ." After all these years, his addiction still embarrassed him. He could never bring himself to come right out and ask for dope.

"Yeah, right—you need to fix," Tyler said. "Tell you what, chief. I'll get Arnie to drop you a dealer's piece after lunch, which ought to keep you going for a spell. Have those cassettes ready for me by tomorrow, okay?"

"Not a problem. Not a problem at all." Rudi busied himself with the recording equipment, and Horst ushered Tyler downstairs to the showroom.

"Mr. Brownlee, I must ask you—how much longer must we do this thing?"

"What thing? You mean the surveillance? Can't say, Horse Man. Maybe another six months, a year. Depends."

"Please do not misunderstand—my brother and I feel fortunate and honored to do work for you and Mr. Cashmore. But this business with the Bowman woman—it's all very distasteful, not to mention time-consuming. Rudi spends most of every day listening to the surveillance tapes, making notes for you, dubbing the recordings onto cassettes. And then there is the matter of maintaining the equipment. The arrangement has become quite costly to us."

Tyler halted next to a huge almond-colored refrigerator, put down his guitar and faced the fat man head-on, grimacing as if he'd just suffered a wound to the heart. "I can't believe I'm hearing this, Horse Man. I pay you and Rudi good money, don't I? And don't I take care of his jones for him? I mean, my God, the man's got a habit as big as the great outdoors, and if it weren't for me, he'd be living in a packing crate somewhere. Way I see it, you should be offering to have my baby."

"As I said, we're honored to work for you, but we have other business obligations. I need my brother's assistance in managing our . . ."

Tyler smacked him on the chest with the heel of his open palm, hard enough to knock the breath out of him. Horst staggered backward, his small eyes alive with terror. Tyler caught a fistful of the Hawaiian shirt and pulled the German's massive face close to his own.

"Listen to me, lard barge. You and I made a deal, and the

Bible says, 'A deal's a deal, and whosoever craps out of it shall have his balls hammered flat.' So don't sling me any more of this shit about *other* obligations, or I'll come for you with a mallet—I shit you not. Your biggest obligation is to me, understand?''

Horst understood.

Tyler left the store and cruised to a vacant warehouse that stood about a dozen blocks east of the King Dome in the International District. He parked the Harley in the alley behind the building and used a key to enter through a rear door, his guitar resting on his shoulder like a musket. The interior was murky and cavernous, full of shadows and empty shipping pallets. He rode a screened-in elevator to the upper level and alighted before a steel door, pushed a doorbell button.

''Hey, old man—it's me, the Blues Beast. How about we jam for a while, get me primed for my gig tonight?'' His voice caromed among the high rafters of the warehouse, creating the auditory illusion of a dozen Tyler Brownlees. ''You in there, old man?''

The door opened with a clanking of dead bolts, revealing a bony figure who seemed to wear the shadows of this place like loose coveralls, whose eyes were dim holes in the dusk. The reek of chain-smoking wafted through the door.

''You know me, boy,'' the man said. ''I'm always ready to jam.''

For the next two hours Tyler and the Ranger played the blues, Tyler on his vintage 1968 Fender Stratocaster, the Ranger on a Stand-up Zeta bass. The old man sang into a portable sound system with a smoky voice that made Tyler think of deep, dark alleys on Chicago's South Side, where the blues was nasty, low-down, and *real* as tuberculosis. Occasionally they paused so the Ranger could show Tyler a certain lick on the guitar, how to achieve the nuance of a Stevie Ray Vaughn, a Kenny Wayne Shepherd, or a Buddy Guy. The way the old man's bony hand flew over the guitar frets reminded Tyler of a frantic white spider.

After calling it quits, they sat together before a musty window, the light of a waning afternoon barely seeping into the apartment. The place had once functioned as an office for the Chinese businessmen who owned the building, but the Ranger had remodeled to meet his own simple needs. Books, magazines, and newspapers stood in man-high stacks among pieces of Goodwill furniture, for the Ranger was an avid reader, a self-taught man, wise in the ways of the world, as is every good blues man. An open area in the center of the clutter served as his recording studio, where sat guitars, amps, microphones, and two costly multitrack tape recorders.

Tyler sipped from a can of Diet Rite and said, "I need to tell you something, old man. It's about Lauren. Maybe I should've told you earlier, but I thought it could wait. I didn't want to bum you, know what I mean?"

"I'm listening."

Tyler waited for the Ranger to light a fresh cigarette, then related what the Stump brothers had told him, that someone *else* had planted bugs in Lauren Bowman's house. The Ranger exhaled smoke, his gaze boring into Tyler's hard, young face. The silence seemed to congeal, and Tyler started to sweat.

"You're right," the old man growled. "You should've told me right off. Where the hell is your sense of priorities?"

"Like I said, I didn't want to upset you."

"*Upset* me? Jesus fucking Christ, how much longer do you think I have in this world? To me, every minute is like an ounce of gold. You waste my precious time, and you waste your own dream, hear?"

"I hear."

"From now on, you hold nothing back—not *ever*. And don't worry about upsetting me. My only reason for living is to help you get what's yours, because you're part of me. Your justice is *my* justice, hear?"

"I hear you. And I understand." Tyler burned with shame for having failed to live up to the Ranger's expectations. His eyes filled with tears. He owed the Ranger better than this—the man who'd taught him how to play the blues, how to ride a motorcycle, how to cut a throat; the man who lived to realize Tyler's reality, as if it was his own.

For the next hour they discussed the meaning of the Stump brothers' revelation about the other set of bugs in Lauren Bowman's house. Then they conceptualized the next outrage that Lauren must suffer in the process of becoming Tyler Brownlee's destiny—her next stop on the road to reality. And by the time Tyler left the warehouse, bound for his gig at the Blue Lion Club, he had his priorities straight.

Later that night, sitting atop a tall stool in the hazy club, the Blues Beast played the blues as he'd never played them before.

Seven

Hyperion heeled over far enough to make Linda Hannigan *whoop* loudly, as if she was on a roller coaster. Before dating Matthew Burgess, she'd never set foot on a sailboat, and—like many newcomers to sailing—she freaked whenever the mast tipped more than twenty degrees.

"Don't worry, we're not going over," Matt assured her while easing the mainsail. "We'll want to tack soon, so stand by to release the genoa sheet."

Linda Hannigan was an attractive though slightly lunchy bookkeeper who was dangerously close to forty, a twice-divorced mother with a craving for a permanent man in her life. She worked for a marine electronics distributorship near Shorty's, lived in a duplex in Ballard with her two kids and an unmarried sister.

Matt executed the tack and swung the bow around to point toward the mouth of the Lake Washington Ship Canal, the sails flapping noisily until filling with wind. Linda looked relieved as *Hyperion* settled into a sedate broad reach.

"This is the way I like it, captain," she said. "Slow and quiet."

"Don't get all comfy," Matt said, chuckling, "because it's almost time to fire up the iron sail. And you know what that means." It was almost 4:30, and the sailing day was nearly spent.

Linda groaned. Starting the engine meant work in preparation for docking—furling the genoa, pulling down the mainsail and

stacking it on the boom, hanging fenders over the transom. She
tackled the chores as soon as Matt hit the starter switch. He told
her that she was doing great, called her a regular old salt.

They motored slowly into the canal from Shilshole Bay and
lined up with a score of other pleasure boats waiting for passage
through the Chittenden Locks. Warm, clear weather on a Sunday
had brought Seattle's sailors out in force, and spirits were high
on the gathered vessels. Beer flowed and music filled the air.
Spectators lined the viewing platforms to watch the locks in action
and take snapshots.

Matt felt good. This had been his kind of day—soaking up the
poetry that flowed from sailing a sound boat, meshing with the
forces of wind and water instead of using an engine to plow
against them. Sailing fit his view of how human beings should
live.

Hyperion belonged to Royal Bowman. Royal had bought her
five years earlier from an orthodontist who'd suffered a nasty hit
on the commodities market. She was a thirty-five-foot Creelock,
outfitted for offshore passage-making with radar, global positioning satellite navigation, single-sideband radio. Her salon was a
paradise of glossy teak and polished brass, her lines graceful.
Royal had let Matt use her whenever he could make time, which
was often. These days Matt had more time than anything else.

He and Royal often talked about sailing *Hyperion* down the
coast to Cabo San Lucas, a shakedown for a blue-water cruise to
Pago Pago in the South Pacific. Like Matt, the old man loved
sailing, loved the ocean, and sometimes voiced regret for ever
having left the merchant marine. The two of them often spent
hours discussing how much water tankage they would need for
their passage to Pago Pago, what kinds of tools to take, how large
a sail inventory to carry, and countless other details of their shared
fantasy.

Matt switched on *Hyperion*'s radio in order to catch the final
outs of the Mariners' game with the Red Sox. Junior Griffey
homered just as the locks started to open, and the Mariners won
the game, three to one. Matt handed the bow and stern lines to
Corps of Engineers personnel, who maneuvered *Hyperion* into the
smaller of the two locks.

A news report came on the radio: *"Seattle police are investigating a double homicide that occurred earlier today in a Capitol
Hill apartment house. The victims have been identified as Kevin*

Hilldahl, formerly of Sioux City, Iowa, and Shannon Joiner of Seattle. The King County Medical Examiner has yet to announce the official cause of the deaths, but a police source says that the two apparently died of knife wounds. The source speculated that the murders are drug-related . . .''

Matt switched the radio off, climbed back into the cockpit and sat behind the wheel. He hated broadcast news, avoided it when he could.

"Why did you stop being a cop?" Linda asked as half a million gallons of water started to pour into the lock.

The question came out of the blue, flattening Matt's mood, but he tried not to show it. He didn't want to tell her about his breakdown in the aftermath of his adopted son's death. Not yet, anyway. And he didn't want to tell her about his long, grinding war with depression. "I became disillusioned," he said, dodging.

"Over what?"

"Lots of things."

"What kind of things?"

"I developed a phobia for doughnuts."

"Hey, I'm serious. Why did you quit?"

"You really want to get into this, Linda?"

She looked at him with needy eyes, notifying him that she did indeed want to get into it. Lately Matt had begun to sense how desperately she needed a partner in her life; and now he dreaded telling her that he no longer wanted to be her lover, only her friend. He'd found much to admire about her, an offbeat sense of humor, honesty, devotion to her kids. But he couldn't be the permanent man she craved, couldn't be her kids' daddy. And he knew that he should tell her this—soon.

He swallowed, thought a moment, then decided that Linda deserved to hear the truth about his past, or as much of it as he could stand to tell. "I was a drug cop," he began. "I worked in a task force that used cops from Seattle, King County, all the surrounding counties, as well as the feds . . ."

"Like the FBI?"

"Sometimes, but mainly the DEA—that's Drug Enforcement Administration. We ran undercover stings, sent people to jail. Sometimes I went out on the street myself, bought drugs or sold them, then collared the folks I did business with."

"I'll bet you were good."

Matt grunted. "Let's say I made a lot of arrests. I've never really thought of myself . . .'' Matt hesitated, searched for words. His police career had become a harrowing tour of innocents' misery. He'd seen kids neglected and abused, left to loiter in alleys for days on end while their parents chased dragons. He'd collared twenty-year-olds for dealing and packed them off to Walla Walla, where the outrages of prison life would harden them into true criminals. Eventually he'd come to understand that no matter how many arrests the cops made, the war on drugs was unwinnable, that the war itself had become a scourge. None of this was easy to say.

"But what?" Linda pressed.

"It occurred to me one day that I wasn't one of the good guys. And it got to me, almost drove me over the edge. I had to get out.''

"But you *were* one of the good guys.''

"A badge doesn't make you good, Linda. It only gives you power over people.'' Power to smash someone's life to smithereens, to vent your darkest prejudice with impunity. Power to manufacture evidence and get away with it. Cops, like so many others in today's graceless world, had quotas to fill, and too often the quotas superseded any consideration of justice or decency. Matt didn't say any of this to Linda Hannigan, however, fearing that he would sound like a cop-hater.

He did point out that more than two-thirds of drug convictions happened to blacks and Hispanics, even though the overwhelming majority of users and dealers were white. He talked about the erosion of civil rights, how the zeal to fight drugs had generated legislation and court decisions that allowed cops to stop and search innocent people on the say-so of barking dogs. He talked about how costly the war on drugs had become, both in terms of precious tax money and the social costs—not enough spent on schools, housing, medical care, parks, and job training; too much spent on prisons and jails. The war was eating America's soul, he said. He'd decided that he couldn't be a part of it anymore. He'd gotten out.

"Forgive me for saying so, but this sounds a little strange coming from a cop,'' Linda said, looking at him with her head cocked, like a befuddled puppy.

"*Ex*-cop,'' Matt reminded her. He grinned and scratched his mustache, having told her as much about himself as he meant to.

Linda became somewhat mopey as *Hyperion* passed through

the lock into Salmon Bay. She helped him dock the boat at Shorty's Landing, helped him tidy up, then made an excuse about needing to go home early, something about her kids needing help with homework. Apparently she couldn't see herself mated to an ex-cop who'd gone soft on crime, and Matt supposed that this was for the best both for her and himself.

He climbed the stairs to his apartment over the tavern and flopped into a leather recliner, the one presentable piece of furniture he'd salvaged from his marriage. He gazed at a work in progress on the easel that stood near the window, a painting of an ancient double-ended salmon trawler. Shortly after leaving the PD and moving to Shorty's Landing, he'd taken up watercolors, bought books on how to paint, even attended classes. He painted scenes from Salmon Bay, mostly the vessels that plied its waters and the people who worked them. To date he'd deemed only one of his paintings good enough to hang, a picture of a mongrel dog in the bow of a trawler, his smiling snout thrust into the wind, his ears blowing back from his head.

Matthew Burgess' tiny apartment was his hideout. Here he felt safe from the tyrannies of the mainstream he'd fled—career, marriage, taxes, other people's expectations and demands. Here he could lie low and peek out only when he wanted to, usually through the Internet, which he preferred to TV or radio because he liked his news in doses that he could manage himself. Thus far he'd allowed no disruption of his measured routine, no disturbance of his lonely peace. He seldom thought about the future, other than misty fantasies about going to sea with Royal.

Had Linda Hannigan represented a disruption? he asked himself—a ripple on his placid little pond? And was this why he couldn't let himself love her? He wondered if he'd found a new demon to wrestle with, the Fear of Disruption.

Pictures of his family and friends hung on the walls, artifacts of a time when Matt Burgess considered himself someone of importance, a man worth loving. Marti, his ex-wife, stood behind her desk, competent-looking in a flannel business suit, the prettiest CPA in Seattle. His late father, Charles Robert Burgess—"Chucky-Bob" to family and friends—mugged for the camera during a party in honor of his retirement after thirty years with the Seattle PD. Matt's adopted son, Tristan, lay in a hospital bed on his twelfth and final birthday, his eyes glistening in the glow of candles on a huge cake.

Matt's mother posed before a table arrayed with Amway products.

His twin sisters waved at the camera, dressed in graduation gowns.

His former partner, Alex Ragsdale, pretended to take a bite out of his detective's badge.

Artifacts.

Someone knocked on the door and Matt hoisted himself out of the chair. He pulled the door open and saw Royal Bowman standing in the hall with his hands in his pockets, looking downcast and miserable.

"I was passing by," the old man said. "Saw your light under the door."

"Yeah, and I was only helping this sheep over the fence."

"You gonna keep me standing out here, or what?"

Matt invited him in, then carried dinette chairs out to the fire escape, where they could sip a couple of beers and enjoy the evening. Royal braced a foot against the railing and tilted back in his chair, made a production of lighting a Camel.

"What's going on, skipper?" Matt asked. "You look like death on a cracker, and I mean that only in the most positive sense."

"It so happens that's exactly what I feel like."

"And you're here to borrow an Ex-Lax, right? Get yourself regular again?"

"I'm here to tell you that Lauren called me this morning. We got together over in the botany garden, where we could talk without anyone hearing." He referred to the Carl S. English Botanical Garden, which was part of the grounds surrounding the Chittenden Locks. No shortage of private places there. "She told me what went down the other night at that laboratory. Told me that one of their people didn't make it out, a young girl named Megan . . ."

Royal laid out the story as his daughter had given it to him, his face dark with worry. Some English asshole had shot the guard, despite the fact that Lauren had banned deadly weapons on the operation. Over Lauren's protest, the raiders had left Megan behind at the scene of the crime. A pair of Seattle detectives had questioned Lauren yesterday.

Then he told Matt about the video that showed Megan's final grisly moments on this earth, and Matt sat wordless as he listened, staring at a gull that had alighted on the rail almost within touching distance. The bird had a streak of dark pigment on its beak, like a mustache. Probably a genetic defect.

"No idea where the cassette came from?" Matt asked.

"No idea."

"Could it be a hoax, some kind of tasteless gag?"

"I asked Lauren that, and she said no way—unless it was done by the best special effects team in Hollywood. The little girl—Megan—wouldn't be a part of any hoax, she said." Royal popped his knuckles and gazed across the marina. "I told Lauren she should call the cops, but she won't do it. Doesn't want to be a traitor to the *movement*."

"Does she understand that she's obstructing justice by sitting on this thing? It'd be another criminal charge on top of the ones she already faces, one she could do time for."

"I said as much, but it rolled off her like water off a duck."

"Better tell her to call a lawyer," Matt said.

Royal flicked his cigarette butt over the railing and took a long pull from his beer. The gull with the mustache stood as still as a wood carving, as if fascinated by the conversation. "No lawyers, she said. Doesn't trust 'em. I suggested she get herself a private detective, somebody who could poke around, find some answers, maybe point the cops to the girl's killer without incriminating Lauren or any of her crowd. But she said no to that, too. She's afraid that word would leak out somehow, blow the whole thing and hurt people she cares about. A PI's secretary might tell her boyfriend, who might tell a buddy who works at the newspaper, who might write a story—you know the drill. I told her that someday she's gonna have to trust somebody. Do you know what she said then?"

"No. What'd she say?"

"She said that the only one she trusts is *me*." Royal lit another cigarette, and Matt thought he saw the glint of a tear in his eye. Behind him, the sky ripened to a deep apricot as the sun settled behind the peaks of the Olympic Peninsula.

"What does she want you to do, skipper?"

"It took me a while to drag it out of her, but basically it's this. She wants me to find somebody to look into this thing for her, somebody reliable. She doesn't trust herself to do it."

"Look *into* it? What the hell does that mean?"

"I don't know. You were a cop—I was hoping you could give me some pointers."

"Christ, you don't *look into* something like this. You pick up the phone and call nine-one-one."

"And I've just told you she can't do that."

"Well, I'm fresh out of pointers."

They finished their beers in tense silence. The gull with the mustache shifted its weight from one foot to the other and glared at Matt as if it disapproved of his attitude in this matter. Matt stared back, and thought, *Groucho. This bird's name is Groucho.*

Finally Royal said, "Suppose I was to ask *you*, Matt."

"Ask me what?"

"You know. To look into it, maybe."

A chill traveled the length of Matt's spine. "Sorry, no can do."

"Why not?"

"Because it would make me a party to a conspiracy to obstruct justice, that's why. Going to prison isn't on my stuff-to-do-this-summer list."

"Then I guess I'm out of luck."

Out on Salmon Bay a file of pleasure boats motored east toward Lake Union and Lake Washington, bound for their home berths. As dusk thickened into night, lights on the opposite shore popped out like fireflies—the neighborhoods of Lawton and Queen Anne with their comfortable hillside homes and three-car garages. Under the Aurora Avenue Bridge a flicker of fire told of some homeless soul cooking his dinner.

"You know," Royal said, blowing smoke into the air, "I hardly got to know my little girl before she grew up. Got myself busted and sent away before she was out of the first grade. I wasn't around when she needed me—never there when she came home crying over something that happened in school. Never there to smooth things over if someone said something mean. I couldn't protect her or provide for her, never really got to be her daddy. These days she even calls me by my first name, like I'm the guy who cleans the pool."

"I'd say you've made up for whatever you didn't do when she was a kid."

"That's bullshit. I've never been able to give her anything. What do you give a girl who's already got the whole world?"

"A lot, seems to me. What money can't buy. Love, under-standing."

"Yeah? So what happens the one time she comes to me for help, the one time she reaches out to her daddy? Nothing, that's what—jack-squat. I'm too damn old and weak to help my own daughter. Do you have any idea how that makes me feel?"

Groucho the Gull switched to his other leg, stretched his wings, but stayed on, like this was getting good. "You're not old and weak," Matt protested. "What makes you think I'd sail off to Pago Pago with someone old and weak?"

Royal turned in his chair, planted his elbows on his knees and stared into Matt's face. "About a month ago I started pissing blood. Made myself believe it'd go away, but it hasn't. It's only gotten worse."

"You've seen a doctor, I hope." Matt felt something cold take root inside his chest. "What did he say?"

"Hell, I haven't seen any doctor. I don't have insurance on myself. By the time I pay the expenses on the bar and marina at the end of the month, make the payments on the boat, I've barely got enough to buy a couple cartons of smokes. Anyhow, I don't need a doctor to tell me what's wrong with me. It's bladder can-cer, same as my old man died of. Comes from bad genes and smokin' like a fuckin' diesel all my life. There's not a thing any doctor can do about it."

"Skipper, you don't know that. We need to get you to a . . ."

"Shut up a minute, will you? I didn't tell you this so you could go all blubbery on me. I only wanted you to know why I've got the guts to ask you this. I'm asking you as a friend, Matt—to help me *be* there this one time for my little girl. Go up to her place in Magnolia, look at the video, check things out. Listen to her story, give her whatever advice you can. That's all I'm asking for."

Matt grimaced, took a deep breath. Another ripple on his placid little pond, the kind that could become a tsunami, an inner voice warned. He felt as if his life was about to change radically, and that he was helpless to prevent it. "I'll do whatever you want, skipper," he heard himself say against his better judgment. "I'll go up there right now, if you want me to."

"Tomorrow's soon enough." Royal leaned back in his chair, his face finally relaxing. "I'll call her tonight, tell her you'll be there around—what—eleven? She's usually free by then. By the way, she called me 'Dad' today. That's the first time, far as I can remember. *Dad.* It sounded good, Matt. You can't imagine how good.''

But Matt could imagine. He closed his eyes and saw the face of a boy in a hospital bed, the light of birthday candles in his dying eyes. Groucho the Gull took flight suddenly, as if he had miles to fly before he slept this night.

Eight

At two minutes before 11:00 the next morning, Matt Burgess halted his rusting Jeep Cherokee at the front gate of the house at 5 Jenkins Way in Magnolia. He stared in through the wrought-iron bars and tried simply to acclimate himself to the scale of the place. The house looked like a movie set, too perfect to be real, a sprawling Mediterranean villa built of creamy stucco, with a tiled roof the color of cinnamon. *Good enough to eat*, Matt thought.

From here he could see a pair of tennis courts, two swimming pools, and a guest house twice as big as the West Seattle bungalow he and his sisters had grown up in. A gazebo the size of a band shell stood at the edge of Elliott Bay, which shimmered like a blue dream. Walkways of crushed granite wound through the grounds, garnished in blooming azaleas, rhododendrons, and roses—a wonderland of color.

Why does anyone need this much? he wondered.

He pressed a button on the intercom box, which summoned a male voice with a Spanish accent. "Good morning. May I help you?"

"Matt Burgess for Lauren Bowman. I understand she's expecting me." He glanced at his watch and saw that he was on time.

"Yes, sir—you are on my list. You may park in the main drive. Ms. Bowman is waiting for you in the guest house, which is at the north end of the grounds, to your right."

"I see it." He doubted anyone could have missed it.

The gate buzzed open, and Matt drove onto the grounds, anxiety coiling in his gut. Someone had killed a security guard, someone else a young woman, both of which were police matters. Meddling in them could only compound the crime of keeping them quiet. He envisioned a nasty headline: *Ex-cop charged in cover-up*. Yet, he could hardly refuse this favor to Royal Bowman, who'd treated him like a son, taken him in after his bout with the dark animal, given him work, a boat to sail. You don't say no to someone who has given you that much.

He parked between a red Bugatti and a black Mercedes, got out of the Jeep and stood a moment in the sunshine, inhaling the sweetness of azaleas and letting the warmth soak into his shoulders. His nose tickled with hay fever, and he sneezed. He reached for the pocket-sized pack of Kleenex he always carried with him this time of year, pulled out a tissue, and blew his nose.

A bull-shouldered man in a well-tailored blazer emerged from the entryway of the house. He had a fighter's blocky face, a thick brow, and closely spaced eyes. "So, who the hell are *you*?" he demanded. His hair was dark and slick, his face a rich man's shade of tan.

Matt stuffed the damp Kleenex into the pocket of his khakis and tried to look dignified. "I'm Matt Burgess. I have an appointment with Ms. Bowman."

"You another one of her space-cadet pals—animal-lover, soldier in the revolution of kindness, all that?"

"Uh, I don't think I've had the pleasure." Matt managed a smile and offered a handshake. He noticed a gold ID bracelet on the man's wrist, diamond rings on his fingers. "I assume you're Mr. Granger."

"What do you say we don't get chummy, okay? This is my property you're standing on, and I don't know you from Adam. I want to know what the hell you and that junker are doing here." He took a menacing step forward, and Matt's old police reflexes came alive. Granger had the build of a linebacker, and he looked strong and fit, even though he appeared to be a decade older than Matt. He also had a good thirty-pound weight advantage.

Matt stood his ground, spoke in an even tone. "I'm here at your wife's invitation, sir. Otherwise I wouldn't have gotten past the front gate, as you well know. I don't want any trouble, believe me." Granger halted, then shook his head as if mortified over the scum his wife hung with these days.

A solid-looking black woman appeared in the door behind him, her hair in shoulder-length cornrows, her fingernails painted silver. She wore pearls over a charcoal business suit. "What is it, Gabe? Is this gentleman a client of yours? I hope you haven't forgotten that we have a meeting downtown in fifteen minutes."

Matt introduced himself to her, feeling thankful for her arrival. He'd feared that he and Gabe Granger were about to go a round of freestyle right there in the driveway. The woman shook his hand and said she was Georgia Pichette, executive assistant to Lauren Bowman.

"We were just leaving," she said, "but I'd be happy to set up an appointment with you later in the week, if you're available. I handle Ms. Bowman's business affairs as they relate to Granger-Bowman Properties. She normally doesn't concern herself with real estate anymore. If you'd give me your card . . ."

"I'm not here about real estate, actually," Matt said.

"He's one of those lovers of furry creatures my wife surrounds herself with," Granger said. "Either that or he's here to get physical with her, like that British twit she's been seeing. Is that what it's all about, Mr. . . . uh . . . what the hell did you say your name was? You come here to get sweaty with my wife?"

"Gabe, *please*." Georgia Pichette smiled an apology at Matt and latched on to Granger's arm, holding him back.

Matt's annoyance with Granger jumped into the red zone, but he took a deep breath and fought down his temper. "My name is Burgess, like I said before. *Matthew* Burgess. I'm here on business, nothing else. Now if you'll excuse me, I'm late for my appointment with Ms. Bowman." He turned and walked toward the guest house, his neck-hairs bristling.

"Give her a message for me, *Matthew*," Granger called after him. "Tell her that she's still my goddamn wife, and that she'd do well to remember that. Tell her there's a price to pay for fucking Gabe Granger in the nose!"

Matt walked on, still breathing deeply, his boat shoes crunching on the crushed-granite path that led to the guest house. He understood now why Royal had gritted his teeth when speaking Granger's name. The guy had all the charm of a Komodo dragon.

He came to the covered entryway of the guest house, rang the bell and heard dogs barking inside. *Big* dogs. A small blond woman answered the door and smiled at him through a smattering of freckles, a nice contrast to the greeting he'd received in the drive.

"You must be Matt Burgess. I'm Jandee Vernon, Lauren's personal assistant. Welcome to Jenkins Way. The boss is expecting you, but she'll be a few minutes yet. She's just getting out of the shower."

A pair of black, shepherdlike dogs accosted him with waving tails and sloppy tongues. Belgian Tervurens, Jandee said, Desi and Lucy. She introduced them as if they were people, and Matt patted their heads, scratched their ears. He was glad they were friendly.

The interior of the guest house looked like a spread in *Architectural Digest*—expanses of wood, stone, and glass; artful sprays of flowers gracing the foyer and the formal living room; recessed lighting everywhere. Jandee showed him to a sitting room, which boasted an array of original art on the walls and a million-dollar view of Elliott Bay and the snowy Olympic Mountains.

"Do you like art?" she asked, noticing Matt's interest in the paintings.

"I do. I don't know much about it yet, but I'm learning. I like this one a lot." He pointed to an etching of two mariners in sou'westers against a background of fog and frothy ocean. They were taking a sight with a sextant on the deck of a ship, their faces taut with the urgency of finding the horizon through the muck. Etched in black ink on misty paper, the scene evoked a sense of hard-to-see realities, of truth hovering just beyond the eye's reach.

"That's a Winslow Homer," Jandee explained. "It's called *Eight Bells*, done in 1887. I think it's easily one of his best."

Matt gazed at it and felt something stir inside him. For a moment the picture made him forget why he'd come.

"If you like Homer, you'll probably like this one by George Maynard, another American of that era." She motioned him to the opposite wall, where hung a painting of a young girl seated with a book under a tall, multipaned window. Beyond the panes a snow-encrusted steeple loomed against a bleak sky. "It's called *Reading at Teatime*. I especially like the feeling of the light infusing through the window—sort of cold and gray, but comforting at the same time, don't you think? And check out the girl's face. Is that serenity, or what?"

Matt gazed long at the work, thought it beautiful in an aching kind of way. He had trouble tearing his eyes from it. "Are you an artist?" he asked.

"I wish I were. I have an M.A. in art history from Columbia, actually. I worked for the Seattle Art Museum a while back, did some consulting on the side. That's how I met the boss. She was a client, and I advised her on what art to buy, what to sell. Still do, in fact. One day we got to talking, discovered we were both animal-rights freaks. She offered me the job as her personal assistant at twice the money I was making at the museum, and I'm like, 'Where do I sign?' "

"So, Ms. Bowman has both an executive assistant *and* a personal assistant?" he asked.

Jandee chuckled. "I take it you've met Georgia Pichette."

"A few minutes ago, up in the driveway. And Mr. Granger, too."

"Yeah, well—Georgia's an executive assistant nonpareil, a real business whiz, Stanford grad. We call her Wonder Woman. She runs the boss's end of the company, works directly with Gabe, which is a perfect fit, because their personalities kind of cancel each other out, like acid and lye. The boss no longer involves herself directly in real estate, as I'm sure you've heard."

Matt then asked what a *personal* assistant does, and Jandee told him—appointments, correspondence, together with the nitty-gritty of LOCA business, which included speech-writing, travel arrangements, and logistics for fund-raisers and meetings. An around-the-clock job, given Lauren Bowman's energy level, and one that required Jandee to live here at the guest house. "Fortunately, opulence doesn't offend me," she added, laughing, "as long as I'm not paying for it. My social life is a little rocky, though."

"Ms. Vernon, do you . . . ?"

"It's Jandee, okay?"

"Jandee. Do you know why I'm here?"

Her expression darkened, as if a cloud had scudded over the sun. "I do. The boss and I don't have any secrets that I know of."

At that moment Lauren Bowman herself breezed into the room, dressed in faded jeans and a burgundy sweatshirt, her dark hair hanging damp around her neck. The dogs bounded to her and lapped at her hands.

"You're Matt Burgess, right? Thanks for coming—sorry to keep you waiting. My trainer was late this morning, which knocks my whole day out of sync."

Matt thought, *A security guard has been shot dead, a young woman butchered, but we don't miss our workout with our personal trainer, do we?* Then Lauren shook his hand, gave him her sunrise smile, and Matt felt something he hadn't felt in a long time.

"Want some tea? Jandee, have Rainy bring us some tea, chamomile for me. What kind do you want, Matt—Earl Grey, maybe? I start with Earl Grey in the morning to get jazzed, then switch to chamomile to calm down."

Matt sat in the indicated chair and asked for a cup of Earl Grey, while Lauren sat on a sofa across from him, her long legs stretched out on a colorful throw rug. She instructed Jandee to tell the cook to set an extra place for lunch, not bothering to ask if Matt would stay, simply assuming that he would.

"You got it, boss." Jandee hustled away.

Matt found himself studying Lauren Bowman as he'd once studied witnesses and suspects in his cop days, reading her body language, interpreting her mannerisms. He liked what he saw, even though she was far from beautiful in the cover girl sense. She was tall and lithe, small-breasted, square-shouldered. Her face was angular, her chin prominent—maybe a bit too much so, the unmistakable genetic influence of Royal Bowman. She had a straight nose and lively brown eyes. She wore no makeup, at least not at this moment, but her skin glowed with a natural vitality. Matt imagined himself touching her cheek, and suspected that he would like the feel of it.

He pegged her right off as a natural-born people-handler, one of those fortunate souls whose charisma hums like a tuning fork. Spend thirty seconds with her, Matt thought, and you want to do something nice for her. Small wonder that she'd proved herself a super-saleswoman or that she'd made a zillion bucks. But then he noticed a tautness in the muscles around her mouth, a hint of darkness beneath her smile, signs that she'd suffered, was *still* suffering. Pangs of regret, he supposed, inasmuch as people had died because of things she'd done or hadn't done, and grief for the dead Megan—which Matt found reassuring. Lauren Bowman was a mere mortal after all, one with a conscience and feelings.

"So, where do you want to start?" she asked, caressing a

dog's ear. "Royal said I should tell you everything, keep nothing back. He said I could trust you like a brother, and that's exactly what I intend to do." The smile again, but fainter now, and a little sad. "He reminded me that you're my only option at this point, short of going to the police."

"Before we take this any further," Matt said, "you need to understand that I'm here as a favor to your dad. I told him I'd give you advice if I could, but that's all. I'm not an investigator, private or otherwise, and I won't have any involvement with your . . . uh, *problem* after this meeting. He did make that clear, right?"

"I really wouldn't have expected any more than that. I only agreed to talk with you because Royal badgered me into it. But don't get me wrong—I'm grateful to you for making time for me. I want you to know that."

Matt frowned. *Badgered* her into it? Royal had said that Lauren had come to *him* for help, that she'd asked for someone to look into the matter of Megan Reiner's death—she couldn't trust lawyers or private detectives whom she didn't know, something like that. She'd called him "Dad."

"I assume my father has told you how important it is to maintain total confidentiality," Lauren went on. "I have friends and acquaintances who'll get hurt badly if any of this gets out." Matt assured her that he would keep to himself everything he learned here today.

A young woman came into the room, carrying a tray with a teapot, cups and saucers, a plate of cookies. Lauren introduced her as Rainy Hales, full-time vegan chef. The girl had a shy, heart-shaped face and a wispy frame, as if a stiff breeze might blow her away.

When he saw her, Matt immediately thought, *Junkie*, for she had that vacuous, empty-eyed expression that many herion addicts never fully rid themselves of, no matter how long they stay clean. Matt had seen the look countless times while working undercover on Capitol Hill, often in the faces of runaway kids who'd gravitated to Seattle with the brittle dream of becoming grunge-rock stars, only to slip into heroin's black hole and lose themselves forever.

"Don't let her tender age fool you," Lauren said as Matt shook Rainy's hand. "She's one of the best vegan hash-slingers around. I'm lucky to have her." Rainy gave a demure smile, muttered a nice-to-meet-you, and left the room.

Matt poured himself some tea, then took a ballpoint pen and a small notepad from the pocket of his sport coat. He suggested that Lauren start at the beginning, with the planning of the raid on the Pacific Northwest BioCenter. He wanted to know who was involved, the actual participants as well as those who had knowledge of the operation. He wanted as much depth on each person as Lauren could provide, together with the details of the raid itself. And then he would need to see the video, of course.

Lauren started with Ian Prather and Vera Kemmis, a pair of British legends in the ultramilitant Front for Animal Freedom. They'd entered the country about a year earlier after waging a long underground campaign against corporate animal abusers in Canada. Lauren voiced mixed feelings toward the pair. They'd shown themselves to be full-blown anarchists, she said, whose cause encompassed far more than animal rights. Matt remembered Gabe Granger's mention of a "British twit" who'd been seeing Lauren, and wondered if Prather was the guy.

Next came Rod Welton and Megan Reiner, the other two participants in the raid. Welton was a juvenile probation officer near retirement, Megan a graduate student and teaching assistant. Before hooking up with the FAF, each had established long records of activism with local animal-rights groups, including illegal rescues of animals from harmful circumstances—minks from ranches in Oregon and eastern Washington, chickens and turkeys from factory farms, even a chimpanzee from a solitary glass cage in a shopping mall in Tacoma.

During the six-month period before the raid on the BioCenter, Ian Prather had trained the three of them—Rod, Megan, and Lauren—in what he'd called *tradecraft*, the techniques of animal rescue and violent protest. The training covered planning and surveillance, penetration of security systems, escape, evasion, and internal security. He'd imparted to them his own discipline and commitment to the cause, his own ironclad altruism, only to shatter his standing with Lauren by carrying a gun on the raid and killing a fellow human being.

Matt jotted notes on his pad, asked questions now and then. While Lauren talked, he noticed that her mouth always seemed to be at work even when she wasn't saying anything, lips pursed or stretched tight in a thoughtful grimace, smiling or pouting or grinning, never neutral or idle. He liked that mouth, tried not to imagine it doing certain other things.

Lauren next recounted the actual events of the raid on the Pacific Northwest BioCenter and all that had happened in the aftermath. She did so in precise detail, her voice quivering at times, her eyes misting as she described the killing of the Pro-Guard security man and the abandonment of Megan Reiner.

Matt jotted the name ''ProGuard'' on his pad, and next to it, the name ''Rags.'' His former partner on the antidrug task force, Alex Ragsdale, now worked for that very firm. Rags and Matt had reached the same conclusions about the hopelessness of the war on drugs, and had left the PD at roughly the same time. Rags had slid smoothly into private security, an industry that had prospered with the dawning of the New World Order.

The matter of the ProGuard security man—a man who should not have been there, if Kemmis and Prather's casing of the BioCenter had been accurate—raised an interesting question: Why had ProGuard suddenly decided to station an on-site patrolman at the facility on that particular night? Had someone at the firm gotten wind of a threat? Matt suspected that Rags could get answers to those questions, if he were to call on him.

''We escaped by driving through Volunteer Park,'' Lauren said, wrapping up. ''Kept the lights off, drove right through the trees and swung back south on Interlaken. Rod had walked the escape route at least twenty times, so he could've driven it with his eyes closed.''

''And from there?''

''North again across the Montlake Bridge. We crossed the U-Dub campus and rendezvoused with Marc in an alley off Laverna Boulevard. He took the van and the animals to a place he owns east of Everett. It's rural and private, and he's outfitted it to take care of rescued animals on a temporary basis. The rest of us split up and went our separate ways. Except for Megan, of course . . .'' Her voice cracked.

Matt chewed the push-button of his pen, thinking. ''Okay, so you'd made everyone promise not to carry weapons,'' he said. ''But Prather carried one anyway. He must've given you some reason to suspect that he'd do that, or you wouldn't have made him promise not to.''

The FAF, Lauren explained, had become increasingly violent against human beings in recent years, to the chagrin of activists like herself. Only last year an FAF cell in England had blown up the car of an executive in the meat-processing industry. A few

weeks later another cell had fire-bombed the front porch of a
noted medical researcher. In Canada, the FAF had sent a wave
of booby-trapped letters through the mail—some were actual
bombs while others contained razor blades taped to the inner
edges of the envelopes, the blades purportedly infected with the
AIDS virus. The devices had gone to the owners of mink ranches
and officials in the fur industry. People had gotten hurt, a few
seriously.

"Until now, there's only been one fatality, thank God—a little
boy hit by shrapnel from a bomb in London," Lauren said. "It's
my view that we've had too many casualties on both sides of the
issue. I'm like the vast majority of FAF and LOCA members—I
don't believe in hurting people. Controlled violence against property is useful, as long as it disrupts the killing of animals and
takes the profit out of it. But violence against other human beings
is reprehensible."

"And Prather had been a part of all this—the letter bombs,
the razor blades?"

"I think so. While he and Vera were in Canada, there were
some gunfights at mink ranches in Saskatchewan and Alberta. The
ranchers decided it was okay to shoot at animal rescuers, and a
few of the rescuers shot back. Several people were wounded, but
nobody got killed, fortunately. It's widely known in the militant
community that Ian led at least one of those raids, and that he's
started to carry a gun."

"A legend in his own time."

"You might say that."

"Okay, we've covered the raid and the participants," Matt
said, taking a sip of tea. "Who else knew about the operation?"

Lauren told him about Dominic Federico and Helga Dunlop,
the cofounders of the League Opposed to Cruelty to Animals and
key figures in the national leadership. They lived in Bethesda,
Maryland, the suburb of Washington, D.C., where LOCA had its
headquarters. Federico served as chairman of the board, Dunlop
as executive director. Before forming LOCA, the couple had spent
years in the more radical FAF, participating in operations that
ranged from ramming whaling ships off Portugal to sabotaging
fox hunts in England. They were blooded veterans of the animal-
rights movement, their bona fides beyond question. At their urg-
ing, Lauren had provided a safe house for Prather and Kemmis
after their flight from Canada, together with financial support.

"I recognize their names," Matt said. "I remember reading about them somewhere." Probably in junk mail that had come to his ex-wife, he thought, when he still lived in a house in the suburbs—appeals for money to save the bunnies in the photos from those evil cancer researchers.

Next on the list were Elise Lekander and her son, Marc, both of whom were like family to Lauren. Elise was a wealthy heiress, a well-known local philanthropist and a major financial supporter of LOCA. Marc, despite personal problems he'd suffered as a young man, had become an important role player in the local animal-rights underground, the "fixer" who was able to find homes for rescued animals of all kinds.

Next came Jandee Vernon, Lauren's personal assistant, whom Matt had just met, longtime animal-rights activist, sometime art consultant, former associate curator at the Seattle Art Museum. Having hired her two years earlier, Lauren trusted her with every facet of her life, both public and private. Jandee had never betrayed that trust, and had proved herself a loving and steadfast friend.

And finally, Rainy Hales, the wispy vegan chef. Lauren had met her several years ago at a meeting of the Northwest Animal Rights Advocacy, a Seattle-based group that picketed animal-products industries, staged demonstrations and rescued endangered animals whenever possible. Lauren had mentioned to Rainy that she needed a vegan chef, and Rainy had expressed interest in the job. But Lauren had hired someone else, an unreliable young man who'd simply disappeared a few months later without so much as a good-bye. Rainy had asked for a second chance at the job, having completed more formal culinary training in the meantime, and Lauren, desperate for someone to run her kitchen, had given her that chance. The girl had performed beyond Lauren's wildest expectations. And yes, Lauren trusted her.

"That's it—no one else?" Matt asked.

"That's it. No one else."

"How about your husband?"

Lauren chuckled. "I've kept him in the dark about my current activities. He's not what you'd call a sympathizer with our cause." She pursed her lips, thought a moment. "Has Royal told you about how things are between Gabe and me?"

"Not in so many words."

"We've been separated for nearly two years, which means that we really only had about one year's worth of actual marriage. I live here in the guest house, he lives in the villa. Our business partnership is still intact, and will probably stay that way until we get around to negotiating some kind of satisfactory split. Once or twice a month he stomps over here and pounds on the door, rails about how we're still married and how I ought to act like a wife. I try to ignore him, but it's a little like trying to ignore a rhinoceros.''

"I met him in the driveway when I came in. He asked me to give you a message . . .''

"Something about my having fucked him in the nose, I'll bet.''

"You've heard it before.''

"Oh, yeah.''

Matt thought, *How did she ever get involved with a barbarian like Gabe Granger?* He couldn't imagine a more unlikely business partnership, never mind a marriage.

Matt refilled his cup and reached for a cookie, which prompted Desi and Lucy to forsake their mistress and sit before him, one at each knee, begging shamelessly and drooling on his Dockers. "I hope you don't think I'm out of line saying this,'' he said, "but you really don't seem like the FAF type. I mean, here you are, a successful businesswoman, rich, personal trainer, the whole shot . . .''

"Our movement has nothing to do with socioeconomics,'' Lauren said, her tone suggesting that she'd heard such comments before and had grown weary of them. "We're businesspeople, professionals, students, rich and poor alike. Come to one of our rallies and you'll find all shapes and colors—boomers, slackers, little old ladies in tennis shoes. We're just people who care about our fellow members of the animal kingdom.''

"I see,'' Matt said, suspecting that he'd just heard a passage from a canned speech. "But you're in real estate. You're a *developer*, for crying out loud. You should be throwing fundraisers for Republican congressmen, not breaking into research laboratories. Hell, you should be summering in Provence and wintering in St. Kitt or cruising around the Sound in a big white yacht.''

"Is that so?''

"It'd be more in character for people like you, seems to me.''

Lauren's face hardened, and Matt saw a new side of her—the

pissed-off side. "So, you think you know about people like me?
I grew up in a run-down neighborhood in southeast Portland, Mr.
Burgess, in a house that would almost fit inside the master bathroom of the villa next door. My mother worked as a secretary for
a furniture wholesaler, so we were always hurting for money. It
was all she could do to put food on the table and keep me in
cheap school clothes. We never went on vacations, never had any
special outings. I won't go into all the problems I had as a kid"—
she breathed in and exhaled, as if to purge old and ugly memories—"except to say that they were problems no kid should ever
have to face. I ran away when I was sixteen, came to Seattle,
ended up on the street because I was penniless, not to mention
young and stupid. I was lucky enough to meet someone who cared
about people like me, someone who felt a responsibility for her
fellow human beings . . ."

"That would be Elise Lekander. Not a bad person to have in
your corner."

"She's a true angel of mercy, Mr Burgess. She *lives* her convictions, like most people don't have the guts to do. She not only
saved my life, but showed me *why* my life was worth saving.
Thanks to her I went back to school, studied hard, went to college.
I even . . ."

"Royal told me your story—right out of Horatio Alger."

"Royal knows I'm not the type who raises money for Republican congressmen or motors around in big white yachts. And now
you know it, too."

"Yeah, you're just one of us down-home folks, a regular Ma
Kettle," Matt said, grinning inappropriately.

Lauren paused, swallowed. "Okay, I've made some money.
I'm in the upper one-percent yearly income category, if you want
to get specific. But money hasn't changed who I am. I haven't
forgotten where I came from or how lucky I've been. If anyone
deserves credit for the person you see in front of you, it's Elise.
She took me into her family, polished off my rough edges, taught
me not to pick my teeth at the table. She taught me values, gave
me a sense of social justice."

"And what else?"

Lauren smiled at him now, but not warmly. "It's no secret
that Elise supplied me with venture capital, more than a million
dollars of it. *That's* how I got rich—I admit it, okay? I used
Lekander money to make money of my own. Like anyone with

average intelligence and a million dollars of someone else's cash in her pocket, I did well financially. I married Gabe Granger, and did even better. I don't pretend to have any special genius. Money begets money, as everyone knows.''

''But why animal rights? Why not homeless people or crippled kids, or the rain forest or the whales? Why not education or drug rehab, something that's . . .'' Matt fished for polite words.

''Go ahead, say it—*worthwhile*.'' Lauren got up from the sofa and went to the glass doors that gave onto a deck, the dogs at her side. She gazed out at Puget Sound, her arms pulled tight over her chest, a dark silhouette against the brightness of noon. ''Who decides which of this world's creatures deserves our mercy and which ones don't?'' she asked, talking to the plate glass. ''Are you willing to be that judge, Mr. Burgess?''

''Look, I'm sorry,'' he said, rising from his chair. ''I don't have any right to question your beliefs.'' He knew now that she'd already done this, as he himself had done after becoming a drug cop—a painful process, like pulling off a patch of skin with a pair of pliers. ''Why don't we pretend that the last five minutes never happened? And I promise to stop being an asshole, okay?''

''Save your apology,'' Lauren said, wiping something from her eye as she turned to face him. ''I don't require kid-glove treatment.''

''Of course not. Can we get back to using first names again?''

''Let's just get on with this, if you don't mind. Do you have any more questions, or do you want to see the video?''

Matt bit his lip, studied his notes. He could find no reason to put off the next step, distasteful though it was. ''The video, right. Might as well get it over with, huh?'' He sat down again. Lauren went to a table, picked up a remote control, and switched on the VCR.

Nine

Matt parked his Jeep in the usual spot behind Shorty's Tavern, next to the Dumpsters. He sat a moment before getting out, collecting himself, still feeling shaky after watching the video of Megan Reiner's rape and murder. He worried that he would never again close his eyes without seeing the poor girl's face, the desperation in her eyes, the *loathing* . . .

The adjacent parking space was empty, where Royal's big green Suburban usually sat. Matt felt uneasy, because on Mondays Royal normally handled the chores of restocking for the coming week. He liked being on hand to sign for delivery of beer kegs, liquor, and canned foodstuffs for the tavern, liked to check each item personally to make certain a supplier hadn't shorted him. In the three years that Matt had lived and worked at Shorty's Landing, he'd never known Royal to vary his Monday routine. Something wasn't right.

Matt used his key to let himself through the rear door into the kitchen, hoping to find Royal's life-partner, Cleo Castillo, bustling around in her huge apron with *The Big Cheese* embroidered on it, running the show with her customary drill-sergeant efficiency. Instead he found Jimmy Jaspero, the assistant manager who normally cooked on Tuesdays, Wednesdays, and Thursdays, a dark man of fifty with a gray mustache and a large gold ring in his ear. He looked as if he could've been Captain Kidd's first mate.

"They're not here," Jaspero said, seeing Matt. "They're over at Cabrini Hospital, somethin' about the old man peein' blood an' fallin' down. Ambulance came an' got 'im, and Cleo went behind in the Suburban. Told me to tell you not to worry.''

Which was like telling the tide not to come in.

After battling a Gordian knot of traffic for half an hour, Matt entered the main lobby of Cabrini Hospital, a tall pile of bricks and glass that stood on a hill on Madison Street. A receptionist gave him Royal's room number. Minutes later he pushed through the door of a semi-private room, which Royal shared with another patient, a young man who had liver problems, judging from his orange skin and yellowed eyes.

Matt fought a wave of nausea—he loathed hospitals. He'd spent too many nights and days in a room like this one, sitting next to the bed of a little boy who wanted nothing more than to breathe, never mind doing the things that other kids did—playing baseball and soccer, swimming, riding a skateboard. Matt hated the antiseptic smell of the place, the rules, the food. Most of all, he hated the memories.

Royal sat in his bed, propped up with pillows and tethered to an IV rack, a hospital gown drooping off his bony shoulders like a toga. His silvery hair stuck out in tufts around his ears, giving him the look of a mad-professor or a psycho ax-murderer—Matt couldn't decide which. Cleo Castillo sat in a chair next to the bed, wearing her trademark apron. She was a large woman in her sixties, well over two hundred pounds, olive skin, Roman nose.

"What some people won't do to get out of work," Matt said, approaching the bed. He patted Royal's arm.

"They told me this was a class place," Royal growled, "and look who they let in."

Matt said hi to Cleo, bent over and kissed her forehead. She smiled, caught his hand and squeezed it. She had the biggest, kindest eyes Matt had ever seen.

"He had some kind of seizure," Cleo said. "I heard a bump, went into the bathroom and found him on the floor with his eyes rolling back in his head. The water in the toilet was all red and . . .''

"It wasn't any goddamn *seizure*," Royal protested. "I got a little light-headed, that's all—too much beer last night. I'll be out of here before you know it."

"They're doing tests," Cleo continued. "Doctor says it might not be anything real bad, but whatever it is, it needs attention *now*."

"Has he gotten any rest?" Matt asked.

"He won't let me lower the bed for him. Wants to sit up like this so he can stay awake and cuss at me. He—"

Royal shook his fist in the air. "Would you people quit talking like I'm not here? I *am* here, goddamn it, but soon as I get some lunch, I'm going home to get some work done."

"The test results should be in by this time tomorrow," Cleo said, still talking to Matt. "The doctor put a rush on it, said she knows how hard it is to wait. Seems like a nice young woman." Cleo turned her attention to Royal. "And you're staying put until we know what's wrong with you, understand? You try to get out of that frigging bed, and you'll deal with me, two falls out of three."

Royal groaned. "I'm sixty or seventy pounds under her weight class. She could throw me through the goddamn ceiling, if she wanted to."

Matt chuckled, tried to look unworried. "You'll be okay, skipper. I feel it in my bones."

Cleo said, "Now that you're here, Matt, I think I'll go down to the cafeteria, get a cup of coffee and a sandwich, give you boys a chance to talk." She stood and slipped off the apron.

"Yeah, you do that," Royal said. "Have a goddamn sandwich. Have three of 'em. We wouldn't want you to lose any weight."

"Take your time," Matt told Cleo. "We'll be fine." After she'd gone, he sat on the edge of the bed. "Why do you have to be such a shithead?" he asked Royal. "She loves you, you know—which I'll admit is a mystery, considering your looks and personality."

"Hell, I know that. She's the best damn thing that's ever happened to me, even though she's not what you'd call pure as the driven snow. I guess you could say I regret treating her like shit all these years, goin' out like I do at night, not coming home sometimes, never telling her where I am. I can't understand why she stays around."

"I just told you. She loves you."

Royal let a minute go by, during which he stared out the window. The room had a decent view of Elliott Bay and downtown Seattle with its imposing vertical architecture—the Space Needle, the IBM Building, Washington Mutual Tower, all the others. Out on the Sound, container ships crawled north toward the Strait of

Juan de Fuca and the San Juan Islands, or south toward the port facilities on Harbor Island. Royal's eyes filled with longing, as if he wished he was in the merchant marine again, standing on the heaving deck of a freighter or a tanker, the wind fresh in his face.

"I've got to ask it," he said, avoiding Matt's face. "How'd it go at Jenkins Way? You see the video, talk to Lauren?"

"Did both. Her cook served lunch afterward—Japanese egg-plant and mushroom sauté over rice, but I couldn't eat. In fact, I'm not sure I'll ever eat again."

"That bad, uh?"

"As bad as anything I've ever experienced."

"Yeah, as far as I'm concerned, God didn't mean for men to eat like rabbits."

"I'm not talking about the food, asshole."

The young man in the next bed coughed. Royal glanced at him, lowered his voice. "Jesus, what's happened to your sense of humor? You gave Lauren some advice, I hope."

"The best I had to give."

"Which was?"

"I told her to call the cops, 'fess up. Work a plea bargain in return for giving them the two Brits, Kemmis and Prather. Get the other guy, Welton, to come along, reinforce her version of what happened at the BioCenter. With a little luck and a good lawyer, neither Lauren nor Welton would do jail time."

"You think the cops might go for that?"

"They'd go for it. Kemmis and Prather are big-deal interna-tional dirt-balls, wanted in Canada and Britain. Taking them down would be much sexier than going after Lauren and some juvey probation officer."

Trouble was, Matt added, Lauren had rejected his advice out of hand. She couldn't turn her back on the movement, no matter what she felt toward Kemmis and Prather.

"I told you she was no stoolie," Royal replied, a perverse pride showing. "Not my little girl. She's true to her friends and her beliefs, that much I'll say for her."

"I just hope she comes to her senses. And soon."

Royal closed his watery eyes, thinking, maybe resting. For a moment Matt feared that he'd passed out. Then he came back again. "What about the dead girl?"

"She's beyond help, skipper."

"But somebody killed her, shot it with a camcorder and sent

the tape to Lauren. The son of a bitch is *interested* in my daughter. He knows who she is, where she lives. I don't mind saying that scares the hell out of me."

"It's a police matter. They're equipped to handle things like this. We're not."

Royal gripped Matt's forearm with his left hand, the fingertips digging into the flesh and causing pain. Matt wondered how the old man had worked up such hard callouses on the tips of his fingers. "Listen, Matt. I've been thinking about all this, the killing, the videotape, the way it all went down. I've got to wonder if there's somebody close to Lauren who means her harm, somebody who knew about the raid on the lab and tipped off the killer, fixed it so he could snatch Megan at the BioCenter. Either that or the killer has bugged her house, knows what's going on in her life. How else could he have found out about . . . ?"

Matt shushed him, fearing that the jaundiced patient in the next bed would overhear. "Let's talk about this later," he said.

"Fuck, no. Let's talk about it *now*. I'm not gonna lie here in this bed while some monster is watching Lauren, listening to her, waiting for a chance to do God knows what. Who can say what's going through this creep's mind? I need to know who he is, what makes him tick. I need to find out where he is so I can get to him before he gets to Lauren."

"Skipper, calm down. You're a sick man."

"I'm not sick enough to sit here on my ass and do nothing. Not at a time like this."

He started to peel away the adhesive tape that held the IV needle in his arm, clearly meaning to be on his way. Matt stopped him. "You can forget about doing something crazy. You're staying here."

"Is that so? You gonna break my arm, or what? You gonna sit here around the clock, watching me? You gonna piss in a jar so you don't have to leave the room? Because the minute you turn your back, I'm gone."

Matt sighed, shook his head. He knew that the old bastard was manipulating him, but what could he do? "Look. Why don't you let me poke a little deeper into this thing, see if I can get some answers? I may have a way of finding out who's watching Lauren, if that's indeed what's happening."

"And you'll make sure she stays safe, right? Make sure nobody gets to her?"

"I'll do the best I can. In return, all I ask is that you stay here until the doc gives the all-clear. Is it a deal, or what?"

Royal looked skeptical, but Matt knew it was a *studied* look. Royal was about to get exactly what he wanted. "Sounds fair enough, I guess. I stay here till I get sprung, you get on Lauren's case, help her stay clear of that pervert. Is that what I'm hearin'?"

Matt nodded and tried not to look ill.

"Okay. You got yourself a deal." Royal settled back onto his pillow, closed his eyes. "Last night I dreamt that you and I sailed *Hyperion* within sight of the south coast of Sumatra," he said, a smile tugging his mouth. "We had Lauren's goddamn dogs along—why, I don't know, but we had 'em all the same—what are their names? Steve and Edie?"

"Desi and Lucy."

"Oh, yeah. They were right there in the cockpit with us, barkin' their fool heads off. It was a paradise, Matt, blue Pacific and a high sun, seabirds, steady breeze about eight to ten knots. What was weird about it was I knew it was just a dream, an idea. But that didn't matter. I realized right then that the *idea* of the thing is sometimes better than the thing itself—know what I mean? Sometimes the reality of a thing just can't measure up to the dream."

Matt said he understood.

"I also knew that I'm not ever gonna sail to Sumatra with you," Royal went on, his eyes open now. "It's been fun talking about it, planning it, but I'm not gonna make it. We both know that, don't we?"

"What are you talking about? Nobody else is nuts enough to go to sea with me. I need another warm body to stand a watch."

"Let's don't bullshit each other, Matt. We both know that this old body ain't gonna be warm much longer. When you come this close to the end of the line, you get a clear picture of what's important—*ideas* and *people*. People like Lauren and you. And Cleo. I know now that I've had more than my share of big ideas, and more than my share of good people in my life. That's something to be thankful for. I'm okay with this, I really am."

Matt saw something in the old man's eyes that contradicted the serenity of his words, a restless flicker that shone through the resignation. Matt looked away, his own eyes smarting.

"You can go now, Matt. I doubt that I'll be kickin' off before the weekend. I'll say somethin' nice to Cleo, if you want me to. Just do me one more favor. Feed the goddamn cats when you get home. There's leftover fish in the cooler, on the right, second shelf. You know where it is.''

''No problem.''

Royal dropped off to sleep within minutes. Matt left the room and went to the pay phone he'd seen in the lobby. He needed to call Lauren to give her the bad news about her father's illness, and to tell her that she was about to get help with her problem, regardless of whether she wanted it.

Ten

Gravity, simplicity, piety. Richardson Zanto mouthed his mantra as he stared at the screen of his laptop, waiting for the encrypted e-mail message from InterActs' headquarters to decode. The computer beeped, and plain-English characters appeared on the screen, a message from the CEO, Brenton Bryson himself.

It was 3:40 P.M.

In the yard next to the apartment building a dog barked, a terrier's high-pitched shrieks—two quick ones, a pause, then three more. Day and night the dog went on like this, always the same pattern, rain or shine—a cruelty that Zanto and his partner had suffered since the operation began six months ago. Lying awake in the small hours, desperate for sleep, he'd fantasized about killing the animal with a weapon he'd used back in 1980 to terminate a Soviet KGB officer in Brussels, a miniature air gun disguised as a ballpoint pen. It fired a tiny flechette coated with cyanogen, a "nondiscernible microbioinoculator," in the sterile vernacular of CIA's science and tech section. The victim had died in his hotel room three hours after Zanto "inoculated" him downstairs in the bar, never having felt the flechette enter his body. The projectile had dissolved and the toxin had dissipated after doing their work, so the autopsy had revealed no trace of foul play. The authorities had concluded that the Russian died of a heart attack.

Gravity, simplicity, piety . . .

The computer finished its work and Zanto cringed as he read the message on the screen. His heart sank. He took off his half-lenses, unplugged the phone jack, then carried the laptop into the living room, where his partner, Stan Goulding, sat on a sofa, hunched over the audio surveillance gear arrayed on the coffee table.

Goulding was a lean, swarthy man of forty-nine whose jet-black toupee seemed too youthful atop a face so severely lined. His three-day beard looked like iron filings glued to an emery board, rough enough to strike a match on. Like Zanto, Goulding was a veteran of the CIA's Special Operations Division. Unlike Zanto, he was a chain-smoker, an inveterate consumer of junk food, a sufferer of chronic indigestion. He chewed four rolls of Tums a day, and he had no use for the wisdom and beauty of classical Rome.

"News from the head shed," Zanto said, handing him the computer. "Read it and weep."

"Who's weeping?" Goulding asked after scanning the message. "The clients are pulling the plug on Operation Undermine. Should've been done long ago." His speech was staccato Brooklyn, his attitude closer to the Bronx.

"I don't like getting a black eye," Zanto said, "especially when I don't deserve it."

"Jesus, Rick, we belly flopped. We said we'd prevent a major act of terrorism. Did we do it? No. We said we'd catch Lauren Bowman in the act, feed her to our clients on a platter. Did we do it? No. So, what do you want, a fuckin' plaque to hang on your wall?"

Zanto stared at the discolored carpet and swore. The operation had started off so well. He and Goulding had recruited a confederate within Lauren Bowman's inner circle, a "fish" who could provide inside information and do critical chores like planting microphones and transmitters in the wall sockets of the guest house on Jenkins Way. Audio surveillance had alerted Operation Undermine to the exact date and time of the FAF raid on the Pacific Northwest BioCenter. The fish had provided additional particulars, critical details about the raiders' plan. Zanto and Goulding had sent an anonymous warning to the top executives of ProGuard, the security firm that guarded the BioCenter, giving them an opportunity to bag a pair of international felons red-handed, Ian Prather and Vera Kemmis, and—as a bonus—a major-league Seattle businesswoman-turned-militant.

But then, in a twinkling, everything had turned to shit. A man was dead. Prather, Kemmis, and Bowman had gotten away. And someone had done something unthinkable to a young woman.

"It wasn't our fault that those buffoons at ProGuard didn't take the warning seriously," Zanto muttered. "They should've put half a dozen trained officers on the site, not a lone fifty-five-year-old part-timer."

"This may come as a shock to you, pal, but our clients don't give a rat's ass whose fault it is. They just want all this expensive cloak-and-dagger shit to cease. As far as I'm concerned, the sooner we get out of this dump, the better. Christ almighty, if I don't get away from that fucking dog . . ."

The dog was at it again—two quick barks, a pause, then three more.

Zanto lowered himself into a recliner that no longer reclined. Like the apartment and everything in it, the chair had seen better days. The building was a shabby fifties-era flat-top that stood in the shadow of the Space Needle, less than a ten-minute drive from Lauren Bowman's estate at Jenkins Way. The location made maintenance of the bugs an easy matter, and the rent was cheap. The clients had become tetchy about expenses.

"I don't see how we can leave it like this," Zanto said.

"It's not up to us, Rick. It's up to the boys who pay the bills, and they've decided the show's over." Goulding starting flipping switches in preparation to pack up the surveillance gear. Four separate spools of audiotape stopped rolling. "Forgive my saying so, but you seem to have forgotten what year this is. We're living in the New World Order, my friend. Principal doesn't matter anymore. Only money matters. You and I are mercenaries, spooks for hire. Better get used to it."

Zanto leaned forward, his elbows on his knees, one rough hand massaging the other. He suffered a twinge of arthritis in his left wrist, where a fragment of shrapnel still lay embedded, a souvenir of his tour in Vietnam. The onslaught of years had ignited other twinges in his thumbs and fingers, a preview of coming attractions, he feared. For the first time in his life, he felt old.

The bugs in Lauren Bowman's walls had told the story of Megan Reiner's end. When Lauren first played the videocassette, Zanto and Goulding had heard the sounds of a woman in extremis, her gagging and gurgling as she choked on her own blood. They'd heard the sinister blues song in the background, the orgasmic huffs and grunts of the rapist as he did his vicious work, the shrieks and cries of Lauren Bowman and her friends as they watched the horror show on the VCR. Zanto's stomach had fluttered like a dying fish.

"A woman's dead, Stan. And some maniac is running around loose. Are you telling me you can walk away from that?"

"Okay, suppose you tell me what choice we have. We can't give the cops what we know without compromising our clients, right? You think these paragons of American industry want it known they hire shady guys like us to spy on people? Besides, what we've been doing for the past six months is illegal as shit, and I'm not in the mood to get busted or sued. Jesus, would you listen to that dog . . . ?"

Goulding went to the window, gave the dog the finger. To no effect.

"I'm not suggesting we go to the cops," Zanto said. "But what about this Burgess character? We could offer to work with him. We're not exactly without resources." Zanto and Goulding had overheard this morning's meeting between Lauren and Matthew Burgess, an ex-cop. Burgess had advised her to take all she knew to the police, work a deal to give up Ian Prather and Vera Kemmis in return for no jail time. Predictably, Lauren had rejected the idea.

"So, you're suggesting we become amateur homicide detectives, is that it?"

"I care about that dead girl, and so do you."

"Yeah? Well, you're delusional, Rick. If you're serious about making a hobby of this thing, you're in it by yourself. I'm getting out, and I'm getting out *now*."

Eleven

At 2:55 P.M. on Tuesday, June 3, the Blues Beast rang the bell in the entryway of Rainy Hales' condo on N.E. 53rd, then leaned against the doorjamb, his guitar hanging from his shoulder, a stick of Slim Jim beef jerky jutting from his teeth. "Surprise," he whispered when she answered the door. "Glad I caught you at home."

Her face fell when she saw him, which made him giggle. He loved imposing himself on her at inopportune times. This was how he kept her just slightly off-balance, never too comfortable or settled-in.

"Tyler, you should've called. I was just about to go out. I . . ." She wore a floor-length calico dress, no makeup or jewelry. A real earth mother.

He pushed past her into the house, kicked the door shut behind him, and went straight to the kitchen. He set the guitar on the counter, took a carton of orange juice from the fridge, and gulped the juice without bothering to use a glass.

"I have needs, Adrienne," he called to her. "Needs that only you can fill."

"Tyler, I can't." She'd followed him as far as the kitchen door. "I was just about to leave. I have shopping to do, a dinner to cook. Lauren's having guests tonight."

"Guests? Who?"

"The Lekanders, Elise and Marc. I'm serving grilled soy sausage and beignets."

Tyler gulped the last of the orange juice and chucked the empty carton into the sink. He bit off another chew of the Slim Jim. "What about the ex-cop, that Burgess motherfucker? He coming to dinner, too?" The Stump brothers had informed him of Matt Burgess' visit with Lauren yesterday, having caught it on tape. They'd also recorded his phone call later that same afternoon, notifying Lauren of her father's illness. Burgess had told her that he'd changed his mind and now planned to help her, whatever the hell *that* meant. Tyler had a bad feeling about this guy.

"He's not on the list," Rainy replied, looking away. "And don't call me 'Adrienne.' You know how that chaps me. Why can't you call me 'Rainy,' like everyone else?"

"Because I'm not *everyone* else. I'm the guy who runs your life. You haven't forgotten that, have you, Adrienne?"

He latched on to her elbow and maneuvered her toward the bedroom. He knew the layout of the place like his own house, having visited regularly in the three years since the Ranger had installed her here. The condo was part of the new life the Ranger had engineered for her after tracking her to an alley on Capitol Hill, where she'd lain in a heap, sick and hallucinating. He'd taken her back to the apartment over the vacant warehouse in the International District, where he'd nursed her through the agonies of heroin withdrawal, detox, and recovery. He'd paid for her culinary training, given her this presentable little house within blocks of the Woodland Park Zoo, bought her a car—all the trappings of a normal, mainstream existence. Only gradually had Rainy figured out that the Ranger had rebuilt her life according to a meticulously laid-out plan, that her own wants and aspirations mattered not a whit to him.

"Tyler, please . . ."

She resisted him, but only halfheartedly. Serious resistance of the Blues Beast was dangerous, a fact Tyler had taught her the hard way. He dumped her onto the bed, hiked her calico dress, pulled off her white cotton panties. Kneeling above her, he peeled away his leathers in order to show her his sculpted muscles, his colorful tattoos, his growing cock. Then he jammed himself into her and pumped her until she moaned, visualizing Lauren Bowman's face, pretending that Rainy's body was Lauren's—the only way he could get a decent nut these days.

Later, after a leisurely shower, during which he soaped Rainy's back and washed her hair, he pulled a packet from the pocket of his leather jacket and tossed it to her. "I need to get into Lauren's house tomorrow night," he said, "so plan on staying over. I need you to fix things for me like before, get me through the security setup. These'll guarantee that everybody drifts off to slumber land, including those fucking dogs of hers."

Rainy eyed the capsules encased in clear bubble wrap. "What are they?"

"*Roofies*—flunitrazepam, actually. College boys sneak them into their girlfriends' drinks—the date-rape drug. It's like Valium, except that it causes extreme intoxication. I've got a guy who gets them for three bucks a hit."

Rainy made a face. "I don't believe this. Are you saying you want me to drug Lauren and Jandee?"

"All you have to do is pull a couple of capsules apart and sprinkle the powder into their zucchini smoothies or whatever the fuck they drink these days. Then give one cap to each dog around bedtime and they'll go down like twenty-dollar whores." He laughed and tossed his blond hair, touched Rainy's face with a fingertip. "They'll probably be hung-over in the morning, but who the hell is a dog gonna tell? As for Lauren and Jandee, they'll just assume that they've gotten some bad tofu."

"Tyler, I can't do this," Rainy declared, pulling away from him.

"Sure you can, earth mama. You've done it before, you can do it again."

"The dogs, yeah, but not Lauren. Not Jandee." Several times over the past year, she'd slipped veterinary tranquilizers to Desi and Lucy, ensuring that they wouldn't bark when Tyler and the Stump brothers sneaked in to service the surveillance equipment. "This is a line I won't cross, Tyler, drugging people. Especially not Lauren."

"Don't make me spank," Tyler said in a playful tone. "You know how I get when you make me do that."

Rainy took a deep breath and held it, tried to hide her fear. The Blues Beast's spankings were no laughing matter. "Whatever you and the old man have been doing, Tyler—that video of Megan, whatever else you guys have in mind—you're making Lauren crazy. Her life is hell, thanks to you. The place feels like some kind of psycho ward, people looking over their shoulders, afraid of their own shadows. Speaking of the video—my God, you guys really outdid yourself with that one. I know it couldn't've been real, but—''

"Who says it wasn't real?"

Rainy's tired eyes widened, and Tyler Brownlee saw the flicker of an old memory in them, one so horrific that she'd long ago banished it to the black realm of childhood nightmares. "It's *not* real, it *can't* be—'' Yet, he could see that she knew better, deep in her heart. "It's some sort of sick joke, right? Nobody could actually *do* something like that, not even you.''

"Oh, people have done much worse, Adrienne. Much worse.'' He gave her his crooked half-grin, did a muscle-man pose. Flexed his pectorals, causing the ears of the tattoo-lion to bounce. "Call me at my cell-phone number after Lauren's been in bed awhile, then be ready to buzz me through the gate. After that you can turn in and sleep the sleep of the innocent.''

"Why do you need to get into the house?''

"Oh, I'm afraid that's classified, child.''

"Jesus, Tyler. Give me some credit. I've done everything you and the old man have told me. I've even *become* what you wanted. You can't keep treating me like I don't have a mind, or a heart. I have a need to know some things.''

Tyler stared at her through his eyebrows, as a kindergarten teacher might stare at a misbehaving kid. He and the Ranger had governed Rainy's life in recent years, having forced her to join the animal-rights movement to get next to Lauren, having sent her to cooking school to become a vegan chef. They'd even arranged the disappearance of Lauren's previous cook, a young man named Bernie Kemper, in order to create a job opening for her.

Rainy Hales had been their eyes and ears in Lauren's household, their pipeline into Lauren's world. She'd proved herself an able spy and a serviceable stand-in for Lauren in the sack. And now, after three years, she'd discovered that she had a backbone.

"What you need to know is this, earth mama,'' the Blues Beast said, moving his face close to hers. "You need to know that you're still a junkie at heart, that without us you would've curled up and retched your guts out years ago. You need to know that you owe us everything you have, everything you are. Without us, you'd have nothing—no house, no car, no job, no *life*—got that?''

"I can't hurt this woman anymore,'' Rainy replied barely

above a whisper, tears welling in her eyes. "She's been good to me. What you're doing to her—spying, listening, terrorizing her—it's sick. It's evil."

Tyler straightened to his full height and inhaled deeply through flaring nostrils. He fought the urge to do something delicious to Rainy right here and now, something with the Redstone knife in his boot. But he couldn't afford to put marks on her, not just yet. Not before the prize was his.

"Forget about right and wrong," he said. "That shit's for lame-os. Worry about what's *real*, like I do."

"Everybody makes his own reality, Tyler. You've said so yourself a thousand times."

"Yeah, well, I've lied, earth mama. What I should've said is, 'Everybody but you.' You gave up your reality years ago when you started shooting junk. *We* gave you a new one, a reality that we created especially for you. That's why you need to keep me grinning. If for any reason I stop grinning—well, you can be sure that Lauren will find out what happened to old Bernie Kemper, and why it happened."

"You wouldn't do that," Rainy whimpered. "Not even *you . . .*"

"Don't kid yourself, Adrienne. Unless you give me exactly what I want, Lauren will find out exactly what kind of bottom-feeder has been cooking her food for the past couple of years. And that's when your reality unravels, okay? That's when your whole life comes apart."

A tear slid from Rainy's eye, and Tyler saw something in her face that he'd never seen before: hatred, pure and black. *Big deal,* he thought. *I don't need her to love me.*

Twelve

The Elysian Pub and Brewery occupied a converted warehouse on East Pike Street, in a slightly seedy neighborhood near Capitol Hill. Matt Burgess walked in and found that a noisy, quit-work-early crowd had already arrived in force, their ties loose and shirt-sleeves rolled. He took a table next to a glass wall that afforded a view of the innards of the brewery, the immaculate stainless-steel vats, the shiny tubing and pipes. A pair of brewers were busy with a new batch of ale, their faces earnest, their brows knitted. They wore rubber aprons and galoshes.

Matt ordered a pint of Elysian, sipped from it and glanced up in time to see Alex Ragsdale arrive, looking prosperous in a well-tailored suit and a conservative rep tie. Life as a senior investigative consultant at ProGuard had apparently agreed with him.

He was an angular, balding man of thirty-seven with severe cheekbones, a cop's sharp eyes, and hands that looked abnormally large on someone with an average build. Like Matt, he was an alumnus of the University of Washington, where he'd taken a degree in chemistry before deciding that his calling was law enforcement. He grinned when he saw Matt, came to the table, eased himself into the opposite chair.

"Here I am, only ten minutes late," he said. "That's a new record. Next thing you know, folks will be calling me punctual." He shook Matt's outstretched hand, then signaled a waiter.

"It's good to see you, Rags," Matt said. "How's the brood?"

"Couldn't be better. They miss their uncle Matthew, ask about you a lot. I never know exactly what to tell them.''

Rags gave a short update on each member of his family—
Ruby and his daughters, Rachel and Kelsy. Ruby had taken on
an important new project at Microsoft, a real feather in her cap.
The girls were busy with summer soccer league. The whole family was planning a trip to Disneyland in August.

''After I got promoted, we bought ourselves a nice condo in
Kirkland,'' he went on. ''Moved in three months ago. It's a great
place, real comfy, view of the lake. And close to Ruby's job.''
The waiter arrived, and Rags ordered a pint of beer.

''So, what does a *senior* investigative consultant for ProGuard
actually do?'' Matt wanted to know. ''Last time we talked, you
were running background checks on people, as I recall, candidates
for jobs, right?''

Rags said that he'd graduated to more important stuff, like
designing commercial security strategies and helping corporate
clients investigate fraud and theft within their organizations. Matt
told him that he thought the work sounded interesting, when in
fact it sounded too much like being a cop for his taste. Rags read
his eyes and laughed. He assured his old friend that ProGuard
had pegged him for bigger and better things. He talked for a few
minutes about his career track, about a training program he'd
entered to learn how to help corporations purge their records of
documents that might someday prove damaging in product-
liability lawsuits. Destroying evidence, in other words, before it
became evidence.

''So, what's this all about, Burge?'' Ragsdale asked finally,
loosening his tie. ''Much as I'd like to, I can't believe you called
because you felt a need for my warmth and friendship. You *do*
realize it's been six months since we last talked.''

Matt flinched. He and Rags had entered the police academy
together, partnered on patrol, made detective at the same time.
They'd joined the interagency drug task force together, leaned on
each other while suffering the vicissitudes of the war on drugs.
And more than anyone else, Rags had helped Matt weather the
storms that had battered his personal life toward the end of his
career—watching a child die, a disintegrating marriage, clinical
depression.

Six months. ''It's hard to believe it's been that long,'' Matt
said, feeling as if he'd just returned from another planet.

''I've called your place, you know, left messages, invited you to dinner, a round of golf. I've been trying like hell to share the rewards of the private sector with my best friend, but you're not an easy guy to share things with nowadays.''

"Yeah, I've gotten the messages. Sorry, Rags. I should've called back, but . . ." No excuse was good enough, so Matt didn't offer one. "In the last year or so I've become a little isolated. I can't deny that it's been—comfortable. And I can't pretend that I miss the aggravation of being out here among you shakers and movers.''

"Still on medication?"

"Wellbutrin every day. Gotta keep those neurotransmitters firing.'' He snapped his fingers three times.

"I thought you were on Prozac."

"I was. And Zoloft, off and on.''

"Therapy, too, I'd guess, hmm?"

"I'm down to once a month instead of twice a week. I've made progress. I'm feeling almost human again.''

To which Alex Ragsdale hoisted his pint in salute.

Matt then told him that Royal Bowman lay in a hospital bed, diagnosed with cancer, the first round of tests having come back today. Rags grimaced when he heard the news. He'd always liked Royal, despite the old man's cantankerousness, and he knew how much Royal meant to Matt. Then Matt told him that Royal's daughter, Lauren, had participated in the raid on the Pacific Northwest BioCenter, and that Royal had enlisted Matt to help her deal with the reality of having become an accessory to murder. This was why Matt had called his old partner. He needed to get Rags' take on the problem. He needed advice.

"Are we talking about *the* Lauren Bowman?" Rags asked.

"*The* Lauren Bowman,'' Matt confirmed.

"Damn, she's fat money, man. She's married to none other than Gabe Granger, the prince of strip malls. You know that, don't you? The guy who tried to buy the Seahawks a couple years back?"

"I knew she was rich, but I didn't know her money was fat.''

"Yeah, well, you've got your *new* money, your *big* money, your *old* money, and your *fat* money . . .''

"I guess you learn stuff like this out there in the private sector, huh? The various ages and sizes of money.''

"What you learn is that money's the root of all happiness, partner, whether it's old or new or big or fat. This shit about money not buying contentment is propaganda the rich folks put out to keep the poor ones from going after their share.''

"My grandfather used to say the same thing."

"So, tell me why this lady with the fat money is out busting up a research laboratory."

"She's a believer in animal rights—a *true* believer. She needed to do something."

"So she goes out, steals a bunch of rats and monkeys, shoots an old guard who was a year from retirement. These true believers sound like real bad actors."

"She didn't shoot the guard, Rags. In fact, she tried like hell to keep anything like that from happening." Matt related the details of the raid as Lauren Bowman had given them to him, emphasizing that she'd insisted on nonviolence, that she'd extracted a promise from the ringleader, Ian Prather, to carry no deadly weapons.

"And you believe her?" Rags asked.

Matt saw Lauren Bowman's face in his mind, her eyes, clear and deep. "Yeah, I believe her," he answered. "I advised her to hire a lawyer and then call the cops, give them Prather as the shooter. I suggested that cooperating might keep her out of the really deep shit."

"Sounds like good advice to me. But she didn't take it, did she?"

Matt shook his head. "There's more. This part's not quite as uplifting . . ." He described what had happened to Megan Reiner, told him about the videotape that had turned up in Lauren's home, the final hellish scene in Megan's life as he'd witnessed it with his own eyes on a TV screen—the blues music, the shiny knife, the rape, the butchery. Rags' jaw dropped open, and he simply stared back at Matt, speechless.

Finally, a low whistle issued through Rags' teeth. "By the time you and I quit the department, I thought I'd seen everything," he said. "I guess I was wrong."

"Yeah, me too. Now you know why I feel a little inadequate, why I called you."

Matt signaled the waiter for another round. Bent over the table, heads close, the two men talked in near-whispers as they'd done countless times over the years, like a pair of conspirators. Matt felt their friendship slip back into its groove. Confiding in Rags felt good, like putting on his old baseball glove.

"Tell me something," Matt said. "Is there any way ProGuard knew about the raid in advance? I've got to wonder why they posted that guard when they normally rely on electronics and roving responders."

"I don't have a clue. That's not my department. But I'll float some innocent questions around the office, see what I can find out." Rags made a show of perusing the menu, as if he could actually eat after hearing what Matt had just told him. "This business with the rape and butchery of young Megan, the blues music in the background—any of that ring any bells for you?"

"Not right offhand. You?"

"I'm thinking I've heard something like it before. Back in the old days—four, five years ago, when you and I were stinging tar pushers on the Hill—there was a rumor going around on Broadway about young girls disappearing. We always figured it was junkie-talk, scare stories like the tar babies tell each other to pass the time. Remember?"

"I *do* remember. They were runaways, right?"

"And they vanished into thin air. Nobody ever saw them again. Except for one."

"And she came back to the street, talked about some asshole who liked to stalk and kidnap girls."

"Her story was he butchered them in the basement of some warehouse, always with blues music in the background. That part of it, the blues music, stuck in my head, because I dig the blues, okay? The old Chicago stuff, like my dad's stash of LP records. The girl never came to the cops, as far as I know."

"Might've been urban myth, like one-hour dry cleaning," Matt said.

Rags tossed the menu aside. "But what if it wasn't? If some lunatic was snatching junkies off the street, the only people who'd know they were missing would be other junkies. And who in the hell takes junkies seriously? Certainly not cops. The son of a bitch could have been taking girls who'd already been reported missing from Cleveland or Omaha or Denver, maybe missing for months already."

"That way, nobody gets suspicious except the junkies, and they don't count. I hear what you're saying."

"Just a thought. Probably nothing to it."

"I'll take it under advisement. I hasten to remind you, however, that Megan Reiner was no runaway junkie. She was a teaching assistant at U-Dub's philosophy department. She had a boyfriend, professional colleagues, family. Somebody's going to report her missing sooner or later.''

''And probably sooner.''

''So, Lauren and her buds can expect more questions from the cops. I'd almost forgotten about that.''

''And I'd guess that Royal would want you to hold his daughter's hand while somebody from Missing Persons interviews her.''

''I wish it was only that.'' Matt took a long pull of his beer, let it go all the way down. He reminded Rags that the killer had sent the video to Lauren, having wrapped it in plain paper and written her initials on it. For some twisted reason the guy had wanted Lauren to experience the final minutes of Megan's life. Hence, Royal Bowman's concern for his daughter and his reason for enlisting Matt to protect her.

''So, you've become her bodyguard, is that it?'' Rags asked.

''In a manner of speaking.''

''You realize, of course, the shit-bag's got an inside line to her, bugs or phone taps, maybe both. Might even have a confederate working for him.''

''This had occurred to me, yes.''

''I can't think of any other way he could've set up the kidnapping of Megan Reiner. Can you?''

''Not really.''

''Let's think it through. The son of a bitch knew exactly when and where he could snatch Megan without running the risk of Lauren and her friends calling the cops, right? He knew they were planning to raid the BioCenter, and that's where he figured he could grab her. What's Lauren gonna do—tell the cops about the abduction and thereby confess that they did the raid? Huh-uh. She's loyal to the cause, a true believer. You said so yourself.''

''So, we're looking at some sick fucker who's obsessed with Lauren Bowman. He's taken great pains, up to and including killing someone, just to impress her. Is that our theory?''

''Works for me. He records the killing on video, makes sure Lauren sees it, gets a major set of yah-yahs. We can only wonder what he does next. With these pieces of shit, there's always a *next*.''

''Christ almighty.'' Matt laced his fingers together, did twirlies with his thumbs, studied his beer.

"I know that look," Rags said. "You start making twirlies with your thumbs, and that means you've got something to say."

"I'm thinking I shouldn't drag you into this."

"What are you talking about? We're partners. We've been on the griddle together before."

"But we're not cops anymore. You're a . . . a senior . . ."

"Senior investigative consultant."

"Right. You're private sector now, great job, growing family."

"I got myself a vasectomy last year. My family's as big as it's ever going to get."

"I meant growing *up*. The fact is, you don't need this shit, Rags. I've probably told you enough already to screw up your job at ProGuard and make you guilty of obstructing justice. I don't have any right to . . ."

"To hell with that. No way I'm leaving my best friend to wade through this lake of shit alone." He reached across the table and gave Matt a gentle punch on the chin with a huge fist. "After all, we're *partners*, right?"

Matt felt a lump in his throat and quickly put on his sunglasses. "Yeah, we're partners. So, I guess our first step is to find out if Lauren's house is bugged. Know anybody who could do an off-the-books sweep?"

"Not a problem. I can line somebody up for tomorrow morning, I think—he's a ProGuard guy who's always in the market for extra work." Rags pulled a cellular phone from his breast pocket, punched in a number. "While he's doing his thing, you and I can figure out our next move. Just like the old days, right? We'll do it the old-fashioned way—protocol, policy, and procedure, the way real cops do it. Sound okay to you?"

Matt swallowed beer and said, "Yeah. I guess. Same as the old days."

Thirteen

Having just heard the news about Megan Reiner, Rod Welton stepped onto the deck of Lauren Bowman's guest house and stared westward at the Olympic Mountains. A tear crept out of one eye and slid down his nose. Lauren moved next to him and shared the dark moment—a pair of soldiers, shoulder-to-shoulder in the aftermath of combat, grieving for a fallen comrade. In a nearby madrona a convocation of crows squawked and cawed, a black-robed choir. The water of Puget Sound played a gentle accompaniment as it lapped against the pilings beneath the deck.

Rod put an arm around her. "You should've told me earlier," he said. "Who else knows?"

She gave him names—Rainy Hales, Jandee Vernon, Elise and Marc Lekander—but made no mention of Matt Burgess. Neither did she mention her father, who lay in the hospital, riddled with cancer.

"How about Ian and Vera?" he asked.

"I haven't told them, yet. But I will. Tomorrow."

"It was my fault," he said, his voice hoarsening. "I was the driver. I could've waited for her."

"You were following the orders of the team leader," Lauren countered. "The police were coming, and Ian decided we couldn't wait. It was his call, Rodney, not yours."

"But another thirty seconds might've saved her. If I'd waited another thirty seconds, she might still be . . ."

"Another thirty seconds and we'd all be in jail now, facing murder charges. The damage to the movement would've been deep and lasting."

Rod Welton pushed his hands into the pockets of his pants. He wore a cheap sport coat full of wrinkles and a tie from Kmart. Juvenile probation officers didn't make much money, which Lauren found hard to comprehend, given the importance of their jobs, their crushing workloads. He'd apparently gotten a haircut since the raid, as his gray ponytail was little more than a stub tied with a rubber band. He looked thin, haggard.

Half an hour ago he'd turned up unannounced at Jenkins Way, hungry for any news about Megan. A missing-persons detective had interviewed him late in the afternoon, as a result of Megan's boyfriend having reported her missing three full days ago. The cops had finally gotten around to contacting her family, friends, and acquaintances, seeking clues to her whereabouts. Because Megan's animal-rights activism was a matter of record—she'd been arrested more than once while protesting or demonstrating—her fellow activists were high on the cops' talk-to list. Rod had warned Lauren that she, too, could expect a visit anytime.

"It's funny," he said. "My conscience has never bothered me about any of the illegal stuff I've done for the movement over the years. It was like another world, you know? Something I kept separate from my day job. But when it came to lying to the police about Megan, I turned into a sweaty mess. I thought of all the time I'd put in as a JPO, serving as an officer of the court, representing the criminal justice system. And there I was, lying to people who I'd always considered to be on my side. I felt like a grade-A hypocrite, Lauren."

"You're not a hypocrite."

"The hell I'm not. I'm a hypocrite and a liar. I told the cops that I hadn't seen Megan in over a month. They believed me, I guess. If they connected her disappearance with the raid on the BioCenter, they didn't mention it."

"That's something, at least. I'll take any good news I can get."

Rod pulled a pack of Merits out of his coat, shook one out and lit it. He exhaled smoke, his eyes narrowed in thought. "I'm having trouble making sense of all this," he said. "First the guard

at the BioCenter . . . where there shouldn't have been one. The
security protocols included no on-site security.''

"You're right. It doesn't make sense."

"And Megan stayed back to free the rest of the rats. Someone
else must've been in the building, someone who . . .''

"Rodney, please. I can't talk about this anymore. It's too . . .''
Too close to the bone. Something in the video had pierced her to
the quick, roused old fears that writhed in her heart like snakes.
She couldn't bear to rehash the details of Megan's final moments.

"I need to tell you something," Rod said, wringing his hands.
"I didn't know Ian was carrying a gun. And I'm not proud of
the way I acted that night. I should've stood up to him, made him
wait for Megan."

Lauren touched his hand, found it cold. "Don't beat yourself
up over this, Rod. There wasn't anything you could've done . . .''

6:20 P.M.

The telephone bleeped in Lauren's study, and Jandee Vernon
picked it up.

"Lauren Bowman's residence."

"Hello—who's this?"

She recognized Matt Burgess' voice. "Matt, this is Jandee
Vernon. Remember me?"

"Yeah, hi. Is Lauren there?"

"She's out on the deck with Rod Welton, deep in conversation. I'll interrupt them if you want me to."

"No, don't do that. You've got an e-mail address, right?"

"Sure."

"Give it to me." She gave it to him. "I'm going to send you
something right now. Make sure Lauren gets the message, okay?
It pertains to you, too."

"This all sounds very mysterious."

"Just make sure Lauren gets it immediately. And thanks."

The line went dead.

Jandee stood for a moment with the phone pressed to her ear,
thinking, "God, this guy's at least thirty-five, probably closer to
forty . . .''

6:28 P.M.

Lauren saw Rod Welton to the door, asked him for the third time if he would stay for dinner, and for the third time he declined. Lauren's social crowd was too rich for his blood, he said. Besides, he had things to do tonight, places to go, people to see. Lauren smiled sadly and hugged him, told him to hang tough. She watched him trudge the crushed-granite path to his battered old Chevy, watched him drive away.

The steel-barred gate automatically clanked shut behind him, which should have made her feel safe. But she knew that high walls and computerized security couldn't protect her from the evil that had bubbled up from her past, an evil she'd buried long ago on the campus of MacArthur High School in Portland. On the fringe of her consciousness hung a fragment of something old and dark—what was it? A song, a poem? Something about blood and tears, she thought, shuddering. Old fears squeezed her heart.

Jandee Vernon entered the foyer and held a sheet of paper out to her. "It's e-mail from Matt Burgess," she said. "Came a couple of minutes ago."

"Christ, I just saw him this afternoon at the hospital. We crossed paths outside Royal's room." Lauren had spent much of the day at Cabrini Hospital, keeping her father company. She read Matt's message, and her knees went weak:

> *Someone may have bugged your house & tapped your phones. Be careful what you say. If you need to get in touch with me, use e-mail. I'll be there tomorrow A.M. with people who can help. Try not to worry.*
> *Burgess*

She and Jandee stared at one another without speaking, each trying to read the other's eyes. Jandee nodded toward the door, and they went out to the gazebo, sat in one of the swinging love seats with their elbows touching.

"Do you think it's safe to talk out here?" Lauren whispered.

"How the hell should I know? I suppose it depends on what kind of microphones they're using, how sensitive they are."

"Who's *they*?"

"Jesus, ask me something I know. Ask me what's the capital of Albania."

Lauren shivered, even though the evening air was soft and balmy, with no hint of breeze off the Sound. She read Matt Burgess' message again, digesting each word.

"He tells us to be careful of what we say, like that's going to do a lot of good. Shit, we planned the raid on the BioCenter in this house. We've held briefings and drills here. We've talked about what happened to Megan. If someone has been listening to us all this time, he's already heard more than enough to hang us out to dry."

"What does he mean about showing up in the A.M. with people who can help? Is he going to get rid of the microphones?"

"That would be my guess. I hope he's being discreet. We can't have too many people getting involved with this thing."

"What're we going to do about dinner, boss? Elise and Marc will be here any minute."

"Tell Rainy we've decided to go out. She's welcome to come along, if she wants."

"God, she's gonna kill me. She's doing her grilled soy sausage and beignets. She's been at it all afternoon."

"Well, we sure as hell can't have dinner here with the walls full of microphones or whatever. Call the Cafe Flora and make reservations for five."

"Okay, but I can't say I'm very hungry. By the way, don't forget that you have a speaking engagement tomorrow, a luncheon at the Emerald City Society. We really should prepare something, unless you want to do it off the cuff."

Lauren winced, shook her head. She'd completely spaced out the engagement. The Emerald City Society was an organization of young professional women who met for lunch once a month in the dining room of the posh Sorrento Hotel. Like other community-service clubs, the Society worked quietly on charitable causes, but unlike most others, it had a reputation as politically and socially progressive. Fertile ground for the seeds of animal-rights activism, Lauren had figured when she'd accepted the invitation months ago. A good chance to recruit new troops, score some contributions.

"You're right, we should prepare," she replied. "Tonight, after dinner. We can pull together some of my usual material, throw in some topical stuff. Better plan on a late night."

"We could, like, cancel," Jandee ventured. "After all, you've just found out your father has cancer. People would understand."

"No. It's important to the movement that I show up for this thing. We all need to go on with our normal routines after the raid. It's what we agreed to do. Otherwise we arouse suspicion." For Lauren, *normal routine* meant spreading the gospel of justice for animals, raising money, recruiting new believers, just as she'd done sedulously for the past four years. She wasn't about to stop doing it now.

Fourteen

The safe house stood on a corner lot on Northwest 67th Street in Ballard, in a claustrophobic working-class neighborhood with narrow streets and overhead utility lines. No view of Shilshole Bay here, the Space Needle, or anything else of interest—only closely spaced houses with aluminum siding, rusty cars parked at the curbs and the occasional sullen-faced passerby. Ian Prather hated the place and said so for the hundredth time. He hated the absence of trees, the preponderance of ragged shrubbery, the lack of color.

"Quit your bellyachin'," Vera Kemmis retorted, taking a swig of Ballard Bitters, a local microbrew. "Next to the dump I grew up in, this is the bloody south of France." She'd often described the dirty flat in Manchester where she'd misspent her youth, an exploited victim of the capital class. Countless times Ian had suffered her stories about insects and rodents, rain blowing in around the window casements, peeling paint, and failing furnaces.

"It's the drabness," he said irritably, lighting a cigarette. "I feel as if I'm living in a fucking George Orwell novel."

Vera scoffed and reminded him that they'd carried out a major operation only five days ago. A man had died, a comrade had disappeared. Drabness! What did he want—a bloody nuclear war?

"I'd like that, actually," he replied, exhaling smoke. He visualized sleek corporate CEOs dying by the thousands in the radioactive rubble of skyscrapers. "At least we'd be rid of those insidious television commercials, wouldn't we? And no more usurious credit card interest. No more telemarketing or McDonalds or Dow Chemical or Mitsubishi. Only sickness, starvation and anarchy—a small price to pay for freedom from the depredations of the corporate establishment." He grinned at his own humor.

"Let's go to a flick," Vera said. "I can't watch another beastly minute of the telly, now that you've mentioned it. Besides, an evening out would do us both good."

Ian walked into the kitchen, where wadded food wrappers littered the countertops, along with beer bottles and heaped-over ashtrays. Vera Kemmis didn't do dishes or housework of any kind. She was a *revolutionary*, not a fucking domestic.

"It's too dangerous," he called to her, pouring scotch into a hazy glass. "By now Interpol has circulated our photographs to the local cops. We need to lie low until the furor over the BioCenter dies down, minimize our exposure. You know that as well as I."

He walked back into the living room with his drink, and Vera sidled next to him. She wore black slacks over her ropy legs, a bulky black T-shirt, red Adidas. Her short auburn hair needed a wash. "We could pack our kits and move on," she said. "This isn't a good place for us, love. The local soldiers are flakes, unreliable. If we're to lie low, why not do it on some sun-drenched beach where the sand is soft and warm? We could have a nice time for a change, just the two of us."

The fading daylight made her prettier than she deserved to be. Ian saw in her face the ghost of the young thing he'd met years ago during an organized sabotage of a foxhunt in Yorkshire. "Don't do this, Vera," he said, backing away from her. "It's not like that with us anymore. Hasn't been for years."

"I'm only saying that we should get out of here, that's all. The BioCenter mission was bad news from the start. The personnel were all wrong, except for Welton, the only real soldier in the lot." If Ian's rejection had affected her, she didn't show it. "As for the birds, one's a bloody socialite and the other's a college girl who's never done anything more violent than slap her boyfriend's face, if that. They were wrong for the mission from the start, and they've bloody well proved it, haven't they?"

Ian wandered to a picture window that afforded him a view of the street corner. A man tinkered with a big Harley Davidson at the curb, apparently having broken down. Blond bloke, well-built, black leather. Ian lost interest and turned to face Vera.

"Whatever happened to Megan certainly wasn't her fault," he said.

"And how would you know that, love? Do you actually have any clue about what happened to her, why she took off like she did?"

Ian had none, but he felt as if he'd come to know Megan. He'd admired her commitment, her mental toughness. She wouldn't have disregarded the mission plan to fly off on her own. He was sure of that.

"As for your little sugar pie," Vera went on, "she's asked you to bugger off, now hasn't she? Wants nothing more to do with you. All that malarkey about not carrying guns, extracting promises from us—what kind of madness is that? What in bloody hell does she think we are, a gaggle of Girl Scouts?"

"You'd do well to remember that Lauren has bankrolled us from the start, Vera. Her company owns this house—"

"Which you loathe."

"And she's paid for the food we eat, the beer and whiskey we drink, the cigarettes we smoke. If it weren't for her, we'd be scrabbling at a pair of menial jobs and living in some flea-bitten motel."

"All I'm saying, Ian, is this is an uncool place for us. Things have gone all wrong. The vibrations are bad, the chemistry is awful. A man's been killed, which destroys whatever good the mission might've done for the movement. You've seen the newscasts—it's all about the bloody security guard, his grandkids, the golden retriever who sits by the door waiting for him to come home. And if it's not that, it's the damage to the research under way at the BioCenter."

Ian couldn't deny that she was right. The news media had played up the human tragedy that the raid had caused, both real and imagined. Colleagues of Dr. Gregory Kirsch, the vivisectionist in residence at the BioCenter, had appeared on camera and had spoken of his work as if it was God's own. *He showed us that severed spinal cords can indeed be reconnected,* one had said, a doctor at Johns Hopkins. *He gave hope to a legion of patients who sit paralyzed in wheelchairs, people like Christopher Reeve . . .* Then came heartbreaking footage of the wheelchair-bound actor, together with his loving family. Followed by crippled children, of course, plenty of them for the camera, with close-ups of precious faces. *Unfortunately, it'll take years to rep-*

*licate the experiments destroyed by the attack on the Bio-
Center . . .*

Watching the coverage had made Ian Prather want to puke.
Nary a reporter had mentioned the plight of the animals impris-
oned at the Pacific Northwest BioCenter, *their* pain or *their* right
to a decent existence. But then what could one expect of news
media owned by the likes of Disney, General Electric, and West-
inghouse? The corporate world owned a huge stake in vivisection,
especially the makers of pharmaceuticals and cosmetics, outfits
that bought great chunks of TV advertising from the networks.

"You may as well save your breath, Vera," Ian said. "We're
staying. It's been years since we've enjoyed a base of support
this strong. We can't afford to blow it off just yet. We need to
stay and make the most of it."

"And that's it—you've made your decision? No more debate,
no consideration of anybody else's thoughts on the matter?"

"Look, you can get out anytime you want to. We're not exactly joined at the hip, are we?"

"Would it suit you, if I left? Are you that much in love with
Lauren Bowman that you can't stand having an old flame hanging
around?"

Ian saw the hurt in her face, disguised by a derisive smirk, and
he regretted what he'd just said. He went to Vera, took her hands
in his.

"No, love, it wouldn't suit me," he told her. "I need your
smarts, your experience. I even need your bloody caustic personality, if you can believe that. I'm better with you than without
you, and the movement is better off having us together. We're
only getting started here, you and I. The BioCenter was a warm-
up. And I need your help to go the rest of the way. After all,
we're a team, aren't we?"

"Yes, I suppose we are," she said, pulling her hands away.
"You needn't worry—I won't leave. Not just yet."

As she went to fetch another Ballard Bitters, Ian Prather
thought, *She doesn't do housework, and she doesn't shed tears.
She's a revolutionary . . .*

And this was what he loved about her, he supposed, if love
was the right word.

Fifteen

Before leaving the guest house for the Cafe Flora, Lauren spoke with Rainy Hales in the kitchen. "I wish you'd reconsider and come along with us," she said to the girl. "I feel terrible, having let you cook this wonderful dinner, only to bail out at the last minute."

"It's okay," Rainy said, acting busy. She'd begun to put food into plastic containers for storage in the refrigerator. "Most of this will keep. We can snack on it later in the week." Busy-busy, no eye contact. Which made Lauren feel worse still.

"I can't promise an evening of unbridled hilarity, but at least you'd get to go out for a meal that someone else cooks," Lauren added. "Now, I realize that my friends and I aren't the best of company these days, but sometimes bad company is better than none." She forced a laugh. "Sure you won't reconsider?"

"I appreciate the offer," Rainy said, "but it's not necessary. You're a good boss, Lauren, the best. You pay me more than I deserve. It's no big deal just because you . . ." She stammered, and Lauren thought, *Maybe she's finally crumbling, like the rest of us.* "Just because you change your dinner plans. When you've got a job as good as this one, you don't sweat the small stuff."

Lauren went to the girl, hugged her. Rainy Hales hadn't participated directly in the planning or the execution of the raid on the BioCenter, but she'd given it her strong moral support. She'd often expressed admiration for Megan Reiner, a frequent visitor to the guest house. Lauren figured that Rainy hadn't yet fully processed the horror of Megan's murder. Perhaps only now had the ugly reality begun to sink in.

"Look, we're going through a bad time around here," Lauren said. "We're entitled to act a little loopy—all of us, even you. God knows I'm doing it, which I'm sure you've noticed."

Rainy smiled around her tears, said nothing.

"I won't press you to come with us," Lauren went on, "but I want you to know that you're welcome. I consider you part of the family, Rainy. Always remember that."

"Thanks, but I'm really beat, you know? I think I'll go home and listen to some music."

"I understand." Lauren turned to leave.

"About tomorrow—" Rainy said, her voice catching. Again she wouldn't look Lauren in the eye. "I should probably, like, stay over tomorrow night, if you don't mind. I need to restock the pantry, reorder a bunch of stuff. I need to put together a list . . ."

"Rainy, you don't need to ask. If you need to stay over, stay over. Your room is always ready."

"Yeah, okay. Do you plan to be home tomorrow night?"

"As far as I know, yes. Dinner as usual. And I promise not to bail out on you without giving plenty of notice."

"Th-thanks. See you at breakfast, then."

"Yeah, breakfast. Take care, Rainy."

Lauren, Jandee, Elise and Marc Lekander all piled into Lauren's Volvo station wagon and departed for Cafe Flora. Lauren had recently gotten rid of the big green Range Rover her husband had given her for Valentine's Day two years earlier, and had bought the Volvo primarily because it had cloth upholstery, not leather like the Range Rover's. She suspected that some of the cloth in the Volvo might be wool, a product that also came from abusing animals, but shearing a sheep of its hair was certainly less barbaric than depriving a bovine of its hide.

During the drive, Lauren updated her passengers on her father's condition, having spent much of the afternoon with him at the hospital. The verdict was in—cancer. No word yet on how much time he had left. For the moment she said nothing about Matt Burgess' e-mail and his warning of unseen ears in the walls. She figured that anyone who'd bugged her house could as easily have bugged her car, and it seemed like common sense not to alert the bastard to the fact that she was on to him.

She tried to guide the talk to lighter matters, but the Lekanders wouldn't cooperate. All Elise and Marc wanted to talk about was the raid on the BioCenter and the implications of Megan Reiner's murder. They worried aloud about Lauren's safety, about the fact that someone—the murderer, presumably—had penned her initials on the videocassette, serving notice that she was the intended recipient, as if to ensure that she witnessed the outrage. Equally worrisome was the question of how the monster had managed to plant the cassette inside the guest house in the first place. If he'd gotten in once, couldn't he get in again?

By the time they arrived at the restaurant, Lauren's guts were in knots, and she doubted that she could eat a bite.

Cafe Flora stood on Madison Avenue in the heart of a rapidly gentrifying neighborhood between Capitol Hill and Lake Washington, the kind of place where affluent health nuts showed up for dinner wearing Versace running togs and two-hundred-dollar-cross trainers, cell-phones pressed to their ears, Wayfarer sunglasses resting atop their heads. Potted plants abounded throughout the airy interior, and a tall tree grew in a central atrium, all emblematic of vegetarian ideology.

Lauren Bowman was more than a regular here. She was a resource who rated special treatment. Her presence lent the place credibility among Seattle's hard-core vegetarians and vegans. Whenever her personal assistant called to make reservations, the maître d' ordered all knives removed from the table that the Bowman party would use, for Lauren's phobia about knives was common knowledge. Her dinner partners were expected to spread their marmalade with spoons and cut their mushroom patties with forks.

The maître d' showed Lauren and her friends to her usual table near the atrium, a spot where they could talk without being overheard. Not until they were safely seated did Lauren disclose to Elise and Marc the reason for the abrupt tossing of tonight's original dinner plans—the possibility of bugs in the guest house. After swearing them to secrecy, she told them about the ex-cop her father had enlisted to help her. She repeated the advice he'd tendered, but quickly added that she'd rejected it because she could never turn against her fellow soldiers, not even Ian Prather, who'd lied to her through his teeth. She could never become a traitor to the movement.

"What's he like, this Matt Burgess?" Elise wanted to know. "Does he seem trustworthy?"

"Royal trusts him, and I suppose that's good enough for me. He seems competent, although . . ."

"Although what?"

"He's made it clear that he doesn't think much of the animal-rights movement. He asked me why I'm not into human charities, crippled kids and so forth."

"But you *are* into human charities, dear. You give tens of thousands of dollars a year to human charities. I hope you told him that."

"I didn't see any reason to. He's not someone I need to impress, Elise."

"He doesn't have beady eyes, does he?"

Jandee giggled, sucking a swallow of water down the wrong pipe. "No, he has large, rather expressive gray eyes," she said, coughing. She incurred a troubled glance from Marc Lekander, who looked more birdlike than usual tonight. And more anemic, too, as if he'd just spent a month in a cellar, protected from the sunlight. "Matt's quite a babe, in fact—lean face, strong jaw, great butt. He likes art, and the dogs love him. Dogs are excellent judges of character, I've heard."

"He sent word that he's bringing help tomorrow morning," Lauren added, "which I assume means that he'll get rid of the bugs somehow. We'll keep you posted."

"Is this guy supposed to do anything more than give advice and look for bugs?" Marc wanted to know. "I mean, is he supposed to be your bodyguard, or what?" Marc wore a tan Hugo Boss suit over an olive T-shirt, with canvas Keds and no socks—clothes that looked more Hollywood than Seattle.

"Why should she need a bodyguard when she has you?" Jandee retorted.

"If he's supposed to be protecting her," Marc said, keeping his voice low, "I can't help but wonder where he is now. I'd feel better if Lauren had around-the-clock protection, wouldn't you?"

Jandee wrinkled her nose as if she smelled something rancid. She no longer tried to hide her dislike of Marc Lekander, who was a spoiled twit, in her view. She'd often voiced to Lauren her contempt for any man whose only vocation was to sit in on board meetings of the family corporation. Real men have real jobs, she'd said. Lauren had reminded her that Marc had done valuable work

for the animal-rights movement, but Jandee had insisted that he'd
only done the work to endear himself to Lauren, with whom he
was hopelessly in love, as any fool could plainly see.

"Marc may have a point," Elise said. "Perhaps we should
consider hiring some armed professionals to keep you safe, at
least until we know precisely what we're up against."

The conversation halted while a waitperson took their orders.
Nobody was hungry, but they all ordered dinner entrées. Lauren
asked for a bottle of merlot, which arrived immediately. The wine
felt good going down, and she drained the first glass in three quick
swallows. Marc poured her another, and she drained that one, too.

"You can't possibly stay at Jenkins Way tonight," Elise declared. "You'll stay with us, both of you, until this business with
the bugs is taken care of. We'll run by after dinner so you can
each pick up a change of clothes."

"And the dogs, of course," Marc put in, looking at Lauren.
"We shouldn't leave the dogs by themselves."

"No, I refuse to be driven out of my own home," Lauren said
with a bravado she didn't really feel. "For the time being we'll
watch what we say and make the best of it. Won't we, Jandee?"

"If you say so, boss."

"But you have no idea who's been listening to you," Elise
argued. "It could be anyone. Who can say how they might use
what they overhear?"

"Whoever they are, they've probably heard enough already to
send us all up the river for twenty years, and maybe longer,"
Jandee pointed out. "The harm has already been done."

"She's right," Lauren said. "Besides, I'm giving a luncheon
speech tomorrow at the Emerald City Society. Jandee and I need
to write it tonight, and I need to rehearse. I frankly don't care if
someone overhears me doing *that*."

"A luncheon speech!" Marc exclaimed. "Are you out of your
mind? Megan's been murdered, your father's in the hospital with
cancer, you've got microphones in your house. Someone may be
watching you, stalking you. And you're worried about a luncheon
speech!"

"Hey, life goes on," Jandee said. "At least it does for those
of us who have lives."

Marc Lekander stiffened in his chair, squared his shoulders.
"That's cute, Jandee. You're a cute kid." Lauren detected real
venom in his voice, something she'd never heard before. "This

is no time for smug self-assurance," Marc went on, covering Lauren's hand with his. "We're dealing with someone who kidnaps and kills, for Christ's sake. We need to be on our guard, take precautions. Lauren, I can't believe I need to tell you this."

"We'll be okay," Lauren said, squeezing Marc's hand. "We'll keep the doors locked. Now, can we please talk about something else—*anything* else? I hear there's an Edward Albee play at the Intiman Theater, *The Sandbox*, I think. Has anyone heard anything about it . . . ?"

Sixteen

At 10:15 P.M., the Blues Beast parked his black GMC Yukon in a dark corner of a strip mall parking lot and cut the engine. He took a bite of his Whopper, munched a French fry, and tried to relax. Arnie Cashmore sat in the passenger's seat, quietly smoking a cigarette, his glasses resting on the tip of his hawk-nose. In his lap lay a zippered canvas bag that bulged with hundred-dollar bills.

The strip mall was in Renton, a suburb that sprawled around the southern tip of Lake Washington. From here Tyler Brownlee could see Interstate 405, a main arterial that ran along the east shore of the lake, connecting Seattle's southeast industrial quarter with the prosperous residential suburbs of Bellevue, Kirkland, and Redmond. Even at this late hour cars choked the freeway as late commuters drove to or from jobs that operated on "flextime," a measure that local government had encouraged to ease traffic.

Renton was home to a vast Boeing manufacturing complex, as well as hundreds of smaller factories and service centers that orbited the world's largest builder of aircraft. Strip malls, convenience stores, and fast-food franchises occupied every square inch of land not taken up by factories, offices, or modest working-class housing. The warm night air buzzed with the sounds of engines. A horde of insects besieged the floodlights above the parking lot.

Tyler nodded toward the relentless procession of headlights on the freeway and said, "That could've been you, Arnie—Mr. Middle America, a regular corporate hamburger. I can just see you hunched over a computer, pounding out reports all day, going to meetings. You'd be good at it, too, with that brain of yours.''

Arnie smiled and shook his head, pushed his glasses to the top of his nose. In the sparse light he looked much older than his forty-odd years, like a rickety prospector who'd just trudged down from the mountain. "And I'd go home every night to my pretty little wifey and my two-point-one kids, right? Nice house out in the 'burbs. Probably have a dog and a cat, a minivan and a riding lawn mower. Oh, I fit the profile, all right, except for my sheet. No corporation in the world would let me into their lobby.''

"Fuck, I'll bet a third of the lame-os out there did what you did or worse, back when they were in college. The only difference is they didn't get caught.''

"That's not the only difference, Ty.''

"Yeah? Let's say you stop every third car out there on the freeway. You're gonna find an ex-drugger, some guy who did weed when he was a kid, maybe sold some to his friends now and then. Probably dropped a little acid back in his hippie days, went on to do some blow when that was fashionable. Now he's a pillar of the community, a doctor, a lawyer, a bean counter for some fuckin' high-tech company.''

"None of them would be pillars of the community if they'd spent six years in Oregon State Penitentiary, I'll tell you that.''

"No shit. But it hasn't been a total loss, right, *compadre*? If you hadn't gotten busted and sent to the joint, you never would've met my brother, and that means you never would've met the Ranger and the Fat Woman. You and I wouldn't be business partners and roomies." He punched the older man playfully on the shoulder.

"True. And I probably wouldn't be in the heroin business, either.''

"And you wouldn't have umpteen million dollars squirreled away in your offshore accounts. You'd be just another drudge out there in the Chinese fire drill, waiting for your gold-watch cere-mony.''

"So, I should be counting my blessings. Is that what you're saying?''

"I'm saying that getting busted gave you a chance to make your own reality, man. You've got what all those poor lame-os on the freeway dream about, but never get.''

"Tyler, don't start with that again, please."

"A world of your own making—that's what you're building, Arn. Everything else is artificial, a dream. Nothing we do in this artificial world counts, because it's not real. If it's not part of the ultimate reality that you create for yourself, you shouldn't waste precious energy worrying about it."

Having imparted this wisdom, Tyler Brownlee stuffed the final bite of his Whopper into his mouth. He felt good about what he'd just said, for he himself believed it fervently, even if he didn't quite understand it. Since his earliest childhood, the Ranger had preached to him about "creating your own reality," and Tyler had never questioned him. After all, the Ranger was a man of the world, a man of learning.

A pair of headlights approached from the street, a low-riding 1975 Monte Carlo painted a searing candy-apple-green, with rumbling exhaust pipes and yellow neon lights inside the wheel wells. The car wheeled into the lot and pulled alongside the Yukon.

"Damn, I wish Paco wouldn't drive that piece of shit when he's making deliveries," Tyler muttered. He wadded the burger wrapper and tossed it out the window. "The fucking thing attracts more attention than a fart in church. Why doesn't he just put a sign on the roof? *Hey, cop! Pull me over—I've got a hundred kilobucks' worth of Mexican tar in the trunk!*"

"Don't worry about Paco," Arnie soothed. "He knows what he's doing. You don't get to be who he is by being stupid." Paco de Leon was the Fat Woman's chief lieutenant, the man who handled her face-to-face contacts with her wholesale customers.

Arnie and Tyler's meetings with Paco never took place in the same place twice, a precaution against surveillance and ambush by the cops. The Fat Woman always notified Arnie of the location by telephone about an hour before the scheduled rendezvous, having sent someone to scout the site thoroughly beforehand.

The passenger's door of the Monte Carlo opened, and a pot-bellied man got out, approached the Yukon with a friendly wave. Paco de Leon was his usual affable self, a smile engulfing his broad face, his black eyes glittering with good humor. Though he and his boss controlled nearly a third of the black-tar heroin that flowed into the Puget Sound area, he looked like any other forty-year-old *campesino* on the street—jeans, cheap cowboy boots, flowered western shirt. His driver and bodyguard was his nephew, Eduardo, who wore the baggy garb of a gang-banger. Tyler glimpsed the handle of a pistol under the kid's Oakland Raiders jacket as he climbed out of the car.

"So, are you happy, *muchachos*?" Paco asked, offering a meaty hand through Arnie's open window. In all the years he'd done business with Arnie Cashmore, he'd never failed to ask this question. *Are you hah-pee . . . ?*

"Oh, we're happy, amigo," Arnie assured him, shaking his hand. "How about you?"

"Yeah, yeah. The old lady's fine, the kids are fine, business is good. I jus' hope they never legalize this shit, y' know?" He handed a plastic-wrapped loaf through the window. "I got a nephew on the old lady's side who wants to be a politician in Mexico, and I'm the guy who's gotta pick up his bills? Bein' a political force ain't cheap these days, even in Mexico. If that ain't enough, I got ten grandchildren who all wanna go to college. This shit ever becomes legal, and the price goes down, I'm fucked."

"Don't worry, Paco," Arnie said, handing over the zippered canvas bag. "It'll never happen."

In the space of sixty seconds, Tyler Brownlee and Arnie Cashmore took delivery of enough uncut Mexican black-tar heroin to keep the junkie population of Capitol Hill partying hearty for two more weeks. Arnie placed the loaf into a gym bag with the Nike swoosh emblazoned on the side, while Paco counted his money with the aid of a penlight. Their business done, they said *adios* and wished each other well until their next meeting. And that was that.

Tyler drove on I-405 west to I-5, the main route into downtown Seattle, and exited north into the International District. He parked in the alley behind the warehouse where his Ranger lived, a featureless three-story structure with dark, unfriendly windows. Arnie got out of the truck and went to the wide overhead door that fronted the alley, unlocked it, and raised it. Tyler drove the Yukon through, and Arnie lowered the door behind him.

On foot they negotiated a familiar obstacle course of empty packing crates and shipping pallets to a stairway that descended to the basement level, Tyler leading the way with a flashlight, Arnie trundling close on his heels with the gym bag. They walked through a musty, damp-smelling corridor to a room crammed floor-to-ceiling with discarded furniture and office equipment—dented metal desks and filing cabinets, swivel-chairs, ancient IBM typewriters, and God only knew what else. In a corner squatted an antique office safe, festooned with cobwebs and coated with grime. Arnie knelt beside it and spun the combination dial while Tyler held the light. The door of the safe opened smoothly, and Arnie tossed the gym bag inside, shoved the door home and spun the dial four times in each direction to randomize the tumblers.

Within the next few days they would retrieve the heroin and transport it to their house in Alki, where they would cut it into half-pieces and dealer-pieces for distribution to the score of retailers who worked their "service area," which included Capitol Hill and its adjacent neighborhoods. Years ago Arnie had negotiated a share of the Seattle heroin market with the Fat Woman and other local distributors—the Crips and Bloods, a handful of Hispanic gang leaders, and the head of an Asian gang. He'd never violated that agreement, even though an occasional interloper had tried to horn in on the lucrative Capitol Hill trade. Whenever this happened, Arnie had dispatched someone to school the interloper on the etiquette of heroin wholesaling. During the past three years, that someone had been Tyler Brownlee, who'd performed the chores with an adolescent gusto that was almost scary. Several of the interlopers had actually survived Tyler's schooling. Several others hadn't.

"There it is again," Arnie said, grabbing Tyler's arm. "That smell. It's strong this time."

"What smell? I don't smell anything."

"Then you've got a defective nose, man. It smells like an open grave."

Tyler laughed. Arnie had often complained of foul odors around here, and Tyler had always scoffed. *Open grave.* "Probably a dead cat," he said, hoping Arnie would let it go at that.

"That's what you always say," Arnie replied, sounding unconvinced.

As they left the building, Tyler glanced up at the top-floor windows and saw a feeble light filtering through a yellow window shade. "I'll be damned," he said. "He's come home. He's been out the past couple of days."

"Who—the old man?"

"Yeah. He comes and goes, sometimes days at a time. I never know if I'm going to find him here. I've always wondered if he's got a woman somewhere, somebody he's never mentioned. He's got another life—I know that much, one he keeps out of sight."

"Maybe he had a gig tonight."

"I doubt it. He would've told me. He likes having me in the audience whenever possible. Says it's good for my musical training."

"Secretive old snake, isn't he?"

"That's putting it mildly."

"Want to stop and say hi?"

"No, I've got things to do tonight."

They took the West Seattle Freeway across the Duwamish Waterway and exited onto Harbor Avenue, bound for Alki. To their right lay Elliott Bay, flat as a mirror and glittering with the lights of high-rises on the far shore. The Space Needle towered prominently over the Seattle Center, a white spear against the black of night.

"There she is—the Needle," Tyler Brownlee said, chuckling. "A junkie told me one time that they built it in case God ever wanted to fix. Man, can you believe that shit?"

"I believe it. You never know what a junkie's going to say."

"Personally, I think the Needle is a dead-on symbol for Seattle. We're the modern Mecca of heroin, after all. No other town in the country comes close to us in the number of junkies per thousand. I read that somewhere, and I'm sure it's true. Don't you think the Needle's a dead-on symbol, man?"

Arnie said nothing, only stared straight ahead through the windshield, which notified Tyler that something troubled him. That's how it was with these reflective types, Tyler had learned through experience. Things *troubled* them. They worried about problems they couldn't do anything about.

After a long silence, Arnie said, "You're full of shit, you know—what you said earlier, about this world being artificial. What we do here counts."

"Oh, Christ. Here we go again."

"Look, we're heroin dealers, okay? A few days ago I asked you to kill a lop, and you did it, like you were going out for pizza or picking up your laundry. And that wasn't the first time or the third. We do bad things, and they count. You've got to start understanding that, Ty."

"I say nothing counts unless we let it. The Ranger taught me this when I was six, and I've believed it all my life. We make our own reality, man, and until we achieve that reality, we live artificial lives, period."

Arnie replied that this was the stupidest thing he'd ever heard.

"Okay, you believe what you want to believe, and I'll believe what I want to believe," Tyler said, his annoyance showing. "I hate it when you get like this, like you're actually starting to grow a conscience after all these years. If you want to carry around a suitcase full of guilt for the rest of your life, that's up to you."

Arguing with Arnie was hopeless, always had been. Arnie was a deep thinker who pondered issues like global warming and the Middle East peace process. Tyler didn't consider himself a dim bulb, but he and Arnie functioned on different planes. They were of different generations. That the two of them ever saw eye to eye on anything was a miracle.

Tyler swung into the driveway of their frame house on Alki Avenue, the ordinary-looking house that Arnie owned through a dummy corporation. Most of the homes along the avenue were modest ranch-styles built in the forties and fifties, but the shoreline location made this an expensive neighborhood. A passerby would never have dreamed that heroin barons lived in this house, unremarkable as it was on the outside, with no exotic cars parked in the drive, no visible symbols of wealth other than the address. And this was exactly as Arnie wanted it. Conspicuous consumption was an invitation to scrutiny, and scrutiny was something that heroin barons avoided assiduously, if they wanted to survive.

Tyler went to his room and changed into a pair of black jeans, a sweatshirt and a short navy jacket. He tossed aside his cowboy boots in favor of high-top Doc Marten combat boots and strapped on his shoulder holster. He wore his Redstone knife in a scabbard on his right calf, his lock picks in a cloth pouch under his sweatshirt.

"So, you're going out," Arnie said as Tyler walked through the living room. "And you're dressed like a cat burglar. What am I supposed to conclude from this?"

"Conclude whatever you want. And don't wait up."

Arnie rose from the recliner, where he'd settled in to watch TV. Behind his thick glasses his eyes were huge with concern. "You've got a gig, right? Tell me you've got a gig, and that you're not up to something crazy."

"Define crazy."

"Crazy means something that could get you busted, send you back to the joint, maybe take me with you. It means wrecking everything we've worked so hard to achieve, watching it all go down the toilet . . ."

"*Work?* Man, did you say *work*? Jesus, Arn, give me a break. What we do isn't *work*. Twice a month we pick up our dope from Paco, spend an hour cutting it up, another two hours delivering it to our dealers. What's that? Maybe eight hours a month between the two of us? *Not* what I call work, *compadre*. You want *work*, talk to some poor fuckin' lame-o who punches a time clock. Don't talk to me."

Arnie scowled. "We're each pulling down seven grand a day, Ty, seven days a week, three hundred and sixty-five days a year. That's value, big-time value. That's the future we both talk so much about. It's worth taking care of, wouldn't you say?"

"Consider me lectured."

Arnie took off his glasses, rubbed his eyes. "This is about Lauren Bowman, isn't it?" he said, sounding tired. "You're out of control, man. You're acting out some dark fantasy about her . . ."

"None of your business, Arn."

"No? Hanging pictures of her all over your room—*that's* none of my business. Writing blues lyrics about her, singing about her, pounding out love letters on your computer—*that's* none of my business. But when you go out at night carrying a bullet launcher and dressed for burgling, *that's* my business, because my future depends on you staying cool. And when you hire the Stump brothers to wire the house of one of the richest women in the city, *that's* my business, too."

"Horst told you, that tub of shit. He told you, didn't he? I'm gonna break his balls."

"Hey, the man has a right to be upset. He called yesterday, asked me if I could reason with you. You're screwing up his whole life, Ty, costing him money, monopolizing his brother with all that surveillance crap. Plus, he's worried about getting cross-wise with Lauren Bowman and her husband—these people aren't exactly shrinking violets, you know. If they ever find out who's been bugging them . . ."

"They won't find out."

"The hell they won't. They *always* find out, Tyler. That's how it goes with these things. They'll find out, and they'll come after you and the Stump brothers with a hook. They'll hire muscle, private detectives, lawyers. And if they don't get you, the cops will."

"Know something, Arnie? You worry too much about things

that don't concern you." Tyler headed for the door, his jaw muscles rippling.

"I worry about *you*," Arnie called after him. "I worry about you not keeping your head in the game. I worry that your fucking obsession over Lauren Bowman is going to do us both in!"

Tyler slammed the door on his way out, climbed into his Yukon, and swung out of the driveway. Before he'd gone a block, he'd already forgotten the row with Arnie, his adrenaline pumping in anticipation of what lay ahead tonight.

Seventeen

Matt Burgess shut down his computer and leaned back in his chair, his eyes burning and his head aching from staring at a monitor for hours on end. He could have used about four Excedrin, chased by a pint of dark microbrew, followed by a neck massage. He would settle for the Excedrin.

He glanced at his watch and saw that it was already after midnight and was now Wednesday, June 4. Time had started to matter again, and he wondered whether this was good.

He'd spent most of the evening surfing World Wide Web sites and news groups that concerned animal rights. The vast majority of them had seemed innocuous enough—pleas for dollars to support shelters and animal-welfare programs, statements of philosophy, advice on how to adopt a "companion animal." Some evangelized about a healthy lifestyle, while others offered nothing more subversive than vegan recipes. A few, however, weren't innocuous. A few contained the ravings of wild-eyed militants for whom the liberation of animals was the first step in bringing down the Establishment.

Matt had seen Web pages that contained gut-wrenching descriptions of the conditions that battery chickens lived in, of slaughterhouses and veal-production operations. A series of photos taken inside a meat-processing plant had made him want to spit up his dinner. He'd read lists of corporations to be boycotted because of their abuse of animals, mostly cosmetics and pharmaceutical firms who used laboratory animals to test their products. He'd even found a manual with step-by-step instructions on how to assemble a delayed-action incendiary device from a milk jug and a handful of common household products, in case he ever wanted to burn down a skinning shed at a mink ranch.

His purpose in undertaking the Internet tour was to enlighten himself about the world that Lauren Bowman lived in, where nobody ate anything that had parents, where trashing medical research facilities rated merit badges. Had someone in that world, he'd wondered—someone who belonged to a competing group or sect—launched a jihad against Lauren and her compatriots in LOCA, possibly because of ideological differences or even jealousy, or maybe for a reason that an outsider couldn't imagine?

He'd explored the Web sites of the League Opposed to Cruelty to Animals, the Humane Society, the SPCA, the New England Association Against Vivisection, as well as those of more radical groups, including the Front for Animal Freedom and its numerous offshoots. He'd found vegetarian sites with scientific essays that spelled out the health dangers of eating meat, which included cancer, hardening of the arteries, and bovine spongiform encephalopathy (the "mad cow disease" that had terrorized Europe and the U.K.). But after hours of wading through stiff prose, he found that he'd achieved precious little real enlightenment. Lauren Bowman's world was still as alien to him as a Jovian moonscape.

Though he could sympathize with those who sought simply to reduce the suffering of animals through reasonable means, he could muster no sympathy for the militants who ransacked research laboratories and mailed letter bombs. Back in college he'd read enough anthropology to know that humans, like countless other species, had eaten meat since the dawn of time. To suggest that this was unnatural, as many hard-core vegetarians did, ignored the realities of natural selection. How could any thinking person deny that predators played an important role in weeding out the weak and infirm, a process critical even to the species they preyed upon?

He found the wild-eyed militants' logic downright laughable. If cattle, pigs, and chickens had a right to freedom from slaughter by humans for food, as the militants claimed, didn't prey animals everywhere have similar rights? The great carnivores of Africa must be as guilty as humans of violating those rights, along with seal-eating polar bears and bug-eating birds. Meat eaters throughout creation should be compelled to change their diets, shouldn't they? Wolves should be forced to give up devouring elk calves and taught to enjoy salads. Sharks should be weaned away from tuna and turned on to kelp.

Having been a cop, Matt understood that rights mean nothing without someone to enforce them. Nowhere in the militants' rhetoric did he find a clue about who was responsible for enforcing gophers' rights against hawks and owls, or wildebeests' rights against lions and hyenas.

Downstairs in Shorty's Tavern someone plugged the jukebox and selected an old tune by Johnny Cash, a song about someone falling into a ring of fire. Matt felt every bass note in his chest and heard every throaty line of the lyrics. Having resided for three years above the pub, he'd found a way to sleep through the racket—an electric white noise generator with settings like *Ocean Tides, Hard Rain,* and *Forest at Night.* Even so, he wouldn't sleep much tonight, he knew, with or without the sounds of crashing surf or driving rain. Tonight he would lie awake and worry about an old friend who was dying of inoperable cancer. He would mull the mysteries surrounding the brutal murder of a young woman and her killer's apparent fascination with Lauren Bowman. And he would try to ignore a nibbling anxiety that caused a pit in his stomach.

He'd first felt it years ago while he was still a cop. A department shrink had suggested that he was working too hard, getting personally involved with his cases. *Learn to detach yourself,* the shrink had counseled. *Don't let the catastrophes of dope pushers and junkies become your own.* But Matt couldn't detach himself from the world he worked in. Like his father, he'd believed that a detached cop was one who didn't care—a dangerous cop, the kind he would never let himself become.

Those first little twinges of anxiety had evolved into outright seizures that had regularly jolted him awake in the dead of night, like electric shocks. In the aftermath of such attacks he'd lain wide-eyed between the damp sheets, worrying about his job, his son's health, his marriage, every facet of his life.

He'd feared that becoming a cop was the worst mistake he'd ever made, because a cop in today's world needed emotional stamina that Matt was sure he lacked. He'd worried that the war on drugs had twisted his own sense of right and wrong, made him into something hateful, a destroyer of civil rights and liberties. Cops, he'd concluded, had become agents of the prohibitionist zealots who considered drug addiction a sin rather than a sickness, folks who preferred the medieval remedy of locking sufferers in jails over giving them medical treatment. He'd begun to feel as much a casualty of the war on drugs as the poor slobs he busted.

Then his son's health had taken a sharp turn for the worse, showing the telltale signs of the end game associated with cystic fibrosis. Tristan's eventual death had brought on the blackness with all its cold weight, dragging Matt into a hole that had nearly swallowed him. His marriage had collapsed, because he'd become totally self-obsessed. He'd lost all confidence in his ability to do useful work. He'd feared that he would never again laugh at a joke or smile at the sight of a child's face, that a sunset would never look like anything but a gray muddle. He'd seriously contemplated putting a bullet through his head, rather than suffer a colorless existence that lacked even small, routine joys.

Was it starting again? Matt wondered now.

Clinical depression, he'd found out over the course of his therapy and recovery, was a chemical imbalance inside the brain, too much of one thing and not enough of another. Some gland goes haywire and your neurotransmitters misfire, plunging your attitude into the toilet. At least one in six Americans endured it at some point in their lives. Famous sufferers included Hemingway, Churchill, Eleanor Roosevelt, Lincoln, countless others.

Fortunately, during the past decade medical science had made dramatic gains in the treatment of depression, mainly on the drug front. Prescription medications like Wellbutrin, Prozac, Zoloft, and Vivactil had proved effective in something like eighty percent of all diagnosed cases. But this didn't mean that recovery was a cakewalk. Not everyone responded favorably to the same drug, while others did not respond to *any* kind of treatment. Some people needed a combination of medications to restore the chemical balance in their brains. None of the drugs worked overnight, and a few took as much as three months to produce positive results. While waiting for the medication to kick in, the victim continued to suffer, slogging through the daylight hours like an insect mired in molasses.

After his breakdown, Matt had qualified for a "partial disability retirement" from the Seattle Police Department, and he'd jumped at the opportunity to get out. Free of the stresses of job and marriage, cocooned in the simple world of Shorty's Landing and fortified by medication, he'd fought off the "dark animal," as he'd come to think of the illness. Gradually he'd regained what his therapist called full functionality.

But during the past few days he'd begun to feel the nibble again, the first inkling that the dark animal might still be near, lurking in the shadows, waiting, sharpening its claws . . .

A knock on his door made him jump. For some reason he thought of his gun, which lay buried in a cardboard box in a corner of his bedroom closet, the SIG Sauer nine-millimeter that he'd carried while serving in the PD. He'd packed it away with his badge and ID, and hadn't laid eyes on it in more than two years. He wasn't quite sure why he'd even kept it.

The knock came again, stronger this time. He went to the door and put his ear against it, asked who was there, a precaution against the occasional drunk blundering up the rear stairs in search of the men's room. It had happened more than once. A few months ago he'd gotten out of bed to find that someone had actually peed on his door.

"Matt, it's me—Cleo. Let me in, will you?"

He pulled back the dead bolt and opened the door, now feeling foolish for having thought of the gun. Cleo Castillo scooted inside, grabbed his hand and squeezed it. She wore her tentlike apron with *The Big Cheese* embroidered on it, which meant that she'd worked a late shift in the tavern with Jimmy.

"It's Royal," she said, her eyes round with worry. "He walked out of the hospital sometime in the last two hours."

"What do you mean, walked out? He's been released?"

"He walked *out*. No discharge, no release. The nurse-supervisor called two minutes ago, said he must've packed up his things and sneaked down the stairs. Nobody saw him. An intern went into his room on his regular rounds and found an empty bed."

Matt's mouth went dry. He pulled Cleo to him and hugged her, not knowing what to say.

"I'd planned to go up there after work and spend the rest of the night in his room with him," Cleo said, her cheek on Matt's shoulder. "I was just about to leave. Jimmy's offered to close up for me."

"We shouldn't jump to conclusions," Matt said, trying to sound hopeful. "He might've flagged a cab, might be heading here right now. You know how he hated that place."

"He won't come here," Cleo said, her voice pinching. "Not

for a while, anyway, and maybe never.'' She whimpered, but
didn't actually cry. Matt figured that she'd used up her tears years
ago.

"Don't say that. Royal loves you . . .''

"Oh yeah, he loves me. But I'm not the only one in his life,
and never have been. He's not the kind of guy who puts all his
eggs in one basket, if you get my drift.''

Matt couldn't deny this. Royal himself had confessed to Matt
on more than one beery occasion that he kept secrets from Cleo,
that he regularly saw at least one other woman. This wasn't something he was proud of, but neither was it something he could
simply stop doing. Like everybody else on the planet, he had his
weakness. *Don't feel too sorry for Cleo,* Royal had said, *because
she's got her secrets, too.*

Matt supposed this was true. He sometimes saw shady-looking
types come into Shorty's and huddle in a lonely corner of the bar
with Cleo, whispering, glancing up occasionally to make sure no
one got close enough to overhear. He'd figured they were relatives
of hers.

He asked whether Cleo had any idea where Royal had gone.

"To *her,* whoever she is. Probably went to say good-bye.
Knowing him, he wants one last roll in the fart-sack, excuse my
French.''

"Listen,'' Matt said, "I still know people in the PD. Why
don't I make some calls, try to get the patrols alerted to be on
the lookout him? He's not a missing person yet, technically, so
they won't be able to detain him if they see him, but at least we
might find out where he is.''

"You can do that?''

"I can try.''

"Thanks, Matt. Thanks a lot.''

He walked Cleo to her apartment, then went back to his own
and spent the next half-hour on the phone with old cop pals, one
of whom turned out to be the downtown patrol watch commander,
a guy who'd served with Matt's father. The watch commander
assured Matt that putting out an informal alert on Royal Bowman
posed no problem, not for the son of the late Sergeant Chucky-
Bob Burgess. Matt thanked him, hung up and punched out Lauren
Bowman's number, needing to notify her about this latest devel-
opment with Royal. After a couple of rings Jandee's sleepy voice
came on the line.

"Lauren Bowman's residence."

"It's Burgess. Hope I didn't wake you."

"Oh—hi. I'd just crawled into bed, actually. Lauren and I have been working on her luncheon speech for tomorrow. What's up?"

"You've got incoming e-mail. I'll be up for a while if you or your boss want to send a reply."

"This can't wait until morning?"

"It's important, Jandee. Lauren needs to read it right now."

"Yeah, okay. I'm on my way to the study."

Matt rang off and rebooted his Macintosh, then pecked out a three-line message and sent if off to Lauren's e-mail address:

Royal walked out of the hospital late tonight. If he contacts you, let me know via e-mail. Remember the bugs.
Burgess.

He sat for a long while and stared through his window at the lights on the opposite shore of the Lake Washington Ship Canal, feeling alone and a little jumpy. The turbulence of other people's lives had churned up waves on his once-placid pond, and his sailor's instincts told him that a storm was coming. He hoped that he was emotionally fit enough to weather it.

Movement gave him a start, a fluttering of white and gray beyond the windowpane. A gull alighted on the rail of the narrow deck where Matt and Royal had whiled away so many evenings with talk of sailing *Hyperion* over the southern horizon. Seeing the bird gave him a strange feeling, for he'd never known gulls to be active at night. He could just make out its markings through the sparse light filtering outward from the lamp on his desk. He noted a streak of dark pigment on its beak, a defect that looked like a mustache, and realized that this particular bird wasn't exactly a stranger.

Groucho had come back, as if to keep him company.

Eighteen

You know you've done some sinnin' woman,
And it's no good confessin' to your priest.
Ain't but one man in the world you should confess to,
And I'm standin' right here—I'm the Blues Beast.

Tyler Brownlee *felt* the music in his soul, though his body was occupied with driving through the shadowy streets of north Ballard at nearly one in the morning. *Felt* his own fingers dancing high on the neck of his Stratocaster, *felt* the lyrics form in his throat while the Ranger's Zeta bass thumped like a pile driver in his chest. None of it was intentional, none of it thought out. This was how he wrote the blues—the music came to life before he ever jotted down a word or a note.

Pure fucking genius, Tyler told himself as he swung his GMC Yukon to the curb in a residential neighborhood, near the opening of an alley. *Nasty stuff—sort of a cross between old Walter Vinson and Robert Cray. Someday people are gonna hear this tune and say, "The Blues Beast has been there, babe—he knows whereof he speaks . . ."* A real blues man was a man of the world, the Ranger had told Tyler countless times, a man with the grit of hard living under his fingernails.

The street was a narrow, hilly byway off Northwest 67th, lined with boxy little houses set closely together. Junkers sat at the curbs and broken toys littered the yards. Here and there a windowpane flickered with the cool glow of a television set, a sign of life lived passively. A couch-potato-kind of life, Tyler thought.

He'd scouted the area thoroughly the previous evening on his Harley, noting the approaches to the house where Ian Prather and Vera Kemmis had taken up residence. He'd pretended to have engine trouble at the intersection near the front of the house, so he could get off the bike and study the scene without attracting attention. Within minutes he'd identified the safest route of ingress and egress, which turned out to be the alley at the rear. He'd noticed Ian Prather himself standing before the picture window in the living room, a drink in his hand and a cigarette hanging off his lip, looking like a regular blue-collar lame-o on his day off.

Tyler Brownlee felt as if he knew Ian Prather and Vera Kemmis personally. He knew their voices, owing to the bugs in Lauren's house. He'd listened to recordings of their tirades against "stateless corporations" and "government by the rich," their invective against a mainstream world that cared neither for social justice nor the institutionalized suffering of animals. He'd listened as they planned the raid on the Pacific Northwest BioCenter, while they coached their worshipful followers in the art of committing glorified vandalism. And he'd learned that Lauren had given them the use of a rental house owned by her company. He'd discovered the address of the place months ago simply by following Prather here from the Bowman-Granger estate in Magnolia.

And now Ian Prather and Vera Kemmis were about to exit Lauren's life forever, taking Tyler one step closer to center stage in her world, a place where he could love her like no other man on earth could.

> *You know you need to suffer, mama,*
> *If you ever expect to get released*
> *From all the trouble you've brought down your head.*
> *I'll make you suffer, girl—I'm the Blues Beast.*

Tyler crouched behind the Yukon and applied silvery duct tape to the rear license plate, then did the same to the one in front, ensuring that no witness would get his license number. He pocketed the roll of tape and took a small vial from the glove compartment of the truck, opened it, and filled a syringe with sodium pentobarbital, a powerful anesthetic that was available only to health-care professionals and those with connections to sources of black-market pharmaceuticals. After placing a protective plastic cap over the needle, he pocketed this, too.

He unsnapped the safety strap of his shoulder holster, hoping he would have no use for the big Smith & Wesson tonight but wanting to make certain that it was handy, just in case. He pulled his Redstone folding knife from the scabbard under his pant cuff and inspected it, put it back again. Checked his penlight, made sure the batteries were strong. Took an aluminum baseball bat from the rear of the truck, slapped it into an open palm, and deemed it suitable for tonight's work. Finally, he bundled his long blond hair into a ponytail and pushed it into a knitted watch cap, then pulled the cap down over his deformed ears. The Blues Beast was ready.

He crept through the alley to the rear yard of the house, the baseball bat brushing against his thigh. No moon tonight. Carports yawned like caverns on both sides of the alley. Unkempt shrubbery loomed black all around him, lilacs and rhododendrons, azaleas and junipers, reaching toward him over splintery cedar fences like creatures from a little boy's nightmare.

He found the gate to the backyard of the house where Prather and Kemmis lived and approached with utmost caution. He couldn't assume that the pair were asleep. They had no jobs, after all, no appointments to keep out in the real world where ordinary folks caught buses and punched time clocks. Why should they have gone to bed by one in the morning when they were free to sleep all day?

He stared over the gate at the rear of the house, his eyes hungry for any glimmer of light, but the house was as dark as the inside of a dead elephant. After two long minutes of staring, he concluded that Prather and Kemmis must indeed be in bed.

Reaching over the upper edge of the gate, he found the latch, ran his fingers over it and encountered a padlock—a strong Yale padlock, from the feel of it, which he could have picked if someone had been there to hold a flashlight for him. *Fuck it, I don't have time for this.* He loped back down the alley to the Yukon and fetched a bolt cutter from the cargo bed, along with an old dish towel. He wrapped the towel around the jaws of the bolt cutter to muffle the pop of steel cutting through steel, and made short work of the padlock.

He approached the rear stoop of the house, striding slowly, his ears tuned for any sound from within. At the top of the stoop he chanced a quick inspection of the door with his penlight. The lock was a common pin tumbler, a Schlage dead bolt, probably as old as the house, which dated back to the late fifties or early sixties—a good lock, but no longer new, which meant that its mechanism had loosened over the years. The lock was pickable.

Tyler tucked away the penlight, set aside the baseball bat and bolt cutter, then put on a pair of tight latex gloves. From his pouch of lock-picking tools he pulled a tension wrench, which was a simple strip of flexible metal that looked like a fingernail file with a wavy point. He located the keyway of the lock with his finger-tips, no longer needing light, and pushed the tension wrench a fraction of an inch into it. Twisting the tool slightly to exert slight pressure on the mechanism, he took a rake pick from his pouch, a wire-thin rod with a hooked tip. He inserted the hook into the lock as far as it would go and began to "rake" it quickly back and forth over the lower pins of the mechanism, making a tiny, inconsequential noise that sounded like a chipmunk gnawing at a walnut. Because the lock was old and worn, the pins readily bounced upward out of their beds, up to the "shearline," allowing Tyler to rotate the plug one notch at a time. Within six minutes he'd bounced the final pin, and the lock turned, pulling the dead bolt out of its hole.

He was in. The Ranger had taught him well.

He fought back an adrenaline rush and paused inside the back door, his nose twitching from the stink of stale food and cigarette smoke. He reminded himself that Ian Prather and Vera Kemmis weren't helpless junkies like Kevin Hilldahl and his mousy girl-friend. They were hardened veterans of a violent underground movement, people who knew how to elude cops and kill security guards. They'd spent years on the lam, living by their wits. Given half a chance, they would likely fight like tigers rather than submit to the tender mercies of the Blues Beast.

Given half a chance—that was the rub. The Blues Beast in-tended to give them no chance at all.

1:12 A.M.

Ian Prather came instantly awake. He lay stone-still in his bed and stared at the ceiling, which the streetlight outside his window had sectioned into shadowy rhomboids. He sat up slowly and listened, his head cocked, his muscles coiled.

He'd heard something.

Years of living in the underground had sensitized him to any hint of threat, be it a noise in the night or a glimpse of a suspicious car in the rearview mirror. Such was the life of a revolutionary: Never a moment of genuine relaxation, not even in bed. The enemy could be anywhere and everywhere, prowling, waiting for the proper moment to spring a trap. It could be FBI or ATF or INS. Or sheriff's deputies, city cops, state cops, or private dicks sent by some giant of the animal-abuse industry. No matter who they were, Ian Prather meant to fight them if they came for him, and he meant to beat them. He had no intention of letting himself be taken again. His hand went to the table next to the bed and found the Glock pistol that he kept with him always, the weapon he'd used only days ago against a security guard at the Pacific Northwest BioCenter.

Any number of things could have roused him from sleep, he knew—innocent things. Vera might have gone to the loo. A neighbor's cat might have dashed through the shrubbery. Then again, a cop might have stumbled over a lawn sprinkler while lining up a shot with a tear-gas grenade launcher.

He swung out of bed, thumbed the safety button on the pistol and moved toward the door of his bedroom. The cool night air made him shiver, since he wore only a pair of Jockey briefs. He slipped into the short hallway that led to the living room and kitchen, the pistol out in front of him. On his left was the door to Vera's room, on his right the bathroom. Except for the luminescent dial of his watch, he could see nothing beyond the bare outlines of walls, floor, and doorsills.

A glimmer caught his eye, and he froze in midstep. It had come from the lower edge of Vera's door, only a wink of light that had died after a mere second or two. He heard a muffled *thump* and the squeak of bedsprings. Vera wasn't a late-night reader, he knew, and she wasn't watching television, or the telly would have been audible through her closed door, even at low volume. And why would she have snapped a light on, only to turn it off again almost instantly?

Ian listened for what felt like an eternity, but heard no hint of what might be happening behind Vera's door. He raised his fist to knock, then lowered it. Ian Prather and Vera Kemmis had been

together long enough to dispense with small formalities like
knocking on one another's door, even in the dead of night.

He reached for the doorknob.

1:15 A.M.

As the bedroom door opened and the overhead light came on,
Tyler Brownlee pushed the plunger of the syringe, injecting into
Vera Kemmis's neck a dose of sodium pentobarbital that would
render her near-unconscious and pliable as a rag doll within three
minutes. He'd attacked her while she slept, having first used the
penlight to make certain that he was in her room and not her
partner's. Slapping one hand tightly over Vera's mouth, he'd ad-
ministered a good hard chop to her right kidney in order to im-
mobilize her with pain. Then he'd pulled the syringe from his
pocket and jabbed it home.

Now he faced Ian Prather himself, the Great English Lame-o,
who crouched in the doorway, wearing nothing but his skivvies,
a sinewy man, craggy-faced and hairy-chested. He was pointing
an ugly automatic at Tyler's forehead. Without even thinking,
Tyler rolled across the bed and pulled Vera Kemmis on top of
him, making a shield of her.

Prather shouted something stupid, a command to freeze, to let
Vera go, something like that. Tyler didn't actually hear it. The
woman fought like a wildcat now, the drug having not yet kicked
in. Her sharp elbows found Tyler's ribs, and she bit his gloved
hand, igniting pain that shot up his arm like a bolt of electricity.
Tyler gave her another chop to the stomach, pivoted on the bed,
and lurched to his feet, hauling her up with him. He pushed her
hard at Prather, then lunged to his right, sprawling headlong onto
the floor.

Prather went to his knees to catch Kemmis as she tumbled
forward, giving Tyler the few seconds he needed to grab the baseball bat that he'd placed next to the bed. Prather now scooted
backward through the door into the hallway, dragging the woman
with him . . .

1:16 A.M.

She made a sound as Ian hauled her out of the room, a nasal
mewing that didn't sound right coming from this tough veteran

of the revolutionary struggle. Her body seemed too light in his
arms, too frail to be that of rawboned Vera Kemmis. She wore
only a pair of gray running shorts and an old T-shirt with a
Tommy Hilfiger logo on the front. Both were stained with the
blood of the intruder's bitten hand. She twisted in pain as Ian
swung her to one side and let her flop to the carpet in the hallway,
regretting that he had no time for gentleness.

Now he squared himself to face the intruder in the bedroom,
intending to fight the bastard and kill him. He saw a dark blur as
the man darted across the doorway. Ian's finger tightened on the
trigger of his pistol, but loosened again as his brain conquered
instinct.

This bloke wasn't a cop, that much was certain, because cops
didn't attack women in their beds. A pistol shot would bring them,
though, as surely as the sun would rise, and cops were the last
things Ian Prather needed right now.

Suddenly the room went black, the intruder having switched
the light off. Ian pressed himself against the wall next to the door
and held his breath, listening for any sound that would betray the
intruder's whereabouts inside the room. But all he could hear was
Vera's labored breathing as she writhed in agony on the carpet.
She mewed again, called Ian's name.

"Get out, love!" he shouted at her. "Get to the car and get
out!"

"Ian, no. What about you? I can't . . ."

"Never mind that, damn it! Save yourself! I'll stay and deal
with this son of a bitch!"

"Ian, I can't l-leave you. Tell me wh-what to do . . ." Her
speech was thick, labored. Ian had no way of knowing what drug
the intruder had injected into her, but it had apparently started to
take hold. "Is it the bloody cops . . . ?" she asked.

"No, love, it's not the cops. Just go! Listen to me, damn it,
and do as I say!"

"I won't go. I won't l-leave you here on your own. I w-
won't . . ."

"Christ, stay then. But keep out of the bloody way, all right?"

1:17 A.M.

Tyler Brownlee swung his aluminum baseball bat as Ian Prather
charged into the dark bedroom, only to connect with a pil-

low that the Englishmen had wadded around his arm. Still, the blow did some damage, and Prather cried out in pain. But he somehow caught hold of the bat with his free hand and pulled on it, hauling Tyler toward him. Both men went to the floor in a tangle.

Something hard and cold caught Tyler across the forehead—the barrel of Prather's pistol, undoubtedly. Sparks exploded behind his eyes. Worse, Prather managed to grab the bottom edge of Tyler's jacket and pull it over his head, severely restricting his arms. A hard fist slammed into his midriff, knocking the air from his lungs. An uppercut found his jaw, causing a second explosion of fireworks in his head.

"Jesus fucking Christ," Tyler Brownlee bleated, and the blows fell on him like rain—ists and hard steel, a good old-fashioned pistol-whipping. The pain gagged him, nearly made him puke.

His world was about to end, it seemed—here in a cramped bedroom of a sorry little house in Ballard. Ian Prather meant to beat him to death, that much was clear, and the Blues Beast's dream of winning Lauren Bowman would die with him. All the scheming and maneuvering, the years spent in the perfection of a vision, the building of a new reality—all dead. Tyler would never feel Lauren's smooth body in his arms or feel her breath in his ear. They would never embark on a tour of respectable blues venues or ride the open road on his Harley. The worst part of it, the most unbearable part for Tyler Brownlee, was knowing that he was about to fail the Ranger, the loving father who'd taught him better than this, the man who'd prepared him for survival in this ugly, biting, bludgeoning world.

Summoning strength he wasn't sure he had, Tyler rolled himself into a fetal ball and pivoted on the floor, then kicked out wildly. The first three or four kicks found no target, but then he connected with what felt like Ian Prather's chest or midsection. The Englishman huffed, having caught the hard sole of a Doc Marten combat boot in some sensitive spot. Tyler managed to scramble away, tearing off his jacket, leaving it in Prather's clutches. He tripped over something—the baseball bat. He snatched it up. Grateful that Prather hadn't gotten his hands on it, he whirled and swung low, felt the bat connect and heard the splintering of bone. Ian Prather screamed and went down.

1:23 A.M.

When the light came on, Ian Prather found that he lay in a lake of his own blood. The intruder's wild kick had caught him square in the sternum, cracking ribs and knocking the wind out of him. The blow with the bat had caught his right forearm and shattered it, blinding him with pain, knocking his gun away. The second and third hits had rendered him helpless and near-senseless.

Now he stared at his useless arm, which hung at a weird angle across his chest, shards of bone poking through purpling flesh. The intruder towered over him, holding Ian's own pistol in his fist—a battered young man with disheveled blond hair, misshapen ears, and a scar to the left of his nose. Squinting through a cloud of pain, Ian strained to make sense of that face, for something about it seemed contradictory—a certain curve of the cheek, the sharp set of the chin, a look that appeared oddly friendly, considering that the man was about to beat him to death with a baseball bat. The face was *familiar*, somehow. Ian Prather had seen this young man before, he was certain.

"I-I know you, don't I?" Ian croaked.

The intruder grinned lopsidedly and pushed the pistol into his belt, looming over Prather like a Nordic demigod in a Wagner opera. He shifted the aluminum bat into his good hand, the one Vera hadn't bitten. The look in his eyes notified Ian Prather that his final moments would be painful.

"I won't beg you not to kill me," Ian said, "but at least tell me who you are. Tell me where we met. Is that too bloody much to ask?"

It was too much to ask. The bat came down and pulverized Ian's left kneecap, inflicting pain of a kind he'd never dreamed possible.

1:27 A.M.

Even though the sodium pentobarbital had rendered Vera Kemmis unconscious, the Blues Beast took no chances. He bound her with duct tape at both the ankles and wrists, ensuring that she couldn't cause trouble when the drug finally burned off. He then wadded one of her dirty socks, stuffed it into her mouth and taped it into place, ensuring that she couldn't scream for help.

He hoisted her into a "fireman's carry," which let him keep one hand free to deal with door handles, the baseball bat, and bolt cutter. Before exiting the house, he stuck his head out the back door and listened, but heard no approaching sirens, no indications that the commotion in the night had stirred the neighbors—a small miracle.

He carried Vera down the alley to the Yukon and heaved her into the cargo bed as if she were a sack of potatoes, then tossed in the bolt cutter and the bat. After checking to make certain that he'd left nothing behind—he accounted for his knife, his lockpicks, his gun, wallet and watch—he slipped into the driver's seat and fired up the engine. He drove the first block with the lights off before stopping to peel the tape from the license plates and throw away the surgical gloves. After getting back into the truck he sat in silence for a full minute, his heartbeat pounding in his ears, his cheeks hot and damp. The night air felt cool on his skin and sweet in his throat.

Despite the throbbing wound in his bitten hand, Tyler felt positively *golden*—bruised and bloodied, but unbeaten. The hand would heal, as would the cuts and contusions that Prather had dealt him. What did a little pain matter to a man who was about to live his fondest dream? The Ranger had been right, as always—good things come to the man who grabs destiny by the balls.

The Blues Beast drew a long, delicious breath and drove on, thankful that the night was still young.

Nineteen

Feeling groggy after a near-sleepless night, Matt Burgess swung out of bed two full hours later than usual, saw that the sun was already well above the horizon and decided to blow off his morning run. He popped his daily dosage of Wellbutrin and took a slow shower, shaved, trimmed his mustache. And because this would be no ordinary workday, he dressed in a freshly pressed button-down shirt, a brown corduroy sport coat and his best khakis.

A check of his e-mail revealed no message from Lauren Bowman, only the usual spam—ads for miracle diets, get-rich-quick schemes, and vacation time-shares. Feeling in need of a blast of caffeine, he went down the back stairs to the kitchen of Shorty's Tavern, where the smell of fresh coffee was strong.

He found Cleo Castillo busy at the grill, beads of sweat glittering on her forehead, her hands moving like well oiled machinery. She barked a continuous stream of orders in Spanish to the pair of kitchen helpers who bustled around in preparation for the lunch crowd, which wasn't due for more than four hours yet. They'd already begun fileting cod, pounding out hamburger patties and stacking them in metal trays, peeling and slicing potatoes for French fries and chips.

Cleo smiled when she saw Matt and offered bacon and eggs, but he wasn't even slightly hungry. He just wanted coffee, and Cleo motioned him to a long row of mugs that hung above the high-capacity coffeemaker. He drew himself a mugful, sat down

at a vacant chopping board next to the grill, and suddenly remembered his new morning chore. He went to the cooler and
removed a pan of yesterday's fish scraps, tossed the contents out
the back door, where the usual gang of cats had congregated for
their daily handout.

"I promised Royal I'd do that," he said, sitting down to his
coffee again. He took a cautious sip, kept his eyes low.

"He loves those scraggly old cats," Cleo answered with a sad
smile. "A couple of them have been around here almost as long
as I have." She cracked two eggs onto the hot grill, where they
sputtered and popped. "They miss him, I think. But not as much
as I do. It seems like he's been gone for years, even though it's
only been a matter of hours."

"Have you heard anything?" Matt asked.

She shook her head. "You?"

"Not a thing."

The police department hadn't called back, which meant that
nobody on the night watch had spotted Royal on the street. The
old man must have holed up with a girlfriend somewhere, just as
Cleo had suspected. Still, Matt couldn't shake the unsettling notion that Royal had hatched some wild scheme to take matters
into his own hands, to take preemptive action against Megan Reiner's killer in order to protect Lauren. Though Matt had no idea
what shape such a scheme might take, he'd learned long ago
never to underestimate Royal.

He and Cleo chatted quietly while she prepared a large breakfast for herself, which she proceeded to demolish in remarkably
few mouthfuls. Eggs, bacon, hash browns, buttered toast—a
woman her size needed lots of fuel. She frowned fiercely as she
ate, as if eating was solemn work that required great concentration.

More than once Matt started to ask her whether Royal had
confided in her about Lauren's involvement with the raid on the
BioCenter, or about Megan Reiner's murder, but each time he
held back. He'd promised Lauren not to tell anyone about these
matters, and he'd already broken the promise by seeking Alex
Ragsdale's help and advice. He decided not to break the promise
a second time, at least not until absolutely necessary.   .

After finishing his coffee, he hugged Cleo, begged her not to
worry. He went down to the marina and puttered around the boats
for a while, making mental notes of work that needed doing. The

Bayliner fisherman in Slip 16 needed new engine oil and filters, the Tartan cutter in 20 had a full holding tank that required pumping out, the Catalina sloop in 39 needed a new rudder cable, and so on, until the list grew too long to keep in his head. In the two short days since he'd first become involved with Lauren Bowman's problems, he'd already fallen behind here at the marina, having spent time interviewing Lauren when he ordinarily would have been taking care of the boats. He'd spent hours sitting next to Royal's hospital bed, hours more talking with Rags. Boat owners would soon start to complain, he was certain.

At 9:15 A.M., he rendezvoused with his once and future partner at the front gate of the Bowman-Granger estate at Jenkins Way in Magnolia, as they'd agreed yesterday. Inside the walled enclosure, steam rose in wispy clouds from manicured shrubbery as dew evaporated under the morning sun. The waters of Puget Sound lay flat and blue beyond the rocky shore, punctuated here and there by white sails. Gulls and crows wheeled in the cloudless sky overhead.

Matt got out of his old Cherokee and walked up to the driver's window of Rags' silver BMW. "Sir, I'm afraid I'll need to see your registration and yuppie license," he deadpanned.

Rags grinned. "But officer, I'm too damn old to be a yuppie. It's my wife's car, honest." They laughed as Rags pretended to offer a bribe.

Matt then became serious and asked where the sound man was, the electronic surveillance specialist that Rags had laid on to sweep Lauren Bowman's residence for hidden microphones. The man's name was Avery Carpenter, and he'd retired from the DEA before coming to work for ProGuard.

"He'll be here around nine-thirty," Rags said. "And he'll need five hundred dollars, off the books. Think Lauren can handle that?"

Matt snickered. "She probably spends that much every month on hair care."

Matt went to the intercom on the gatepost, punched the call-button and identified himself to the Hispanic man who answered. The gate buzzed open. Matt got back into his Jeep and drove into the circular brick drive, with Rags following in the BMW. They parked, got out of their cars.

"Welcome to the lifestyles of the rich and shameless," Matt

said. "From this point on, no smoking, no spitting, no peeing in the shrubbery."

Rags glanced around at the grandeur and shook his head in awe. "So, this is how the fat money lives. Too bad I'll never know what it feels like."

"Hell, you're upwardly mobile. I predict that ten years from now you'll own a controlling interest in ProGuard. You'll have estates like this on both coasts."

"Yeah, right. And pigs will fly."

Matt nodded toward the guest house, which stood well apart from the main mansion. "Lauren lives in that one," he said.

"I've heard of his-and-her bathrooms, but this is ridiculous."

"She and her hubby are on the outs. They don't see much of each other, from what I gather."

"That's in keeping with Gabe Granger's reputation for being an asshole."

"One he richly deserves, believe me. I ran into him the other day, right where you're standing. He came at me like a pit bull." Matt described his encounter with Gabe Granger, and wondered aloud how anyone with Granger's personality could have made millions in real estate, a business in which personality mattered big-time. And how someone like Lauren Bowman could have fallen for him.

"Which brings up a related matter," Rags said. "I floated a few discreet inquiries around the office this morning about why ProGuard stationed a security officer at the BioCenter on the night of the raid. It seems that IP and R got a mysterious message from . . ."

"IP and R? What's that?"

"Our 'Intrusion Prevention and Response' unit. They handle the anti-intrusion accounts, security patrols, and such. Anyway, the head of the unit received an anonymous letter a week before the raid on the BioCenter, outlining when it would go down, who was involved, et cetera, et cetera. The bosses didn't take it seriously, figured it must be a hoax."

"I don't believe it. How could they *not* take it seriously? Isn't it their business to take these things seriously? Christ . . . !"

"Let me finish. The letter fingers Lauren Bowman as one of the perpetrators, right? It so happens that Lauren and Gabe are major clients of our little company. We handle security and patrolling at all their retail malls and office buildings, and it's a big,

lucrative contract. The bosses couldn't believe that Lauren Bowman would be involved in something like busting into a research
laboratory, but to be on the safe side, they laid on a live guard
for the night.''

"The old guy who got himself killed."

"As it turned out, one guard wasn't enough, obviously."

"So the moguls at ProGuard are aware that Lauren was involved. And now they're going to take this tidbit to the police, I
suppose."

"Not on your life. Outfits like ProGuard have a privileged
relationship with their clients, sort of like lawyers. They're
obliged to keep stuff like this confidential."

"Even if it means obstructing justice?"

"That's the way they're interpreting it—for the time being,
anyway. They certainly don't want one of their major clients to
end up in the slam. It might affect the cash flow, and we can't
have that, can we?"

Matt let out a long puff of air. "You know what this means,
don't you? There *is* a mole in Lauren's crowd, just like we worried. Someone took it upon himself to arrange for Lauren and her
pals to get caught in the act of demolishing a research lab."

"Maybe more than one mole, seems to me."

Matt thought a moment and decided that Rags must be right.
Someone in Lauren's circle had collaborated with Megan Reiner's
killer, planting bugs or passing on information about the raid. But
this probably was not the same person who tipped off ProGuard,
unless he or she actually meant for the killer to get caught right
along with the FAF raiders. More likely, someone *else* had done
that, someone with an altogether different agenda.

Two moles.

Matt and Rags strolled the crushed-granite path toward the
guest house, bantering and wisecracking as they'd always done,
as if they never had stopped being partners and gone their separate
ways. But Matt's easy manner hid the dark misgivings he'd begun
to feel again over any further involvement in the matter of Megan
Reiner's murder and the raid on the BioCenter. Withholding
knowledge of a crime from the police was bad enough, a clear
case of obstruction of justice, which Matt had been willing to risk
for Royal's sake. Luring Rags into complicity was unforgivable,
however. You don't do that to a friend, he'd told himself again
and again while lying awake in the small hours of the morning,

his white noise machine issuing the sound of surf at high tide. He told it to himself again right now.

Try though he might, Matt could not envision a happy ending to this matter. Even if Megan Reiner's killer got caught, the cops would eventually figure out who knew what and when they knew it. The DA would slap Lauren Bowman and her entourage with obstruction charges in addition to the various charges associated with the raid and the murder of the security guard. Matt Burgess and Alex Ragsdale would get special treatment, naturally— *tougher* treatment, because they were ex-cops. They were supposed to know better. If they managed to avoid jail time, which was problematic at best, Rags would certainly lose his PI ticket, along with his job and career.

Furthermore, Matt had growing doubts about his own emotional fitness. He wondered whether he could handle the stress that would surely come with the task of protecting Lauren Bowman from some sicko killer. And he worried whether he could be a dependable partner to Rags if things got sticky.

He halted in the entryway of the guest house before reaching the door, and stared level in his friend's face. "What in the hell are we doing here, Rags? Let's walk away from all this while we still can."

"We're not walking away from anything, Burge."

"Why? Why can't we get back in our cars and leave, go back to our normal lives, maybe shoot a round of golf, as long as you're playing hooky from work?"

Rags rolled his eyes the way he did when he felt he was dealing with a moron. "Because this is for Royal, that's why."

"Doesn't it bother you that we're obstructing justice?"

"Look, we don't really know about any actual crimes, do we? All we've really got is hearsay. Someone *told* you she participated in the BioCenter raid, *told* you about Megan Reiner's murder. We don't have any actual evidence that this stuff really happened. For all we know, Lauren Bowman is a congenital liar. She could've made all this up to get attention or something."

Now it was Matt who rolled his eyes. "I've seen the video. I watched Megan get her throat cut."

"It could've been a fake. We have no way of knowing that tape was authentic. Hell, with a computer and a modern video-editing program, you could create footage of Hitler doing the hokeypokey with Hillary Clinton, and it would look like the real thing. We're just here to scope things out, that's all. The minute we find any evidence of a real crime, we'll call the authorities, like any other good citizen.''

Matt looked away, incredulous. He couldn't understand why Rags was so fired-up to involve himself in this madness.

"We'll talk more about this later," he said, pushing the doorbell button. "If we're not going act like sane people and get the hell out, we might as well get started."

Jandee Vernon answered the door, looking pert in a mint-green cotton dress. She smiled hugely at Matt, her big blue eyes dancing. Matt introduced Rags as a "professional associate," whatever the hell that meant, and Jandee shook his hand. She showed them into the sitting room with the art collection and the magnificent view of Elliott Bay. Matt mentioned that someone else was due to arrive within the next ten minutes or so, a man named Carpenter, and Jandee promised to make sure that he got through the gate.

A moment later Lauren Bowman entered the room, dressed in a lightweight business suit like the ones Matt remembered his ex-wife wearing—navy blue, conservative, and correct, appropriate for a lawyer or a CPA. Her footwear, however, provided a bizarre touch—white canvas Keds. But then a hard-core vegan wouldn't be caught dead in leather, Matt remembered. At her side were the Belgian Tervurens, Desi and Lucy, who wagged their tails in welcome.

Lauren said hello to Matt, introduced herself to Alex Ragsdale and suggested they all use first names. Matt saw through her smile, saw the turmoil in her eyes, the tension in the muscles of her face. She looked as if she hadn't slept much last night, which was understandable. Her father was missing and, in all probability, someone had bugged her house—someone who had killed a friend and might try to kill again. Matt marveled that she could smile at all. Nonetheless, he thought she looked beautiful.

"Have you heard anything from Royal?" she asked him in a low voice.

"Not yet. I take it you haven't either."

She shook her head.

"Don't worry, he'll get in touch," Matt said, feeling a need to offer comfort. "It's only a matter of time."

Lauren looked at Rags and said, "I assume that Alex is here to deal with the problem we talked about in our e-mail." She glanced around to indicate the possibility of ears in the walls. "Why don't we go out to the veranda, where we can enjoy the fresh air and have some tea?"

"Call me Rags," Rags put in. "Only my great-aunt calls me Alex."

Lauren led the way out to an open veranda paved with colorful Italian granite. In the center stood a cluster of hand-built redwood deck chairs and a low table with a glass top. A madrona provided sparse shade, its leafy limbs reaching skyward in graceful twists. Matt suffered a sudden attack of hay fever and sneezed before getting a pack of Kleenex out of his pocket.

"I think we can talk safely out here," Lauren said, motioning her visitors to the chairs. "No place to hide microphones, as far as I can see." Rags conducted a quick visual inspection of the undersides of the furniture and found nothing suspicious. The three of them sat. Rainy Hales brought tea and croissants from the kitchen, avoiding eye contact with everyone but Lauren.

"I have a confession to make," Matt said after sipping his tea. "I've confided in Rags here concerning the BioCenter and Megan."

"I thought we agreed to keep it between the two of us," Lauren said, her eyebrows arching with chagrin. "When I make a deal with someone, I expect him to honor it."

"This won't go any farther, I promise. The truth is, I need Rags' help with this case. You're better off with both of us, instead of just me."

"We were partners in the PD," Rags added, "and we were pretty good, actually. Even did some undercover work. Matt's right—we work best as a team."

Lauren swallowed hard, staring a dagger at Rags. "You're not still with the police?"

"I work for ProGuard Security and Investigation these days. I'm here on my own time as a favor to Matt. The company will never know about any of this, I assure you. And neither will the cops, if we're careful."

"You're with *ProGuard*," Lauren said. "Our company, Granger-Bowman Properties, uses your firm. Did you know that? ProGuard has the security contract for all our retail malls and commercial buildings."

Matt and Rags traded glances. "Yes, I'm aware of that," Rags said. "Small world."

"I'm a little confused about what you intend to do exactly," Lauren said, looking at Matt now. "Did Royal talk you into becoming my bodyguard—is that it?"

"I told him that I'd do all I could to keep you safe from whoever killed Megan Reiner," Matt replied. "The first priority, like I said before, is to clear your house of audio surveillance devices. Rags here has laid on an expert to sweep the place. In fact, he should be here any minute."

Lauren put a hand to her forehead and closed her eyes. "I hope you haven't told this expert about Megan. Or the BioCenter, for that matter."

"Of course not," Rags said. "All he knows is that we want the house clear of bugs. He does this kind of thing all the time. You'd be surprised how many people eavesdrop on each other. No one believes in the sanctity of a private conversation anymore."

"He charges five hundred dollars," Matt added. "He'll need cash, since this'll be an off-the-books kind of thing. You understand."

"Cash," Lauren repeated, looking dubious. "I guess I can arrange that. You said that getting rid of the bugs is your first priority. Does that means there's a second priority?"

"We'll need to start talking to people," Matt said. "If your place really is bugged, we can only assume that someone you know is working against you."

Lauren's tired eyes grew large with new worry. "Why would you assume that?"

"You've got a sophisticated electronic security system here, put here by ProGuard, no doubt," Rags said, gesturing. "If I wanted to bug your house, I'd need to get inside to do the installation. I'd need somebody to shut off the sensors and the cameras, someone to give me the activation codes for the locks. Then I'd need to know when you and your people plan to be out, so I could slip in, do my thing, and get out without you knowing about it. I'm talking about an insider."

"Okay, I hear what you're saying," Lauren said. "What's this about talking to people? What exactly do you mean by that?"

"Interviews," Matt answered. "We need to check up on the folks close to you, find out why anyone would want to hurt you."

Lauren sat rigidly upright. "You're not serious. You can't talk to people about this stuff. You might as well put an ad in the

Seattle Times. The whole idea is to keep it quiet, for the love of God.''

"We'll be discreet," Matt promised.

"*Discreet?* How can you possibly be discreet about something like this?"

"We'll use a cover story," Rags said. "We'll tell people that you've gotten some threatening mail and phone calls, and that you've hired us to do a little checking. It's not unusual for celebrities to have this problem."

Lauren hunched forward and braced her elbows on her knees, rested her head in her hands. "God, things are so out of control," she said, barely above a whisper. She rocked back and forth for a few seconds, then straightened up and gazed at Matt with steady, dry eyes. "Shit. All right. Do whatever you need to do. Just be cool about it, I implore you. Remember that lives and livelihoods depend on keeping this matter in-house. Now, if you'll excuse me, I'll go try to scrape up five hundred bucks in *cash*. Then I have a speech to give." She stood and strode into the house, Desi and Lucy trotting at her heels.

The men sat quietly for nearly a full minute before Matt said, "That went well, don't you think?" He sneezed again and dug for his Kleenex.

Twenty

While waiting to be introduced as the featured speaker of today's meeting of the Emerald City Society, Lauren became physically sick. Just moments earlier she'd thought again of Megan Reiner—a thought that had recently begun to invade her skull at random moments, at all hours of the day or night, bringing with it gut-twisting images of the girl's final moments. Every invasion contained a new element of the horror, some aspect of it that Lauren hadn't yet quite focused on. At this moment it was the pain that Megan's family and friends must be suffering over her disappearance, a pain that would surely linger as hope faded for her ever turning up safe. Lauren felt culpable for having learned the black truth, while the girl's loved ones languished in ignorance of Megan's fate, a fate that Lauren feared she could have prevented.

Blood dries faster than tears.

Though Megan's blood might have dried by now, Lauren knew that the girl's family hadn't stopped shedding tears. Does a mother ever stop crying for a murdered child? Lauren took a sip of ice water to dowse her growing nausea. She couldn't shake the crawling sense of reaping the fruit of seeds sown years ago in Portland—the deaths of Megan and the security guard, the listening devices in her house, the likelihood of a traitor within the cell of her most trusted comrades. All related. All part of a justice that she must suffer for sins committed long ago.

The dining room of the Sorrento Hotel, where the Emerald

City Society held its monthly meetings, had walls of dark hard wood and high ceilings hung with glittering chandeliers, the leather-and-mahogany look of an exclusive men's club. The luncheon-goers sat around tables covered in white cloth, garnished with elaborate centerpieces of fresh flowers. Lauren picked at her garden salad and tried to make conversation with the gregarious young woman sitting next to her, the president of the Society, whose name tag identified her as Lupe Rocha, director of human resources in a firm called Cognitronix. Rocha talked at length about the coming economic crisis in Asia and its potential damage to the local economy, and Lauren pretended to listen, even feigned fascination. The nausea persisted.

Blood dries . . .

The members of the Emerald City Society were professional women like Lupe Rocha, all under forty, most dressed to the nines. They were shakers and movers in the business community, people who knew how to think "outside the box," which perhaps explained why the Society had invited a high-profile, left-leaning activist to address their monthly luncheon. Not so long ago Lauren would have felt at home among them. She would have swept into this place and shaken the hands of as many Society members as she could reach. She would have schmoozed, circulated, and worked the room like a politician questing for votes. But not today. Today she felt like an impostor, a criminal. Today she kept her hands to herself.

Rocha went to the podium, switched on the microphone, and introduced Lauren Bowman as a "paragon of modern business-womanhood," an icon of feminine success in a business world still dominated by men, a walking testament to what everyone in this room could aspire to be. As Rocha sang her praises and listed her accomplishments, Lauren swept the crowd with her eyes, found Jandee Vernon in the rear of the room, hovering over a slide projector, smiling, conveying encouragement with a wink. And next to her stood Matt Burgess, lean and watchful, his arms folded, his rusty mustache twitching as he studied the crowd. He'd insisted on accompanying her to this event, leaving Alex Ragsdale and the "sound man" to prowl the guest house in search of hidden microphones.

How could it have come to *this*? Lauren asked herself.

Applause now. Lauren somehow got to her feet, walked to the podium and smiled her trademark smile, waved to an old acquaintance in the audience, blew a kiss to no one in particular. As the applause died, she suffered her customary pang of stage fright, which normally went away as soon as she started her remarks. But today it hung on, a lingering low-grade panic that caused her voice to quiver and her eyes to tear. She fought it and forged ahead, only vaguely aware of what was coming out of her mouth.

She thanked the president for her kind introduction, thanked the program committee for the invitation and the hotel catering staff for preparing a single vegan meal just for her. She struggled through an old joke about a real-estate broker in a sinking boat with a lawyer and a used car salesman, and received far more laughter than she expected. Feeling a little better now, she signaled Jandee to dim the lights and switch on the projector.

A collective gasp went up as the first slide hit the screen, a shot of a tabby cat on a vivisection table, its front and rear paws clamped down at grotesque angles. A researcher had peeled back the animal's scalp and had cut a hole in its skull to expose its brain. An electrode prod was poised above the bare cranial tissue, apparently to carry out some sort of neurological experiment. Lauren heard murmurs among the listeners, people in danger of losing their lobster salads.

"Sometimes I'm asked why I've become so deeply involved with animal rights," she said, her voice ringing through the loudspeakers. "*That's* why." She gestured toward the screen, not daring to look at it herself. "This kitten was fully conscious when this picture was snapped, and we have no indication that anyone had bothered to anesthetize her. The bad news is that this kind of cruelty goes on worldwide, day after day, hour after hour. The good news is that activism by people who care—people like you and I—has had an effect. Take the fur trade, for example . . ."

She thumbed the advance button on the projector remote control, and the next slide came up, a color photo of a mink caught in a leg-hold trap. The terror-stricken animal was trying to gnaw off a rear paw, the one pinched between the steel jaws. More murmurs in the crowd, and an undercurrent of whispers.

"Nine years ago, more than twenty-three million animals were killed for their fur in the United States, three-quarters of them trapped like this one. Today, thanks to the efforts of LOCA and its allies, fewer than five million animals a year die this way. Since 1988, we've cut the number of active fur trappers in America by roughly two-thirds. We've reduced the number of mink farms by better than half . . .''

She was on autopilot. The words came out without any conscious effort, words she'd uttered in countless speeches to civic organizations, clubs, coffees and teas, rallies. While her mouth and voice box performed their robotic work, her brain coped with an onslaught of old fears, memories, secrets. She saw the skinny little girl she'd once been, the shabby rented duplex where she'd lived in northeast Portland, the face of her mother, ever tight and accusing, a face with restless eyes.

"In 1988, we had more than a thousand mink farms in America. Today we have fewer than half that many . . .''

She thought of an old friend, a calico cat named Mandrake. She remembered how soft his fur was, how good it felt against her hand, the keen intelligence in his eyes, the way he sidled against her ankle whenever she returned home. An ache took hold in her throat as she relived his final moments, the excruciating price he paid for having loved her. She remembered the *knife* . . .

Twenty-one

Matt watched and listened with a fascination that verged on awe. Words rolled out of Lauren Bowman's mouth and washed over the crowd like an inescapable wave, full of pain and passion and exhortation, troubling words that crackled with conviction while painting harrowing pictures.

"I can think of nothing more cruel than confining an intelligent, thinking creature to a few cubic feet inside a cage, and later murdering it in order to strip off its skin—just so that some misguided man can decorate his woman with fur . . ."

Matt tried to gauge her effect on her listeners. A few of them wrinkled their noses, rolled their eyes or threw sidelong glances at each other, as if to question the appropriateness of uttering such remarks and showing such pictures to a luncheon audience. But most listened as Matt did, captivated, even though their stomachs might be roiling.

A picture of the interior of a slaughterhouse hit the screen, with steers lined up in front of a gate where a hard-hatted worker operated a hydraulic stunner. A rapid succession of slides showed the conveyor that hauled the stunned bovines into a hell of chain saws and mechanical knives. Blood was everywhere, the walkway ankle-deep in gore.

Lauren likened the animal-products industry to the Holocaust, a systematic and massive murder of innocents. She recalled the work of Hannah Arendt, the Jewish writer who spoke of the "banality of evil" in Nazi Germany, an evil perpetrated not by wild-eyed psychopaths, but by devoted husbands and loving fathers, the same kind of people who operated today's meat-packing plants and battery farms. They weren't monsters, these people. They were fathers and husbands who loved art and culture. Their only sin was falling victim to a twisted, wrong-headed belief system that validated torture and murder. Was it much different in this age, when the massive killing of innocent animals was as widespread and banal as using an ATM machine or getting a bikini wax? Was a modern slaughterhouse so much different than a death camp?

She told each mother in the audience to imagine the anguish of watching someone apply an acetylene torch to the face of her child, an anguish no less insufferable than that inflicted on cattle, hogs, and fowl during the process of mechanized slaughter. Could anyone seriously believe that exploited animals don't suffer? she asked.

"Sometimes people tell me to lighten up," she said, "or to get over it, or to chill out. After all, it's not *people* we're butchering, is it? Only animals. But I refuse to lighten up or chill out, because if I do that, I give up everything that I know in my heart to be good and decent.

"I refuse to be a good sport about what's happening in the world, because we are indeed talking about *people*. We're talking about a day when *people* will show universal compassion and love for one another, when we stop having silly wars, and stop imposing sanctions that deny food and medicine to the poor—all because of some stupid argument over ideology, or some imagined insult, or the violation of some rule that only politicians care about.

"I say, let's start with the animals, and maybe—just maybe— if we show kindness to them, we'll elevate our own spirits and start being humane to one another. In the end, that's what this movement is all about."

And suddenly she was finished, having talked for precisely twenty-five minutes, the mark of a pro. She said a final thank-you and stepped away from the podium, and the crowd slowly comprehended that it was time to clap. A handful of Society members pressed around the head table to talk with her and ask questions, as Matt supposed must happen routinely to people with Lauren Bowman's kind of charisma. Were these the converts, he wondered, the new recruits for LOCA, new sources of money and moral support? Or were they merely captives of another Lauren Bowman moment? The rest of the crowd migrated toward the rear exit, having had enough of animal rights for one day.

"Well, what did you think?" Jandee asked Matt as she folded up the projector. "Can the boss wave a bloody shirt, or what?"

"It was quite a show, I'll give you that."

"God, you make 'show' sound like a four-letter word."

"It *is* a four-letter word."

Jandee laughed. "So it is. But you need to understand that it's so totally *not* just a show. The boss believes what she preaches."

"I don't doubt that for a minute."

"And she makes a difference, which is more than ninety-nine percent of the rest of us can say. The world's a better place because of what she does. Can you, like, say the same about what you do?"

"No, I can't," Matt confessed, his eyes wandering over the faces of the crowd as they passed by en route to the hotel lobby. "But then I don't have your boss's money. I can't lay a buck on a panhandler without feeling the pinch."

Three people entered the dining room from the lobby, a woman and two men, swimming against the current of the crowd. Matt instantly spotted them as cops, an ability that came from having been one himself, he suspected. The woman, a squat red-head in her forties, looked familiar, but Matt couldn't dredge up her name. He figured that he'd probably made her acquaintance at some point during his aborted law enforcement career. He doubted that he'd ever laid eyes on either of the men.

The trio threaded their way toward the head table, where Lauren conversed with a few remaining well-wishers.

"Lots of people think they can't work for justice because they can't afford the time, or they don't have the resources," Jandee was saying. "But really, a person doesn't need to be rich in order to . . ."

"Can we talk about this later?" Matt asked. He set out toward the front of the hall, following on the cops' heels.

"Excuse me, Ms. Bowman," the female cop said to Lauren, "can we have a word with you? We visited you last weekend in your home, remember? I'm Sergeant Henness and this is Detective Cosentino, Seattle PD. And this gentleman is Special Agent Brunsvold of the FBI, Seattle office." She indicated the blocky blond man next to Cosentino.

"Of course," Lauren replied, not missing a beat. "Nice to see you again. Your first name is Connie, as I recall, and you're Aaron. Am I right?" She begged the pardon of the remaining knot of Society members and led the cops to a corner of the room, then shook hands with all three. "So, did you like my speech?" she asked.

"Actually we just got here," Henness said. "We went to Jenkins Way first, but your executive assistant told us about your engagement here today—a Ms. Pichette, I think her name was."

"Georgia Pichette, yes. It must be important, whatever it is that brought you all the way up here. I *have* been known to return telephone calls, you know."

"I'm sorry if we've embarrassed you in front of all these people," Henness said with apparent sincerity, "but we need to ask you a few questions concerning—" She became aware of Matt's presence as he approached the group, and turned to face him. "I'm sorry, sir, but this is police business. We need to talk with Ms. Bowman in private." She held up her badge packet in front of Matt's face.

"*Connie,*" Matt said, seeing her name on the ID, "it's me— Matt Burgess. How the hell are you?" He threw his arms around her and hugged her, like she was his long-lost buddy. The officer pulled away from him, her brow pinched in bewilderment.

"Burgess, did you say? I'm not sure I remember . . ."

Detective Cosentino took a firm hold of Matt's elbow. "Sir, you're interfering with official business. I'll have to ask you to . . ."

Matt thrust out his hand to him, and the young detective instinctively shook it. "I'm Matt Burgess, formerly *Detective* Matt Burgess, SPD. My old man was Chuck Burgess—something of a legend around Metro Patrol. You're probably too young to have heard of him."

"Chucky Bob," Henness put in. "I remember—a sergeant, right? Retired sometime back? And now I remember *you* now, too, . . . sort of. Narcotics, weren't you?"

"Regional Antidrug Task Force," Matt confirmed. "I worked Capitol Hill and Mercer Island with a ne'er-do-well named Alex Ragsdale. He's gone private, works for ProGuard now, hauls in major cash."

Henness grinned. "You two were in the class behind me at

the Academy. What are you doing these days? And how's your dad?''

Matt was about to tell her that Chucky Bob had been dead for five years when the blocky FBI man intervened. "I hate to break up Old Home Week, but we've got things to do here. Can we get on with it?"

"I was about to offer the same suggestion," Lauren said, throwing a questioning glance at Matt. "I hope this won't take long."

"Don't mind me," Matt said to Henness. "I'm with Ms. Bowman. She has retained me as a consultant on security and personal safety."

"You're her bodyguard, is that it?" Cosentino said. Matt saw a mean glint in the young cop's eye, which looked out of place in his baby face. For some reason the kid had taken a dislike to him, it seemed.

"I guess you could say I'm her bodyguard. Actually, I hope I'm a little more than that." Matt moved close to Lauren and snaked an arm around her waist, pulled her to him. "We don't keep secrets from each other, do we, sweetheart?"

Lauren forced a smile, went along. "No secrets," she said.

"Ho-kay," Henness said, looking skeptical. "Ms. Bowman, we're here about a friend of yours, Megan Reiner. As you may know, she's missing. Her family has become quite worried."

With his arm still around Lauren's waist, Matt felt her body stiffen. "No, I didn't know that," she said. "How long?"

"Six days. We were wondering if you might've heard from her since last Thursday."

"Uh, no—I don't think so. It's been well over a week since I've talked to her."

Cosentino then asked whether Lauren had ever heard Megan say anything about leaving town, perhaps running away with someone. Any secret lovers? Any fantasies about escaping the grind of city life? Lauren replied that she'd never heard Megan say anything of the kind, that Megan was a dedicated scholar and teacher. Matt thought to himself, *No doubt about it, the woman can act.*

Henness asked whether Lauren had heard any mutual acquaintance say anything about having seen or spoken with Megan since last Thursday. Again Lauren answered no.

Any strange behavior of late on Megan's part? No again.

"Now I have a question for *you*," Lauren said. "I thought you people were homicide detectives, and that you were investigating what happened at the BioCenter last week. But here you are, looking for Megan. Does that mean you think she's . . . *dead*?"

"We think her disappearance is related to what happened at the BioCenter," Henness replied. "The security system at the lab included video and audio monitors. The security company turned over the tapes, which we've viewed and analyzed. In the audio portion, you can clearly hear someone call out the name 'Megan' three times."

"And in the video?" Lauren asked.

"It shows someone dragging a woman out the rear door of the building," Cosentino answered. "Unfortunately, they were all wearing ski masks, and the video's a little choppy. But that's what it shows."

"And since Megan disappeared shortly before the incident at the BioCenter," Henness added, "it doesn't take a quantum leap to conclude that she was involved, and that maybe her disappearance is related to that incident. We think she was the one being abducted."

"Sounds like a reach to me," Matt said, putting in his two cents' worth. "Megan is a common name. Sometimes I think a third of the female population under thirty has that name with one spelling or another."

"But not all those Megans have Ms. Reiner's record of criminal activism in the cause of animal rights," said the FBI man, Brunsvold. Matt noticed that his face was a near-perfect square. "Considering her background, not to mention the fact that she's been missing since the day of the raid, I'd say there's a strong probability that she's the woman on the videotape."

"If you don't mind my asking," Matt said, "what's the federal government's interest in this matter? I'm only asking as a curious taxpayer, you understand."

"I *do* mind your asking," Brunsvold replied.

"Oh, come on, Ken," Henness said, "this guy used to be one of us. The Pacific Northwest Biomedical Research Foundation is a recipient of federal grant money," she said to Matt. "Some of the equipment and research data destroyed at the BioCenter actually belonged to Uncle Sam, and that makes . . ."

"Makes the raid a federal crime," Matt said, finishing the

sentence for her. "Well, I wish Lauren and I could help you with this, Connie, but we can't. Neither of us knows anything about the raid or that girl. So, if you'll excuse us, we have a heavy schedule today."

"Not so fast," Cosentino said, stepping in front of Matt like a high school bully with an itch to rumble. "We're not exactly done here."

"We're not, exactly?" Matt asked.

"Maybe we're not so sure that Ms. Bowman has told us everything she knows. Maybe she'd like to have another chance to do the right the thing, spare herself a bunch of grief later on."

Matt appealed to Sergeant Henness. "Connie, let's get real. You can't think that someone of Ms. Bowman's stature and standing would have anything to do with abducting a young woman or demolishing some laboratory. She's one of the leading citizens of this city, for crying out loud. She doesn't wreck things—she builds them."

"You missed your calling," Henness said. "You should've been a lawyer. The problem is that the voice on the tape—the one screaming Megan's name—sounds a lot like Ms. Bowman's." She winked at Matt, one cop to another, which Matt found oddly offensive. "The DA might think it's reason enough to bring her in for a chat."

Matt laughed, though he felt Lauren stiffen again. "If you had any real evidence, you would've already had your chat—we both know that."

"We could voiceprint the tape," Brunsvold said, "and compare it to a recorded sample of Ms. Bowman's voice. It's called forensic biometric identification, and it just might put her at the BioCenter last Thursday night."

"Good luck convincing a judge that it's admissible in a criminal proceeding," Matt said, "even if you somehow manage to talk Ms. Bowman into giving you a voice sample for comparison, which I doubt that her lawyer would let her do. Are we done now?"

"Oh yeah," Henness said. "But don't worry. If we think of anything else, we'll be in touch."

Jandee chauffeured Lauren and Matt back to Jenkins Way, which took almost forty minutes, thanks to midday traffic. Matt sat in the rear seat of the Volvo station wagon and listened to Lauren describe to Jandee the encounter with the cops in the dining room of the Sorrento Hotel. She worried aloud over the fact that the cops had a recording of her screaming Megan's name at the BioCenter, then damned herself for not heeding the rule that Ian Prather had laid down to the troops—not to use each other's names when they were inside the building. How could she have been so lax? she asked. This was exactly the kind of mistake that could land them all in jail, she was certain.

While she berated herself, Matt couldn't stop thinking about how good it had felt to put his arm around her, even under less than ideal circumstances. She'd leaned on him, *needed* him. He'd *been* there for her.

Then he reminded himself that she was a felon—a well-meaning one, but a felon nonetheless. She'd helped in the commission of a crime that had caused the death of two people, and she'd actively undertaken to cover up her involvement in it. If this wasn't enough, she was a certifiable crackpot, a zealot with a cause that mocked logic. Among her kind, breaking the law was acceptable if it promoted the "higher good," an idea that Matt had always disliked.

So, why did he feel drawn to her? he wondered. He couldn't believe that it was a purely physical thing.

Jandee halted the Volvo in the circular drive of the estate to let Lauren and Matt out, then drove on to park in the six-car garage. Matt walked with Lauren along the crushed-granite path toward the guest house, watching her dark hair bounce around her slim neck with every stride. Again he noticed that her mouth never stopped working, her lips pursing and puckering when she wasn't talking, a sign of a busy mind or an uneasy soul, maybe both. The sunlight betrayed the bottomlessness of her brown eyes, the clarity of her skin. She moved with grace atop her long legs, her hips swinging subtly beneath the fabric of her blue business suit. Matt wanted more than anything in the world to put his arm around her again.

I've got to stop this, he told himself.

"I want you to know something," Lauren said as they approached the covered entryway to the guest house. "I appreciate your running interference for me with those cops. I'll have to admit that I was feeling a little vulnerable when they swooped down on me right there in front of God and everybody."

Matt felt warm inside. He was about to say something—he wasn't quite sure what—when his hay fever attacked. He sneezed three times, struggled with his pocket-size pack of Kleenex. *Must be the fucking rhododendrons*, he thought. Lush, blooming bushes loomed on both sides of the path, fountains of yellow and orange.

"I'm sure you could've handled them on your own," he sniffed through a wadded tissue. "I just thought, well, since I used to be a cop myself, maybe I could help."

"What was that business about you and I being an item?" Lauren asked, a coy smile playing on her lips. "Are you trying to start an outlandish rumor, or do you just want to put yourself squarely on my husband's shit list?"

Matt wadded the Kleenex and poked it into the pocket of his khakis. "I had to tell them something so they'd let me stay, that's all. That Cosentino kid was ready to muscle me out the door, as you'll recall. Sorry if I embarrassed you."

She laughed. "Nothing embarrasses me, Matt. Ask anyone who knows me."

"I'll remember that."

"So, in your professional judgment, how much trouble are we in?"

"You're talking about the recording?"

She nodded. "Can they really get a voiceprint and prove I was at the BioCenter that night? I know that voiceprints are in vogue as replacements for computer passwords."

"Even if they could prove you were there, I've never heard of anything like this being admitted as evidence in a court. It's one thing to use a voiceprint to boot up your computer, but it's something else to convict someone of murder with it."

Lauren cringed visibly. "Shit, that's what we're talking about, isn't it? A murder charge."

"I'm afraid so. No matter who actually shot the guard, everybody who had anything to do with the raid is an accessory. That's the way these things work."

"Yeah." She turned toward the door, but Matt caught her arm.

"Tell me something," he said. "All the trouble, the pain and agony you've been suffering over this—is it worth it?" She gave him a frosty stare, and he worried that he'd ventured into forbidden territory.

"I'm not sure I understand you."

"I'm talking about people getting killed, people spying on you. I'm talking about what you must be feeling right now, the grief and uncertainty, not knowing if your world is about to blow up in your face. Is any cause worth all that?''

She stared at the ground, then stared at the sky. "What do you want me to say, Matt—that I'd undo what happened to Megan and that guard, if I could? Of course I would. I'd undo it in a minute, even if—'' Her voice caught.

"Even if it meant selling out the movement?''

"A week ago I would've denied that. Now I'm not so sure. In fact, I'm not sure of anything anymore. Is that what you wanted to hear?''

"I don't know what I wanted to hear.''

"The things I've been working for, my convictions, my hope for the world—it's really all I have. Can you understand that?''

Matt glanced around at the grounds, the conspicuous display of wealth and consumption. "None of this counts?''

"Not in the greater scheme of things. You don't justify your existence by making it big in real estate. You do it by improving the world. That's what I'm trying to do. That's *all* I'm trying to do.''

Matt said he understood.

Twenty-two

Alex Ragsdale met them in the foyer, said a warm hello to Lauren, and pulled Matt into the sitting room, where the two of them huddled with Avery Carpenter, the sound man. They stood in a corner next to the Winslow Homer painting that had captured Matt's attention on his first visit here, the one that depicted two mariners on the heaving deck of an old sailing ship. Matt even remembered the title: *Eight Bells.*

"We've discovered something very interesting," Rags said. "And it fits in with what we talked about before. Tell him, Avery."

Avery Carpenter was a tall black man in his early sixties, dressed in baggy golf slacks and an ample polo shirt. He had the loose-skin look of a man who had recently lost a great deal of weight.

"What we've got here is two sets of bugs," he said, holding out both his palms. In each hand lay an electronic device, one of which looked exactly like a common electrical outlet. "This one," he went on, holding up his right hand, "is a VHF low-band transmitter, battery-powered, made in Sweden about fifteen years ago. Operates on a frequency range of thirty-five to thirty-nine megahertz. Found them in every room of the house, placed on the undersides of furniture, behind bookcases, like that. They're well-built, reliable, but inconvenient, because the batteries go dry. You need to come in regularly and install fresh ones if you want to keep on recording, see what I'm sayin'?"

"I'm with you so far," Matt said.

Carpenter then held up the one that looked like a wall plug. "Okay, *this* one is state-of-the-art technology, built by an outfit in Maryland that makes them for the government and law enforcement. Like the other one, it's low-band VHF, but it takes power from the house current and functions like any other standard duplex outlet. You just substitute it for the regular wall outlet, and it transmits all audible events that occur within its range. And keeps on doin' it until it's disconnected, like that damn rabbit pounding the drum in the TV commercial."

"And you found these in every room, as well?" Matt asked, pointing to the device that looked like a wall outlet.

"That's right."

"Sounds like overkill to me. You figure this guy's some kind of anal-retentive, using two separate sets of devices, or is that common practice in the eavesdropping industry?"

Carpenter scowled. "It's not one guy. It has to be two guys, and they probably don't even know about each other. Whoever put in this set"—he held up his left fist—"is into cut-rate electronics, takes whatever he can find on the casual market. He's probably an amateur, though a talented one, based on how he planted the things. But *this* guy"—the right fist now, the one with the modified wall socket—"is a pro, has access to all the latest gear. My guess is he's had government experience, probably with law enforcement or the intelligence community."

Matt stared at the Homer painting and imagined himself part of it, one of the pair of old salts struggling with a sextant on the deck. Like them, he felt blinded by fog, adrift on a raging sea in search of elusive truth. A pang of anxiety shot through him, and he thought of the dark animal. "I suppose it was the same story with the phone bugs," he said.

"Same story," Carpenter said. "One guy used simple drop-in transmitters, the kind you put into the phone receiver. The other guy's more sophisticated—used what we call 'parasitic series in-line transmitters,' which he hooked up on the exterior connection box. Either one gives a good copy of both sides of a phone conversation."

"Two sets of bugs, two sets of bad guys," Matt muttered. "Jesus, the fun just never stops."

"But it makes sense," Rags said. "Two moles, two sets of bugs. Mole Number One is whoever's helping Megan's killer.

Mole Number Two is whoever tipped off ProGuard about the raid on the lab. Now all we have to do is find them.''

Avery Carpenter held up a hand. "I don't want to hear this shit. I'm just here to pick up a little spare change, if it's all the same to you guys. I got no interest in picking up any guilty knowledge of any crimes that may or may not have been committed on these premises."

"I understand," Matt said. "The place is clean of bugs now, right?"

"Cleaner than Mother Teresa's Diner's Club bill," Carpenter answered.

"How do we keep it that way?"

"I'm glad you asked that," Rags said, reaching down to pick up a carrying case that leaned against the wall. It was the size of a large briefcase. "Avery has graciously consented to lend us a detector-locator for our very own personal use." He popped open the case to reveal a contraption that looked something like a hand-held Geiger counter. It had a digital readout display and a tele-scoping antenna. "Ever see one this nice? Check out the fit and finish."

Having spent years as a drug cop, Matt was no stranger to such equipment. "But can it make a decent corned beef sand-wich?"

"All you need to do," Rags said, "is walk through the place every morning, holding this thing in your hand, and it'll tell you if anyone has planted any ears in the walls. You gotta remember to turn it on, that's all. Right, Avery?"

"Pretty much," said the sound man. "It'll sound a directional alert if it detects any RF transmitters, tape recorders or AC line carrier transmitters. You get an alert, call me. Don't try to deal with it yourself." Carpenter gathered up his detection tools in preparation to leave. "Oh, and one more thing: Please, please, *please* don't drop it on the floor. You break it, ProGuard takes it out of my hide. Then I take it out of yours, see what I'm sayin'?"

"Don't worry, Avery, we'll be careful," Rags assured him.

After Carpenter had left, Matt went out to the veranda where he, Rags, and Lauren had sat this morning. He took off his cor-duroy sport coat and tossed it into one of the cedar deck chairs, then stood with his hands in his pockets and stared at the blue Puget Sound. The sun felt good on his shoulders. His stomach relaxed, the dark animal having momentarily lost its grip. He savored the smell of the water, and wished that he was at the helm of *Hyperion*, bound for the San Juan Islands or Canada's Gulf Islands. He wished that Royal was in the cockpit with him, a cold bottle of beer in his hand, a cigarette between his lips. How beautifully simple life would be out there on *Hyperion*, with good company and no worries more complex than finding an anchorage for the night. No psycho killers out there, and no electronic eavesdroppers. No dark animals.

Rags came out and handed him a cellular phone. "Keep this with you and call me whenever the spirit moves you. I'm off to the office now, unfortunately—meetings all afternoon. Need to do some real work every now and then."

Matt took the phone, slipped it into his pocket. "Are you ready for the latest? The PD has a tape of Lauren's voice at the BioCenter, screaming Megan's name. They're threatening to do a voiceprint comparison in order to place her at the scene."

"Big deal. They're just trying to scare her into 'fessing up, same kind of thing you and I used to do to folks."

"Suppose the big dogs at ProGuard decide they can't sit on the anonymous letter any longer, and they send it downtown to avoid an obstruction of justice beef. Suddenly the cops have Lauren's voice on tape *and* an anonymous tipster saying she was in on the raid. That's pretty strong stuff, wouldn't you say?"

"You and I both know that voiceprinting is a bunch of mumbo jumbo, which no judge in the whole fucking state of Washington would let in as evidence. Tell Lauren to be cool, stick by her guns."

Matt looked at him. "You're loving this, aren't you? Here we are, wading into a cesspool, and you're loving it."

Rags grinned like a little kid caught with cookie crumbs all over his face, and clapped a huge hand onto Matt's shoulder. "You know, we should open our own PI outfit, you and me. It'd be like the old days, only better, because we'd never have to do anything we didn't want to. 'Burgess and Ragsdale, Confidential Investigations.' Sounds solid, doesn't it—like a Big Eight accounting firm. We could make a ton of money, my man."

"You're off your knob. You should get yourself looked at."

"That's what my wife says. Oh, I almost forgot—" He pulled out a small notebook and tore out a page, which he handed to Matt. "While you were at the luncheon, I talked to the cook, Rainy Hales, and a lady named Georgia Pichette next door in the main house, Lauren's business aide, something like that . . ."

"Executive assistant."

"Right. Between them, they gave me a list of all the people who come through this place regularly, more than three dozen people, if you can believe that."

Matt glanced down the list, saw the names of gardeners and grounds people, pool-maintenance guys, house cleaners, and the like. Then he giggled. "Would you look at this? They have a florist who comes in every week. And two personal trainers, a manicurist, a hair stylist, a fucking *cosmetologist* . . ."

"If you're rich, you've got to keep yourself looking nice. That's in the rule book, man."

Matt harrumphed. "These people all have keys or pass codes or whatever?"

"That's right. Of course, the system's programmed to let them in between specified daylight hours—no other times. Their access gets electronically logged, which means there's a record of each person's visit, showing when they checked in and when they checked out. Except for the last two."

Matt's eyes went to the bottom of the list. "Elise and Marc Lekander," he read aloud. "They both have the run of the place, with no automatic log."

"Yup. The cook says they're close friends of Lauren, and they come and go like family. ProGuard will have a record of everyone else's visits. It shouldn't be too much trouble for me to print out a copy."

"Then we can eyeball it for visits that look out of the ordinary."

"Yeah, the ones that happen when no one else is around. Or times when someone shuts the system down for whatever reason."

"You can do this printout without getting your *schwanz* in the ringer?" Matt asked. "Aren't you required to show some sort of need-to-know?"

"I'll dummy-up something, make it look legitimate. Don't worry."

"Jesus, I hope you know what you're doing."

"I'll be fine. In the meantime, you can start talking to people on this list. Stoke up your old cop's instincts, see if anybody strikes you as wrong."

Rags left in his BMW, and Matt went into the house in search of Lauren. He needed to tell her that the sound man had indeed detected bugs, that until a few hours ago, her home life had been under constant surveillance by *two* separate entities. He found her in the study with Jandee, chatting over tall glasses of what looked like some sort of fruit freeze. Both women had changed into shorts and T-shirts. Desi and Lucy were asleep under the desk.

Matt gave them the bad news, then asked the obvious question: Could either of them think of anyone who would want to spy on them—anyone who had the resources to find and pay audio surveillance experts to install the bugs?

Lauren took a long, thoughtful sip from her glass. "No, Matt," she answered, her eyes not meeting his. "I don't know anyone who would do such a thing."

Jandee snorted. "Of course you do, boss. Do you want to tell him, or should I?"

"I don't know what you're talking about," Lauren said.

"You know exactly what I'm talking about—that scumbag husband of yours, soon to be *ex*-husband, I hope."

"Jandee, will you please control your mouth?"

"Hey, we're looking for the ugly truth here, aren't we? And the ugly truth is that Gabe Granger is a jealous, vindictive brute. His idea of a marriage is out of the Middle Ages. Women are chattel to him, like every wife is the personal property of her husband. The fact that you can actually live without him is a festering boil on his ass."

"Is this true?" Matt asked Lauren. "Should we be looking at your husband for one set of the bugs?"

"He may be an asshole, but even Gabe has his limits," Lauren answered. "He wouldn't go so far as to bug the house."

"I wish I could be as sanguine about his limits as you are," Jandee retorted. "The fact is, he'd have a right to bug this place, according to his fucked-up logic. It'd be part of his husband's prerogative."

"He wouldn't do *this*," Lauren said to Matt with a tone of finality. "I know him."

"You're positive about that?" Matt asked. "No chance you could be wrong?"

"I've never been more sure of anything in my life." Looking away from him, Lauren reached into a drawer and took out a leather-bound checkbook, penned a check, walked over to him, handed it to him. His eyebrows arched when he read the amount—five thousand dollars.

"What's this? I thought I made it clear that I'm not working for money."

"You are now," Lauren replied. "You can give as much of that to your partner as you see fit."

"You don't understand. I'm helping you as a favor to your old man." He tried to hand the check back to her, but she pushed his hand away.

"You told the cops at the Sorrento that I'd hired you to consult on—how did you put it?—'matters involving security and personal safety.' I'm only making an honest man of you, Matt. No sense in lying to the cops unnecessarily, is there? Lying to the cops can be dangerous."

Matt fought down his annoyance. What she was doing was obvious—formalizing their relationship with payment of a retainer, making herself the boss, the client, the one who called the shots. A typically rich-bitch kind of thing. Matt was about to protest further when she announced that she was leaving for Ballard in order to pay a call on Ian Prather and Vera Kemmis. She'd tried to telephone them earlier to tell them what had happened to Megan, but they hadn't answered. She confessed to being a little worried.

"I should go with you," Matt said. "If I'm on retainer as a bodyguard, I might as well earn my money."

"Thanks, but I'll go alone. Ian and Vera don't take to outsiders."

Jandee said, "I think he's right, boss. You shouldn't be going out by yourself these days, not after all that's happened. How do we know somebody isn't stalking you right now?"

"We don't have any real indication that anyone means me any harm," Lauren countered. "Besides, I need a little time on my own, time to think. I'll be back in a few hours, I promise."

Matt watched her go out the front door, watched her walk to the garage and drive away in her Volvo. Jandee stood beside him, silent, a frown pinching her freckled face.

"I don't like this," Matt said under his breath, not really meaning to say it aloud. "I don't like this one bit."

"Neither do I," Jandee said.

Twenty-three

Lauren parked in the driveway of the modest rental house in Ballard, got out of the car and walked to the front stoop, rang the bell, waited. She expected to hear someone stirring inside, footfalls coming to answer the doorbell, but she heard only the ordinary sounds of a spring afternoon in a middle-class neighborhood—the laughter of children at play somewhere down the street, a jetliner rumbling in the distance, a crow cawing as it teetered overhead on a utility line.

She stepped back from the door and eyed the picture window that fronted the street, a window that needed cleaning. Through it she could make out the outline of a cheap sofa, a print of a soulless landscape on the wall, a few other interior details. Someone had carelessly strewn an article of clothing over the back of an armchair, a green breaker that she recognized as Vera's.

She rang again, but drew no response, then rang again. The thought came to her that Ian and Vera had decided to vanish, inasmuch as the BioCenter operation had turned into a gory debacle. Quite possibly they had fled to Mexico or Central America to hook up with other activists and wait for the situation in Seattle to normalize. But in her heart Lauren couldn't believe this. Leaving without saying good-bye—without staging a dramatic exit—wasn't Ian Prather's style. Unlike old soldiers, swashbucklers never faded away quietly. They went out with a flourish, with a maximum of Sturm und Drang.

She pawed through her shoulder bag for a key, found it, and

pushed it into the lock, shoved the door open. A troubling odor hit her as she stepped into the living room, something like rancid butter commingled with the stink of cigarette smoke. The house was in its usual state of dishevelment, since neither Ian nor Vera had any inclination to do housework. Lauren figured that the stink was attributable to some English cooking experiment gone awry.

"Ian? Vera? Is anybody home?" The house answered with unsettling silence.

She called their names again as she ventured into the kitchen and the dining room, where dirty dishes lay in piles on counter-tops and tables, along with empty booze bottles and wadded food wrappers. A nameless fear wormed in Lauren's chest as she moved down the hallway toward the bedrooms, past a reddish smear on a wall. She came to a door on her right, Vera's room.

"Vera, are you . . . ?"

A man's body lay on the floor in a dark, sticky lake, attended by a host of flies buzzing and feasting. So battered and broken were his head and face, so puffed out of shape and discolored, that Lauren wouldn't have recognized him. Where the skin wasn't purple and blue from a savage beating with some blunt weapon, it was chalky gray. Shards of bone poke through the naked flesh of his arms and legs.

How long she stood there before realizing that the body belonged to Ian Prather, she had no idea—stood there with her eyes tearing, her breath coming in sharp hiccoughs. Only his genitals were recognizable, the plump penis with its uncut foreskin, his underwear having slid down over his thighs during the beating that ended his life. A brutally absurd thought hit her, the scenario of a police interrogation—*"And tell us again, Ms. Bowman, how you recognized the victim . . ."*

She would have screamed if her stomach hadn't erupted. Somehow she found the bathroom and the toilet bowl. She stayed there a long time, her fists gripping the cold porcelain rim of the toilet as her digestive system emptied with painful, wrenching spasms. When it was over, she went to the sink and washed herself with cold water, found a bottle of Scope and gargled.

She walked unsteadily into the hallway, forcing one foot in front of the other, determined to check the other rooms for some sign of Vera. But Vera was not in the house, which was a relief, in a way. And not in the backyard or the garage. If Vera had fled the scene, she'd done it on foot, inasmuch as the beige Taurus that Lauren had leased for her and Ian sat in the garage with its key in the ignition, ready for a quick departure if the need ever arose.

Lauren suddenly found that she didn't want to touch anything in the house, lest Ian's killer had touched it and left some microscopic trace of himself that she might absorb through her pores. The thought of inhaling the air that the killer might have breathed revolted her, and she wanted nothing so desperately as to leave this place. She'd felt this brand of revulsion before, long ago in Portland, a revulsion that had driven her from home and school, from everyone and everything she'd ever loved.

She went to the living room and stood motionless in the center of the worn carpet, her arms pulled tight around her. She forced herself to think, to focus, to banish the wild and fanciful fears that swarmed in her head. Ian's death was simply a problem that demanded a solution, she told herself. A *creative* solution. And who better to help with improvising a creative solution than her trusted "fixer?"

Twenty-four

Hello, you've reached Marc Lekander's message service. When you hear the tone, please leave a message, and I'll get back to you . . .

"Marc, pick up if you're there, will you? It's me. I need to talk to you. Something has happened, and I don't know where else to turn. *Please*, Marc . . ."

Click. "Lauren, hi. Are you okay?"

"I'm—yeah, I'm okay. I think. Look, Marc . . ."

"Sorry I didn't pick up right away. I'm screening my calls today, only taking the ones I want."

"I . . . understand."

"You don't sound so good, sweets. Are you at home?"

"I . . . no. I'm at Ian and Vera's, actually. Do you know where that is?"

"Of course, in Ballard. I've seen the place. I might ask what you're doing there, though. I thought you and Ian had split the sheets."

"I can't talk about it on the phone. Can you come over here? *Now?*"

"Well, sure—I suppose so. Lauren, what's going on?"

"Just come. And don't use one of your fancy cars, okay? Use something that won't attract attention in this neighborhood."

"I'll use my van, if you think it's appropriate."

"Yes, good. Use the van. And Marc—*hurry!*"

Forty-five minutes later Lauren heard Marc Lekander's Chevy

van wheel into the driveway, and she glanced out the window in time to see him park behind her Volvo. She met him at the door, pulled him quickly inside.

"God, what's that smell?" the little man asked. "Has the refrigerator broken down?"

"No, nothing like that. Marc, I don't know how to tell you this . . ."

He touched her face with his slender hand. "Christ, you look awful. You must be as pale as I am on a good day. You're not sick, are you, sweets?"

"No, I don't think so. Not anymore."

"What's this all about? Where are Ian and Vera?"

"Come with me," she said. "It's probably best just to show you." She took his hand in hers and led him slowly down the hallway to Vera's room. But she halted before reaching the door. "You'll need to brace yourself."

An uncertain smile pulled at his mouth. "Okay."

With her hand on his arm, she guided him into the doorway of Vera's room, not looking in herself. She looked only at his face, which went blank with disbelief as he took in the spectacle. His steely eyes widened and traveled slowly from left to right, registering the grisly details, the lake of blood on the floor, the bits of bone and hair stuck to the wallpaper, the busy flies. His spare cheeks whitened beyond the usual shade of pale.

"Is . . . it Ian?" he asked.

"Yes."

"God, how can you say for sure?"

"Believe me—it's Ian."

Marc backed away from the door, turned and walked past her into the living room. He eased himself into a tatty arm chair and ran a hand through his wispy yellow hair, took out a handkerchief and wiped his mouth. "What about Vera?" he asked.

"She's not here. I have no idea where she is. The car's still in the garage, and it doesn't look like she packed any of her things." Lauren sat on the sofa across from him, leaned forward and took his hands in hers. "Marc, what are we going to do?"

"Let me think. We certainly can't call the police."

"No, we can't. It would take them about two seconds to connect Ian to the raid on the BioCenter. They'd want to know why he and Vera have been staying in a house that I own, why I leased a car for them, who knows what else."

"And they'd probably find his gun, run a ballistics test on it and discover it was the same one that killed the security guard. You're right, we can't have the police swarming over this place."

He got up and paced the room, his twiggy legs swimming inside his pleated Armani slacks. He went to the picture window and gazed out a moment, then turned back to Lauren. "Could Vera have done this?" he asked.

"No, Marc. She loved him. That was obvious to anyone with eyes."

"Who, then?"

"No one I know, I hope. It had to be some kind of monster."

"The same monster who killed Megan?"

Lauren shuddered. "I suppose it's possible. But do we have any reason to think that? Why couldn't it have been a burglar who got caught in the act and went berserk?"

"Whoever it was, he must be one formidable dude. Ian Prather was no cream puff."

Lauren closed her eyes and tried not to imagine the details of Ian's final moments in this world. She also tried hard to disbelieve that Megan's killer and Ian's were one and the same person, because the implications of that notion were simply too huge, too unthinkable. And yet . . .

Marc sat down next to her, wrapped a brotherly arm around her. "The important thing now, sweets, is for you to go home," he said. "You were never here, understand? As far as you know, Ian and Vera have simply disappeared. That's what you tell everyone, even Jandee and my mother. Nobody can ever know that you have any knowledge of this."

"Except for *you*."

"The secret's safe with me." He hugged her, kissed her forehead. "Are you okay to drive?"

"Yeah. But I can't leave you here with"—she glanced toward the bedrooms, then glanced quickly away—"*that*. We've got to do something, Marc. Sooner or later my rental people will want to put this place on the market . . ."

He pressed a finger gently against her lips, shushing her. "Leave it to me. There are a thousand places on my Little Green Acre that would serve as a decent burial site, places that no one would ever find."

Marc Lekander's "Little Green Acre," as he called it, was a rather large acreage in the wooded hills east of Everett, less than an hour's drive from the Lekander family estate in The Highlands of northern Seattle. He'd put a small bungalow on the acreage, as well as several outbuildings equipped to house liberated animals on a temporary basis. A paid caretaker kept the weeds down and made incidental repairs.

"I can't leave you to deal with this thing alone," Lauren argued. "It's too dangerous. What if someone sees you?"

"No one will see me. My caretaker lives in Everett, and he goes home at night to his three-hundred-pound wife and six screaming kids. I'll just wait until he's gone for the day. As for this place, there's nothing wrong here that a little soap and water won't cure. I may be rich and indolent, but I'm a madman with a mop and bucket." He actually smiled.

Suddenly Lauren wanted to cry. The loss of Ian Prather lay in her chest like a great stone. For despite his glaring flaws, he'd fought for justice as he saw it, which wasn't something that many could claim.

And here was Marc, having charged to her rescue, ready to undertake the gruesome and hazardous chore of disposing of a murdered human body. She wondered whether a real brother could have shown any greater devotion. She doubted that she deserved it.

"Thanks, Marc," she managed, struggling. "Someday I'll try to make this up to you—I swear it."

"I know you will, sweets," he answered, patting her head as she pressed her face into his shoulder. "I know you will."

Twenty-five

"I'm worried about Ty," Arnie Cashmore said to the old man. "He's starting to act goofy. This obsession of his with Lauren Bowman—it's making him do dangerous things."

"Is that so?"

"Ordinarily I wouldn't come to you about this, Ray, but I can't afford to let him fuck himself up. If he starts drawing heat—well, I don't need to tell *you*."

"What kind of dangerous things, Arnie?"

They sat in a cloud of cigarette smoke in the old man's apartment on the top floor of the empty warehouse in the International District, where the noise of the rush hour seeped in through locked doors and shaded windows. A battered Gretsch guitar lay across the bony knee of the old man whom Tyler Brownlee called the Ranger. At Arnie's feet lay the gym bag that he'd fetched only minutes ago from the safe in the basement of the building. Inside the bag was the loaf of Mexican black-tar heroin that he and Tyler had bought from Paco de Leon last night.

"He's wired the Bowman woman's house," Arnie answered. "Got the Stump brothers to do it, paid them big time. Remember the Stump brothers? You and I used to do business with them back when we were getting started. They're the electronics guys. They tap phones, do sweeps."

"I remember them. I may be old, but I'm not senile."

"Yeah, my apology. What I'm trying to say is, it's bad medicine to wire somebody like Lauren Bowman. If she ever finds out, she'll bring all fifty-seven varieties of grief down on our heads. She'll call the cops, hire private investigators and muscle men . . ."

"*If* she ever finds out. My guess is she never will."

Arnie took a long drag from his cigarette, exhaled smoke into the general cloud that surrounded them, tried not to let his face display his doubts and suspicions. For the past fifteen years Ray Brownlee had been a kind of silent partner to him, having set him up in the heroin trade and vouched for him with important people like the Fat Woman and Paco. In return, Arnie had taken care of the old guy's material needs, which were few—the lease on this warehouse, groceries, a modest cut of the profits, an occasional cash bonus when Ray wanted it. Only because of this long and advantageous relationship had Arnie agreed to take in Tyler as a partner when Ray floated the idea three years ago. It was the least Arnie could do for an old friend.

"There's more," he said.

"I'm listening."

"He went out last night, carrying that howitzer of his, dressed like he was going to steal the Hope Diamond. I don't know where he went, but he came back this morning looking like he'd gone ten rounds with an earth mover—all black and blue and bloody. I can only hope that he gets away with whatever he did."

Ray Brownlee looked down at his guitar and picked out a few bars of a solo bridge, the amplified notes slicing through the smoky air like flying shards of glass. "That's a little piece of Walter Vinson," he said. "Can't quite do it like I once could, back when I was the Blues Ranger. Tyler can do it the way it was meant to be done. That's the beauty of youth—strong, nimble fingers, the kind of fingers you need to play the blues."

Arnie dropped his cigarette butt into an empty beer bottle that sat on the floor next to his chair, then took off his glasses and cleaned them with the tail of his T-shirt. "Look, Ray—I don't care if the kid is off his nut for Lauren Bowman. When I was a kid, I had it bad for Olivia Newton-John. I put up a big poster in my dorm room with her picture on it, bought all her records, even got the fan magazines. I'd get a hard-on every time I heard her sing 'Xanadu.' But I didn't bug her house and I didn't stalk her, for Christ's sake. I didn't become *obsessed*."

"What do you want me to do, Arnie?"

"Talk to your son. Get him to forget about Lauren Bowman.

Bring him into the real world before he does something that flushes our future down the shitter.''

Ray Brownlee scratched the stubble on his jaw. ''I'm afraid I can't do that,'' he answered.

''Why not?''

''Because—in the first place—Tyler is no kid. And in the second place, he's got a right to love Lauren Bowman, a right like nobody else on earth has.''

''I don't understand.''

''No, you don't. And you never will, Arnie.''

''But he doesn't even *know* Lauren Bowman. He's seen her picture in newspapers, magazines. He's read about her. How can he love somebody he's never even met?''

Arnie Cashmore couldn't see the old man's grin as much as sense it, for the room was murky with smoke, and the light was ebbing as the afternoon aged. ''Let me give you some advice, Arnie. Never stand in the way of a young man's dream. Never try to keep him from his fulfillment. That's the worst kind of sin, the kind that can bring you misery.''

Arnie now understood something for the first time. He picked up the gym bag and rose out of the chair, a chill stuttering along his spine. ''You're part of it, aren't you, Ray? I should've known. Nothing that kid says or does comes from inside himself. It's all from you, isn't it? The blues music, the obsession with Lauren Bowman, all that crap about creating your own reality.''

''If you're uncomfortable with the situation, you're free to get out,'' Ray Brownlee said. ''Christ knows you've made enough money. You've done like I told you, haven't you? Stashed it in offshore banks? It's okay by me if you want to hit the road. I won't hold it against you, and neither will Tyler. It might be the best thing for everybody.''

Arnie strode to the steel door, disengaged the dead bolts and pulled it open. ''I was hoping it wouldn't come to this—me just walking away. I wanted to see you through to—well, you know.''

''The end, yeah. Fact is, the end's not that far off for me, so you don't need to feel guilty about anything. Go off to your Caribbean island or wherever you've been planning to go, spend your money, make a new world for yourself. Forget about all this. Get yourself a woman, Arnie, or better yet, get two or three of 'em. You deserve it.''

Arnie Cashmore winced. "To be perfectly honest with you, Ray, I hope to shit I *never* get what I deserve."

He rode the creaking freight elevator down to the loading bay where he'd parked his Nissan Altima, threw the gym bag into the trunk, and started to raise the jointed garage door. As the shrill notes of an electric guitar caromed around the high rafters of the warehouse, he smelled it again—the stink that he'd smelled so often over the years, always thickest in the basement where there were locked rooms. It had always made him think of something dead, always made him wish that he didn't have business here.

After today, he reminded himself, he would never have business here again. And that was something to be thankful for.

Twenty-six

While Lauren Bowman was away, Matt Burgess spent nearly two hours studying the layout of the estate on Jenkins Way, sketching diagrams of the guest house and scribbling notes in his spiral pad. He verified what he'd already known: The Bowman-Granger estate was a fortress guarded by a high stucco wall and an elaborate array of automated closed-circuit TV cameras, passive infrared motion detectors and acoustic sensors, both short-range and long-range. That anyone could have gotten in without help from someone inside was next to inconceivable.

Jandee Vernon showed him the security control console in an alcove off the foyer, then walked him through the process of turning the system on and off. "There's a sister console just like this one next door in the villa," she explained. "During the day, Gabe's butler monitors it, lets people in and out of the front gate when they call . . . people who don't have pass codes, of course."

Matt checked the list that Rags had given him earlier, ran down the column of names. "The butler would be—let's see—Manuel Esparza?"

"Right. Nice man, very competent. Goes to night school, wants to be a cultural anthropologist." Jandee frowned. "We're talking about an inside job here, aren't we? Like, nobody gets in or out of this place unless someone pushes the right buttons."

Matt studied her young face as a cop would, instinctively looking for the tiny telltales of duplicity—the faint twitch of a cheek, a soft fluttering of an eyelid, an unsteady gaze. But he saw only genuine worry. "I'm afraid you're right," he replied. "An inside job."

At that moment the front door opened, and Lauren Bowman walked past the alcove into the sitting room. Desi and Lucy bounded to her, barking a rowdy welcome, but Lauren ignored them and flopped into a stuffed chair. She leaned back and closed her eyes, as if exhausted.

Jandee asked about Ian and Vera, but Lauren didn't answer for a long time. Finally she opened her eyes and stared through the plate-glass doors at the mountains of the Olympic Peninsula, purpling now against a sunset's fiery finale. "Gone," she said.

"I don't get it."

"I don't either, Jandee. They're gone, that's all."

"*Gone*, as in 'flew the coop?' "

"*Gone*, as in I don't know where the hell they went, or why. They didn't leave a good-bye note."

Matt came into the room and sat on the sofa opposite Lauren's chair. He started to say something, but held back. He wondered why she'd been away so long.

Jandee broke the silence, wanting to know whether she should prepare one of the guest rooms for Matt, since he would probably stay on the premises tonight, now that he was a paid bodyguard. But Lauren replied that this wasn't necessary. She didn't expect him to give up his home life for a five-thousand-dollar retainer.

"I don't have a home life," Matt said. "And it wouldn't be an imposition. In fact, it might make me feel like I'm actually earning the money you forced on me."

Lauren gave him a weary stare. "Maybe you don't value your privacy, but I value mine. Go home, Matt. You've put in a good day's work. Come back tomorrow if you want to." Her head lolled back against the cushion of the chair, and she closed her eyes.

"Fine," Matt said with annoyance in his voice. "I'll be back in the morning to do a sweep for bugs." He stood, looked around for his sport coat. Jandee handed it to him and escorted him to the door.

"You don't really think someone might try to get in tonight to plant more bugs," she said. "Tell me that's not what you think."

"It's certainly not impossible. Considering everything that's happened up to now, I say we do a sweep."

"I guess this means I don't sleep tonight. Hey, I apologize for the boss's abruptness a minute ago. Normally she's not like that, you know. It's the stress."

"No apology necessary. Think you'll be okay tonight?"

"We'll be fine. Rainy plans to stay over, so there'll be three of us, not counting the dogs. Three tough broads and a pair of slavering canines."

Matt smiled. "Call me if anything spooks you. Or if you hear from Royal."

He said good-bye and walked to his Jeep in the circular drive, the fumes of blossoming rhododendrons and azaleas tickling his throat. After exiting the front gate, he took care to wait for the iron bars to clank shut, just to make certain that no one sneaked in behind him.

When he arrived at Shorty's, he found Cleo behind the bar, coping with the evening rush. "Busy as a one-armed wallpaper hanger," Royal might have said. She saw Matt and shook her head, telling him that Royal hadn't gotten in touch. Matt had a quick beer, then climbed the back stairs to his room and booted up his computer. He checked his e-mail but found nothing of interest, surfed the Web for a while to catch up on current events, then logged off.

Before going to bed, he went to his closet and crouched to paw through the cardboard box in which he stored some artifacts of his past life and career. He found his badge and ID packet, the saucer cap that went with his dress uniform, the framed citations he'd received—chief's commendation, meritorious service award, certificates of promotion, all the others. *Why do I keep this stuff?* he asked himself.

He found a photo album with portraits of his classmates at the law enforcement academy, some candid shots of his fellow members on the antidrug task force, and one that showed Rags dressed like the Easter bunny, clowning for a group of kids in a park. *That's why,* he thought, answering his own question.

Finally, in the bottom of the box, he found what he was looking for—a SIG Sauer pistol in a stiff leather holster. He pulled the pistol out of the holster, held it for a moment, tasted its weight and no-nonsense solidity with his hand. He ejected the empty clip and replaced it with a full one, twenty rounds of nine-millimeter, cocked the weapon and snapped on the safety. He laid it on the table next to his bed.

Later, as he lay sleepless in the dark, with the electronic thunder of high tide filling his ears and the sharp scent of gun oil teasing his nostrils, he told himself that the dark animal wasn't stirring to life in his gut. That he had his life well in hand, and he wouldn't go to prison for the crime of obstructing justice and hindering prosecution. That Royal would turn up alive and well.

He told himself that he was doing the right thing, getting mixed up in Lauren Bowman's life, that a decent man would do no less under the circumstances, even if it meant bending the law. He'd learned long ago that the letter of the law wasn't always synonymous with goodness and decency. Sometimes the letter of the law kept a good man from doing what his heart told him he needed to do.

"Everything will be all right," he said aloud, and he believed it just long enough to drift into a fitful sleep.

Twenty-seven

Inland from Jenkins Way the shoreline rose to a heavily vegetated plateau that overlooked Puget Sound. Sumptuous houses clung to the woody hillside, most of them outfitted with layers of decks and long banks of windows that afforded their Brahman owners a magnificent vista of water, mountains and urban skyline. Narrow byways twisted back and forth among tall stands of Douglas fir and cedar, occasionally giving onto gravel turnouts where sight-seers of lower caste could park and enjoy the view.

At one such turnout, directly overlooking the Bowman-Granger estate, Richardson Zanto had installed a powerful radio retransmitter that relayed signals from the phone tap and hidden microphones in Lauren Bowman's guest house to his rented apartment in downtown Seattle. He'd fastened the device and its battery pack to the trunk of a mature cedar, having climbed the tree to a height of almost twenty feet, clawing through heavy branches and stinging needles every inch of the way. He'd worried that a curious hiker or picnicker might eventually discover the transmitter and disable it, or perhaps report it to the authorities. In either case, InterActs stood to lose an expensive piece of equipment.

Around noon today the signal from Jenkins Way had abruptly gone dead.

Only yesterday he'd received a warning from his "fish" that the ex-cop named Burgess, as a favor to Lauren Bowman's father, would mount an effort to rid the guest house of bugs. Zanto could only assume that Burgess had already accomplished this, but he couldn't confirm it. The fish hadn't answered the telephone all day.

So, Zanto had decided to conduct *visual* surveillance of the house on Jenkins Way, physically taxing and downright exhausting though it was. Megan Reiner's killer, he'd reasoned, had shot footage of her death and had sent the video here to Ms. Bowman, betraying some sort of sick interest in her. Zanto was willing to bet that the maniac would try to interact with her again, and long shot though it was, he wanted to be on hand for the attempt.

Sitting on a picnic table at the very edge of the overlook, he stared through binoculars at the estate that sprawled along the shore, searching for any hint of what was afoot behind its stucco walls but seeing nothing of interest. Now and then a human figure moved along one of the white stone walkways, bent on some domestic errand—household staff members, Zanto assumed, gardeners or housekeepers. As the twilight faded to night, shadows filled the spaces between the guest house and the villa. Electric yard lights switched on automatically. Cars departed one by one as the help left for the day, their headlight beams winking between the trees. The two swimming pools shimmered in soft aquamarine, while warm yellow light spilled from the windows of the villa and the guest house.

Gravity, simplicity, piety, Zanto said to himself, as he had countless times throughout his adult life. His career with InterActs, he knew, was history. He'd ignored a direct order from the CEO to fold up Operation Undermine. Then he'd failed to report back to the Washington office for a new assignment. By now his ex-partner, Stan Goulding, had surely tried to explain to management why a seasoned company operative had abruptly kissed off his job in order to chase some personal notion of justice that had little or no relevance to the realities of today's world. Zanto didn't doubt that Goulding had tried valiantly to put a favorable spin on the story, but neither did he doubt that old Brent Bryson, the CEO, had failed to empathize. Business was business, after all.

Zanto put down the binoculars and massaged his aching wrist, the old shrapnel wound having acted up. He wished he was back in his comfortable house in Falls Church, Virginia, ensconced in his worn leather armchair and surrounded by his books—Livy, Julius Caesar, Dio Cassius, Pliny the Elder, countless others. He closed his eyes a moment and saw the paintings on the walls of his study, his favorite being a nineteenth-century oil of the Arch of Septimius Severus, a sight that always made him feel connected to that earlier time, that *better* time. On his desk stood his prized reproduction of Vulca's statue of Apollo, a graceful Etruscan work. Here stood a bust of the historian Suetonius, there one of Marcus Aurelius, the philosopher-emperor.

A man needed such things, he'd come to understand long ago, the small treasures that beautify his life—paintings, books, sculpture—especially if his duty required him to wallow in ugliness, as Zanto's so often had. The small treasures made the rest bearable.

He'd never shrunk from ugliness, never balked at getting his hands wet. While working for Clandestine Services he'd killed—or arranged to kill—terrorists of every stripe, including Islamic fundamentalists in Iran, Brigatti Rossi in Italy and Rote Verbände in Germany, as well as agents of the Soviet GRU in Mexico and the KGB in Austria and Belgium. In all those years, he'd never questioned an order nor stinted his devotion to duty, not even when Ronald Reagan's right-wing zealots took over the CIA's Covert Operations and used it to pursue their misguided obsessions over "creeping Marxism" in Central America. Zanto had gritted his teeth and followed orders, even to the extent of planning and executing the kidnap of a leftist newspaper editor in El Salvador.

Such devotion to duty had ruined his marriage. His wife, Loretta, had lacked his capacity for sacrifice, wanting a normal life with a conventional family routine, regular hours and vacations that nobody could cancel at the last minute. She'd detested secrecy. Worst of all, she'd misunderstood his piety, believing that he was indifferent to her happiness, since the demands of his damnable work always superseded her wishes.

Their tumultuous two-year marriage had produced a daughter, Meredith, whom Zanto seldom saw these days. A year ago she'd graduated from Georgetown with a degree in comparative literature, but she'd sent her father no announcement, no invitation to the graduation festivities. Zanto had heard that she'd enrolled in the Master's program at his alma mater, Cornell. He had no idea when or if he might see her again.

Over the years, he'd become an out-and-out loner. He had precious few casual friends and no close ones, only *associates* within a tight circle of former CIA colleagues and fellow InterActs operatives, people for whom close *friendship* wasn't necessarily a viable concept, given the uncertainties they lived with. In place of friends, Zanto had his books, his paintings and treasured Roman artifacts—a life of gravity, simplicity, and . . .

Piety.

Face the stormy winds with steady oars and uncomplaining hearts, Marcus Aurelius had written. Stoic that he was, Zanto had no choice but to point his chin into the storm and follow the dictates of his conscience, just as the philosopher-emperor would have advised. *This* was true piety . . .

He saw something. He instinctively glanced at his watch, marked the time at 2147 hours. A black or dark blue sport utility vehicle cruised slowly past the front gate of the Bowman-Granger estate, slowed nearly to a crawl as if the driver wanted to get a look at the place, then proceeded north on Jenkins Way. The SUV looked like a Suburban, though not quite as large. A Yukon or a Tahoe, Zanto said to himself, a smaller version of GM's behemoth.

He followed the vehicle with the binoculars until it vanished around a bend in the road, its taillights leaving violet smears in his field of vision. He waited. Less than a minute later, headlight beams swiped across the stucco wall of the Bowman-Granger estate, and the SUV came into view again, having made a U-turn on Jenkins Way to backtrack past the front gate. Again the driver slowed as if to get a good look, then drove on.

As the vehicle rounded a curve to the left, its brake lights flashed, and it swung off the road, jouncing onto what appeared to be little more than a mountain bike path. It climbed fifty or sixty feet up the face of the hill and halted. The headlights and taillights went black, and the dome light came on briefly, indicating that the driver had dismounted the vehicle.

Zanto spun the focus wheel of the binoculars and tried to get a clear look, but dark masses of trees and shrubs obscured his view. He wished that he had a night-vision device.

Movement now, between the SUV and Jenkins Way. He focused the binoculars and caught a glimpse of a human figure trekking downhill toward the road, a man. The figure disappeared again briefly into an amorphous mound of dark foliage, then reemerged in a tight clearing north of the bike trail. Carrying a small parcel of some kind, he moved laterally along the hillside and

waded through a riot of ferns and low bushes until reaching a
fallen log that lay almost directly between Zanto and Lauren
Bowman's gate. He sat on the log and folded his arms, facing the
gate, his back to Zanto.

He's waiting for something, Zanto said to himself, studying
the figure in the light of a rising moon.

Twenty-eight

"Boss, you really should eat," Jandee said, setting the tray on the table next to Lauren's bed. "You need to keep your strength up."

"I'm afraid my stomach can't handle anything right now." Lauren sat on the edge of her bed, facing a panoramic sweep of windows, beyond which the Sound lay black under a velvet sky. Now and then a shard of moonlight danced across a wavelet, a mere suggestion of silver. Desi and Lucy sprawled side-by-side on the huge bed, ready to call it a night.

"Will you at least *look* at it?" Jandee begged. "It's sautéed tempeh with lemon-mustard sauce, and I must say Rainy has out-done herself this time."

"Jandee, I'm telling you I don't want anything. I only want to get some sleep, okay? And I'm not a little kid, so quit treating me like one."

"All right, whatever—don't tear my head off. Dry up and blow away, for all I care. I'll just have Rainy make you a mango-raspberry smoothie . . ."

"I don't want a mango-raspberry smoothie. I don't want any sautéed tempeh, and I don't want a dish of cinnamon oatmeal or anything else you're pushing. I just want to be left alone, for the love of God."

Jandee sat down next to Lauren, making clear that she had no intention of leaving her alone at a time like this, not for the love of God or anyone else. A long silence endured. "Mind if I, like, ask you something?" she ventured.

"Yes. Go away."

"You don't really think Ian loves you, do you? I mean, a man doesn't just bail on the woman he loves, okay? A man who does something like that isn't worth the spilled tears. It's better for you to forget about him, give him up for a lost cause."

"Jandee, please."

"You did the right thing when you told him you didn't want to see him again. After the promise he made to you and broke—the one about carrying a gun on the raid—and the way he's taken advantage of you, fading into totally thin air without even leaving a note."

"Jandee, shut up. You don't have any idea what you're talking about."

"The hell I don't. I'm not exactly inexperienced in these things, you know. And you're not so old and wizened that you couldn't use some sound advice now and then. Forget Ian Prather, boss. He's gone, and he won't be back. He's probably sunning himself in Costa Rica right now, or sniffing after some Latina . . ."

Lauren let herself collapse backward onto the bedspread. When she spoke, her voice sounded thin, ready to crack. "What will it take to make you leave me alone? I'll do anything."

Jandee stared at her with worried eyes, shaking her head. "Are you serious? *Anything*?"

"Anything."

"Have a mango-raspberry smoothie with me. And promise me that you'll see a doctor if you don't feel better tomorrow."

"All right, whatever. Anything for a little peace."

Twenty-nine

The Blues Beast brushed a frond of sword fern away from his face and popped a Hillshire Farms Li'l Smoky into his mouth. He chewed slowly, because his jaw hurt from the pistol-whipping Ian Prather had given him the night before. He shifted his weight on the log, letting blood flow into the numb half of his butt, stretched first one aching leg and then the other. One of the Ranger's old blues songs shambled through his mind:

> *Bein' patient for your lovin', girl,*
> *It's makin' me an angry man.*
> *Ain't gettin' any stronger,*
> *Can't hold out much longer,*
> *Ain't sayin' that I can . . .*

He stared at a patch of blackness that until a minute ago had been a rectangle of soft yellow—the skylight in Lauren Bowman's bedroom. The blackness could only mean that she'd retired for the night, a thought that started a new fire in his innards. His mind suddenly lit up with the image of Lauren lying atop twisted sheets, her legs stretched out in the freeze-frame pose of a runner caught in midstride. She wore only high-cut panties and an athletic bra. He imagined putting his hand on her ankle and running it upward, slowly and smoothly, past her knee to her thigh, and then higher and higher still, until . . .

Can't hold out much longer.

His cellphone rang.

"Yeah."

"Tyler, it's me." Rainy. "Where are you?"

"How many times do I have to tell you? No names on the phone. Try, try, *try* to get that through your head, or you'll make me spank."

"I-I'm sorry. I forgot. It won't happen again."

"I know, I know. Are we ready to rumble?"

"I did like you wanted, gave the drugs to Laur—I mean, the women." She sounded miserable, as if she was close to breaking down. "I emptied the caps into their mango-raspberry smoothies."

"And?"

"They drank them. It was touch and go at first, because one of them was determined not to have anything, but the other one talked her into it. That was about twenty minutes ago."

"I assume the medication has had the desired effect."

"Uh, yeah—I guess. They're both asleep."

"What about the dogs?"

"I coaxed them out of the bedroom and gave them the caps. They thought I was giving them treats. They went to sleep right away."

"So, everybody's sawing logs, right?"

"Uh . . . there's still some lights on in the villa, but that's normal. I'm sure Ga—" She almost said Gabe Granger's name. "I'm sure the man next door is in bed—he's never up late on weekdays. You'll be okay if you don't make any noise."

Tyler fished another little sausage from the plastic wrapper and snaked it into his mouth, chewed slowly, carefully. He took a long, slow breath, told himself to take it easy. "Okay, now listen, babe. I'm going to switch off the phone and head down to the gate. You get ready to shut down the security, but don't do it yet. Call me in exactly ninety seconds, and I'll give you the word. Got that?"

"I got it."

"Good. You're doing fine, makin' me proud."

Tyler switched off the phone, stood, and stretched to work the kinks out of his bruised body. A fierce throb in his left hand, the one Vera Kemmis had bitten, reminded him that women could be brutal in defending themselves, a lesson he'd vowed never to forget. He took a blue watch cap from the pocket of his jeans, pulled it down over his misshapen ears, and tucked his blond hair into it. He started trekking down the hill toward the gate of the estate on Jenkins Way, carefully stepping over logs and boulders, dodging the fronds of sword ferns and the limbs of fir trees. By the time he reached the street, his heart was pumping like a pile driver, and his cock was so hard he could barely walk.

Thirty

Richardson Zanto glanced at his watch and marked the time at exactly twenty-six minutes past midnight. With the moon cresting the hill behind him, he had no trouble following the man's progress down the hillside toward Jenkins Way.

The guy was broad-shouldered and muscular, dressed in dark clothing. A moment ago he'd put on a knitted cap and tucked his long hair into it. A white bandage covered his left hand, suggesting that he'd recently suffered an injury of some kind. Zanto sensed pain in the way he walked, a stiffness in his movements, like a man walking away from a car accident.

Zanto watched him emerge from the wooded hillside onto Jenkins Way, saw him look in both directions before crossing quickly to the gate of the Bowman-Granger estate. The man needn't have hurried, for traffic was nonexistent. The night was silent except for the twang of insects and the occasional honk of a nautical horn out on the Sound.

The man reached the gate and stood still, his shoulders hunched in a nervous, expectant pose, like someone waiting for a bus in a downpour. A half-minute went by. He pulled out a cellular phone, talked into it, then switched it off and pocketed it. Suddenly the gate started to slide open, and he quickly slipped past the bars onto the grounds, the gate immediately clanking shut again. He trotted along the curving drive until reaching the crushed-granite path that led to the guest house, where he swerved to his right and disappeared into the deep shadow of manicured shrubbery. Zanto waited a full five minutes, but saw no more sign of the man.

Zanto went to his rented car, got in, started it up, drove down the road to the intersection with Jenkins Way. He turned right and headed toward the Bowman-Granger estate, but went less than a quarter of a mile before swinging into a turnout normally used by picnickers and hikers. His was the only vehicle in the area, for city regulations prohibited hiking, picnicking and biking after sundown.

From where he now sat, Zanto had a good view of the roadway. He knew that when the man in the stocking cap finished his business at Lauren Bowman's residence, whatever that was, he had no choice but to pass this spot, since Jenkins Way dead-ended a short distance north of the Bowman-Grangers' gate. And Zanto meant to wait for him, no matter how long it took, no matter how hungry or thirsty he became.

Gravity, simplicity, piety.

Richardson Zanto was a patient and pious man.

Thirty-one

A sound reached Lauren's brain, fabric moving over skin, *close*, within touching distance. *Someone slipping out of his clothes.* Horrors that she'd suffered long ago had sensitized her to such tiny warnings in the night, and no drug could completely shut them out. She stirred, tried to move her arms and legs, but she felt as if she'd blundered into a tar pit and sunk to the bottom.

A touch sparked against the skin of her ankle like a live electrical wire. She struggled and tried to scream, but every movement met an avalanche of warm tar, stifling, smothering. Another touch. A man's coarse hand moving upward over her calf, her thigh. She felt the moist heat of his breath on her neck. All part of a nightmare, she prayed. This was nothing real, only a harmless memory dredged up from the cellar of her mind. A nightmare, yes—and knowing this, she could bear it.

She was fifteen again, lying paralyzed with fright, as now.

Cringing against every caress, trying not to breathe.

Willing herself into another world, where young girls were safe from creatures like this man with his gaggy tobacco breath and his cold, calloused fingertips.

She'd wanted so desperately to fight him then, but she'd lacked the strength and bravery. She wanted to fight him *now*. Hauling in a lungful of air, she now tried to scream herself awake, to burst through the curtain of sleep into the clear air of reality. But she could only croak and whimper.

Sleep was an enemy now, falling upon her like black snow.

Throughout her adult life, she'd suffered dreams about the outrages she'd suffered at his hands, about the things she knew he'd done to other girls, other children. The dreams had always featured bolts of bright light reflected off the blade of his knife, and spatters of red blood—somebody's blood, maybe her own. *God*, how many years had she fought those dreams?

Blood dries faster than tears . . .

She felt his hands on her panties, pushing them down past her knees, past her ankles, his hands on her hips pulling her toward him, his hands between her legs, pushing them apart. His breath hit her flat in the face and nearly made her retch, for it was the breath of a meat eater, rich with the stink of the slaughterhouse. He entered her from behind, and she shrieked loudly enough to shatter glass, but only in her mind. Filled with tar, her mouth gave out only a low moan. He stayed with her a long time, pumping, grunting, his breath coming in putrid huffs. Sometime during this seeming eternity, her mind switched off, and she plunged into nothingness.

Thirty-two

Twenty minutes after receiving Jandee's frantic call, Matt Burgess arrived at the door of the guest house. Jandee answered the doorbell.

"I've never seen her like this," she said, clutching the lapel of Matt's corduroy sport coat. "She's completely out of her mind. She's been in the shower since the sun came up, washing herself, rinsing herself, over and over again, washing and rinsing and *washing*—"

"That's almost two hours," Matt said, looking at his watch. "You're saying she's been in the shower for two hours?"

Jandee pulled him into the foyer, closed the door after him and locked it. Matt expected Lucy and Desi to come bounding toward him, their toenails clicking on the tiles, barking their usual welcome. But the dogs were nowhere in sight, and the guest house was strangely silent.

"Matt, I'm scared," Jandee said. "The boss has always been the iron woman, the one we count on to be tough. I can't handle her going to pieces like this." She clung to him as if he was a lifeguard who'd swum out to the deep water to rescue her.

Matt wondered if Jandee was the one going to pieces. Her eyes were red and swollen, her cheeks pale. Her freckles stood out like a rash across the bridge of her nose. She looked as if she'd won a beer-drinking derby the night before.

"Yeah, I know I look like shit," she said, reading his face.

Matt suggested that she sit down, have a glass of water or

some tea. No stranger to hangovers himself, he'd found that taking on fluids was the best remedy. But Jandee insisted that she wasn't hung over, that she'd had no alcohol of any kind last night.

"Whatever you say," Matt replied, looking skeptical. "Now tell me what's going on here. And start from the beginning."

Jandee told the story in slow, precise syllables, her voice quivering occasionally. She'd heard a scream that had jolted her out of a dead sleep—Lauren's scream—and she'd opened her eyes to find that the sun was just coming up. She'd tried to get out of bed, but her own body had felt as if someone had weighted it with lead. She'd managed to stumble into the master suite, where she'd found Lauren naked on her bed, kneeling, her fingers buried in her hair, screaming at the ceiling.

"I tried to calm her down," Jandee went on, "but she was a wild woman. Wouldn't let me touch her, tried to claw me whenever I got too close. I asked her what was wrong, tried to get her to talk to me. Finally she ran into the bathroom, got into the shower. She turned the water on, like, really hot. She's been in there ever since, and . . ." Jandee's voice faltered, and she took a moment to gather herself. "I tried to pull her out of the shower, but she's too strong for me. She actually hit me in the jaw with her fist. I was ready to call an ambulance, you know? I mean, it's like she's having some kind of episode or something."

Matt glanced around as if he expected to see someone else. "I thought Rainy was staying the night. Didn't you ask her to help?"

"She *did* stay the night. But I couldn't get her to come out of the guest room. I could hear her in there, crying like the world was ending, but would she come out and lend a hand? No fucking way. I actually picked up the phone to call nine-one-one, but then I thought of you, and . . ."

Jandee's eyes were suddenly moist with tears, and Matt put his arms around her, held her. She sobbed quietly against his chest. He offered her a Kleenex from his pocket pack, and she dabbed her eyes with it, blew her nose.

"There's more," she said, sniffing.

"More?"

"We got another video."

Matt's stomach did a flop. "Where?"

"In Lauren's room, on the bed."

"Christ. That means someone got in here last night."

"No shit. I guess we'll need to look at it, right?"

"First thing we do is take care of Lauren," Matt said.

"Sure, of course. I'm ready anytime you are."

"Show me the bathroom."

The master bathing suite was a spectacle of Italian marble, handmade ceramic tiles and chromed fixtures, potted ferns and vines. The dual sit-down shower stood opposite a four-person bathtub and spa. Sticking his head through the door, Matt became aware of Lauren's voice amid the swirling steam, singing a slow, mournful song over the hiss of dual water spigots. He saw her naked form huddled in the corner of the shower, just visible through smoky glass doors. He could barely make out the lyrics:

> *You know you've done some sinnin' woman,*
> *And it's no good confessin' to your priest . . .*

The song gave Matt gooseflesh—the *way* Lauren sang it, the resignation in her voice. She sounded as if she'd accepted total, utter defeat.

> *Ain't but one man in the world you should confess to,*
> *And I'm standin' right here—I'm the Blues Beast.*

Matt breathed in the steam, the thick scent of soap and shampoo, and for a moment he felt dizzy. He felt like a trespasser, a Peeping Tom who'd happened upon a scene of some wrenching private catastrophe. He fought the urge to run away.

"She's been singing for the past hour or so," Jandee said, standing behind him. "Same song, over and over. I don't mind saying that it, like, totally creeps me out, man."

"We've got to get her out of there," Matt said. He moved into the cloud of steam toward the shower, moving one foot in front of the other. He called Lauren's name, but she didn't hear him. She continued to sing.

"Lauren, it's Matt Burgess. I'm coming to help you, okay?"

> *You know you need to suffer, mama,*
> *If you ever expect to get released*
> *From all the trouble you've brought down on your head . . .*

He halted inches from the glass doors, his hand reaching for the handle. Moisture condensed on his eyelashes, ran down his face. He wished intensely that she would stop singing that hideous song.

"Lauren, I'm going to open the door now. Jandee's here with me. We're going to help you dry off and get dressed, okay? Then we're going to talk awhile, have some tea . . ."

I'll make you suffer, girl—I'm the Blues Beast.

He pulled on the door handle, and the door swung open, but Lauren didn't look up at him. She huddled in the confluence of two streams of water—water that was much too hot, Matt judged from the redness of her skin. Her nakedness mattered nothing to him—she reminded him of a child, helpless, needing rescue. Bars of soap and bottles of shampoo littered the tiled floor around her, as well as a bottle of Lysol bathroom disinfectant that she'd apparently used on herself. Matt wondered what on earth could make anyone feel so dirty.

> *No use runnin' from the past, my girl,*
> *Of all your dumb ideas, that's the least.*
> *There ain't a woman alive who can outrun me.*
> *Chasin' is my specialty—I'm the Blues Beast.*

He turned off the water, and Lauren's eyes popped open. She stared up at him, her face beet-red from the hot water. She screamed.

"Sweetheart, it's okay," Matt said, reaching down to take her arm. But she flailed and fought him, as if he was the most hideous creature on God's green earth. She hit and slapped, tried to scratch and bite. Matt had no choice but to engulf her in his arms and haul her unceremoniously from the shower. She tried to knee him in the groin, but he turned sideways to dodge the blow.

Jandee joined the fray, helping him pin Lauren's arms to her side. Somehow she managed to wrap a long terry-cloth robe around the struggling woman. Together they wrestled her into the bedroom, then onto the bed, where they lay with Lauren sandwiched between them, holding her as she shuddered and screamed and fought. They tried to soothe her, reassure her, but the best they could do was keep her from hurting herself. Finally her panic started to ebb along with her energy, and the screaming subsided to long, low moans.

"I'll stay with her," Matt said to Jandee. "Go call someone, a friend—we need help here. Make sure it's someone you trust."

"I'll call Elise," Jandee said. "She'll know exactly what to do. She always does."

"Yeah, good. Tell her to hurry, for God's sake."

Thirty-three

Alex Ragsdale arrived at the estate shortly after noon, looking dapper in a blue blazer, his hair freshly barbered to minimize the prominence of his balding crown. "What's for lunch?" he asked as Matt led him from the foyer into the sitting room.

"Nothing you'd want. They only eat vegan stuff around here, lots of tofu and eggplant. Settle for a banana?"

"I'll take it."

Matt fetched a banana from a fruit bowl in the kitchen, where Rainy Hales was busy preparing the noon meal. She barely acknowledged his presence, keeping her eyes glued to a cutting board and the task of slicing fresh vegetables. *Avoidance*, Matt thought as he left the kitchen. A junkie's phobia for cops, he figured. Or an *ex*-junkie's phobia for *ex*-cops.

He gave the banana to Rags and suggested that they retire to the gazebo at the rear of the house, where they could talk in private. They sat opposite one another, Rags in a cedar rocker and Matt in the swinging love seat.

"Sorry I couldn't come earlier," Rags said around a mouthful of banana. "I've been in meetings all morning. I left as soon as I got your voice mail. Hey, I don't mean to be unkind, but you look a little rumpled, Burge. What did you do—run through a sprinkler with your clothes on? And there's this thing all us guys do—it's called *shaving* . . ."

"There's another video," Matt said, ignoring the ribbing.

Rags' jaw froze in mid-chew. "Another homicide?"

Matt nodded, his face grim. "I'm the only one who's seen it so far. The victim looks to be about thirty-five, reddish hair, pretty green eyes. The killer did her the same way he did Megan, with a knife, blues music in the background. It's not any easier to watch than the first one."

"Did he rape her?"

Matt nodded again, his eyes fixed on a wedge of white sail out on the Sound. The sky was blue under a high, golden sun. The light westerly was perfect for sailing.

"Any idea who she was?"

"My gut says Vera Kemmis. She and Ian Prather are missing as of yesterday, no good-bye, no farewell letter, nothing. Jandee thinks they went south to dodge the heat. Plus, the girl on the tape was no pussycat. She fought the son of a bitch every minute right up until the end, even though she was tied up—cussed him out, told him exactly what kind of lowlife he was. It fits with everything I've heard about Kemmis. On top of that, she sounded British."

Rags put the banana down, no longer hungry. In fact, Matt thought he looked a little green around the gills, the way Matt himself felt. "You think the killer's got Prather, too?" Rags asked.

"Who the hell knows? It certainly wouldn't surprise me."

Matt heard footsteps on the walk behind him, the clip-clop of sensible Birkenstocks. He looked over his shoulder and saw Elise Lekander climb the steps to the gazebo, holding herself in an imperious, ramrod posture that evinced old money and good breeding. She wore fitted white jeans that looked good on her lean, middle-aged frame, and a flouncy green "pirate" shirt. A sickle of honey-blond hair drooped over her high forehead.

She went immediately to Rags and thrust out her hand. "I'm Elise Lekander," she said, wasting neither time nor words.

"And I'm Alexander Ragsdale," he replied, getting to his feet. This was maybe the second or third time that Matt had ever heard him use his full first name. Old money apparently had an effect on him. "It's truly an honor to meet you, ma'am. I'm Matt's partner."

"I didn't realize he had a partner. I trust that I can speak candidly, then."

"Absolutely."

She turned to Matt, whom she'd met earlier in the day. "I'm

happy to report that Lauren seems to be feeling more herself again, though she's very tired. Unfortunately, she has vetoed my suggestion that we call a doctor to examine her, but I suppose I should have expected that." Elise managed a small smile. "I want to thank you, Mr. Burgess, for coming to her aid this morning. It was well beyond the call of duty."

"Not at all. I only wish that I'd insisted on staying over last night. Maybe we could've prevented this."

"I couldn't agree with you more. From now on, that's exactly what you'll do, of course. I want to ensure that Lauren is never left without an armed protector, no matter *what* she says."

"I understand," Matt said.

Rags coughed, signaling that he wasn't yet in the loop. "Something happened to Lauren?"

"We have reason to believe that she was raped last night," Elise answered bluntly. "Someone managed to gain entry to the estate, then slipped into her room and assaulted her. He left the video as a sort of calling card, it would seem. I assume that Mr. Burgess has told you about the video."

"He told me," Rags answered. "But this is the first I've heard about an assault on Lauren." He threw an accusing look at Matt.

"Hey, you've only been here a few minutes," Matt said.

"Did anyone hear anything, see anything?" Rags wanted to know.

"Regrettably, no," answered Elise Lekander. "It's my theory that everyone in the house was drugged."

"Drugged?" Rags scowled as if he'd just gotten a whiff of sour milk. "Why would you think that?"

"I've worked for many years as a volunteer with the People's Resource Center down in Belltown," she declared, "and I've had close contact with countless runaways and addicts. I may not be a doctor, but I know a hangover when I see one. Both Jandee and Lauren display all the symptoms—headache, nausea, redness of the eyes. Neither of them, however, abuses drugs or alcohol, which leads me to conclude that someone gave them some kind of strong sedative, perhaps a barbiturate. That's how the assailant was able to get in without anyone hearing him—the women were in a drug-induced stupor. It also explains how he was able to force himself on Lauren and escape without having his eyes clawed out."

"You didn't mention the cook, Rainy Hales," Matt said. "Does she have a hangover, too?"

"She has an intense headache," Elise answered, "although I can't say that her eyes look abnormal in any way. She reports that she slept very heavily last night, which could've been the effect of a sedative. The room she uses is on the opposite end of the house from Lauren's and Jandee's rooms, so it's quite possible that she wouldn't have heard the intruder, even if she hadn't been drugged."

"What about Desi and Lucy?" Matt asked. "Aren't they supposed to be watchdogs? You'd think they would've barked their heads off."

Elise frowned as she considered this. "I've scarcely noticed them all morning, now that you mention it. I did see Lucy lying in a corner of the pantry, which doesn't seem quite normal. They're usually such lively animals."

"Maybe they're hung over, too," Rags said with a snigger, drawing a disapproving frown from Elise. Matt pointed out that the idea wasn't so far-fetched. Burglars had been known to disable watchdogs by tossing them hamburger laced with pills.

"Actually, this drug theory only reinforces what we've thought all along," Rags said. "Somebody around here is working for the bad guy. It's no stretch to assume that whoever drugged Lauren and Jandee also planted the bugs in the walls. Any reason why we shouldn't narrow the field of suspects to those who were here last night?"

Elise thought a moment, staring a dagger at Rags. "Am I to understand that you're accusing Rainy?"

"Well, she'd be on my short list. For one thing, she cooks for everybody in this house, right? She'd have the opportunity to slip a couple of mickeys into the drinks, then a couple more to the dogs. After Lauren and what's-her-name—Jandee—are amply doped up, she could turn off the security system and let somebody in. It's almost too obvious."

"Rainy Hales has been in Lauren's employ for nearly two years," Elise declared, her dander up. "In all that time she hasn't once done anything untoward. She's proved herself steady and reliable, not to mention a gifted vegan chef. I can tell you unequivocally that Rainy would never do anything to harm Lauren."

Rags backed off. For now. He glanced at Matt, an eyebrow raised.

"Mrs. Lekander, I hate to ask you this," Matt said, "but I—"

"I appreciate being called Elise by those I know and like."

"*Elise*. I need you to look at the video. We've got to try to ID the victim. The sooner we do this, the better."

Elise Lekander's jaw tightened, but she didn't look away. "Yes, of course. I'm at your disposal."

"Rags, I want you to see it, too, if you don't mind."

"I mind. But I'll look at it. Any time you're ready."

Matt led the way back into the sitting room, where he plugged the videocassette into the VCR. He waited until Elise and Rags had settled into their seats before hitting the play button.

As with the video of Megan Reiner's murder, the intro was blues music, sung in the now-familiar sandpaper male voice, accompanied by an electric guitarist who clearly knew what he was doing. To Matt's untrained ear, the performance sounded good enough to be the work of a professional.

> *Don't you worry 'bout this one, woman.*
> *No way she's fit to lick your boot.*
> *She don't mean a dirty whit to me.*
> *She ain't nothin' but a substitute.*

The camera panned a woman's nude body, which lay on an incline of about forty-five degrees, her hands bound above her head with leather straps, her ankles tied down. The woman fought the bonds, twisted and squirmed like a worm on a hook. The microphone picked up her screams over the bluesy music, the curses and insults that she hurled at her tormenter. She called him a bloody maniac, a slimy pervert. She vowed to rip his balls off if she ever got free. Then the camera zoomed in close to her face . . .

"It's Vera," said a voice behind Matt, and he flinched, not having heard anyone approach. He turned and saw Lauren standing in the mouth of the hallway, her shoulder braced against the doorjamb. She still wore the bulky terry-cloth bathrobe, which she'd drawn tightly around her body. Red blotches on her face and neck told of exposure to hot water and detergents not meant for human skin.

Elise bolted out of her chair and went to her, but Lauren waved her off. "I'm all right, now," she said, not taking her eyes off the television screen. "I had to see this . . ."

Yeah, she's a stand-in, playin' second string.
Scratches my itch, don't mean a thing.
Hear me, woman, you got nothin' to fear.
She's only gonna do me till you get here.

Matt studied Lauren's face as she watched the video. To his surprise, it registered no horror as the bloody spectacle unfolded on the screen, no grimace of revulsion as the killer forced himself on the doomed Vera Kemmis, no shiver as the shiny knife pressed into the poor woman's throat. Still, Matt thought he saw *something* in Lauren's face . . .

She ain't even all that cute.
She ain't nothin' but a substitute.

"At least she didn't go quietly," Lauren said, watching as Vera's life drained away through the wound in her neck. Matt sensed that Lauren had used up her inventory of tears. Her face was as lifeless as a carving, her eyes as empty as glass—except for a small, almost imperceptible glimmer of . . . *something*. Was it recognition?

"Darling," Elise pressed, "you really should go back to bed, don't you think? You've been through a terrible ordeal."

"Nothing that compares with *that*." She nodded toward the TV screen.

A man can't wait forever, y' see,
A man might take what he can get.
Get me a girl, I might get three.
You're just the one I ain't got yet.

The video ended, and no one spoke for more than a minute. One of Lauren's dogs—Matt thought it was Desi—ambled slowly into the sitting room from the hallway and flopped onto an oval throw rug next to Rags' chair, paying no one any heed. The animal looked sick.

"Matt, I need to talk to you," Lauren said. "Alone." She went into her study, and Matt followed, feeling Rags' and Elise's curious eyes on his back. She shut the door, motioned him to a chair. She herself then sat, tucking her long legs underneath her.

She closed her eyes and began to massage them with her finger-tips in a slow, circular motion.

Matt watched her a moment, thinking how different she looked from the first time he'd met her, only three days ago—it seemed like a decade. With her dark hair hanging lank to the base of her neck, her skin reddened by hot water and corrosive chemicals, she didn't much resemble the charismatic, uncompromising activist who'd welcomed him with a blinding smile and a cup of Earl Grey. Today she had the depleted look of a refugee, the empty face of someone who'd suffered the grossest kind of violation. He felt sorry for her, and wished that he could comfort her, that he could restore all she'd lost. He also yearned to get his hands on the animal who'd raped her.

"Ian Prather's dead," she said, not opening her eyes. "I thought you should know, given the job I'm paying you to do."

Matt held his breath a moment, then let it out slowly. He said nothing.

"I found him yesterday in Ballard," Lauren went on. "He was alone in the safe house I'd lined up for him and Vera. I think someone had beaten him to death."

"Is the body still there?"

"I don't know. I don't think so. I . . . uh . . . asked someone to take care of it for me. I haven't said anything about this to anyone else, not even Jandee."

"You asked someone to take care of it for you. What does that mean?"

She looked straight at him now. "What do you think it means? Take the body away, clean the place up."

"Must be nice to be able to afford that kind of help. A man gets killed in a house you own, you get someone to come in, clean up, make it disappear."

"It's not like that. I asked—a friend."

"Who?"

"Matt, I'm not really free to say."

Matt was suddenly on his feet. "Jesus Christ! Why did you even bother to tell me this?" He snatched a magazine from the table next to his chair, a copy of *Animal Realm*, and flung it against the wall, the pages fluttering and flapping like a wounded bird. "What's *with* you, anyway? Do you think we're playing some sort of fucking game here?"

"It's no game, Matt."

"You're fucking right it's not! People are getting *killed*, Lauren . . ."

"And that's why you're here, isn't it? To help me."

Matt sputtered, looked around for something else to throw. Who in the hell did this bitch think she was? "Let me tell you something," he said, struggling to keep his voice down. "You can't make a murder disappear by hiring someone to clean it up for you. We have *laws*, Lauren—laws against covering up crimes. You cover up a homicide, you get burned. Even you."

"What would you have me do?"

Matt ran his hand through his hair, paced up and down the room, stopped and stared at her. "I think you know the answer to that question," he said.

He sat down again, put an ankle on a knee, made twirlies with his thumbs. He hadn't lost his temper in years, and he damned himself for having done it now. He apologized without looking up.

"You've been very patient, actually," Lauren replied. "And I want you to know how grateful I am for what you did this morning. I have no idea why I acted like I did. Elise thinks someone drugged me, and that I've been suffering some kind of toxic reaction . . ."

"She's probably right." Matt leaned forward, his hands pressed together to make a point. "Look, Lauren. We're way beyond worrying about obstructing justice here—that's small potatoes now. We've got something bigger to worry about, a killer who's . . ."

"Who's killing people close to me, yeah." She tapped her temple with her index finger. "Mind like a steel trap."

"This prick can apparently come and go as he pleases—in and out through your goddamn gate, most likely. Your personal safety has become the issue now, don't you see? After what happened last night, we've got to face the ugly fact that we're not equipped to fight this guy on our own. We need the cops, Lauren. We need to get a homicide team on the case—real pros, not goofs like Rags and me. We need to get after him before he does somebody else, namely *you*."

Lauren bit her lower lip, grimaced—her mouth always working, working. "You want my life to end, in other words," she said. "You want me to give up the only thing that makes me feel like a real human being."

"I'm not saying that."

"That's *exactly* what you're saying. If I go to the police, I rat out Rod. And I put other good people on the hot seat, people I love, like Jandee and Rainy and Elise and Marc. They're all co-conspirators in their own ways, because they all knew about the raid, and they encouraged us, helped us. And suppose—just *suppose* that by some miracle, I come out of this without serving a prison term. Do you think I could still be an effective member of the movement? Do you think anyone in the movement would ever trust me, ever take me into their confidence? I'd be a pariah. I'd be finished, Matt—literally."

Matt started to say something. He wanted to point out that she was still a young woman, an extremely rich young woman, that even though she might face shunning by the animal-rights movement, the world was her oyster. She could set up a foundation to rescue baby sea otters or chimpanzees or elephants, if she wanted. She could buy a ship, put to sea, and ram Japanese whalers. Hell, she might even decide to do something for *people*, just for a change of pace—God knew the world teemed with sick and desperate people who would welcome a little help from the top one-percent tax bracket.

But looking into her disquieted brown eyes, Matt knew that he needn't waste his breath. Lauren Bowman truly believed that the animal-rights movement was her life. Admitting her role in the Northwest BioCenter raid was tantamount to forsaking her convictions and betraying her compatriots. Matt leaned back in his chair and shook his head slowly. "I see," he said.

He noticed that her eyes were wet. She hadn't used up all her tears after all.

"You're not going to leave, are you?" she asked in a thin voice.

"No," he muttered. "I made a promise to Royal, and I intend to keep it. But from now on, I need to know everything you know. I need you to level with me. No more games, okay?"

"Okay."

He got up out of the chair, wandered to the window and watched a flock of noisy gulls circle the deck. For a split second he actually thought that he spotted Groucho among them, then decided he was seeing things. "Let's start with whoever took care of Ian Prather's body," he said. "I'll want to talk to him. Or her."

Lauren cleared her throat. Matt could almost hear her mental gears grinding. Finally she said, ''Marc Lekander. It was Marc Lekander. I couldn't have asked anyone else to do something like this. I don't expect you to understand.''

Thirty-four

In an alley off First Avenue in downtown Seattle, three blocks from Pioneer Square, hung a vague rendering of a lion's head on a musical staff, all in shivering blue neon. The sign marked the entrance of the Blue Lion Club, which occupied the basement of a dismal nineteenth-century brownstone that had seen service as a whorehouse, a flophouse, and a warehouse. Few tourists ever saw the place, unless they happened to be inveterate lovers of the blues, the kind willing to brave an alley that was dark and unencouraging even in the light of a summer noon hour.

Tyler Brownlee was such a lover. For more than half his life, the Blue Lion had been his second home.

He parked his Yukon on Cherry Street, the closest spot he could find. He walked across Pioneer Square to Yesler Way, twining through a horde of tourists, office workers, street people, and pigeons, his guitar case brushing his leg, the heels of his snakeskin boots popping satisfyingly against the brick pavement. People gave way before him like the Red Sea before Moses. They stared at him as if he was someone famous, a big-time musician, maybe. Tyler loved it.

Today was Friday, June 6, and the noon rush was in full swing, the weather warm and bright. Lunch-goers in shirtsleeves and sundresses thronged to the entrances of fancy restaurants sprinkled among dusty antique shops, furniture boutiques, galleries, and import shops. Less discerning customers crowded into bars and hamburger joints, or sat at sidewalk tables to sip microbrews and people-watch. The air smelled of greasy cooking, salt water, and seaweed.

This was *old* Seattle, a place of cobblestones and squat Victorian buildings. Despite the bulbous presence of the King Dome a few blocks to the south and a vertical clutter of skyscrapers to the north, a visitor could squint his eyes and slip backward a hundred years, to a time when tall-masted ships crowded the piers along Alaskan Way and horse-drawn hansoms clattered around the Square.

Tyler had grown up near here in the International District, in a cramped apartment house known as the Klondike Hotel, which had catered to sea captains in its heyday, according to the local lore. He'd attended school within spitting distance of the interchange of I-5 and I-90, under which he'd taken his first hit of dope and gotten laid for the first time. He'd hung out in Rizal Park and roamed the surrounding neighborhoods, doing what streets kids do, always hoping not to get caught, often succeeding. He knew this neighborhood and its secrets. Nothing could surprise him here.

Ignoring a small, hand-lettered sign on the door that said CLOSED, Tyler trotted down the stairs to the entrance of the Blue Lion, shouldered through another door and paused a moment to let his eyes adjust to the gloom. Tables clustered around a low stage, each with a potted candle planted in the lid of a Kerr jar. Plumbing pipes and heating ducts ran overhead, painted black. Onstage, a band rehearsed its gig for tonight, seven pieces, including the front man.

Tyler recognized the voice immediately, a voice with a black man's ring and a touch of the gospel in it, even though the face that it came from was white. This was one of Tyler's idols, none other than the great Curtis Salgado from Portland.

Tyler closed his eyes and savored that voice as it waded through a doleful song about a woman who breaks her man's heart and immediately takes up with another, just to pour salt in her old lover's wounds. Low-down stuff, Tyler thought, and full of emotion—vintage Salgado. Then came a harp solo, with Salgado blowing out notes that hung in the air like the smell of ozone during an electrical storm. The sound nearly moved Tyler to tears. *This* was what Tyler wanted for himself—a band this good, a front man like Curtis.

This and Lauren Bowman, of course.

Someone touched his arm, a shrunken man in his mid-seventies, wearing a frayed apron and carrying a tray—Packy Barker, the owner of the Blue Lion since long before Tyler was born. He wore a week-old beard that looked like aluminum filings. He had a glass eye.

"What'dja do to your hand?" Packy asked, a cigarette bouncing on his lip.

"Got it bit. Hurt like hell, too."

"What was it—a dog?"

"Yeah, a dog," Tyler answered, smirking. "Big one, too. Big teeth. Had to cut its throat."

"That's too bad," Packy said. "I like dogs." He poked a thumb toward a rear corner. "The Ranger's waitin' for you at his usual table. Want a beer or sum'n, a sandwich?"

"Give me a Red Hook, nothing else."

"You got it."

Tyler walked to a table buried in shadow, just as Salgado and his band took a break to discuss how to play this or that passage. If not for the orange dot of the Ranger's cigarette, Tyler wouldn't have noticed that the table was occupied. The old man possessed an uncanny ability to blend into the background of wherever he happened to be, a kind of behavioral camouflage.

"I've been trying to reach you since yesterday," the Ranger said, his oily eyes glittering. "Why didn't you call me back?"

"I . . . uh, I've been real busy. We've had some developments." Tyler's face grew hot, and his stomach cramped the way it always did whenever the Ranger called him to task for some shortcoming. "Arnie's hanging it up, quitting the business. We're doing our last drop-offs together, having one last payday." He leaned his guitar against the table, pulled out a chair and sat. And acted casual, or tried to. "I guess this means I go it alone from now on. Should be an adventure."

The Ranger let a tense silence endure as he lit a fresh cigarette. "What aren't you telling me?" he asked.

Tyler felt his throat constrict, but at that moment Packy Barker showed up with his beer. "It's on the house," Packy gruffed, dropping the mug on the table. He made a production of lighting the stubby candle on the table, then shuffled away.

"I . . . nothing," Tyler responded to the Ranger's question. "I'm not holding anything back from you. What's this about, anyway? I thought we were going to listen to some music, relax a little."

The Ranger sucked smoke from his cigarette and blew a cloud across the guttering candle. "Rainy tells me you went into Lauren's house night before last. Says you forced her to drop some roofies in the food, put Lauren and her girl to sleep. Then you snuck in and dipped your wick."

Tyler sipped his beer, even smiled in his crooked, noncommittal way. "I couldn't wait any longer. I needed a taste, that's all. I went in, did my thing, got the hell out. Everything's cool, I assure you."

"You needed a *taste*?"

"Yeah, that's all it was. I've been waiting so long for her, you know? All these years. I had to find out what it was going to be like."

"So, what did you think? Is she worth it?"

Tyler felt a warm tingle in his balls, a stirring. "She's something else, man," he replied, grinning all the way now, something he rarely did. "She's everything you've always said she'd be. She's the *world*, man."

The Ranger's face twisted into a savage scowl, its furrows deepening and darkening. "You broke a rule, you silly son of a fuck. You acted without clearing it with me."

Tyler gulped. "It wasn't any big deal. I had to get the video into the house anyway—that was part of the plan. I just elaborated on the plan a little."

The Ranger's hand shot under the table and grabbed a fistful of Tyler's gonads. Red pain burst into his abdomen and shot upward into his throat, causing him to spill his beer on the table. "You don't elaborate on the rules, boy. You follow them to the letter. The rules are all you've got going for you, and you're not smart enough yet to change them. You hear me?" The fist tightened, and the pain in Tyler's stomach grew redder.

"I . . . hear you."

The *rules*.

Since his early boyhood, Tyler had lived according to the Ranger's rules. The rules governed how long he practiced on his guitar every day, how many songs he would write about Lauren every week, how he went about scouting out "lovers" for the old man. The foremost rule said simply, *Nobody's rules matter except the Ranger's*.

He'd never taken a hit of heroin, even though he sold the stuff to the tune of megabucks per year. He'd never stored dope in his house. He'd never dealt with anyone he didn't know, either on the buying end or the selling end. And he'd never gone on spending sprees, lest he attract unwanted attention. *Rules.*

Only when he'd broken the rules had he gotten into any real trouble, as had happened when he was fifteen. He and a pair of homeboys had burgled a sporting goods store, hoping to steal guns, a violation of the Ranger's rule against breaking the law without getting his clearance and guidance. They'd gotten caught, of course. And because this was his third offense, Tyler had drawn an eighteen-month sentence in a juvey lock-up, another year in a halfway house. What a lesson *that* had been.

Tough though the Ranger's rules were, Tyler had reached the understanding early in life that the rules represented *freedom*— freedom from the restrictions imposed by the lame-os who mistakenly believed that they ran the world. The Ranger's rules gave a boy from the streets a shot at the good life without regard for conventional notions about right and wrong. The Ranger's rules let a boy take whatever he wanted, within carefully constructed parameters, naturally—like tasting certain forbidden pleasures. Like chasing certain forbidden dreams.

The Ranger pulled his hand back, and Tyler coughed, tried to breathe again. The pain took its sweet time going away.

"If you'd done what I told you and sent the tape in with Rainy, nobody would've had any real reason to suspect her," the Ranger growled. "But no. You go in and do the root dance on Lauren. Now everybody knows for sure that someone got in, that someone *else* had to turn off the security for him so he could do it. They start lookin' at Rainy, wondering about her, asking questions. Now we can't use her anymore, 'cause she's worthless to us."

"I'm sorry."

"Yeah. You're sorry, all right."

Tyler studied the white bandage on his hand, saying nothing for a long time. Finally: "I guess Rainy probably told you what happened to the bugs, huh? That Matthew Burgess dude brought in some lame-o to sweep the place."

"So I heard."

"If you want, I can chop him, get him out of the picture."

"Not yet."

"How about Rainy? Should I bring her in so you can do her? It'd make a nice video for Lauren."

The Ranger scowled again, causing Tyler to expect his fist

under the table again. Tyler turned sideways in his chair, a reflex. "You see, that's why you need to check with me before you do anything," the Ranger said in a chiding tone. "Doing Rainy would be stupid, because both you and I have been talking to her on our phones. You know what that means, don't you?"

Tyler screwed his eyes shut, nodded. Phone logs. If Rainy were to turn up dead or missing, the cops would look at the phone logs and start checking the numbers she'd called, as well as the ones from which she'd gotten calls. They would find the numbers of the cellular phones that Tyler and Ray Brownlee used. And then they would come sniffing at the house in Alki, because this was where the accounts were billed. They would ask questions, poke around. The Brownlees didn't need this.

"But that's not all we have to worry about," the Ranger added. "Someone *else* bugged Lauren's house, someone we don't know. We can't make our final move until . . ." He cut himself off.

Tyler looked up and saw Curtis Salgado walking toward this corner of the club, a man in his forties, heavy-browed and well-built. He wore his dark hair in a short ponytail, and looked as if he would be a good ally in a bar fight.

"Excuse me," the singer said, approaching the table. "Packy just told me that someone special is here, a man named Ray Brownlee. That man wouldn't be you, would it?"

"Might be."

"Didn't they used to call you 'the Blues Ranger' down in Portland?"

"That was a long time ago."

Salgado extended a hand, and the Ranger shook it. "People still talk about you, know that? The way you played the guitar, the way you sang. I even heard you a couple times when I was a kid—dirty little place in the Hollywood District, on Sandy Boulevard. Can't quite remember the name. I was too young to be in there, but I found a way in. No way I was gonna miss the Blues Ranger."

"That could be," the old man said, tapping his calloused fingertips on the table. "I played most every blues joint in town."

Salgado smiled. "Are you still doin' it?"

"Packy asks me in now and then, when nothin' else is doin'. I can sit in on bass or lead guitar, but I don't do much singing anymore."

Tyler listened to them chat, a pair of seasoned bluesmen, and tried to work up the nerve to say something. This was *Salgado*, for crying out loud, one of the best in the country. He heard Salgado say that at least once a year he did a gig at the Blue Lion for old times' sake, a favor to Packy in return for Packy's having given him work before anyone knew who the hell Curtis Salgado was. Which wasn't exactly news to Tyler, of course. He'd heard the man perform more times than he could count.

Salgado and the Ranger traded words about people they'd known in the business, common acquaintances—drummers, keyboard guys, horn men, singers, agents. Tyler expected that at any moment the Ranger would introduce his son, and say something like, *This is the future. This is the man, the Blues Beast. You ought to give him a listen.*

But the Ranger never said it. Tyler felt hollow, as if some mean little animal had begun to eat him from the inside out. The Ranger had promised that the day would come when someone important would hear the Blues Beast play, someone like Curtis Salgado. Someone who could help him along, make his dream come true. Why shouldn't that day be today?

Tyler decided to seize the moment. He introduced himself to Salgado, said that he too was a bluesman. And yes, he was the Blues Ranger's son. It just so happened that he had his ax with him, if Curtis had a minute.

Thirty-five

Lauren saw Rod Welton and waved, but he didn't yet see her. He stood outside the entrance of the Seattle Art Museum, scanning the crowd of passersby, just as she was doing. A three-story sculpture of black metal towered over his head, something that looked like a man with a hammer, its motorized arm pounding away at something. It was a monstrosity that someone had passed off as art, in Lauren's opinion.

Finally Rod saw her and loped across First Avenue. They hugged. He wanted to know what was so important that they couldn't talk about it over the phone. Unable to think of any way to soften the message, she blurted it out. Ian Prather and Vera Kemmis were dead, murdered. Rod's face went pale as milk. With jittering fingers he lit a cigarette.

"How?" he wanted know.

She slipped her arm into the crook of his elbow and steered him to the top of the Harbor Steps, a descending walkway that consisted of five concrete plateaus connected by gently graded stairs. They started downward toward Western Avenue, past a large Asian-import retailer called Amandari. Along the way were fountains that provided the comforting sound of running water. They sat next to one in the shade of a potted tree. Pigeons strutted around them, begging for food, and the sound of water covered their voices.

She told him all that had happened since she'd last seen him—Ian's murder, her own rape, her discovery of the video of Vera's last moments. She told him that she feared for his life, since it was now brutally clear that someone had undertaken to kill the people associated with the raid on the BioCenter. Megan, Ian, and Vera had all become victims, so a reasonable person could only assume that either Rod or Lauren herself would be next. She told him that she'd acquired a bodyguard.

"We don't have a clue about who this person is or why he's doing these things," she told him, trying to keep her voice strong and steady. "It could be anybody." She tightened her grip on his arm. "So be careful, damn it. Now might be a good time to take a vacation. You probably have some time coming, don't you?"

"I'm more worried about *you*," Rod said. "Where's this bodyguard you mentioned? Why isn't he doing his job?"

She confessed that she'd sneaked out of her house, that she'd been going stir-crazy. Anyway, no one could hurt her in broad daylight in downtown Seattle. Cops were everywhere.

Rod finished his cigarette, tamped it out and flicked the butt into the potted tree. "Maybe you should take a vacation, too," he said. "Might be a good time to get out of the country."

"That's what Marc says. He thinks I should hole up in the Lekanders' house at Poipu Beach."

"Where's that?"

"The island of Kauai, in Hawaii. They also have a place in Pedregal, outside Cabo San Lucas. But I can't leave. You know that."

"Why not? Who needs the aggravation of being stalked and slaughtered?"

"This is where I live, Rodney. This is where I work. I have unfinished business here."

"For the movement?"

"Yeah, for the movement."

Rod stood, pushed his hands into his pants pockets. "I understand," he said. "I feel exactly the same way."

Thirty-six

Tyler Brownlee hardly noticed the ache in his bitten hand. He finished the guitar solo with a flourish that featured a spurt of notes high on the neck of the Stratocaster and a crashing C-minor chord. Then he switched off the amp, unplugged the guitar and hopped off the stage. He walked to the rear table where the Ranger sat with Curtis Salgado.

"So, what's the verdict?" he asked. "Is the Blues Beast for real, or what?" He saw Salgado look to the Ranger, who looked at nobody. The silence became burdensome.

Salgado got up from the table. "You're looking for a paying arrangement somewhere, is that it?"

"Yeah. Aren't we all?"

"Look, man—I'm gonna say this right out, okay? I respect you enough not to jerk your chain. You do a nice job with your ax, nice for somebody who just wants to have fun, jam with his friends, like that. But there's a whole lot of really talented guitarists out there, guys who do blues, jazz, rock, and they're all lookin' for gigs, hear what I'm sayin'? A lot of them are playin' for peanuts all up and down the Coast. Unless you're a Johnny Lang or a Terry Robb, you really can't expect to find a paying arrangement—not these days."

Something thudded in Tyler's heart. "Are you saying I'm no good?"

"All I'm saying is, you're not a Johnny Lang or a Terry Robb.

That's why you need to keep it cool, keep it loose. And don't quit the day job, man.''

"Don't quit the day job?"

"That's all I'm saying."

They stood a moment, facing each other in the tenebrous air of the Blue Lion. Onstage, Salgado's band gathered around their instruments to resume rehearsing. "Hey, I gotta go," Salgado said. He turned to the Ranger and extended a final handshake. "I enjoyed meeting you, Mr. Brownlee. It was a real honor."

Tyler unhooked his guitar strap, set the Stratocaster on a table, and headed for the exit, his boot heels popping on the hard floor. Pieces of cold truth came together in his mind and knitted like broken bones. Anger welled up in his chest, for the truth was ugly, hateful. He understood now that he'd been a chump for most of his life.

Salgado and his group began tuning up and testing microphones, so Tyler wasn't sure whether he actually heard the Ranger call his name. It didn't matter. The Blues Beast was his own man now. And the Blues Beast felt like killing somebody.

Thirty-seven

The following week tested Matt Burgess' patience and physical stamina, not to mention his civility. At Alex Ragsdale's suggestion, he tried to set up a "security protocol" to ensure Lauren Bowman's safety, which meant providing armed protection around the clock in her home and an escort whenever she left the estate. The problem was that Lauren wouldn't cooperate. She failed to give him advance notice of her intentions to go somewhere, which was bad enough. She also sneaked off on her own whenever she got a chance, which defeated the very concept of a security protocol. When Matt challenged her on the issue, she said simply that she valued her privacy and her freedom of movement. She had work to do, a life to live. She could not and *would* not seek anyone's permission to come and go from her own house.

"You promised no more games," Matt reminded her. "I can't do my job if you won't help."

She gave him a pained look. "I can't become someone else, Matt. I'm sorry. Let's just try to work around each other, okay?"

Work around each other. Like he was here to redecorate. He cursed himself for having let Royal rope him into this mess, but he kept his temper. He threw no magazines.

He spent most of Monday and Tuesday interviewing the people on the list that Rags had given him a week earlier—the various gardeners, housekeepers, and maintenance people who trooped into and out of the estate on a daily basis, even the per-

sonal trainer and the florist. He told each person that he was a
security consultant whom Ms. Bowman had hired to check out
some threatening phone calls she'd received. *Can you think of
anyone who'd want to hurt Ms. Bowman for any reason?* he'd
asked. And each had given him an emphatic "No." Matt had
seen no twitching eyelids, no quickly averted eyes, none of the
small signals that cops look for.

On Wednesday he'd made the acquaintance of Rod Welton,
who'd arrived in the evening to have dinner with Lauren and the
Lekanders. Welton came across as a quiet, no-nonsense type
whom you could confide in and count on—exactly what you need
in a juvenile probation officer. Matt liked him immediately, in
spite of his way-out views on animal rights. After dinner, the two
men sipped a couple of tall Jack Daniels over ice and leaned
against the rail of the deck outside Lauren's sitting room. They
talked frankly.

Matt expressed his frustration over trying to set up a security
protocol when he should be out looking for a certifiable psycho-
sexual killer. He confessed that he had no idea what he would do
if by some miracle he caught the guy. He felt inadequate, untrained for what he'd promised Royal he would do and what
Lauren had hired him to do. And he was worried about going to
jail for obstructing justice.

Rod volunteered to help in any way he could. He also mentioned that he was licensed to carry a concealed firearm.

"I might be a ragged old Vietnam vet, but I'm not totally
useless," Rod added. "I can be here at six on any weekday and
pull a shift until seven the next morning. I can work all weekend,
if you need me. Just be advised that my beeper might go off
anytime day or night, and I might need to go out and deal with
some poor juvey's personal crisis."

"I thought you animal-rights types frowned on carrying guns,
except for a few wild-eyed extremists like Ian Prather."

"We frown on it, yeah. But sometimes we don't have any
choice, do we?"

Matt slapped him on the back and shook his hand. "Consider
yourself signed-up."

Matt had also enlisted Alex Ragsdale's help with the security
protocol, but Rags was a family man with a big job and a mul-
titude of domestic responsibilities, meaning that he could only be
on hand two or three hours a day at the maximum. So Matt him-

self shouldered the main load of guarding Lauren Bowman. He moved bag and baggage into her guest room, in order to be close. He accompanied her whenever she left the estate during the day—whenever she didn't sneak off without him, that is. And he monitored the comings and goings of her coterie and household staff. It was exhausting, frustrating work, a 24–7 life. Matt acquired a new appreciation of the bodyguard profession.

Despite the fact that he lacked a concealed weapons permit, he started carrying his SIG Sauer in a shoulder holster. Rags assured him that obtaining a permit from the King County Sheriff's Office would pose no problem for a former Seattle cop, but Matt recoiled against the idea of submitting paperwork and answering bureaucrats' questions. Moreover, carrying a gun without a card paled next to the much bigger crime of obstructing justice, the one he committed every time he took a waking breath.

It was Thursday before he managed to land an audience with Gabe Granger, thanks to the personal intervention of Georgia Pichette, Lauren's executive assistant—a twenty-minute "squeeze-in" during a lull in the great man's heavy schedule. Lauren promised Matt that she would stay in her study while he was away, where she was at work on an article for *Animal Realm*.

Granger's head butler, Manuel Esparza, showed Matt into the study in the rear of the main villa, a long room with an expanse of glass that fronted the Sound. It had a fifteen-foot ceiling, lots of teak paneling and several groupings of wine-red leather furniture. The mounted head of an African Cape buffalo glowered down from the wall with eyes that looked alive enough to give Matt the creeps.

Everywhere stood gleaming trophies that proclaimed Granger's prowess as a racer of speedboats. Here and there hung framed photos of him atop some mountain summit, shots of him with the governor or some congressman, portraits of his relatives, candids of Lauren.

Sitting behind his curved teak desk, Granger seemed the apotheosis of the go-get-'em real-estate tycoon, the poor kid who'd made good. Subtlety and restraint were concepts unknown to him. Today he wore a tan suede blazer, a large diamond ring and a gold ID bracelet.

"Mr. Burgess, nice to see you," he said, getting up to shake Matt's hand. "Sit anywhere. Want a drink or something?" With his bull shoulders and barrel chest, he looked as if he'd lettered in football back in high school, or maybe the hammer throw. He looked fit and strong.

"No thanks," Matt said, taken aback. It was eleven in the morning. "I appreciate your seeing me. I know how busy you are." Based on his first brush with Granger, the last thing he'd expected was courtesy.

"I understand you're a security guy, and you're working for my wife," Granger said, pouring himself a scotch. "Something about threatening phone calls?"

Matt gave him the canned spiel, then asked whether he could think of anyone who'd want to harm Lauren. Did she have any enemies in the business world, for example? Was there a disgruntled former employee or associate, someone who'd lost a bidding war with her for some property? Or any customers who weren't happy with what Lauren had sold them?

"No, nothing like that," Granger answered, lowering himself into a leather armchair near the one Matt sat in. "If you ask me, it's far more likely to be someone in that legion of weirdos she hangs around with." He smiled broadly, his capped teeth standing out against his tanned face. "Lauren and I don't see eye-to-eye on some things, and animal rights is just one of them. But I'm sure you've heard chapter and verse on that."

"How much do you know about her associates in the animal-rights community?" Matt asked.

"More than I want to. When we were first married, I made a real effort to understand those people. I went to some of their meetings, just to find out what they were all about, even gave them some money. Unfortunately, it didn't take me long to conclude that they're a bunch of sorry-ass nutcases. I made the mistake of trying to woo Lauren away from them, tried to talk sense to her. And that was when things started to go downhill for us." He sipped his scotch, causing the ice cubes to tinkle.

"Forgive me for asking, but how did you and Lauren come to be an item? You seem so—*different* from each other."

Granger laughed. "That's the understatement of the fucking century, my friend. I could say, 'Opposites attract,' but that would be just a skosh too simple, wouldn't you say? It's never that cut and dried between a man and a woman, is it?"

"No, it's not." How well Matt knew.

Granger drained his drink and chewed on an ice cube. "For starters, she's attracted to he-men types—adventurers, sportsmen, guys with muscles and guts. She enjoys glamor, excitement, going places. I'm no shrink, but I'd bet a pile of money that it's got something to do with the way she was raised. Her mother was some kind of religious zealot, and she kept her kid on a tight leash. Until Lauren got out on her own, she lived a pretty drab life." He chomped another ice cube and swallowed it. "She's never talked much about her childhood, and I only know what I've managed to piece together over time. But I think I can make an educated guess and say that she's attracted to the type of man her mother would've hated—the kind of guy who goes out and makes his own life. Her mother liked quiet little men with Bibles in their pockets, whose idea of fun was the weekly choir practice. Lauren, on the other hand, likes men who climb mountains and build empires."

"*Your* kind of man," Matt said.

"I married her, right?"

Matt nodded.

"The problem, of course, is that she only likes a man until she gets to know him," Granger went on. "It doesn't take her long to start noticing his shortcomings, like he enjoys a good steak, or he considers it relaxing to fish for Chinook out in the Sound, or he tells politically incorrect jokes. I'm a special kind of ogre, you see, because I like to hunt African game animals. You can just imagine how this goes down with Lauren's space-cadet friends."

But hadn't she known about Gabe's tastes and proclivities before she married him? Matt asked. Gabe Granger's exploits weren't exactly unknown to the readers of Seattle newspapers. His pals included people like Ted Turner and Mario Andretti. How could she *not* have known?

"She thought that she could change me," Granger answered, his expression darkening. "She actually thought she could make me over into somebody she approved of. Can you believe that shit?"

Matt could believe it.

"I don't know why I'm telling you all this," Granger said, "because it's really none of your business, is it?"

"No, I guess not."

Granger got up and went back to the wet bar to freshen his drink. "About the other day," he said. "Sorry I acted like such an asshole. I didn't have any right to insult you like that."

"Hey, we all have our moments."

"I still love my wife, you know. Until recently, I actually held on to the hope that I'd get her back someday. But that hope's gone now. I've accepted the fact that I've lost her for good, and it's not an easy pill to swallow, Mr. Burgess. Sometimes I get testy, you know? Maybe even a little jealous."

Matt accepted the apology.

"Now tell me what's *really* going on," Granger said. "This isn't about crank calls, is it?"

Matt suddenly wished he'd accepted a drink instead of the apology. "I don't know what you mean," he said.

To which Gabe Granger replied that he wasn't blind. He'd seen folks coming and going at the guest house, their heads hung low, their faces ashen, as if they were attending a funeral. The police had visited not once but twice, wanting to talk about one of Lauren's friends, Megan Reiner, who was missing. Any idiot could see that something major was afoot. Granger was willing to bet that it concerned the raid on the research laboratory a couple of weeks ago.

"As much as it pains me to say this, I can see Lauren being mixed up with something like that," Granger said. "She's become an out-and-out radical you know. And she hangs out with a crowd who thinks it's noble to bust up property to get their point across. That's what this is about, isn't it?"

Matt cringed. "I really can't tell you anything more than I already have. It's a matter of confidentiality. I hope you understand."

Granger frowned at him. "I hope you find whatever it is you're looking for, Mr. Burgess."

"Thanks, You've been helpful." Matt got to his feet.

"By the way, you're not fucking her, are you?"

Matt blinked. "No, Mr. Granger, I'm not."

"Good. Because that would complicate things for you, maybe even screw up your life. Take it from somebody who knows." He shook Matt's hand with a grip like a blacksmith's, then showed him to the door. "One last word of advice: If you're trying to figure Lauren out, don't believe anything she tells you. I've learned this through on-the-job training. Look to her past, her childhood in Portland. That's where all her secrets are—the ones that count, anyway."

Matt paused in the doorway of the study. "Is that how you figured her out?"

Granger snorted and knocked back the rest of his scotch. "I stopped trying to do that a long time ago."

Thirty-eight

Richardson Zanto walked into the Blue Lion Club and sat at the bar. The crowd was sparse, for the club had opened only half an hour earlier, and the entertainment wasn't due to start for three hours yet.

"What's it gonna be, young fella?" the bartender asked.

"I'm looking for somebody," Zanto said. "I'm told he spends time here." He pulled a snapshot from the pocket of his jeans and laid it on the bar.

The bartender picked the picture up and stared at it with his one good eye. It was a candid shot of a young man on a huge Harley Davidson motorcycle, a man with flowing blond hair, a square jaw, and a strange, handsome meanness in his face.

"Where did you get this?"

"A friend of mine lent it to me," Zanto lied. In truth he had taken the picture himself several days earlier, while standing on Alki Beach, using a powerful telephoto lens. He'd been surveilling the man whom he'd followed from the Bowman-Granger mansion a week ago, watching him come and go from a nondescript house in Alki, taking note of his habits and movements. More than once he'd followed him here to the Blue Lion, but Zanto hadn't risked venturing into the club, lest the blond man notice him and make further surveillance dangerous. The time had come to find out who this guy was, *what* he was.

"Who're you?" the old man demanded, his real eye full of suspicion, the glass one full of nothing.

"Name's Rick Wilson," Zanto answered, offering his hand across the bar. He wore black jeans, a black sweatshirt with the sleeves cut off, and a black Greek fisherman's cap—clothes that suggested a familiarity with the hard life of the street. He'd let his beard grow out to stubble. He could have been an aging poet or a painter, a roadie for a band, or a grifter. "You?"

"Packy Barker. I own this place. You want sum'n to drink?"

"I'll take a beer."

"Does it matter what kind?"

"Nah."

"Didn't think so." Packy drew a beer and set it before Zanto on a cocktail napkin, watched as Zanto took a sip. "You some kind of cop?"

Zanto smirked. "Do I look like a cop?"

"Looks don't mean shit anymore. I've seen cops you'd swear was junkies."

"I'm no cop," Zanto said, staring Packy hard in the eye.

"What do you want with this kid?"

"I need to talk to him, that's all. You know him?"

"Sure I know him. But you don't want to, believe me."

"Why's that?"

"Because he's a fuckin' freak, that's why. He's as likely to stick a blade in your gut as buy you a beer. It all depends on what side of the bed he got up on."

"Have you known him a long time?"

Packy whispered a curse, fetched a shot glass and poured himself a shot of Jameson's Irish whiskey. He threw it down and cringed from the liquid heat. "I've known him since he was a little kid. He does a gig here once a week, on Sundays—pick-up band, strictly amateur. I don't pay them, but they don't care. It's a way to get experience in front of a crowd, work on your licks, learn how to play the blues."

Zanto nodded. More than once during the past week he'd seen the blond man carry a guitar case. "What else can you tell me about him?"

Packy scowled, shook his head. "I must be gettin' stupid in my old age, talkin' about this shit."

"Nobody needs to know you ever told me anything," Zanto said.

Packy poured himself another shot and disposed of it. His good eye became a little bleary as he sized Zanto up again, more thoroughly this time. He must have seen something in Zanto's face that he liked. He started to talk, keeping his voice low. Every few minutes he broke off to fill an order for drinks, as the crowd was starting to grow.

The kid in the picture was Tyler Brownlee, Packy confirmed, the son of a man named Ray Brownlee, who himself was something of a blues legend in these parts. Some thirty years ago, Ray had begun dividing his time between Portland, his hometown, and Seattle, playing any joint that would give him a gig. The Blues Ranger, he'd called himself. Eventually he'd moved to Seattle and taken up residence here full time.

Rumors had always swirled around Ray Brownlee, like flies around a turd. He was into drugs, some people had whispered, not merely as a user, as many blues musicians were, but as a dealer. Others had whispered about blacker crimes, like murder and manslaughter, maybe worse. But the Blues Ranger had never done any jail time that anyone knew of, and no matter what sins he might have committed in his private life, nobody could deny that he was a damn fine bluesman. His singing voice reminded old-timers of Walter Vinson, the famed front man for the Mississippi Sheiks, a down-and-dirty Chicago blues outfit. His guitar work was a cross between Eric Johnson's and Buddy Guy's. As if this wasn't enough, he could play a stand-up bass that brought to mind the great Roscoe Beck. The Blues Ranger was the real deal.

"So—did you believe the rumors?" Zanto asked.

"I always got the feeling that old Ray had a dark side to his life that he kept to himself," Packy replied. "It had nothin' to do with the rumors. It was just a *feeling*. I never had any real knowledge that he's ever done anything ugly to anybody." Packy shook a cigarette from a pack of Camels and lit it with a potted candle that sat on the bar.

"I take it the kid's trying to follow in his old man's footsteps," Zanto said.

"Way I hear it, he never really had a choice."

Tyler Brownlee's mother was some junkie that Ray had fished out of the gutter and cleaned up, Packy explained. That was the kind of thing Ray Brownlee did, according to whispered rumors. He took young women in, cleaned them up, used them for a while, then turned them loose. It was like a hobby. Some guys restored broken-down cars; Ray restored broken-down girls.

For some reason Ray had decided to keep this one around longer than any of the rest. It was possible, Packy supposed, that he'd actually loved her, though this seemed unlikely. More likely he'd liked the idea of having a son. And a son needs a mother—in the early stages of his life, at least. Ray had installed the woman and the kid in the old Klondike Hotel, which stood not more than a dozen blocks east of the Blue Lion, on the other side of I-5. Though Ray hadn't lived there himself, he'd visited the apartment regularly to check up on little Tyler. And he'd put a guitar in the kid's hands before he was barely old enough to walk.

"All this would've been just peachy," Packy went on, "except the kid doesn't have his old man's musical talent. Oh, he's competent enough on guitar, but he's not *great*. And he can't sing worth a rusty fuck. The trouble is, playin' the blues is what he wants, 'cause that's what Ray has put in his head since he was a baby. He wants to make the big time, become another Stevie Ray Vaughn or a Robert Cray. And I'm here to tell you, it won't happen."

"He wouldn't be the first kid to watch a dream go pop," Zanto said. He took a token sip of his beer. "When I was a kid, I wanted to play center field for the Baltimore Orioles. I didn't see the light of reality until I was a senior in high school."

"Well, you're not Ty Brownlee," Packy said, squinting from the sting of cigarette smoke. "He don't take no for an answer. Not even from fate."

Like his father, Tyler had been the center of juicy rumors over the years. People talked about knifings, beatings, shootings, the possibility of his being in the drug business. Long story short, people were scared of him. And Packy was no exception.

"Why do you think I let him hang out here?" Packy asked. "I'm scared shitless of what he might do if I tried to throw his ass out."

"What does he do to support himself?"

Packy grinned around his cigarette. "If I knew the answer to that, do you think I'd actually tell you? I wouldn't want to be the one to put the finger on that evil son of a bitch."

Zanto grinned back and nodded. "Where can I find the Blues Ranger?" he asked.

Packy shook his head, signaling that he didn't know. Besides, Ray would never talk to him, he added. Ray wasn't what you'd call the outgoing type.

"What about the kid's mother? Is she still around?"

"Never really knew her. Only saw her once or twice in all the years I've known Ray." He thought a moment, a faraway look on his wrinkled face. "Her first name was Bonnie. Don't think I ever heard her last name. If you was to go over to the Klondike, you could ask the manager, a mean old fart named Ron Keen. He's been around here as long as I have. He'd remember her if you told him she was Tyler Brownlee's mother. He might even know if she's still alive."

Zanto pulled a frayed notepad from his jeans pocket and wrote the name with a stubby pencil. "What about friends and acquaintances?"

"He don't have any friends, not even the guys in the band. They only get together when they practice and when they play their gigs. I've heard some of 'em say they wish they could be rid of him."

"Mmmm. Anything else I should know?" Zanto dug for money to pay for his beer.

"Shit, you should know enough by now to stay away from that son of a bitch," Packy said. "By the way, he calls himself the Blues Beast. That should tell you sum'n."

"Thanks for the conversation," Zanto said, laying money on the bar. "Like I said, nobody'll ever know we talked."

He walked toward the door, thinking about the music that had accompanied the videotaped scene of Megan Reiner's murder. He'd heard it himself through microphones hidden in Lauren Bowman's house as Lauren played the video of Megan on her VCR. *Blues* music. And then, five days later, a man had visited the Bowman-Granger estate in the dead of night, a man who called himself the *Blues Beast*.

It figured. Only a beast could've done what someone had done to Megan Reiner.

Thirty-nine

Rod Welton showed up at the front door of Lauren Bowman's guest house promptly at 6:00 P.M., looking wrung-out, as if he'd put in a grueling day in the world of juvenile crime and punishment. When he saw Matt, he pulled the front of his frayed sport coat aside, showing off the old army .45 that hung in his armpit.

"Loaded for bear," he said with a grin.

Matt gave him a thumbs-up, and said, "Listen, I've got some errands to run, but I shouldn't be gone more than a couple of hours. Here's the number of my cell phone. Call me if you need me."

"Roger that," Rod said, sounding like the army vet that he was. "What does Lauren have on tap tonight?"

"She, you, and Jandee are having dinner at the Lekanders' around seven-thirty. They're planning to come back here immediately afterward. Shouldn't make for any problems. Just keep your eyes open during the trip there and back."

Rod patted the .45. "I'll be extra-careful. Today's Friday the thirteenth."

"You superstitious?"

"Let's say I don't take anything for granted anymore."

Matt drove to Ballard and went directly to Shorty's Tavern, found the parking lot already full. He glanced toward the marina and saw a long parade of boats lazing westward on Salmon Bay toward the Chittenden Locks, where they queued up for passage into Puget Sound. Sailboats, mostly—their hulls white against the rich background colors of a late afternoon in early summer. Seattle boasted more sailboats per capita than any other city in the country.

Matt hungered to fire up *Hyperion*'s iron sail, take her through the locks and point her bow toward the Strait of Juan de Fuca, with nary a thought about when or if he might return. But he couldn't do this, of course. A promise is a promise. He remembered Lauren Bowman looking at him with huge, troubled eyes: *"You're not going to leave, are you?"*

Inside the tavern a raucous crowd was well into its celebration of the weekend. The air was alive with country music and the warm smell of Cleo's killer fish and chips. Cleo herself, as usual, was behind the bar, slinging drinks and shouting orders to the help. Matt thought she looked as if she'd lost weight, though she was still an imposing figure in her huge embroidered apron. He caught her eye and motioned her into the back room.

"Heard anything from Royal?" he asked.

"No," she answered, lowering her eyes. "If you want to know the truth, Matt, I've given up. It's time to go on, pick up the pieces of my life."

"Jesus, don't talk like that. It's only been nine days. You don't give up on someone after only nine days."

Cleo looked up at him and gave him a smile that had a touch of bitterness in it. "That's nine eternities," she replied. "Remember what Royal always used to say?"

"He used to say a lot of things."

"A day is like a thousand years, and a thousand years is like a day. I think it's from the Bible. I never knew what in the hell it meant. But now I do." She wiped a tear away, tried to laugh. "How do you suppose Royal ever picked up a saying like that? In all his life he never cracked a Bible or saw the inside of a church."

Matt put his palm to her cheek. "I've been such an asshole," he said. "I should've been staying here with you, helping you through this." He wanted to tell her why he'd moved into Lauren Bowman's house, wanted to explain everything. But his promise of confidentiality to Lauren held him back.

"We all do what we have to do," Cleo said, as if she'd read his heart. "Someday you'll tell me all about it."

Matt took out his checkbook and wrote her a check for $2,500. "This is half of what I've been paid so far," he said, handing it to her. "Use it to hire someone to take care of the marina until I'm back." She didn't want to take it, so he folded the check and slipped it into a pocket of her apron. "Tack up a card on the bulletin board in the marina," he told her. "You'll snag some college kid who needs a job for the summer. Try to get somebody who knows which end of the boat is the front."

"It's the pointy end, right?"

Matt laughed and promised to keep in touch. He climbed the back stairs to his apartment and let himself in. The place looked like a foreign country, even though he'd been away less than a week. He checked his e-mail, found nothing of interest, then checked his refrigerator. Just as he'd suspected, an open quart of milk had soured. He poured it into the sink and tossed the carton into a recycling bin.

He went to the bathroom and stared at his own face in the mirror—a face craggier and more leathery than it should be for a man who was still three years shy of forty. If he looked closely, he could see a gray hair here or there amid the auburn thatch. He had bags under his eyes.

This was the face of a man who needed sleep, something that Matt Burgess had gotten precious little of during the past week. Despite the quiet comfort of Lauren Bowman's guest room, he'd found it impossible to drift off. Worries had buzzed in his head like bees in a hive. He'd worried about Royal and Cleo. He'd worried about Lauren, about going to jail. And he'd worried about a faceless killer who'd targeted the people closest to Lauren, a killer who might strike again, unless Matt himself found some way to stop him.

Within the past few days, he'd begun to feel the first telltale signs of total exhaustion—a heaviness in his limbs, difficulty in concentrating, a constant need to yawn. It wouldn't be long, he feared, before the dark animal went to work in earnest, hurling lightning bolts of anxiety at him and imposing long, crippling periods of self-doubt and hopelessness. Thinking about this very real possibility made him nauseous.

He opened the medicine cabinet, took out a prescription bottle that contained a hundred small, white pills. *Xanax*, said the label. Active ingredient: alprazolam, a powerful trank in one-milligram tablets. His therapist had prescribed the drug to combat the anxiety that had typically presaged an attack of depression, but only in doses of one or two milligrams per day over short periods.

Even relatively short-term usage could result in dependence, she'd warned, frightening Matt to his bone marrow.

In the past, he'd used Xanax in conjunction with his antidepressant, Wellbutrin, without negative side effects, but he'd always felt uneasy about doing so. Having been a drug cop, he'd seen the ravages of every kind of drug abuse—not just heroin, cocaine, and speed. He'd seen countless cases where people had derailed their lives with prescription drugs, sometimes unwittingly, often in combination with other prescription drugs.

But I've got to sleep, Matt told himself, his fist tightening around the bottle. He crammed it into his pocket.

His cell phone rang. It was Rags. "You. Me. Beer," Rags said. "I've got something for you. Name the place."

They rendezvoused half an hour later at the Red Hook Brewery, which occupied a corner in a cluttered industrial neighborhood near the shore of the Lake Washington Ship Canal. The tavern was a cozy room with four communal oak tables and a bar that accommodated six comfortably, eight in a pinch. A cluster of used living room furniture offered more seating around a vaguely art-deco fireplace. Matt liked the place for the relaxed atmosphere and the somber expressionistic oil paintings that hung on the walls.

He met Rags outside, and they went immediately to the bar and ordered pints of Red Hook hefeweizen. They found a pair of chairs near the fireplace and scooted close together so they could talk with a modicum of privacy.

"Here's the printout of the security system log for the Bowman-Granger estate," Rags said, showing Matt a thin bundle of papers. "None of the authorized parties logged in at any weird hours, so that's pretty much a dead end."

"Meaning that none of the gardeners or house cleaners or personal trainers tried to get into the place during their off-hours," Matt said.

"Right. The system wouldn't have let them in anyway, unless they'd somehow laid their hands on an override code. But the exercise wasn't a total waste. The log does show a system shut-off at ten-seventeen on the night of the fourth. That's a *total* shut-off, Burge, gate locks, auto-cameras, the works. It happened again a few hours later, which would've been in the wee hours of June 5th. It's like someone got in, stayed a while, then left."

Matt stared at the printout, focusing on the relevant lines.

"That's the night Lauren got raped," he said. "The video of Vera Kemmis' murder turned up in her bedroom the next morning."

"Exactly. And because it was a total shut-off, we've got no video record of the event, no picture of whoever came and went, so to speak."

Matt scratched his mustache and stared into space. "Are you thinking what I'm thinking?"

"I don't know about you, but I'm thinking about a certain Vulcan cook whose initials are Rainy Hales."

"It's *vegan*, Rags. Not *Vulcan*."

"Yeah, okay. But I've got more, yessiree. *Much* more." Rags tucked the sheaf of papers into his attaché case and pulled out a manila folder, which he opened to reveal yet more papers. "I took the liberty of doing a computerized background check of everybody on the list," he said.

"How in the hell did you bring that off without setting off all kinds of alarms?"

"I billed it to Lauren Bowman. It's perfectly natural. As far as ProGuard knows, she wants backgrounders on a couple of friends and everybody who works for her, right? No big deal, we see it all the time. Rich people need to know who they're dealing with."

"How much is it costing her?"

"Not important. Anyhow, I ran every name through a series of standard databases, like the ones the big credit-check companies use. Then I ran them through a couple of *non*standard ones, the kind that gives you public-record poop on criminal convictions and so forth."

"Find anything juicy?"

"You be the judge." Rags handed Matt two sheets stapled together, one labeled *Adrienne Hales* and the other *Marc Lekander*. "Don't waste your time with the speeding tickets," he said. "Go straight to the good stuff at the bottom."

Rainy Hales' sheet showed two convictions in the state of Washington for possession of small amounts of illegal substances, with suspended sentences and mandatory rehab for heroin addiction. It also showed a long list of charges and convictions for public intoxication, loitering, and shoplifting. If she'd done any time, the record didn't show it. Her latest brush with the law had occurred nearly four years ago, and she'd failed to show up for the court hearing on prostitution charges. Chances were good that the criminal justice system had simply forgotten about her by now, having bigger fish to fry.

According to Marc Lekander's sheet, the state of Washington convicted him for possession of marijuana in 1981 and gave him a suspended sentence. A year later the city police of Newark, New Jersey, busted him for possession of a small quantity of cocaine, upon which he pled guilty and received a suspended sentence with probationary rehab. Since then he'd had two convictions for driving under the influence, the latest having occurred five years ago.

"What do you suppose he was doing in New Jersey?" Matt wondered aloud.

"Attending Princeton. They threw him out after the drug beef. He transferred to U-Dub, but dropped out after a couple of years. Not what you'd call a dedicated academic."

"You got all this from a database?"

"Everybody's life is an open book these days," Rags said with a wry smile. "Kind of creepy, isn't it?"

Matt laced his fingers together and made twirlies with his thumbs. "So Marc Lekander has a past, but don't we all? I'm more concerned about Rainy Hales, frankly."

"As well you should be. A junkie is a junkie is a junkie, and who knows it better than you and I?"

Matt nodded. A junkie was weak. A junkie was susceptible to manipulation, blackmail. Some cops doubted that any junkie could ever recover fully and become a real person again, despite the occasional success story in the warm-and-fuzzy section of the newspaper. Matt had never been one of those cops, because he'd always believed in second chances. Yet, he couldn't deny that Rainy Hales' history of heroin addiction only strengthened his and Rags' suspicions about her. He no longer doubted that she was the mole in Lauren Bowman's household. Or *one* of the moles.

"So, what do we do?" he asked. "Lauren refuses to believe that Rainy would ever do anything to hurt her, never mind become a party to serial murder. As far as she's concerned, Rainy's part of the family and always will be."

"Maybe one of us should have a talk with Rainy," Rags suggested. "You know—give her some avuncular advice, point out a few realities, like the state of Washington still hangs people for murder. She might decide to unburden herself."

"Forget that. The woman is a sphinx. She'll only close her eyes and pretend you're not there."

"You got a better idea?"

Matt thought a moment, his eyes wandering around the crowd. He caught sight of a young blond dude at the bar, big and well-built, a short scar on his right cheek. With his shoulder-length hair and square jaw, he looked like a refugee from a soap opera. Despite the warm weather, he wore a black leather motorcycle jacket. For the tiniest moment his eyes met Matt's, but he quickly looked away and gulped a mouthful of beer.

Matt, too, looked away. Told himself that the guy hadn't been watching them. This was what lack of sleep could do to you, he figured—make you jumpy, make you start seeing things.

"Let's bird-dog her," Matt suggested, "find out who she hangs with, where she goes. Somebody in her crowd likes to butcher women and shoot footage of it. If we're lucky we just might spot a likely suspect. I mean, a guy who does that kind of stuff should stand out somehow, wouldn't you think?"

Rags liked the idea. He suggested that Matt notify him by phone just before Rainy left the estate tonight. Rags himself would tail her. If she went home, he would surveil her residence until she went to bed, then pick it up again in the morning.

Matt protested. This was the beginning of the weekend, and the Ragsdale kids needed their daddy. Matt wanted to do the tailing himself, inasmuch as he'd delegated security duties to Rod Welton for the evening.

"Negative," Rags said. "Your eyes look like a couple of sphincters, and you need to get some sleep. Besides, you know what all work and no play did to that kid named Jack."

Matt thought of the bottle of Xanax in his pocket. "Okay, but be careful. We're dealing with a certifiably evil dude here. You don't want to cross paths with him."

"Don't worry about me," Rags said with a wink. "Friday the thirteenth has always been my lucky day."

Forty

Tyler Brownlee eased his purple Harley Davidson Shovelhead to the curb, snapped off the headlight and killed the engine. In the driveway of the house where he'd lived for the past three years stood a United Van Lines moving truck, illuminated by a floodlight over the garage door. A trio of young men were muscling a few remaining cardboard boxes into the maw of the cargo bay. Next to the truck sat Arnie Cashmore's nondescript Nissan Altima.

Tyler strolled through the front door of the house into the dusky living room, which seemed huge and full of echo now that the furniture was gone. Arnie leaned against a bare wall with his hands deep in the pockets of his jeans, surveying the emptiness through his thick glasses, apparently deep in reflection. For some reason he wore the green visor that he normally only wore while cutting up loaves of black-tar heroin or doing bookkeeping.

"What brings you here?" Arnie asked. "Forget something?"

Tyler had moved out three days earlier, having transported the bulk of his belongings to a commercial storage facility—except for his precious posters of Lauren Bowman, of course. He'd taken up residence with the Ranger on the top floor of the warehouse, in a dingy corner room with just one small window. He'd hung the posters on the walls, even though the light was bad. Fortunately, the arrangement wouldn't last forever.

"Dropped in to say one last good-bye," Tyler said. "Also, I wanted to drop this off." He tossed Tyler a cellular phone. "The

Ranger and I have new ones, billed to some guy he knows, some crooked accountant. It's the guy who handles his money, I think.''

"Yeah. You can't run a heroin business without a cell phone. Or an accountant, either.''

Tyler chuckled and extended his hand. "Things are cool between us, right?''

Arnie shook hands. "Things are cool.''

At that moment one of the movers came through the door and handed Arnie an invoice. Everything was loaded and ready to go, the man said. Arnie signed the invoice and handed it back, along with three hundred-dollar bills—a healthy tip for each of the movers. The man thanked him enthusiastically and left, leaving the front door open. The truck's big engine grumbled to life, and the truck rolled out of the drive, leaving silence in its wake.

"I should probably be on my way,'' Arnie said, moving toward the door. "No sense hanging around this dump any longer.''

"You're headed off to your island now, right? What's the name of it again?''

"Martinique. It's in the Caribbean, French West Indies. I've bought a house on the north end of the island with a view of the ocean. You should come visit sometime.''

"Yeah, for sure. Like, you'll have room for me, right?''

"Room is one thing I'll have plenty of. And time, too. Lots of room, lots of time—all a man really needs. You'll need to brush up on your French, by the way.''

"No way I'm learning French, man. I've got all I can handle with English.''

They both laughed.

Tyler offered to drive Arnie to the airport, but Arnie said that he had some business to wrap up, something about arranging for the electronic transfer of a large sum to an offshore bank. For the past week he'd made the rounds to old friends and associates on Capitol Hill, saying his final good-byes, and he had a few left to see yet. He planned to spend a few days in the Mayflower Park Hotel, living the good life, the kind he'd avoided until now in order not to be conspicuous. His aim was to run up a $1,000 room service bill, get a little drunk, eat lobster every night. Arnie hadn't been drunk in years.

Tyler grinned with more than his customary commitment, a full grin this time. "You've done it,'' he said. "You've made your own reality, man. Want to know something? You're an inspiration, Arn. You're the proof that it's really possible. You've given me my faith back.''

Arnie Cashmore smiled a slow, sad smile and shook his head. ''I've been lucky,'' he said. ''I've sold drugs for fifteen years and haven't gotten caught or killed. Now I'm going to live like a tourist for the rest of my life and try to forget that any of it happened. I might succeed, I might not. That's all there is to it, Ty. Nothing mystical or miraculous. And it sure as hell isn't inspiring.''

''Well, I beg to differ,'' Tyler said. ''You've taught me a lot, and I'm grateful. You've been like a big brother to me. I'm going to miss you, know that?''

Arnie shrugged his bony shoulders. ''Yeah.'' He walked through the door onto the stoop, then paused and turned to stare at Tyler. ''You need to grow up, Ty. You need to start living in the real world.''

''What's that supposed to mean?''

''Forget about Lauren Bowman. Throw away all those pictures of her and all those posters you've made. Stop writing songs about her. And for God's sake, stop trying to get next to her. Find yourself a nice girl your own age, and get yourself a new dream, a *healthy* one.''

Tyler's blood began to rise. ''Why should you care who I love, man? Why is that so fucking important to you, anyway?''

''I don't want you to screw yourself up. This thing you've got for Lauren Bowman—it consumes you, makes you do stupid things. That's dangerous for a man in the heroin business.''

Tyler balled his fists, took a step forward. ''I can't just forget about her. She's all I've got.''

''Wrong. You've got your music, you're young. You've got a big stash of money, probably enough to last you a lifetime. If you were smart, you'd quit selling tar and find a blues singer who needs a guitar player. Maybe then you'd live to see twenty-five.''

''You don't know what the fuck you're talking about, Arnie. My music is shit, strictly amateur—and I've got that from somebody who knows. As a bluesman, I'm in the toilet. The only dream I've got left is Lauren. She's my reality, my destiny. That's the way it is.''

They stood for another moment, neither saying anything, each staring across the emptiness of the dim room. Then Arnie shrugged again, a gesture of frustration. He took off his green visor, looked at it briefly, and tossed it onto the bare floor of the living room. Then he gave Tyler a small wave and walked down the steps to the driveway. Without looking back, he got into his drab Nissan Altima and drove away, leaving Tyler Brownlee to believe that he would never see him again.

Forty-one

Matt studied his favorite painting in Lauren Bowman's collection, *Eight Bells*. When he'd first looked at it eleven days ago—eleven eternities, as he supposed Cleo Castillo might say—he'd gotten a sense of hard-to-see realities, of truth hovering beyond the eye's reach, obscured by mist and rain. He'd *felt* for those imperiled seamen. He'd felt their desperate need to sight the horizon through the storm's miasma so they could navigate their ship to safety. He'd been *one* of them.

Today the painting struck him altogether differently. Today the truth seemed brutally clear and unobscured. The storm itself was truth, together with the waves, the mist, and the ship. It was a truth that wouldn't compromise or cut you any slack. Either you faced it and dealt with it, or it killed you.

Rainy Hales was in the kitchen, betrayed by puttering sounds—an occasional clink of kitchen utensils, a soft thud of a cupboard door. Matt glanced at his watch, and saw that it was nearly nine o'clock. Rainy would soon leave for home.

No one else was in the house. Lauren Bowman and Jandee Vernon had left nearly two hours ago for dinner at the Lekander estate in The Highlands, accompanied by their new bodyguard, Rod Welton. Several times during the evening, Matt had felt the temptation to confront Rainy and tell her that he knew the truth, that she'd been working for whoever killed Megan, Vera, and Ian. But he'd held off, for he couldn't predict how she would react. Confronting her might simply put her on guard, cause her

to harden her defenses and take precautions against letting the
rest of the truth come out. For all Matt knew, she might pull out
a gun and blow his head off. Better to let her go on thinking that
she'd fooled everyone, he'd decided. Better to give her a chance
to lead them to the killer.

She appeared at the door of the sitting room, looking wraith-
like in a long calico dress, her dishwater-blond hair hanging limp
to her shoulders. She carried a valise, which Matt figured contained recipes or notes about how to prepare this or that vegan
dish. Without establishing eye contact, she informed him that she
was finished for the day, and because she didn't work on weekends except by special arrangement, she wouldn't see him again
until Monday. Did he need anything before she left?

Matt said no and thanked her. He smiled, but he doubted that
she saw it. She turned away and walked out the front door, the
valise pulled tight to one scant hip. Matt went to a window and
watched her get into her Saturn coupe, watched her drive toward
the front gate.

Does she really think we don't know? he wondered. *Does she
think we're idiots?*

He picked up a telephone and punched Rags' cell phone number.

"It's me," Rags said on the other end.

"She's on her way. She's heading out through the front gate."

"I'm all over it, buddy-boy. I'm parked down Jenkins Way
about a quarter of a mile. She'll come right past me, and I'll be
on her tail like ugly on a baboon's ass. Now do me a favor and
get some sleep."

"Be careful, Rags. Remember what we're dealing with here."

"When the day comes that I can't handle a skinny Vulcan
cook, I'm gonna hang it up."

"It's *vegan*, not Vulcan. And you know fucking well it's not
Rainy Hales I'm nervous about."

"Well, I'm nobody's weak sister myself, okay? I'll be fine."

"Call me if you need me."

"I will. Plus, I'll call you first thing in the morning and give
you a full report. Now stop your hand-wringing and hit the sack.
Someday we'll look back on all this and laugh."

"I hope you're right," Matt said, although he didn't believe
it for a minute.

After switching off the phone, he strolled out to the deck and gazed across Elliott Bay at the glittering skyline of Seattle. He wondered where Royal was at this very moment, and hoped that the old man wasn't in pain. The thought struck him that perhaps Royal had slunk off to die in darkness and privacy, like a decrepit old cat who knows that the end has come.

He checked the locks on the doors and made certain the windows were all closed tight. Then he went to the guest room that had been his home for the past week, sat on the bed and stared at the bottle of Xanax in his hand. Weariness swept over him, and he wanted nothing more than to fall back onto the mattress and sleep until the end of the world. But he knew that the moment he closed his eyes, his head would begin to hum with worries and anxiety. He would become hot and flinchy. The day's events would play inside his mind like a movie, over and over again, the volume too loud, the projector slightly out of focus. Sleep would be impossible, and his exhaustion would grow. *Unless* . . .

He looked again at the bottle in his hand.

Forty-two

Tyler strode into the circle of light where the Ranger sat with a guitar on his knee. A single bare bulb swung on a cord above the old man's head, the only source of light in the apartment. The Ranger stopped playing when he looked up and saw his son, causing an abrupt silence that hung in the air like a bad smell.

"It's time for Rainy," Tyler said.

"Is that so?"

"I need her now. And so do you."

The old man set aside his guitar and stubbed his cigarette into a mounded-over ashtray on the floor next to his chair. "Maybe you're right. Maybe that's what we both need."

"The phone logs don't matter anymore," Tyler said, feeling a new surge of eagerness. "If the cops look up who's talked to Rainy, they'll find the address of Arnie's place, but that's no big deal now, because the place is full of nothin'. And there's no record that I ever lived there. Arnie made sure all our records were sanitary—our driver's licenses, license plates, everything registered to some bogus corporation with a bogus address. Not even the lame-o who bought the place knows who we are, or where we are."

"Who do you think taught Arnie how to do all that?" the Ranger asked, squinting through the haze of cigarette smoke. "You're talking about forty years of experience here. You see, Arnie played it right by the book, did things exactly the way I told him to. And because of that, he never saw the inside of a jail cell—after his first stretch in OSP, that is. That should tell you something, Ty."

"Yeah, I know. I should be like Arnie, listen to you, do what you say."

"Have I ever steered you wrong?"

Tyler grimaced and stared at his snakeskin boots. "You told me that I'd be a great bluesman someday," he said. "And I believed you. What am I supposed to think now? You heard what Salgado told me—Don't quit your day job, he said. Do you think anybody ever said that to Robert Cray or Johnny Lang?"

The Ranger got to his feet and walked toward his son, his gait stiff and painful. Tyler glanced at him and winced, for he looked so very old, as if his bones might break under their own weight. He placed a cold hand on Tyler's neck.

"Like I've told you all your life, every man creates his own reality," the Ranger whispered, his voice rasping. "You'll create yours. Not overnight, but in time. And it'll be whatever you want it to be, Ty. If you want to become the greatest bluesman in the country, that's what you'll become, no matter what Salgado told you. All you need to do is believe, and do exactly as I say. It worked for Arnie, and it'll work for you."

Tyler's pulse throbbed in his temples. "Will I get Lauren?" he asked.

"Yeah, you'll get Lauren. She's part of your reality, always has been."

"Soon?"

"Very soon. We're almost there, Ty. We've almost succeeded in knocking down that little castle that she's built for herself. After that's done, she'll have nowhere to turn but to you. You'll charge into her life like a prince on a white horse, sweep her up in your arms and rescue her from the ashes of destruction. And she'll love you for it, Ty. She'll love you like no woman has ever loved a man."

Knocking down her castle. Tyler liked that thought.

Forty-three

Tyler used a pay phone at a Chevron station to call Rainy Hales.

"Hey, what's happenin', Adrienne? Got a big weekend planned?"

"You just called me by name. That's supposed to be verboten on the phone, isn't it?"

"Not anymore. I've quit the pharmaceuticals business. It's a whole new world for me, Rainy-my-girl, and I'm in the mood to party. How about you?"

"You're not serious."

"Have you ever known the Blues Beast *not* to be serious?"

"Tyler, it's late, and I've had a hellish week."

"Aw, c'mon—don't be that way. An upstanding working girl like yourself needs to get out every now and then, have a little fun. Tell you what—" He'd rehearsed this to make it sound like a spur-of-the-moment idea. "Meet me in the parking lot of the Shilshole Bay Marina. I need to go over there anyway to drop something off for a friend."

"You just said you weren't in the business anymore."

"This is, like, my last delivery, okay? Don't bust my balls, earth mama—I'm not in the mood for that. Be there in an hour, and I'll take you out on the town. We'll actually have a good time, I promise. And I won't keep you out all night."

"Tyler, there's something you should know."

"What's that?"

"I'm being followed."

Tyler swallowed wrong and coughed. "Followed by who?"

"One of the guys Lauren brought in to get the bugs out of the house. I think he works for ProGuard. His name is Ragsdale. He's parked in the street across from the parking lot at my place, in a gray BMW."

Tyler's palms grew sweaty almost instantly. The implications of what Rainy had just told him were not good. One of Lauren's hired goons had followed Rainy, which meant that Rainy was under suspicion, just as the Ranger had feared. This Ragsdale lame-o had followed her in order to find out who she hung with, where she went in her free time. The guy knew that someone in Rainy's circle of acquaintances was the killer of Megan Reiner, Ian Prather, and Vera Kemmis. And this made Ragsdale a dangerous dude.

"Tyler, are you still there?"

"Yeah, I'm still here. Okay, this is what I want you to do, earth mama. Go to Shilshole Marina and leave your car at the north end of the lot, as close to Golden Gardens Park as you can get. Then walk south along the marina, like you're looking at the boats. Sit at one of the benches, and I'll pick you up."

"What about Ragsdale?"

"I'll deal with him, Rainy. Not to worry."

Tyler hung up the phone and thought, *Let 'em look up that call in the phone logs. Only about a hundred people a day use that phone.* He bought a pack of Slim Jims and ripped the wrapper off, thrust one into his mouth and bit the end off. He chewed hard enough to make his jaw hurt.

Forty-four

He parked his Yukon in the southern end of the parking lot of the Shilshole Bay Marina in Ballard and glanced at his Audemars Piguet. It was 11:22. The moon, according to the watch, had just entered its "new moon" phase, not that it mattered—the sodium vapor floodlights made the lot as bright as a summer afternoon. Which was fine, because Tyler Brownlee didn't need darkness for tonight's mission.

We're knocking down her castle...

The marina sat in a shallow bay on Puget Sound, just north of the Chittenden Locks in Ballard, on Seaview Avenue. It was Seattle's biggest marina, home to fifteen hundred boats, with guest facilities for a hundred more. At the northern end of Shilshole Bay lay Golden Gardens Park, a favorite picnic spot among the locals. Directly across the Sound was Bainbridge Island, the lights of its fine homes twinkling through the trees on the shore.

Before getting out of the truck, Tyler checked his equipment one final time. His .357 Magnum revolver was loaded and ready. His Redstone folding knife was in his right boot, within easy reach. In an inner pocket of his motorcycle jacket were two capped syringes that contained carefully measured doses of sodium pentobarbital, one of which was a spare. He had brass knuckles in one pocket of his jeans, a can of CS tear gas in the other— not the comparatively tame self-defense product that any lame-o could order out of a catalog, but real U.S. Army chloroacetophenone.

He sat very still a moment, breathing slowly and deeply in order to control the frenzy building in his chest. Pro football players must feel this way before a game, he imagined, fully charged both emotionally and physically, every nerve eager for combat.

After opening a fresh Slim Jim, he got out of the truck and looked around. This being Friday night and the start of a summer weekend, not many parking slots were open in this section of the lot. Rock music came from somewhere in the marina, probably from a boat. He heard laughter out on the water, both male and female. *Party hearty*, Tyler thought.

Though full of vehicles, the lot was nearly empty of people, just as he'd hoped it would be. He reminded himself that the Shilshole Bay Marina was a regular patrol stop for the cops, that he needed to be extra careful here. No telling when a cop car might swing into the lot. Moreover, the marina headquarters building housed two restaurants and a lounge, and just south of the marina stood Anthony's Home Port, a well-known seafood joint—all of which were still open for business at this hour. Restaurant patrons could pop up at any moment, walking to their cars.

He crossed the parking lot to a walkway that ran the length of the marina, well over half a mile from end to end. From the walk a pedestrian could gaze out at the forest of masts and spars, perhaps with longing for the sailor's life, or envy of those who could afford to keep their boats here. Locked gates kept the riffraff away from the docks and the boats, making the marina a "gated community" where the affluent could feel safe. Beyond the breakwater sprawled the Sound, as black and deep as dreamless sleep.

Tyler turned south and strolled at a leisurely pace toward Golden Gardens Park, his sweaty hands pocketed, his boots clopping on the cement. At this moment he wished that he looked like an ordinary guy out for some evening air, but he knew that he didn't look ordinary, not with his long blond hair and black leather. In fact, he feared he looked downright suspicious. He hoped to God that he wouldn't meet any cops.

Near the park, the lot was less crowded with cars and trucks, which meant that he could anticipate a good view of any vehicle that entered it. He left the sidewalk and walked a hundred paces to a park bench that faced the Sound, sat sideways with one leg stretched out, keeping an eye on the lot behind him. It was dark here, for the park had no floodlights. And probably dangerous,

too, Tyler figured, though he almost felt sorry for any creep who
might accost him. He almost wished someone *would*.

A pair of headlights veered into the parking lot directly opposite the boatyard at the Marina, and continued north toward the
park. Excitement fluttered in Tyler's chest, and he wondered if—
yes, it was Rainy's blue Saturn. His heartbeat accelerated, and he
tossed away his half-eaten Slim Jim.

She took a parking slot next to an empty boat trailer, got out
of the car and stood a moment in the stark purplish glow of the
floods, gawking. Then she remembered her instructions, and
started walking north along the route by which Tyler had just
come.

Another pair of headlights appeared on the avenue, and Tyler
strained to make out the car itself. The headlights slowed at one
of the entrances to the marina lot, but then sped up and continued
toward Golden Gardens Park. The car came into view, a silver
BMW, and Tyler knew that this was his guy, Ragsdale, one of
the lame-os Lauren had hired to debug her house.

The Bimmer made a slow U-turn at the entrance of the park
and pulled to the curb on Seaview Avenue. The headlights and
taillights went black. But Ragsdale didn't get out of the car. From
this spot Ragsdale could maintain visual contact with Rainy until
she'd walked at least another block along the edge of the marina.
Why get out of the car and run the risk of being spotted? This
guy was no dummy.

Rainy came to a bench and sat down, as Tyler had instructed.
Good. All the actors were in place. Time to bring this little drama
to its conclusion . . .

Time to knock down another wall in Lauren's castle.

Tyler stood and reached into the pocket of his jeans for the
tear gas canister. He unlocked the safety switch and pushed the
canister up the right-hand sleeve of his leather jacket. Then he
unsnapped the retainer strap of his shoulder holster.

He moved toward Seaview Avenue, keeping to the shadow of
the park, darting among trees and picnic tables. Upon coming to
the street, he made directly for the BMW, approaching from the
rear on the driver's side, walking softly to keep his boot heels
from giving him away. When he'd closed to within twenty feet
of the car, he could see the rear of Ragsdale's head. *This lame-o
is going bald,* Tyler said to himself. *He's got nothing to live for.*

He saw, too, that the driver's window of the car was open,

which would make his job even easier. He crouched and pressed himself against the rear fender, then inched forward to the driver's door. Ironically, he could stare level into the exterior rearview mirror and see Ragsdale's face. But Ragsdale's eyes were glued to Rainy Hales.

Tyler shook his arm, and the CS canister slipped out of his sleeve into his hand. He rose up and pushed the canister to within six inches of Ragsdale's face, then hit the button. Ragsdale immediately choked and gagged as the chemical permeated his nasal passages and eye membranes. The concentrated dose blinded him instantly and caused his lungs to seize up. Mucos flowed from his nostrils and tears streamed down his face. He clutched his throat, clawed at the door handle.

As Ragsdale lurched out of the car, Tyler pocketed the canister and pulled the Redstone knife from his boot, whipping the folding blade into position with the same smooth motion. He struck with quick, pistonlike strokes, the nine-inch blade sinking deep into Ragsdale's torso—four times, five, half a dozen times. Ragsdale stumbled forward, gurgling, hemorrhaging, trying to scream. He fell facedown onto the asphalt and twitched like a dying fish. Ribbons of dark blood crawled past the front tires of the BMW into the gutter.

Tyler spent no more effort on the lame-o. He went straight to the bench where Rainy sat, nearly half a block away, and sat next to her, grinning his half-grin, showing her his pearly whites.

"It's about time you showed up," she said. "Sitting here alone was starting to creep me out." She coughed and waved her hand in front of her face. "What's that awful smell?"

Residue of the CS on his clothes, Tyler figured. "My new aftershave," he said, still grinning. "Like it?"

"It makes me want to puke."

"Not the effect I was hoping for. Oh, well. What do you say we go somewhere and do nasty things to each other?"

Rainy turned away from him. "Tyler, I only agreed to meet you tonight so I could say something to you, something I've been meaning to say for a long time."

"And that would be?"

"I can't do this anymore. I can't be your spy in Lauren's house. And I can't have anything to do with you, or the Ranger, either. It's over, Tyler. I'm sorry."

The Blues Beast laughed without really smiling. "You're forgetting something, aren't you? Somebody named Bernie Kemper, the vegan chef who disappeared from the face of the earth, like he fell into a sinkhole or something? It wouldn't be cool if Lauren found out what happened to him, would it?''

"I don't care about that. If Lauren finds out, she finds out. If I lose my job, so be it. But I can't go on with things the way they are. I can't look at myself in the mirror."

Tyler stared at her face, which was ghastly pale in the light of the sodium vapor streetlamps. He noticed every little freckle and blemish, the redness of her eyes, the fact that her lank hair needed washing. She was way too thin, probably from never eating any meat, he figured. He longed to cut away what little meat still clung to her fucking vegan bones, preferably while she was still alive to appreciate it.

"Okay," Tyler said. "I can see you're serious about this. And I guess I can't really blame you."

Rainy's head snapped around, and she stared at him, incredulous. "What did you say?"

"You're free. You're square with the Ranger and me. We won't bother you anymore. You have my promise on that."

A smile pulled at the corners of Rainy's mouth. "You mean it?"

"You bet I do. Just do me the favor of having a good-bye drink with me. Let's go downtown, somewhere nice. Or maybe to some place on Lake Union. You decide."

Rainy stared hard at him, searching his face. Her quivering little smile withered. "Tyler, I . . ."

She sensed something, he could tell. He threw a glance over his shoulder at Seaview Avenue, where Ragsdale lay beside his BMW. A car might drive by at any minute, and the driver would see the body, call the cops. It was time to go.

"No more screwing around," Tyler said, grabbing Rainy's hand. "One last drink, that's all I ask." He started walking toward the north end of the marina with Rainy in tow. She seemed as if she weighed nothing, like tissue.

"I don't want to go," she protested. Her eyes were round with fear. "I want to go home."

Tyler whirled, grabbed her around the neck and slammed her against the steel railing that ran along the walkway. He leaned into her and pressed his mouth over hers, indicating to any passerby that they were just a pair of overheated lovers. He maneuvered a syringe out of his jacket with one hand, and popped the cap off with his thumb. Rainy struggled and tried to twist away from him, but she was no match for the Blues Beast. Still smothering her mouth with his, he plunged the needle into her neck and pressed the plunger.

Within thirty seconds he felt her start to go limp. He just managed to walk her to his Yukon before she lost consciousness, a man walking his inebriated date, from outward appearances. Driving away with Rainy slumped in the passenger seat, Tyler thought, *Your castle is crumbling, sweet Lauren. Your castle is crumbling . . .*

Forty-five

The persistent bleep of a telephone prodded Matt out of a murky dream that involved a sailboat, a kangaroo, and a set of bagpipes. Daylight streamed through a window, notifying him that morning had come—notifying him, too, that the Xanax had worked. He'd actually slept.

The phone wouldn't stop ringing, and he thought, *Why doesn't Jandee pick it up?* Then he realized that the ringing came from the cellular phone Rags had lent him. He rolled out of bed and groped for the sport coat that he'd thrown over a chair last night, dug the phone out of a pocket and answered it.

"Matt, it's Ruby," said a female voice on the other end. It was Ruby Ragsdale, Rags' wife of eleven years. Her tone sounded urgent.

"Ruby, hi. To what do I owe this pleasure?"

"Matt, it's Rags. He's—he's . . ."

Matt felt his breath go out of him. "Sweetheart, what is it? What's happened?"

"Rags has been—stabbed. He's just come out of surgery, and . . ."

"*Stabbed!* How, when?"

She told him what she knew, which wasn't really much. Police had responded to an emergency call late last night near Shilshole Bay Marina. They'd found Rags lying in the street, unconscious and bleeding. He'd spent the night in surgery and had just now entered intensive care.

"Ruby, is he . . ." Matt could hardly bear to ask this, but he needed to. "Is he going to make it?"

She whimpered, but managed not to cry. "We don't know yet."

Matt rang off, then dialed Rod Welton's number. Something had come up, he told Welton, an emergency. He needed Welton here now to stay with Lauren and Jandee. Welton said he was on his way.

Forty-five minutes later Matt dashed into the waiting room outside the intensive care unit of Virginia Mason Hospital on the corner of Ninth and Seneca in downtown Seattle. The hospital smell hit him like a blast from a kiln, made him want to retch. Images of the ordeal he'd suffered during Tristan's dying days flashed through his head, conjuring panic, a sense of hopelessness, a longing to be anywhere but next to the deathbed of someone he loved.

He spotted Ruby Ragsdale immediately, a tall brunette of thirty-five with hair cropped to about an inch all over her head. She stood next to a window, holding a disposable coffee cup in her hand, her face drawn and depleted. She looked like a woman edging toward collapse.

Matt went to her, hugged her, offered what comfort he could. He asked about the kids, and she told him that they were with friends. No sense bringing them to the hospital until Rags woke up, she said—*if* he woke up. As for Rags, the surgeon had reported that he'd suffered six stab wounds, resulting in a punctured lung and lacerations of the spleen and a kidney, both of which he'd lost. He'd also sustained chemical burns on his face and in his eyes, the effects of tear gas, one of the doctors had said, judging from the odor.

Then she told Matt that two detectives had interviewed her earlier in the morning—she couldn't remember their names. They had wanted to know if Rags had maintained any connection to Matt, either professionally or personally. And they'd asked if Rags had ever done any off-the-books work for Lauren Bowman.

"I didn't know what to tell them," Ruby said, dabbing her eyes with a Kleenex. "I knew that you and Rags had been getting together regularly during the past few weeks, but I didn't know anything about his working for Lauren Bowman. Matt, you've got to tell me what this is all about."

At that moment a middle-aged man dressed in a lab coat came

out of the ICU and put his hand on Ruby's shoulder. His name
tag identified him as J. Alvarez, M.D. He reported that Rags appeared to be gaining slightly, that his life signs had strengthened.
He was far from out of the woods, but if he suffered no setbacks
by midday, the staff would upgrade him from critical to serious.

Ruby wept with joy and pumped Alvarez's hand. Matt asked
the doctor if he knew any of the circumstances surrounding the
assault, but Alvarez replied that that was somebody else's loop.
He suggested that Matt talk to the police if he wanted to know
more, then excused himself and walked back into the ICU.

Matt noticed two people in the corridor outside the waiting
room, talking to a uniformed policeman. He recognized them as
Sergeant Connie Henness and Detective Aaron Cosentino, Seattle
PD. Henness wore baggy denim shorts, an equally baggy red shirt,
and a shoulder bag that Matt supposed contained her gun and
badge. She looked like a middle-class mom who'd gone out to
do the weekly grocery shopping. Cosentino wore white painter's
pants and seersucker sport coat.

"That's them," Ruby said, nodding toward the corridor. "The
two cops who talked to me earlier." Matt told her he would be
in touch, then walked out to the corridor and approached the
detectives. He wasn't quite sure what he would say to them. Part
of him wanted to blurt out everything he knew, regardless of the
legal consequences, purely in the interest of catching the man who
had attacked Rags. But another part of him, the stronger part,
remembered the promises he'd made.

"Well, well, well," Cosentino said, noticing Matt, "this is a
surprise. What brings the infamous Matt Burgess out to a hospital
on a sunny Saturday morning?"

Infamous. Cosentino must have asked around the department
and found some cops who didn't hold Matt in high esteem, probably because of his lack of enthusiasm for the war on drugs. Or
he'd found people who considered Matt a weakling for suffering
a breakdown and quitting the force.

"I could ask the same of you," Matt replied, trying to smile.
"I didn't know Homicide worked on weekends."

"Hey, Homicide works *all* the time, day and night, weekends
and holidays," Henness said. "That's why we're all so happily
married."

Matt wondered if she was trying to be funny. He forced another smile, then volunteered that he'd come to visit his friend,

Alex Ragsdale, who'd been the victim of an assault last night, a stabbing. Unfortunately, Rags was still unconscious and the doctors weren't allowing visitors.

Well, wasn't this a coincidence? Cosentino asked with a sneer that Matt found annoying. Ragsdale was the reason he and Sergeant Henness were here, too. They'd seen today's morning report in the squad room, which had noted the stabbing incident last night at Shilshole Bay Marina. The victim's name, Ragsdale, had leapt out at Henness. Was it possible, they'd wondered, that the incident was somehow connected to the raid on the Northwest BioCenter and the disappearance of Megan Reiner? After all, Ragsdale and Burgess were old buds, and Burgess and Lauren Bowman were sweeties. Lauren and Megan were fellow soldiers in the animal-rights movement. And, unless Cosentino's instincts were misfiring badly, Lauren Bowman knew much more about both matters than she'd let on.

Matt's anger mounted as he listened to all this. "Your instincts are full of shit," he told Cosentino. "I don't have any idea what Rags was doing at Shilshole last night, but I can guarantee that it had nothing to do with the raid or Megan Reiner."

"How can you be so sure about that?" Henness wanted to know. "Does he check with you before going out at night?"

"I know my partner," Matt said. "He works for ProGuard now. And he's a straight-ahead guy."

"Well, that's got to be news to the people at ProGuard," Cosentino said. "We talked to his boss on the phone a few minutes ago, and he swears that old Rags was not on assignment for the company last night. *Which* leads me to wonder if Rags was out looking for some companionship of the female persuasion, and maybe got crosswise with somebody's pimp."

Matt could barely keep himself from smashing a fist into Cosentino's boyish face. When he spoke, his voice trembled. "Listen, fuck-stick. Alex Ragsdale is a devoted husband and father. He was also a first-rate cop, the kind you'll never be unless you lose the Generation-X attitude. If you were half as bright as he is, you'd know that Shilshole Bay isn't a neighborhood conducive to trolling for whores."

"What did you call me?" Cosentino asked, puffing out his chest.

"Boys, boys," pleaded Sergeant Henness, stepping between them. "Let's can the testosterone and get civilized, shall we?"

"Keep him away from me," Matt said, thrusting a finger at Cosentino, "or I'll put a shoe up his ass. You might also teach him some respect for the law-abiding taxpayers."

Cosentino started toward him, but Henness and the uniformed officer held the young cop back. "Look, I apologize for all this, Matt," Henness said. "We're just doing our jobs, that's all."

"Yeah, right," Matt said, walking away. He needed to be out of there, out of that damned hospital.

"We're not going to let this thing lie, Burgess," Cosentino called after him. "You haven't seen the last of us." Without looking back, Matt gave him the finger.

As he walked to his car, he thought of Rags lying in the ICU, and his throat became hot and tight. His eyes welled with tears. Since Tristan's death, he'd found that crying had become alarmingly easy.

Forty-six

During the drive back to the Bowman-Granger estate, Matt made
a decision: no more playing defense. He decided that he needed
to go on the offensive against the maniac who had killed Megan
Reiner, Vera Kemmis, and Ian Prather. Reactive measures had
proved unsatisfactory. Despite sweeping the guest house of listening devices, and despite his best effort to provide around-the-
clock protection for Lauren and her friends, the killer had gotten
into the house and had assaulted Lauren, then left a video of
Vera's torture and murder. And last night the bastard had nearly
killed Rags.

No more, Matt told himself.

The problem was that he didn't have a plan. Yet.

Jandee Vernon met him at the door of the guest house, handed
him a mug of coffee, and wanted to know what had made him
leave in such a hurry. He briefly related that Rags had followed
Rainy Hales last night in order to surveil her comings and goings,
and that he'd ended up at the Shilshole Bay Marina with somebody's knife in his gut. Had Rainy set Rags up? Or had she
become another victim? Matt asked whether Jandee or Lauren
had heard from her since last night.

"No, she hasn't called," Jandee replied, "but then why would
she? She doesn't work weekends. Lauren and I cook for ourselves
on Saturdays and Sundays, unless Lauren plans to entertain, that
is. In that case, Rainy will come in, cook a meal, and leave."

"What's her number?" Matt asked, picking up a telephone.

Jandee gave it to him, and he dialed. Rainy's answering machine came on, asked him to leave a message. He switched off the phone and stared at Jandee. "She's not there," he said.

Jandee put a hand over her mouth. "Oh, God."

"Let's not panic just yet. She might've gone out shopping or something. If she was working for the killer, it doesn't make much sense that he would do her in. Does it?"

"You're asking *me*?"

"Try calling her every fifteen minutes or so."

"I will," Jandee said, taking the phone from him.

"Where's Rod?"

"Last time I saw him, he was out in the gazebo, having a smoke. He's wearing a shoulder holster—did you know that? A shoulder holster on the outside of a Hawaiian shirt. It looks positively ridiculous."

"He's *supposed* to be armed. Be thankful that he is. Where's Lauren?"

"In her study. She's working on an article for *Animal Realm*."

Matt went into the guest room where he'd been staying and fetched the two videocassettes that contained the gruesome scenes of Megan Reiner's and Vera Kemmis's last moments in this world. He replayed them on the VCR in the sitting room and made notes in his little spiral notebook. After stowing the cassettes in his room again, he went to Lauren's study, knocked on the door, and pushed it open.

Lauren sat on the deck with a notebook computer in front of her, with Desi and Lucy sleeping in the shade of a madrona. She wore a tan pullover tunic with matching pants, hemp sandals, and sunglasses. Matt liked the way a few strands of her dark hair swung down over her forehead.

"Come in," she said, not looking up. "Forgive me if I seem distracted. I've got to e-mail this article to LOCA national headquarters tomorrow, and it's only half-finished." Her fingers continued to fly over the keyboard. "You know, working is the only way I stay sane these days. It keeps my mind occupied, keeps me from thinking about . . ." The flurry of typing slowed a moment, then sped up again.

Matt walked out to the deck and sat across from her in a padded patio recliner. "You need to take a break and listen to me," he said.

Lauren looked up at him. "What is it?"

He told her what had happened to Rags. He told her that there could be no doubt of Rainy Hales' complicity with the killer of Megan, Vera, and Ian. And he told her that he needed to know all she knew about the killer.

Lauren's face went ashen.

"I don't know what you mean," she said, her voice shaking. "What could I possibly know about him?"

Matt let his eyes wander over the scenery. Another sparkling summer morning was under way, full of sunlight and salty breezes. Already a hundred white sails speckled the Sound. It was beautiful.

"It's the music, isn't it?" Matt said. "The lyrics mean something to you, right? At least, the singer thinks they should mean something to you."

Lauren stared at her computer screen, said nothing. But Matt saw turmoil in her eyes, in the way her restless mouth worked, smiling, then grimacing, the lips puckering, then stretching tight. Turmoil. And pain. *What is it?* Matt wondered—a memory so horrific that her conscious mind refused to process it? An old wound, an old sin?

"When I pulled you out of the shower," Matt went on, "you were singing a song—a *blues* song. Do you remember it?"

She shook her head.

"Well, *I* remember it. I can't carry a tune in a bushel basket, but I remember the lyrics. You kept singing them over and over again . . ." Matt recited what he remembered of the song that Lauren had sung on that excruciating morning nine days ago, the morning after the killer had invaded her bedroom:

> *You know you've done some sinnin' woman,*
> *And it's no good confessin' to your priest.*
> *Ain't but one man in the world you should confess to,*
> *And I'm standin' right here—I'm the Blues Beast.*

Lauren turned away from him, her eyes shut tight. For a moment, Matt thought that she was about to have a seizure of some kind, and he readied himself to jump out of his chair and rush to her. Then, to his astonishment, Lauren began to sing in a strong, measured voice. Though hardly a polished blues singer, she rendered the melody perfectly, hitting and slurring all the right notes.

You know you need to suffer, mama,
If you ever expect to get released
From all the trouble you've brought down on your head.
I'll make you suffer, girl—I'm the Blues Beast.

A chill crept over Matt's shoulders. After she'd finished the song, he walked over to where she sat and leaned close to her. "Where does that song come from?" he asked.

She closed her eyes again, as if to shut out the world. When she opened them, Matt witnessed a sudden transformation from beleaguered victim to self-assured fighter for justice. The change startled him, and he stepped back from the table.

"Have you ever heard of Estrin?" she asked.

Matt shook his head. *Estrin?*

"It's the most widely prescribed drug in the country for estrogen replacement therapy. Most women don't even know that there's an alternative. The manufacturer makes close to a billion dollars a year on it. Do you know where it comes from?"

"No. Where does it come from?"

"The urine of pregnant mares. The company gets it from more than five hundred farms in the American Midwest and Canada. On these farms, the mares are confined to tiny stalls for seven months a year. In a horse's lifetime, she's impregnated twenty times or more. The operators give them only enough water to keep them alive, in order to ensure that the estrogen concentration in their urine is high. They collect the urine in plastic bags attached to the animals' legs, which causes chafing and painful infections. And because the horses can't move or lie down to rest, they go lame—not even a horse can bear to stand on a concrete floor for seven months straight. As for the foals, well—the industry produces something like seventy-five thousand a year. They're all slaughtered and sold to pet-food manufacturers, or exported to places where people willingly eat horse meat. When a mare matures to the stage where she can't produce as much estrogen, she suffers the fate of her young."

Matt ran a hand through his hair, wondered what to say. He nodded toward the computer on the table in front of her. "Is this what you're working on—your article for *Animal Realm*?"

"Yes. LOCA has obtained some photographs of conditions on the farms, and they'll be printed with this article. *If* I ever finish it, that is." She put her hands to the keyboard again.

Matt stared at her for a long time, worrying that her mind had begun to take evasive maneuvers from the ugly realities of murdered friends. Not so hard to understand, really. Hadn't something similar happened to him, back when Tristan was suffering the final throes of cystic fibrosis?

"To answer your question," Lauren said suddenly. "I heard the song from the man who raped me. He must've been singing it while he was doing it. I don't have a clear memory of it, because I was probably drugged while it was happening. The song must have become imprinted on my mind."

Matt licked his dry lips. "What does it mean, this business about your having sinned, your needing to suffer?" he asked. "And who's the Blues Beast?"

"I—don't know. It's just a sick song, Matt. It might not have been written for *me*."

"Oh, it was written for you, just like the songs on the videos." He pulled out his spiral notebook and consulted the notes he'd made while watching the videos. On the first tape, the song was about a woman who had *more money than Oprah Winfrey,* a woman who needed to pay what she owed—as if she'd wronged the singer somehow. On the second, the singer referred to Vera Kemmis as a *stand-in* and a *substitute,* ending with the line, *You're just the one I ain't got yet.*

Matt dared Lauren to insist that the singer wasn't talking to *her.* The woman with Oprah Winfrey–class money, after all, had to be Lauren. The context of the songs that accompanied all three incidents—Megan's and Vera's deaths, and Lauren's rape—suggested that the killer felt he'd suffered some injustice at Lauren's hands, and that the murders were part of a plan to exact justice from her.

"*You're* the target," Matt reiterated. "This guy thinks that you've done something to him, or taken something from him. And I need you to tell me about it."

Lauren's face became the picture of misery. "I *can't.* I—don't know anything about him, I swear." She made a fist and pressed the knuckles to her teeth. "I'd hoped that it was over—can you believe that? I'd hoped that he'd gotten what he wanted, me in bed. I'd let myself believe that Megan and Vera were only the warm-up acts, and that Ian had merely gotten in his way. They all died within a week, and it's been more than a week since he got to me. But now . . ."

"Now Rags is in the hospital, and Rainy may or may not be missing."

Lauren closed her eyes and whispered, "Shit." A tear splashed down her cheek when she looked up at Matt again. "I'm so sorry about what happened to Rags. I know that you and he are close."

"We went to college together. We were in the academy at the same time, and we partnered while we were cops. He's my best friend."

She got out of her chair and approached him, her hands out. "I wish there were something I could do," she said.

They stood a moment and stared at one another. A breeze caught a sickle of Lauren's hair and tossed it over one eye. Matt marveled at how soft her cheek looked, how clear and clean her skin was. He felt an urgent need to take her in his arms, but he didn't dare—only nine days earlier she'd endured a sexual assault that had left her in a state bordering on psychotic. If she wanted never to touch a man again, Matt couldn't blame her.

But then she reached out to him, found his hand, and the sensation of her touch shot through him like a surge of electrical current. In her face he saw a hunger for something, or was it merely longing? He couldn't read it. She moved close, pressed her cheek to his chest. He inhaled the scent of the shampoo she'd used that morning. Her hand traveled to his face, traced the line of his jaw upward to his ear, moving over morning stubble. Matt's own hands went around her waist, and he pulled her close.

She raised her face to his, and she waited—for what? A kiss? Matt couldn't believe this was happening. He was a lowly ex-cop, yet he had his arms around Lauren Bowman, the Wonder Woman of Real Estate, the tycoon-turned-animal-rights activist. They were as different as night and day, he and she. They held different beliefs about nearly everything.

"Lauren, what is this?" he asked.

"I don't know," she said. "And I don't care." Then she pressed her lips to his.

It was a long, deep kiss. The feel of Lauren in his arms, the feel of her mouth and tongue, overwhelmed him. Lauren finally broke the embrace and led him into her study, to the long sofa across from her desk. She took the precaution of locking the door before slipping out of her clothes.

Forty-seven

The Mayflower Park Hotel, an elegant brick Victorian that looked like it would tell many a juicy story if only it could talk, stood in the shadow of the towering Westlake Center, a contemporary study in stark glass and steel. At 9:00 P.M. on Saturday, June 14, Richardson Zanto strode through the main entrance of the Mayflower and crossed the hushed lobby to the registration desk, carrying a sharkskin attaché case.

"Mr. Cashmore's room, please," he said to the registration clerk. He'd tailed Arnie Cashmore to the Mayflower only yesterday, watched him check in.

"Yes, sir. Pick up the courtesy phone, please."

Zanto moved to the end of the counter, picked up the courtesy phone, and waited for the clerk to put the call through.

"Hello?" someone said on the other end. Zanto pictured the thin, sickly looking man whom he'd shadowed intermittently over the past week, the man with whom Tyler Brownlee had shared a beach house in Alki.

"Mr. Cashmore?"

"Yeah, who's this?"

"I'm someone who's willing to do you a big favor, one that might save your butt. Interested?"

"What kind of favor? What're you talking about?"

"I have something that you've lost. I'm willing to return it to you. This isn't an opportunity you can afford to miss, Mr. Cashmore." Zanto paused for effect. "I also figured that you might be willing to do a favor for *me*. You see, you've got something that *I* need.''

Zanto actually heard Cashmore grind his teeth as he considered the possibilities. The caller might be a cop, luring him to arrest. Or a blackmailer. Or a past rival in the black-tar business, looking to settle an old score. ''I need to know who you are,'' Cashmore said finally. ''How do I know this isn't a shakedown?''

''No shakedown, believe me. Meet me downstairs in the bar in ten minutes. Take a table and get yourself a drink. I'll find you.''

''Jesus, this is bizarre, man. I can't just . . .''

''Ten minutes, Mr. Cashmore. Don't be late.'' Zanto hung up the phone.

The bar was the kind of dim, leather-upholstered cavern typical of lounges in fine old hotels. Zanto found a stool with a view of the door. Wearing his Brooks Brothers suit, carrying his sharkskin attaché case, he could have been a banker or a stockbroker. He ordered a Chivas Regal, sipped it.

Arnie Cashmore arrived a full two minutes early, sporting a fresh haircut and a blue blazer over gray slacks, the image of cleanliness and respectability. He glanced cautiously around, obviously looking for the man who'd just called him, but spotted nobody who looked the part. He found a booth in the rear of the lounge, sat down, and lit a cigarette. A hostess took his order and returned a few minutes later with a drink in a tall glass, a whiskey sour, Zanto guessed.

Gravity, simplicity, piety, Zanto said to himself as he eased off his stool and headed toward Cashmore's booth. Would Marcus Aurelius approve of what he was about to do? he wondered.

He set his Chivas next to Cashmore's whiskey sour and slid into the booth next to the little man. Cashmore stared at him with wide eyes, apparently not having expected anyone who looked like Zanto.

''Hi, Arnie,'' Zanto said, spinning the combination dial of his attaché case. ''It's nice to finally see you face-to-face.''

''Who the fuck are you?''

Zanto opened the case, took out a green sun visor and tossed it onto the table next to Cashmore's glass. Cashmore stared at it, didn't touch it. ''I found this in the living room of the house where you lived until a few days ago,'' Zanto said. ''I guess you must've dropped it on your way out.''

Cashmore took a nervous gulp of his drink and sucked on his cigarette. "How do you know it belongs to me?"

"I've seen you wear it. In fact, I have pictures—nice ones, too, taken with a telephoto lens. In several, you're sitting in front of the television set. In a couple of others, you're at the dining room table, eating a frozen dinner. It's a good thing you kept your windows so clean."

"An old visor and a couple of Peeping-Tom shots don't prove anything." Another gulp of the drink, another drag of smoke.

Zanto described some of the other pictures he'd taken of Cashmore over the past ten days. Telephoto shots of meetings with slacker-types in parking garages on Capitol Hill, in alleys, in apartment houses. Meetings in which parcels changed hands, along with wads of money. You didn't need an advanced degree in quantum physics to conclude that Arnie Cashmore was in the drug business.

Cashmore, to his credit, kept his cool. The cops weren't likely to find a handful of snapshots very compelling, he insisted. Nothing he'd heard so far constituted probable cause, much less a case against him. He floated the theory Zanto was a wayward cop who was trying to shake him down.

"You couldn't be more wrong," Zanto said. "I do have many close friends and contacts in federal law enforcement, however, notably in customs, DEA, and the FBI. I could arrange to create a truckload of grief for you when you attempt to try to transfer money out of the country. That's what you're planning, isn't it—a getaway to some tropical paradise? It seems like every drug dealer I've ever met nurtures the same dream."

Cashmore denied that he planned to leave the country, causing Zanto to *tsk-tsk*. Zanto had followed him on his round of farewells to various friends and acquaintances around town, and had noticed that one such pal looked particularly down and out, an aging graduate student who'd put his tuition money and everything he owned into his arm. Wave a hundred dollars in the face of such a man and he'll tell almost anything you need to know, Zanto said. *Which* that man had done, and gladly, too. He'd told Zanto all about Arnie Cashmore and his business history on Capitol Hill, his recent and abrupt retirement from the Mexican black-tar business, the permanent vacation he'd planned.

Cashmore drained his whiskey sour or whatever it was and took off his thick glasses. He reached into the breast pocket of his blazer, upon which Zanto whipped out a Beretta .40-caliber pistol and shoved the muzzle into his ribs. Cashmore choked on a clot of saliva and turned as white as a round of Swiss cheese.

"I was only going to clean my glasses," he stammered, taking a handkerchief out of his pocket. His upper lip was shiny with sweat.

"My apology. I thought you were about to do something stupid. You should be more careful."

"Shit, would you have capped me here in this bar, with all these people around?"

"Without hesitation, Arnie. Then I would've walked out calmly, hailed a cab and gone to the airport. By this time tomorrow I would've been in a safe house in Manila."

Arnie Cashmore stared at him a long time, his mouth hanging open. "Who the fuck *are* you, man? *What* the fuck are you?"

Zanto holstered the pistol and suggested that they get down to business. He'd kept his part of the bargain by returning Arnie's green visor. Now he expected Arnie to hold up *his* end.

"Tell me about Tyler Brownlee," Zanto said, sipping his Chivas.

"Who?"

"No more games, Arnie. I'm talking about the young dude who lived with you until several days ago. Were the two of you just roommates, or were you a gay couple?"

"What's your interest in Tyler?"

"I think he may have harmed some people I know. I need to find out for certain. I'm hoping you can help me."

Cashmore leaned back from the table and wiped the sweat from his face with the handkerchief. "So *that's* what this is all about. You work for Lauren Bowman, don't you? I warned him that this would happen."

Zanto said nothing, only stared at him with his opaque hazel eyes.

"Look, the kid's got an obsession with your client," Cashmore went on, leaning forward again. "But it's not his fault. It's his old man's fault. For years his old man has drilled into him this bullshit that Lauren Bowman is his destiny, that someday she'll be his wife and lover, and they'll go off together to play in blues clubs all over the country. It sounds crazy, I know . . ."

Cashmore was eager to talk now. He told Zanto about the posters that Tyler had made and hung in his room, the photos of

Lauren at various stages of her life. He talked about the blues music Tyler had written, all of it about Lauren. He talked about the sickly sweet poetry the kid wrote about her, together with the love letters that he saved in a locked box with the cockeyed notion of someday giving them to her.

"I didn't find out that he'd wired her house until almost two weeks ago. The guys who did it for him called me to complain. It was taking up all their time and energy, and they had other things to do."

Zanto could sympathize. Audio surveillance was both expensive and exhausting. It was akin to giving up your life in order to listen in on someone else living his.

"And that's when I knew he'd gotten totally out of hand. I tried to talk sense to him, but I might as well have been talking to a fire hydrant. I tried to tell him to forget about Lauren Bowman, get his head back in the game . . ."

"The *heroin* game?"

Cashmore shrugged. "I even went to the old man and asked him to rein Tyler in, but he refused. Told me not to get in the way of the kid's dream." Cashmore emitted a bitter chuckle and crushed his cigarette butt into an ashtray. "I finally put two and two together. It was the *old man* who'd planted this obsession in the kid. I'm surprised that it hadn't occurred to me before."

The *old man*. The source of everything Tyler was or hoped to be. Cashmore tried to describe the silly, ill-thought-out philosophy that the old man had drilled into his son's head, something about every man creating his own reality. "He has Tyler believing that he's not accountable for anything he does. I guess it's a way to justify doing any fucking thing you want to, no matter how sick or ugly it is."

Zanto folded his hands in front of him and tried to ignore the twinge in his left wrist. The old shrapnel wound had started to act up. "Have you ever heard of a woman named Bonnie Harrell?" he asked.

"Doesn't ring a bell. Who is she?"

Zanto didn't tell him that old Packy Barker had advised him to visit the manager of the Klondike Hotel, where Tyler had grown up. The hotel manager would remember the name of the kid's mother, Packy had said. Zanto had followed the advice, and the manager had remembered. *Bonnie Harrell.* He'd even known where Zanto could find her.

Neither did Zanto relate that he'd driven down to SeaTac early this morning to find a certain diner a few blocks off Pacific Highway, where Bonnie Harrell had worked as a waitress for the past six years. He'd caught her on a break, bought her a late breakfast, and given her a twenty just to talk to him.

She was a loose-fleshed woman of fifty, with waxy-looking skin, puncture scars on her arms. She'd worn a long wig that looked as if it belonged on a mannequin. Zanto had asked her to tell him about her son, Tyler.

"He's no son of mine," she'd said with a scowl. "Ray moved him in with me over at the Klondike when he was four or five, told me I was gonna raise him, and that was that. What was I gonna do—me bein' a junkie and all? Ray had gotten me clean and was payin' my bills. I couldn't hardly tell him no."

Who was the boy's real mother? Zanto had asked.

"Some bimbo down in Portland, I think. Back in those days, Ray did a lot of traveling back and forth between Portland and Seattle. Sometimes he'd stay down there for weeks at a time. Said he was playin' gigs with some band—Portland was a big blues town. I always figured he had a wife down there, but he never told me nothin' about her. Anyway, he shows up one day with this five-year-old and drops him in my lap, tells me I'm gonna be his mom. And that's what I was for the next ten, maybe eleven years, until the kid went off to the juvey lockup. Sometimes I wonder how I kept from going crazy . . ."

She'd never felt close to the boy. Ray Brownlee had presented her a list of rules for him to follow, making Bonnie something like a drill instructor as well as nursemaid and nanny. The rules covered every aspect of the kid's life—the exact hours of the day he spent on homework, practicing the guitar, listening to music, reading, and . . . *other* things.

"Ray taught him to fight with a knife, how to shoot a gun, how to pick locks—Christ, I can't remember what all. Later he taught him how to hot-wire cars, and—God, I just remembered this—he taught him how to break somebody's fingers. I swear, it was like he was groomin' the kid for a life of crime. It made me sick."

By the time Tyler entered his teens, Bonnie had grown thoroughly frightened of him. He'd developed a mean streak. More than once he'd raised a fist to her after refusing to follow some rule or another, forcing Bonnie to call Ray and plead for help. His only friends were juveys who got their jollies by stealing things or beating people up. But what could anyone expect of a kid whose dad had taught him the things that Ray had?

And then, of course, there was the *Lauren* thing.

Bonnie had never understood, never known just who *Lauren* was. She'd known only that around the age of nine or ten Tyler starting hanging pictures of some dark-haired woman on the walls of his room. He'd written songs about her, which he'd performed for Ray, as if to get his old man's approval. As if that weren't enough, he'd written letters to her, and Bonnie had sneaked a peek at them one day while he was at school—gooey letters like no little kid should write to a grown woman.

"It was like some kind of obscene secret that they kept between them. If I was in earshot, they'd snicker and whisper. Sometimes I got the feeling that both of 'em had a crush on this Lauren, whoever the hell she was . . ."

But there'd been something else, too. Something even darker and more unwholesome, and . . .

Bonnie had been unable to talk about it, not even when Zanto had slipped another twenty under her coffee cup. Anyway, she'd never really *known* about it, but had only caught snippets of whispered conversation between father and son, conversation that had made her sick to her stomach. Something about women and girls and *knives*.

And that had been as far as Bonnie Harrell would go.

Zanto finished his scotch. "She's the lady who most people thought was Tyler's mother," he said to Cashmore. "I talked to her this morning. She suggested that Ray Brownlee made him into a kind of blues-playing monster."

"And?"

"I'd like to hear your take on that."

Cashmore lit another cigarette, blew smoke toward the ceiling. He allowed that while "monster" wasn't the word he would use, Tyler Brownlee did have a scary side to him. The black-tar business, Cashmore said, sometimes demanded aggressive measures against people who threatened you—lops who might sell you out to the cops, other dealers who tried to squeeze into your market area, people who stole from you.

"We call it 'wet work,' in my business," Zanto interjected.

Tyler had proved himself a willing muscle man, Cashmore said. Willing and even enthusiastic. Sometimes a little scary.

"To your knowledge, has he ever killed anyone?" Zanto asked.

Cashmore gazed back at him like a statue, moving not a muscle. Only the ribboning smoke of his cigarette ruined the freeze-frame effect. After many long seconds, Zanto got the message: Arnie Cashmore didn't plan to answer the question.

"You need to understand something," Cashmore said finally. "This kid never had a chance. It must've been hell for him, growing up with a father like Ray. How could anyone expect anything different from him?" He explained how Tyler and he had become business partners and roommates. Cashmore had agreed to the arrangement as a favor to Ray Brownlee.

"Tell me how you and Ray became so tight," Zanto said.

"He had another son who was eighteen or nineteen when Tyler was born, closer to my age. His name was Ben. Not really a bright kid, but he was tough, full of adventure. Rode Harleys, wore leather jackets—kind of like Tyler that way. I ran into him in Oregon State Prison . . ."

Cashmore himself had grown up in Gresham, a suburb of Portland, the son of a reasonably successful insurance salesman. While attending the University of Oregon in Eugene, he'd gotten busted for cultivating and selling marijuana. He'd drawn a sentence of ten years in OSP, six of which he'd actually served. While there, he'd met Ben Brownlee, who was serving ten on a burglary beef. They'd become friends.

"When I got out, I visited Ben's old man, who turned out to be Ray Brownlee, the Blues Ranger. It seems that Ben had mentioned me in his letters, talked about how smart I was, college boy and all that. Ray made me an offer. He'd gotten next to a lady known as the Fat Woman up here in Seattle, a real heavyweight in the tar business, and she was setting him up with a wholesale territory of his own. He needed somebody to run it—somebody smart and reliable. He figured I was the guy."

And because a recent graduate of OSP could count on few if any real prospects for a successful mainstream life, Cashmore had accepted Ray Brownlee's offer. Ray had schooled him on the ins and outs of running an illegal enterprise, taught him the ropes, introduced him around. Ray, it seemed, had vast experience in such matters.

"He had three cardinal rules," Cashmore went on. "Never do dope yourself, never deal with anyone you don't know, and don't spend enough to attract attention. Follow these rules, he said, and you'll retire with more money than God."

"Which is exactly what you've done," Zanto said.

Cashmore shrugged.

"I need to know where I can find Ray Brownlee."

"Sorry. I can't give you that information."

"Can't or won't?"

"He's been good to me. I owe him everything I've got."

Zanto sat quiet a moment, massaging his aching wrist. Would a man who'd gotten rich by selling heroin, he wondered, have a sense of decency that someone could appeal to? Not likely. But what the hell?

"I have reason to believe," he said, just above a whisper, "that your former roomy has killed two young women . . ." No, not just *killed* them—tortured them and raped them before butchering them alive. Zanto himself had heard the audio track of the first killing, and a source close to Lauren Bowman had notified him of the second. The killer had taken pains to record the atrocities on videotape, and to send the tapes to Lauren Bowman. A final touch: He'd overlaid the action with blues music.

"Ten days ago, I watched your roomy sneak into the Bowman-Granger estate," Zanto added. "A couple of hours later, he sneaked out again. I followed him to your place in Alki. That's how I became interested in *you*."

"Lucky me."

"Did you hear what I just told you, Arnie? Your boy Tyler is a sex killer."

"I don't see how that's my problem."

"It's your problem, Arnie, because I'm making it your problem. Remember what I said on the phone, that I was willing to do you a big favor?"

"Yeah."

"Actually, it's two favors. The first is that I'll keep quiet about your pending decampment from our fair shore, meaning that I won't alert Customs or the FBI to your transfer of funds offshore."

"And what's the second?"

"I won't tie you up and break your ankles."

Cashmore cringed visibly, but made a show of stoutheartedness. "You're not the type who could do something like that. I can see it in your face."

"Don't make the mistake of thinking that, Arnie. For your own sake, don't make that mistake..." Zanto jotted his cell phone number on a cocktail napkin and pushed it toward Cashmore. "Call me," he said, "when your instinct for self-preservation kicks in."

Forty-eight

The next morning, Sunday, Matt awoke in Lauren's bed, his body spooned around hers. From the sound of her even-paced breathing, he figured she was still asleep.

He was wrong.

"Let's go for a swim," she said, wriggling out of his clutches. When Matt worried aloud about running into her husband, Lauren assured him they wouldn't. Gabe had left town on business and wouldn't return for a week. Besides, she and Gabe had separated long ago, and she'd since stopped caring whether he approved of the men whose company she kept.

She and Matt swam for an hour in the huge pool behind the villa, then took a sauna. Later, they made love in the shower, and Matt wondered if this was a dream. He couldn't remember when he'd been so aroused, so in need of sex, even though he'd gotten it only yesterday. He took her from the front *and* the rear, cupping his hands around her soapy breasts while doing it. He felt like a college kid again, capable of conquering the world.

Lauren prepared breakfast. Actually she warmed leftovers from two days earlier, cherry muffins and a sweet porridge made of rolled oats and hazelnuts, one of Rainy's many specialties. They ate on the private deck outside Lauren's study, the morning sun warm on their shoulders.

"Something's bothering you," Lauren said.

"What could be bothering me—unless you count the psycho-sexual killer who's been butchering your friends? Or the fact that

Royal has been missing for two weeks? Or the fact that my best friend is lying in the hospital, fighting for his life?''

''No need to get sarcastic.''

Matt put down his spoon, having found that he wasn't hungry. Lauren caught the meaning in his stare.

''You're confused about all this, aren't you?'' she said, covering his hand with hers. ''So am I, a little. I never imagined doing the boy-girl thing with you, Matt, but now that it's happened, I can't pretend that I'm not glad. I want you to be glad, too.''

Matt picked up his spoon again and used it to draw circles in his porridge. ''It's what I wanted from the moment I first laid eyes on you,'' he admitted. ''But I never expected it to happen. You and I are from different galaxies.''

''All I know is that I've never felt safer than I do with you. Or more loved.''

''But I don't race speedboats or climb peaks in the Himalayas. And I know damn well I couldn't shoot a Cape buffalo.''

She laughed and leaned across the table to kiss him.

They finished eating, then strolled out to the gazebo, hand-in-hand. Lauren became quiet.

''Something's bothering *you* now,'' Matt said. ''Don't tell me—you're wondering why I wear my boxers inside out. It's because the label in the waistband gives me an itch.''

''There should be a law,'' she replied, only smiling.

''I totally agree. Except that's not what's bothering you, is it?''

She went to the swinging love seat, sat down and motioned him to join her. Which he did.

''Royal told me you had a son once,'' she said. ''You lost him, I understand.''

Matt endured the familiar wave of grief that always washed over him whenever he thought of Tristan. Yes, he'd had a son, he confirmed, and he had indeed lost him. ''My wife and I signed up to be foster parents, and Tristan was our first assignment. He came to us when he was four, and he had cystic fibrosis. It was supposed to be a temporary deal, but we fell in love with the kid, couldn't let him go. We adopted him, and he became—*ours*.''

''Jesus, Matt. I'm sorry. If you don't want to talk about this . . .''

Actually he did want to talk about it. His therapist had told him that talking about it was good.

He told Lauren about the harrowing eight-year war of attrition that he, his wife, and their adopted son had waged with cystic fibrosis, an inherited genetic disease that causes chronic lung problems and digestive disorders. He told her about the treatments that Tristan required every four hours, twenty-four hours a day, to loosen the mucos in his lungs and bronchial tubes—forced inhalation of a saline aerosol, followed by "percussive postural drainage," a euphemism for violently slapping the kid on his back with a cupped hand. He tried to describe how it felt to do such a thing to a crying child, but failed. He tried to relate how he and Marti, his wife, had coped with the frequent hospital stays that Tristan had required, but he failed at that, too. He spoke of the strain that the ordeal had inflicted on his marriage, the near-continuous state of exhaustion that he and Marti had endured, the scrimping and saving to pay for numerous medications, antibiotics, and enzyme supplement therapies. Inasmuch as Tristan was an adopted child, neither Matt's nor Marti's health insurance policies covered such costs.

But the worst part of it, he told Lauren, was knowing that no matter how hard they fought, no matter how valiantly they soldiered on, the disease would win in the end. Despite huge gains that medical science had made in recent years, sufferers of cystic fibrosis seldom lived beyond thirty. What compounded the tragedy for Tristan was the fact that his birth mother had been a drug addict, and she'd been unable to take proper care of him when he was very young. Thus weakened, he'd faced the likelihood of dying much earlier than the average sufferer.

"In a way, it was a miracle that he'd lived long enough for us to get him," Matt said. "He was a good kid, a strong kid, even though he was sick. In spite of everything, he loved life, loved to talk and sing and paint pictures. I figure he could've been an artist or an actor, maybe a writer . . ."

Matt coughed and took a breath to hold back a flood of emotion.

"We lost him a week after his twelfth birthday," he said finally. "I brought a big birthday cake to his room at the hospital, and I blew out the candles for him, because he didn't have the wind for it. But you should've seen his face—it was like I'd brought him a basket of puppies. Then I told him I'd get him anything he wanted, anything at all. Do you know what he asked for?''

Lauren sniffed and blinked away tears. ''No. What did he ask for?''

''A *Penthouse* magazine.''

''You're kidding.''

''Twelve-year-old boy, right? Not so strange, I guess. His hormones were just starting to kick in.''

''What did you do?''

''I went around the corner to the newsstand and bought him a goddamn *Penthouse*. We looked through it together, talked about the girls. Marti walked in on us as were looking at the centerfold, and I thought she was going to kill me.''

Lauren couldn't talk.

''A week later, he was gone,'' Matt said, wrapping up. ''I look back on it now—that horrendous eight-year period, all the agony, the sense of hopelessness, the grief—and I'd go through it again in a minute. They were the best years of my life, because I was a *dad*. And I'd do anything to have that kid back.''

Lauren pulled his hand to her cheek and wept silently. After a long while, she said, ''He could've made the world a better place, couldn't he—with his art, or his writing?''

Matt nodded.

''And you did everything you could to save him. That's the important thing. You never gave up, no matter how bad it got.''

''You're right, we never gave up, Marti and I—not on Tristan. After he died, we gave up on each other, but we never gave up on *him*.''

Lauren clutched his hand so hard that it started to hurt. He sensed that she wanted to say something more, but that she was holding back. He wondered if she, too, knew the hurt of losing a child.

Just then Matt heard his cellular phone ring—he'd left it on the deck outside Lauren's study. His breath caught, because the only people who had that number were Cleo Castillo and the Ragsdales. Cleo might be calling with news about Royal, or Ruby about Rags. He jogged back to the deck, snatched up the phone, and answered it.

The last voice he expected to hear was Royal Bowman's.

Forty-nine

"Royal, where the hell are you?"

"That's not important. What've you found out, Matt?"

"Damn it, Royal, I want you to tell me where you are. Cleo has fucking-near given you up for dead, and Lauren has been beside herself. We need to get you to a hospital and . . ."

"I just talked to Cleo a couple of minutes ago. It was her who gave me your number. How's Lauren? You takin' good care of my little girl?"

"She's fine, fine. How are you? How do you feel?"

"Like I've been sat on by an elephant—how do expect me to feel? You haven't lived till you start pissin' blood. It makes every day feel like a thousand years."

"When are you coming home?"

"That depends. I've been out here doin' a little investigating, poking around with some of my old contacts. We've put the word out that we're looking for information about people who wire houses. It might turn out to be a dead end, but shit, I've got to do *something*, Matt. You can understand that, can't you?"

"Who are these *contacts* you're talking about?"

"Some of 'em are folks I knew in the joint down in California, others are contacts I got through the merchant marine, people who know how to handle hot goods, stuff like that. And some of 'em are just plain old grifters who found their way to Seattle. They might not be social-register types, but they're good people to have on your side if you're in trouble. Anyhow, I need to know what you've found out, Matt.''

"It's a goose egg on this end. I'm sorry. We've debugged Lauren's house, and I sweep it every day to make sure it stays clean. The weird thing is that we found *two* sets of bugs . . ."

Matt filled Royal in on the rest of the news. Ian Prather and Vera Kemmis were dead. Rags was in the hospital with stab wounds, and Lauren's cook was missing. Matt made no mention of the fact that someone, presumably the killer, had gotten in and sexually assaulted Lauren.

"Jesus. I'm sorry to hear about Rags," Royal said. "He's a stand-up guy. Hope he makes it."

"Thanks. So do I."

"About this business with the two sets of bugs. You don't know who put in either one?"

Unfortunately this was true. All Matt could say for certain was that the killer accounted for one set. Not that this mattered much: Matt had no idea who the killer was.

"What I do know is this," he went on. "The killer knows Lauren, or thinks he does. He also thinks that she owes him something, that she's done him some kind of wrong. The tapes of Megan's and Vera's murders had blues music with them, songs that the guy believes Lauren will understand and respond to."

"*Blues* music?"

"That's right. Lauren says she can't think of anyone in her past who could possibly be this guy. But I get the definite feeling that she's holding out on me—maybe unconsciously. I think the songs mean something to her, and that she's repressed that meaning. It might involve something that happened deep in her past, something so bad that her conscious mind has switched off the memory of it."

"Sounds like bullshit to me, Matt. It reminds me of the psycho mumbo jumbo your shrink feeds you. Why couldn't it be some asshole who saw Lauren's picture in the paper and fell in love with her—some fat guy with pimples who can't get a woman in the real world? That's the kind of guy I'd be looking for if I was you—a stalker type."

Matt admitted that Royal might be right. But he had nothing else to go on, no other avenues to explore. He couldn't begin waylaying fat guys with pimples and working them over with rubber hoses.

He asked if Royal knew of anything in Lauren's past that might fit the repressed-memory theory. Any jilted boyfriends who might have become obsessive? Any disgruntled real estate customers or business rivals? Anything from an even earlier era, from Lauren's adolescence or childhood?

"I'm not the man to ask," Royal answered, sounding miserable. "She'd lived a lot before she made contact with me. I wasn't around when she was a girl, as I told you before. I was coolin' my heels in Pelican Bay. And she'd made it big in real estate long before she and I got back together. When it comes right down to it, there's a whole lot of my little girl's life that I don't know about and never will."

Matt said he understood.

Royal asked to speak with Lauren. But before Matt could get her on the phone, Royal said, "I appreciate what you're doin', Matt. Someday I'm gonna make this right with you, wait and see. I know Lauren is safe in your hands."

Matt wished to God that he himself could believe that.

Fifty

Tyler Brownlee left the warehouse in the International District on his Harley and cruised past the King Dome on Fourth Avenue, then swung toward the Sound to Third Avenue. He turned north and took a leisurely ride through the main business center of the city. At the stroke of noon he rounded a corner onto Cedar Street a few blocks south of the Seattle Center, where the Space Needle loomed into a hot blue sky. He parked in the drive of a presentable six-story apartment house called The Morgana.

He knew the doorman, called out to him by his first name. "Hey, *que pasa*, Freddy?"

Freddy's real name was Alfredo, and he spoke little English. Tyler knew that he kept a submachine pistol under the counter. Most of The Morgana's residents were native Spanish speakers, so Freddy's lack of English mattered little. He grinned and waved Tyler to the elevator.

Tyler took the elevator to the top floor, and rang the bell at number 606. The door opened to reveal a handsome, middle-aged woman who wore an apron and rubber gloves. Though Señora de Leon was busy preparing Sunday dinner for her large family, she greeted Tyler with a warm smile and invited him in.

The house was full of rowdy kid chatter, the smells of spicy cooking, and Mexican music. Tyler glanced into the living room and saw what looked like a rather large family reunion, with kids ranging from toddlers to high schoolers. Most of them, he figured, were Paco's. Others were probably cousins or neighbors.

Paco de Leon met him in the foyer of the spacious apartment, congenial as ever. He pumped Tyler's hand, asked about the Ranger, said how sad he was to learn that Arnie Cashmore had left the business. Then he led Tyler to a rear bedroom and closed the door for privacy. On the walls were pictures of the Pope, the Virgin Mary, and John F. Kennedy.

"Now, what's this all about, amigo?" Paco asked.

"I need a crew," Tyler said, "a couple of guys, at least. They've got to be professionals, not wannabes. You know people in L.A., right?"

A frown crept into Paco's round face. "A crew, you say. What do you need this crew to do, man?"

"I need them to do somebody, an ex-cop, then stay around to supply some muscle for a few days. Don't worry—it's got nothing to do with the business. I'm willing to pay major greenies, including finder's fees."

"Cap an ex-cop? Man, I don't like the sound of this."

"Don't sweat it, amigo. This won't bring any heat, believe me. It's a personal thing."

Tyler watched as Paco mulled the request, as he considered the potential benefits and liabilities. As Arnie had said many times, Paco hadn't become the Fat Woman's right-hand guy by being stupid.

"Does your old man know about this?" Paco asked, his frown deepening to a scowl. He'd lost his affability. He seemed like a cautious man not given to snap decisions.

"The Ranger knows. And he's given it his blessing. It's really no big deal."

After a long silence, Paco said, "Okay, I can set you up with a crew. They're major smoke, though, and they ain't cheap, know what I'm sayin'? I'll give you the name of my man in Riverside. You'll deal with him direct. You and me never talked about this, right?"

"Right. Now about the finder's fee. I'm ready to pay . . ."

"Forget that. I don't want no part of cappin' no ex-cop, and I don't want no fuckin' finder's fee. I don't even want to know about it, hear what I'm sayin'?"

"I hear you, Paco. Thanks."

"One more thing. You fuck up and bring trouble for the business, I got to take you out."

Tyler grinned his half-grin and slapped Paco on the shoulder. "I understand."

"Good. Now, you want to stay for dinner, or what? The old lady's cooked up enough to feed half the people in this building."

"Yeah? Maybe just a burrito or two. I don't have a lot of time."

Tyler wolfed down three of Señora de Leon's beef burritos before leaving.

Fifty-one

The package arrived at the Bowman-Granger estate via commercial messenger service just before 1:00 P.M. Matt Burgess and Rod Welton went together to the front gate to accept delivery. The sender had wrapped it in brown butcher paper and had jotted Lauren Bowman's name and address on it with a blue felt-tip pen, as with the previous two. And like the others, it was about the size of videocassette.

Matt read the carbon copy of the invoice before signing it. In the box labeled *Sender* someone had written *Meat Eater*.

"Who's 'Meat Eater?' " Matt asked the young driver, an overweight kid with pimples.

"No clue. Sorry."

"Where did you pick it up?"

"Abnor's Steak and Chop House up on Denny Way—just this side of I-5. Guy called our dispatch, said he had a package for immediate delivery, and gave the restaurant as the address. Said he'd be having a drink in the bar."

"He didn't give a name?"

"Nope. Just 'Meat Eater.' I figured he was, like, somebody's secret admirer, and didn't want her to know who sent the present. That happens a lot."

"What did he look like?" Rod asked.

"Young dude, built like a ceramic defecatorium, wore a black leather motorcycle jacket. He had long blond hair—like, to his shoulders, right? He looked like he could tear a telephone book in half.''

The description tickled Matt's memory. He'd seen someone like that recently, but he couldn't remember where. Long blond hair, black leather . . .

He asked whether the sender had paid with a credit card, because a credit card slip would have a name on it. But the kid said no. The guy had paid with cold cash, $125, the going damage for immediate pick-up and delivery of a small parcel on a weekend. Matt's heart sank.

He and Rod trudged back to the guest house, neither saying anything. As they reached the entryway, Rod held him back.

''There's no doubt about what this is, is there?'' the older man said, his face full of misery. ''It's a video. And we both know Rainy's on it. We don't really need to watch it, do we?''

Matt turned the thing over his hand, stared at it and fought the compulsion to throw it as hard and as far as he could. ''We need to watch it, Rod,'' he said. ''I'm sorry.''

''Fuck.'' Rod turned away, shuffled his feet, studied the blue sky. ''You'll excuse me if I take a pass.''

''Not a problem.''

Matt went to the sitting room, where Jandee Vernon was engrossed in a tennis match on TV. Her face fell when she saw the parcel in his hand. She switched off the TV and went immediately to Lauren's study to give her the news. Both women emerged a moment later, their faces bloodless and grim.

''You don't need to see this,'' Matt told them. ''I can take care of it.''

Lauren shook her head. ''I *do* need to see it. If it happened because of *me* . . .''

She broke off, but Matt knew her meaning. If Rainy's death was a message, a *gesture* from a madman to Lauren, then Lauren owed Rainy something, a debt far too huge ever to repay. The least she could do was share Rainy's pain in some small way.

''I need to watch it, too,'' Jandee said, her voice shaking. ''The more eyes, the better. One of us might see something that the others miss—a clue, a lead.''

Matt nodded, and got on with it. Following his cop's instincts, he carefully removed the wrapper from the cassette and set it aside, knowing that it might have the killer's fingerprints on it.

Never can tell, he said to himself. *Someday, somebody might actually report this asshole ...*

Handling the cassette itself by the edges in order to avoid smudging any prints, he maneuvered it into the VCR slot and switched on the power. He quickly sat down next to Lauren

The screen flashed to life with a now-familiar scene—a naked young woman bound to a plank on a forty-five-degree incline, her hands bound above her head, her scant breasts and pubic mound exposed to the devouring eye of the camera. Matt suffered a painful stomach cramp when he recognized Rainy Hales, her face wet with tears, her eyes shiny with terror. The microphone picked up her whimpering.

He became aware that Lauren had linked her arm with his, as if to seek his protection. He felt her stiffen at the first sight of Rainy on the screen, but she didn't gasp or cry out.

Rainy looked straight into the camera, and her mouth moved, formed words, but just then the music kicked in and covered her voice.

> *You know what I want for dinner, baby,*
> *And you know I don't like to eat alone ...*

The singer was the same gravel-throated man who'd performed the songs on the previous videos. Behind his lead vocal were an electric guitar and a bass. The music felt like a cold rain on a dark day.

> *And you know just how to cook it, baby.*
> *I'm talkin' red meat, talkin' blood and bone.*

The camera zoomed in tight on Rainy's face. At this range, injuries were visible, evidence of bludgeoning. Her lower lip was split and swollen, her cheek deeply bruised. Now that the mike was closer, her whimpering was audible again. She spoke. *"Lauren, I'm so sorry. I didn't want to hurt you. I didn't want to hurt anybody ..."*

Lauren turned away and pressed her face into Matt's shoulder. Her fingers dug into his arm like steel bands. Matt swore under his breath.

> *I'm a meat eater, woman—yes, I am,*
> *A meat eater day and night.*

I'm a meat eater, honey.
You've got to cook it just right . . .

Rainy's face twisted into a rictus of anguish, and Matt knew
that her tormentor had begun to rape her. As had happened before,
the man's shoulder occasionally came into view at the lower edge
of the screen, a rounded mass of muscle and bone. For the first
time, Matt became conscious of the fact that someone *else* had
operated the camcorder. The rapist could not possibly have
achieved this camera angle, given his groin-to-groin position with
Rainy.

Hey, I'm bringin' home the best cut, baby,
Because you know I like to eat it rare.
I like my meat like I like my women—
Naked, ready to eat and layin' bare.

The knife appeared now, and soon Rainy Hale's blood flowed.

Fifty-two

"She won't talk to me," Matt said, collapsing into a chair on the deck off the sitting room. Jandee sat across from him in the shade of a madrona. "I don't think she can. There's a roadblock in her mind."

He was talking about Lauren. Two hours had passed since they'd viewed the video, and Lauren had retreated to her bedroom suite, where she sat with her two dogs at a window, staring in silence at the Sound. Matt had spent more than an hour with her, prodding her to tell him what she knew about the killer, pleading with her to give him some hint concerning the meaning of the man's twisted message. But Lauren had merely continued to stare in silence, one hand stroking Desi, the other Lucy.

Rod Welton emerged from the wet bar in the sitting room, carrying two glasses of scotch over ice, one of which he handed to Matt. He sat down and lit a cigarette. "So, what's our next move?" he asked.

"We do some digging," Matt answered. He looked at Jandee. "Do you have any documentation concerning Lauren's past— school records, old yearbooks, correspondence from childhood friends, things like that? If you do, I'd like to see it."

Jandee replied that stuff like that did indeed exist, and she could put her hands on it. The main villa had a walk-in vault where Lauren and Gabe stored such material—fireproof, burglar-proof, you-name-it-proof. Like many rich people, they felt an obligation to preserve material essential to the writing of their biographies and memoirs.

"How much is there?" Matt asked.

A *lot*, Jandee answered. Since her youth, Lauren had been an inveterate saver of cards, letters, mementos, and even newspaper clippings. Sometimes Jandee wondered if her boss had ever thrown anything away.

"Then we'd better get busy," Matt said.

Jandee picked up a telephone and called Manuel Esparza, the butler in the villa. She told him that she and Matt needed access to the documents vault and that they would need to use the adjacent reading room. No, they wouldn't need meals or refreshments, she said, except for coffee, of course. They would bring their own snacks.

"Neither he nor his cook does vegan," Jandee whispered to Matt.

Then she called Elise Lekander, and asked her to come stay with Lauren. She didn't say why, only that Lauren needed a friend right now. Elise promised to arrive within the hour.

"We're all set," she said to Matt, switching off the phone. "Just let me fetch my laptop. Why don't you grab some fruit from the pantry?"

Matt swallowed the rest of his drink and stood. "Take care of things," he said to Rod. "I'll be next door, if you need me. Call me on the cell phone."

Rod stood, too. "I'm thinking that I should arrange to take some time off," he said. "Sounds like you're going to be busy for a while, and you're going to need someone to pull a security shift."

"You can do that?"

"I've got enough leave time stored up to grow a redwood. Count on my being here for the duration. All I ask is that you keep a full bottle of good scotch in the cabinet."

Matt and Jandee walked over to the main villa and entered through the south veranda, she carrying her laptop, he carrying a sack of apples and pears. She led him down a circular staircase to the basement level, where they walked past a huge wine cellar, an armory where Gabe Granger stored his arsenal of big-game guns, and an actual movie theater with a projection booth and an old-fashioned popcorn machine. At the end of the hall was a comfortable room that had a long table of polished mahogany,

six padded chairs and individual reading lights. On the far wall
was a steel door that looked as if it belonged to a bank vault.

Jandee set her computer on the table and spun the combination
dial, then put all her weight into heaving the door open. The vault
was ten by fifteen feet, divided by a walkway down the center.
On either side were document racks that accommodated hanging
folders, floor to ceiling, most of them full.

"Gabe's stuff is on the left, Lauren's is on the right," Jandee
said. "It's all in alphabetical order according to subject. I keep
an index on my computer that tells where everything is."

Matt gawked at the volume of material and asked if Jandee
had read all of it. She laughed and confessed that she had not.
She'd only begun working for Lauren two years ago. But she *had*
inventoried the material that belonged to Lauren in order to catalog everything and create the electronic index.

"Well, I guess we'd better get to work," Matt said, despite a
sinking feeling.

"Just one thing before we start," Jandee said. "I'm glad about
you and the boss—you know, you guys becoming an item, all
that."

"You know about it, huh?"

Jandee smacked a palm against her forehead. "Hel-*loh!* Like,
how am I going to miss it? It's not too obvious or anything. I
mean, like, you spend the night in her bedroom, and you sit
around holding hands? What am I supposed to think?"

"I guess we could've been more discreet."

"Hey, we're all adults here. And like I said, I'm glad. The
boss needs somebody like you, a regular guy—not some titan of
the business world or some international fugitive, but a regular
guy who cares about her. I can see that you do—*care* about her,
I mean."

"I care about her. But I wouldn't jump to conclusions, if I
were you. There's no telling where we'll be a month from now."

"Yeah, I know what you're saying. You're both stressed out
and needy. Like me. Even so, I'm glad. You're a good person,
and so is the boss. People like you guys should be together."

She sat down at the mahogany table and switched on her laptop. "Let's get to it, or we'll be at it all night," she said.

So they got to it. And they were at it all night.

Fifty-three

Matt and Jandee plowed through a mountain of paper, including letters Lauren had received from friends and relatives, invitations to parties and charity events, and messages both from supporters and opponents of her political views. They sifted through reams of receipts and order forms for clothing, furniture, cosmetics, objets d'art, and a hundred household items. They skimmed abstracts of research pieces sent to her by various experts in zoology, sociology, economics, and medicine—material she'd used for speeches and articles promoting veganism and animal rights. After working through the night to the brink of dawn, they'd actually read only a fraction of what was there.

"I've had it," Jandee said at four in the morning. She looked haggard. Her blond hair stuck out in misshapen fists from her head. "I feel like the bottom of a birdcage."

"Me too," Matt said. He felt as if he was bleeding to death from the eyes, and his back ached from hunching over a table all night. Even so, the ample supply of espresso from Manuel Esparza's kitchen had launched him on a caffeine jag that he feared would last for hours yet. "What do you think? Do we have anything here?"

Jandee consulted the notes she'd made. "Nothing that looks like a Rosetta Stone. The problem is we might have something, but simply not recognize it. When it comes right down to it, we don't really know what we're looking for, do we?"

"You're right. Maybe we should get help."

"Help from who?"

Now Matt looked at *his* notes, where he'd circled and underlined three names. The first was Angela Quilici, who was Lauren's aunt on her mother's side. Matt had seen nearly a dozen letters from Angela to her favorite niece, dating back to Lauren's college days. The second was Carlotta Lovitz, a high school friend who'd sent Christmas cards and occasional Where-Are-They-Now? letters about old acquaintances. And the third was the Reverend Danny Jayquist, pastor of the Foursquare Tabernacle of Galilee Church, which Lauren had attended as a girl. The pastor had written numerous letters imploring Lauren to repent of her sin, give up the ways of Mammon, and return to the fold of the Good Shepherd, if not for her own sake, then for the sake of her departed mother, a sister in Christ.

Quilici, Lovitz, and Jayquist all lived in Portland.

"Are you suggesting that we call these folks and ask if they know who's been cutting the throats of Lauren's friends?" Jandee asked.

"I'm suggesting that we pay them a visit and engage in some polite conversation, get them talking about the old days with Lauren. Maybe one of them will let slip some tidbit that will mean something to us."

Jandee paced around the table, her arms wrapped around her chest as if the room was cold. "God, it seems so flimsy, like such a long shot."

"It *is* a long shot. But it's the only shot we have. Lauren knows something about the killer—I've seen it in her eyes, some flash of memory or recognition, and it has something to do with the damn music." He hoisted his aching body out of the chair where he'd sat throughout the night. He rubbed the back of his neck. "We'll need to keep our ears perked for any reference to blues music, or anything that happened to Lauren that might cause someone to think she owes him something—something traumatic and life-changing."

"Owes him *what*? Her life, the lives of her friends?"

Matt shook his head. "We're dealing with a psycho, Jandee—bear that in mind. Whatever this guy thinks or believes won't make sense to you and me."

"So what happens if we come up empty-handed?"

"Then we try something else."

They walked back to the guest house as the eastern sky red-

dened with dawn. Jandee went immediately to her room and
flopped onto her bed, not bothering to undress. Matt paused before the door of Lauren's bedroom suite and grappled with the
question of whether to climb into the sack with her. While he
craved the feel of her body next to his, he was unsure about his
status with her. Were they full-blown lovers now, boyfriend and
girlfriend? The question became moot when he inched the door
open and saw Elise Lekander asleep in a chair next to Lauren's
bed. Matt had forgotten that Jandee had called Elise to request
her presence.

Matt got another rude awakening when he entered the guest
room. Marc Lekander lay asleep in the bed, apparently having
come along with his mother. *Shit.*

He went into the sitting room, thinking he would stretch out
on the sofa there, only to find that Rod Welton had already ap-
propriated it. Finally, he ended up on the couch in Lauren's study,
where he and she had first made love yesterday, which felt like
months ago. With the help of a tab of Xanax, he actually got
some sleep.

Fifty-four

Richardson Zanto's cell phone bleeped, and he pulled it out of his pocket, answered it.

"I'm at the north end of Pike's Place Market," said the man on the other end. "Do you know where that is?"

"Yes," Zanto said.

"I'll be sitting on the grass with the pigeons. Can you be here in an hour?"

"Oh, I think so."

"Don't be late. I've got a plane to catch this afternoon." *Click.*

Zanto smiled, because he stood less than two hundred feet from where Arnie Cashmore sat among the pigeons. A throng of tourists milled around the stalls in the market providing Zanto a perfect defilade. Since meeting Cashmore at the Mayflower Park Hotel two days earlier, Zanto had hardly let the little man out of his sight.

Cashmore sat cross-legged in the noon sunshine, facing the Sound. Zanto's sudden appearance startled him. "What the hell—? How did you get here so fast?"

"I'm faster than a speeding bullet," Zanto said.

"You've been watching me—is that it? Why did you even bother giving me your phone number?"

"Let's get down to business," Zanto said. "I take it you've had a change of heart. You're going to tell me where I can find Ray Brownlee, aren't you?"

Arnie raised his sunglasses to rest atop his balding head. "I'm going to reach into my pocket for a key," he said. "Don't shoot me, okay?"

"Okay."

Arnie took a key out of his pocket and handed it to Zanto. Then he described the warehouse where Ray Brownlee lived, and gave Zanto directions on how to find the place. Zanto didn't tell him this, but he knew the building, for he'd followed Tyler there. He hadn't known that this was the old man's home, however.

"That key will get you into the old man's apartment, which is on the top floor," Arnie said. "Getting in there would be like trying to get into Fort Knox. He uses a steel door and five, maybe six dead bolts."

"How did you come to have this key?"

"The old man and I have been sort of like partners for the past fifteen years. There's a safe in the basement where I stored merchandise and cash for the business. I came and went on a regular basis."

"Mmm. Anything else I should know?"

Arnie hesitated, glanced around nervously. "The basement stinks, always has. Smells like something dead. I don't know— it's probably nothing."

"What are you trying to tell me?"

Arnie swallowed, his Adam's apple bouncing. "I'm not trying to tell you anything. Except . . . there are a lot of locked rooms in the basement of that warehouse, places I've never gone and never want to. When you told me what happened to those women—Megan what's-her-name and the other one, Vera—I got to wondering, that's all. Like I say, it's probably nothing."

Zanto nodded. The two men stared at each other a moment. "Thanks," Zanto said at last. "I'm glad I don't have to tie you up and break your ankles."

Arnie Cashmore grimaced. "You wouldn't've done it. I know guys like you. You talk a tough game, but it's all talk."

"Oh? Then why did you call? Why did you give me the key?"

Cashmore looked away. "I can't remember doing anything in my adult life that I can be proud of. Maybe I'm taking a shot at doing that for once, doing something good. Sounds like bullshit, right?"

"No. It doesn't. If Tyler's killing women for fun, we need to stop him. If you help, you can be proud of that."

"You're serious?"

"Dead serious." Zanto got to his feet, brushed his trousers off. "Have a good life on your island," he said before walking away.

Fifty-five

At 1:15 on Monday afternoon Matt received word from Ruby Ragsdale that Rags was out of intensive care, and that the hospital had upgraded his condition to serious. He could see visitors. Matt immediately drove to Virginia Mason Hospital and spent an hour with his old friend, who lay in a bed with tubes coming out of his nose, his arm, his abdomen. Rags' face was rashy and blistered from the CS agent, his eyes inflamed.

"You look like shit," Matt told him, patting his arm.

"It's an act to get sympathy," Rags said.

They watched two innings of a Mariners' game, but because Ruby was in the room, they didn't talk about the Lauren Bowman case. Matt said that he needed to leave town for a few days in order to take care of some business. He planned to catch a plane to Portland later in the afternoon.

"Keep me posted," Rags said.

"I will. Take care, okay? By the way, you owe me a round of golf." He left the hospital and drove back to Magnolia.

Marc Lekander accosted him as soon as he arrived, and said that he was deeply concerned about Lauren's emotional state. As one who had known her for many years, Marc believed that the best thing for her was to leave Seattle immediately and go somewhere safe, preferably far away. He asked Matt's help in persuading her to go with him to the Lekanders house in Kauai.

"She needs to decompress," Marc said, "to feel safe and protected. I can give her that in Hawaii. You *will* talk to her, won't you? Jandee tells me that you and Lauren''—he blinked several times, as if having trouble finding words that didn't taste bad— "have become *close*. I'm sure Lauren would listen to you.''

Matt protested that he couldn't tell Lauren where to spend her time. Besides, he had confidence in Rod Welton's ability to keep her safe, as long as Lauren cooperated with him. Then he excused himself, and went to Lauren's study, knocked on the door. Elise answered it and ushered him in.

Lauren sat on the deck with the dogs, wearing a scarf over her head and sunglasses. Matt sat next to her, kissed her cheek.

"I like the Jackie-O look,'' he quipped. ''It makes me feel like we're on a Greek island.'' She gave him a feeble smile. ''I'll be gone for the next few days, but Rod will take care of things here. Do whatever he says, okay?''

"We'll muddle through,'' she said in a thin voice. Matt now appreciated how profoundly Rainy Hales' death had affected her, this third hammer stroke against the brittle shell of her emotional armor. ''You're going to Portland, aren't you? You and Jandee. I know why. And I hope—'' She caught his hand, brought it to her lips. ''I hope you find what you're looking for.''

"We'll find it,'' he assured her.

"Promise me that . . . if you find it . . . you won't *hate* me.''

"I could never hate you,'' Matt said, his heart brimming.

He went to the guest room and packed his shaving gear and a change of clothes into a sailor's duffel. He stashed his SIG Sauer in the bottom drawer of the handsome teak bureau, knowing that he couldn't bring a gun with him on a commercial airplane. That he felt vulnerable without it surprised him.

Fifty-six

On the forty-five-minute flight to Portland, Jandee informed Matt that she'd reserved adjacent rooms at the posh Heathman Hotel downtown. Why go slumming, she asked, when Lauren Bowman was picking up the tab?

She also confirmed that she'd contacted each of the people they wanted to see—Angela Quilici, Carlotta Lovitz, and the Reverend Danny Jayquist. She'd arranged appointments with them over the next two days. She'd used the cover story that Matt had suggested: She and a writer named Matt Burgess had begun work on an authorized biography of Lauren Bowman, and they needed background information from relatives, old friends, and acquaintances.

Also, she'd rented a car, bought notebooks and pens.

Matt now understood the value of a personal assistant, and vowed that if he ever struck it rich, he would get one.

At six the following morning he woke to the ringing of the phone in his room. "Rise and shine," Jandee told him. "I'll be there in half an hour with some fresh fruit and the best organic bran flapjacks you've ever had. That should give you time to shit, shower, and shave, as an old boyfriend of mine used to say."

"You're telling me they cook vegan here at the Heathman?"

"Only if you give them enough advance notice. Which I did, of course."

Matt made a mental note to himself: *If you ever get a personal assistant, make sure he's a meat eater.*

Over breakfast in Matt's room they put the final touches on their cover story and rehearsed their lines. Then they left for a neighborhood named Laurelhurst in northeast Portland, Matt driving the rented Chrysler Concorde, Jandee navigating with a map of the city splayed on her lap.

Matt had visited Portland many times, and he knew the city fairly well. Like Seattle, Portland had developed a traffic problem, which he and Jandee experienced in full force as they drove east across the Willamette River on the Burnside Bridge.

"I forgot to allow for the rush hour," Jandee said.

"That does it—you're fired," Matt said.

They arrived fifteen minutes late at Angela Quilici's home, which stood in a pleasant, shady neighborhood near Laurelhurst Park. The house was a neat clapboard bungalow trimmed with rounded junipers and dazzling red roses that made Matt's nose itch. He managed to stifle a sneeze as Angela Quilici herself answered the doorbell. She invited them in, offered them coffee and cookies.

She was a tall woman in her mid-sixties with short black hair that showed not a trace of gray. Matt could see a definite family resemblance between Angela and her niece, Lauren—the long face atop a slender neck, intense brown eyes, severe cheekbones. She seated them in her living room, where a huge Siamese cat kept watch atop a spinet piano.

"Well," Angela said, "I understand that you're writing a book about Lauren. I'll be glad to help you any way I can. Just don't expect me to give you anything juicy . . ."

Fifty-seven

Tyler Brownlee escorted the two men from L.A. to the Ranger's regular table in the rear of the Blue Lion. With a nod of his head, the Ranger motioned them to sit. Though the club wouldn't open for hours yet, Packy Barker approached the table and offered to bring drinks. Nobody wanted one, so Packy retreated to the back room.

"Gentlemen, allow me to present the Blues Ranger," Tyler said, pulling up a chair and sitting on it backward. "And this is the crew, up from L.A.," he said to Ray. On his right sat a short, blunt-looking man of thirty, dark-haired and heavily bearded—he could have been an Arab or a Turk. Tyler introduced him simply as Shafiq.

The other man was a light-skinned black with hazy blue eyes, slender, tall, maybe thirty-five. His name was Cyan, and like Shafiq, he had no last name. He wore a black blazer over a red T-shirt and a single strand of gold around his neck.

Both men shook hands with Ray Brownlee.

And Ray Brownlee wasted no words. "You're here to kill a man who needs to die," he said without preamble. "Then, you'll stick around for a while, do some chores for me, provide some security. Shouldn't take more than a week out of your busy schedules. Got any problems with that?"

"Not me," Shafiq replied. Cyan merely shrugged.

"Good. You know about the money?"

Tyler explained that he'd offered each of the men $50,000 up front, with another fifty thou for each at the end of the job. "Everything's cool," he said. "I showed them the money."

"Tell you what I'm going to do," Ray Brownlee said. "I'll make it seventy-five up front, and another seventy-five when it's over, just to show good faith. That's a hundred and fifty each. Not bad for a week's work, eh?"

Shafiq and Cyan glanced at each other. Cyan then spoke with a voice that seemed too deep for a man of his size. "Just so you know—we work for some very major dudes out of Colombia and Mexico."

"I know exactly who you work for," Ray Brownlee said.

"Yeah, well—here's the deal, dawg. Anything happens to us—like, it's popular to hit the hit men when all the dirty work's over, hear what I'm sayin'? If that happens, or if anybody tries to stiff us for our greenies, there's gonna be some major smoke out of L.A."

"I don't believe in stiffing people. The people in L.A. know that, or they wouldn't have let you come."

"Yeah, well—jus' so we understand each other, dawg."

Tyler's excitement mounted as he listened. He could see that things had finally started to come together for him. Soon the last wall of Lauren's castle would crumble, and she would be his. A new world would begin.

His old world held little magic for him anymore.

Fifty-eight

Over dinner in a small vegan restaurant in northwest Portland, Matt and Jandee discussed their conversation with Angela Quilici, who was Lauren's only living relative on her mother's side of the family. The truth was that they hadn't really learned much of interest during the five hours they'd spent with her.

Angela had confirmed that Lauren grew up poor, that her mother, Marlene, had worked as a bookkeeper for a furniture wholesaler after Royal had abandoned them, a job she'd kept for more than thirty years. They'd lived in a tough neighborhood between Fremont and the notorious Killingsworth Street in northeast Portland, in a cramped unit of subsidized housing.

In 1972, when Lauren was twelve or thirteen, Marlene had undergone a conversion to militant fundamentalist Christianity, which Angela had disdainfully called "going off the deep end." Lauren's life had become a hell. Marlene had forced her to attend church services three times a week, to sing in a choir, attend Bible studies and join a Christian youth group that didn't believe in dating or rock music. Marlene had turned every meal into a lecture on *evil*—the evil of cigarettes, drugs and alcohol, sex, even dancing and makeup. Angela had felt sorry for her niece. When Lauren finally rebelled against the enforced piety, it came as no surprise to her aunt.

"She started to run with a bad crowd," Angela had said. "Motorcycle hoods, mostly—boys who smoked and drank, and ex-

pected their girlfriends to . . . well, I'm sure you can just imagine.
That's when Lauren met that Ben Brownlee kid, and things went
from bad to worse. He was just plain no good, that Ben Brownlee.
He was at least three years older than she, maybe four . . .''

Jandee suggested that they follow up on this Brownlee, find
out who he was, what had happened to him. Matt agreed. In his
mind he pictured someone who looked like James Dean in *Rebel
Without a Cause*, though Brownlee could as easily have looked
like a Hell's Angel.

Matt had sought Angela's clarification on something. She'd
said that Royal Bowman had abandoned his family. But Matt had
learned from Royal himself that he'd gone to prison in California,
which wasn't the same thing, strictly speaking.

"Don't you believe it," Angela had said. "Royal had love
interests all over the West Coast. He told Marlene he was going
to jail so he could get free of her without going to the trouble of
getting a divorce. Why, I heard people say they'd seen him right
here in Portland, living with another woman and raising another
family."

"I can't believe that Royal would've abandoned his wife and
daughter," Matt said to Jandee over dinner. "He's not the type
to do that. He feeds stray cats, for crying out loud."

Maybe Angela had exaggerated, Jandee offered.

The next morning they drove into the neighborhood where
Lauren had spent her childhood. Most of the homes were small
and rundown, many in need of paint and repair. Here or there
stood an abandoned house, like a rotting tooth in a skull's face.
From nearly every overhead utility line dangled a pair of sneakers,
signifying the territorial claim of some gang. Junked-out cars sat
at the curbs, and broken toys littered the yards.

The Foursquare Tabernacle of Galilee Church was an outpost
of neatness and orderliness on a residential corner, its stumpy
steeple thrusting proudly into a bright morning sky. In the church-
yard stood a back-lit marquee with the name of the church on it,
the name of its pastor, and the title of next Sunday's sermon:
WARRIORS IN CHRIST.

Next to the church was the parsonage, a small but nicely maintained house that boasted the same white paint as the church. Matt
and Jandee climbed the stairs to the front porch, but before they
could ring the bell, the door opened, revealing Pastor Danny Jay-

quist himself, a trim man in his sixties with a shock of white hair
that hung down over his forehead. He had twinkling eyes, a broad
smile and a ruddy complexion that suggested high blood pressure.
He welcomed them with hearty handshakes and invited them in.
His wife served scones with homemade blackberry preserves and
coffee. He would be pleased, he said, to give whatever help he
could toward the writing of a book about one of his favorite
parishioners, Lauren Bowman.

The pastor then proceeded to sermonize for the next four
hours.

By the time Matt and Jandee left, both had splitting headaches.
"Is it okay for vegans to drink beer?" Matt asked.

"Not only is it okay, it's encouraged," Jandee said.

They drove back into downtown Portland and found a bar that
Matt remembered from a past trip—the Pilsner Room, which had
a nice view of the Willamette River. He and Jandee each ordered
a pint of microbrew. He ordered a burger, she a salad.

They discussed their conversation with Jayquist, and decided
that they'd learned little if anything new. He'd confirmed that
Lauren had been a rebellious girl, and that her life had gone to
hell in a handbasket when she took up with that reprobate, Ben
Brownlee.

"This Brownlee character certainly seems to have made an
impression on people," Matt said.

After lunch they motored out to the western suburb of Beaverton to keep their appointment with Carlotta Lovitz, who lived
in a condominium that overlooked a park. When she greeted them
at the door, Matt was surprised to see how much older than Lauren she looked, but then he reminded himself that she was probably a middle-income lady who hadn't enjoyed the benefits of a
personal trainer, a personal cosmetician, and extended stays in the
world's major health resorts.

Ms. Lovitz welcomed them into her home, then showed them
into her office. She was a freelance tax accountant, she told them.
She was also divorced and the mother of two energetic teenagers,
whose pictures graced the wall next to Carlotta's diplomas from
Portland State University. She asked how Lauren was, causing
Matt and Jandee to lie like a couple of Bedouin carpet peddlers.
She's great. Very busy. Sends her love . . .

"It's exciting that someone is finally writing a book about

her," Carlotta said. "I'd once thought about doing it myself. But alas . . ."

Matt remarked to himself on how completely this woman had shaken off the dust of the neighborhood she'd grown up in. She seemed cultured, well spoken. Her college education had transformed her, he thought.

Five hours later, Matt and Jandee headed back downtown. They dined in the same vegan place that they'd patronized last night. Once again, it was debriefing time.

"I must say, the news about the baby was a shock," Jandee said around a bite of tofu. Lovitz had disclosed that Lauren had been pregnant when she ran away at the age of sixteen. "The boss has never uttered a peep about ever having had a kid."

"She never actually told me about it," Lovitz had said. "I'm sure she thought that she'd kept it a secret. She'd taken to wearing these huge dresses of her mother's, thinking she could cover it up. But it's tough to keep something like that a secret from your best friend."

That Carlotta had laid bare the secret after all this time surprised Matt, and he said so to Jandee. Don't friends keep each other's secrets?

"It's clear she doesn't feel close to Lauren anymore," Jandee said. "She's probably a little jealous, which would only be human. Your best bud from high school goes out and makes a bazillion bucks, and where do you end up? In a condo in Beaverton, Oregon, a divorced mom, doing somebody else's tax returns. I'd probably be jealous, too."

"I've always assumed the baby was Ben Brownlee's," Carlotta had added. "It's probably a good thing that Lauren took off when she did, because she could never have made a go of it with Ben. She'd grown to hate him . . ."

Carlotta had reinforced the impression that Ben Brownlee had been a reprobate of the first order. He'd dealt drugs, stolen cars, burgled houses. Worse, he'd abused Lauren.

"He was a chip off the old block, Ben was. His father was as bad as he was, if not worse. Everybody called him the Blues Ranger, but his real name was Ray Brownlee. He was a musician, a singer I think—I never heard him perform. He played in clubs

downtown and all over the east side. It was common knowledge
that he was a drugger.''

That Ray Brownlee had hit on his son's young girlfriend, Lauren, was not common knowledge, however. Several times Lauren
had recounted ugly episodes at the Brownlee house on North
Borthwick Street. Ray and his boy had taken turns slapping her,
doing things to her. Whether the old man had actually forced her
to have sex with him had remained Lauren's secret.

"I think it was her fear of those two that drove her to run
away . . .''

As he heard this, something twisted inside Matt's gut. He felt
a breed of anger that he hadn't experienced in a long time, a
craving to punish any grown man who could intentionally harm
a child, be she a toddler or a teenager. At such moments he jet-
tisoned his cop's devotion to notions like *probable cause* and *due
process*. Matt knew that if he ever caught some son of a bitch in
the act of committing such an outrage, he would kill him. Having
listened to Carlotta Lovitz's story, he could think of nothing more
satisfying than finding this Brownlee and blowing his head off.

"The more I think about your suggestion that we track this guy
down, the better I like it," Matt said to Jandee.

"How do we do that?"

"Carlotta gave us the address of the house where the Brownlees lived, right?''

Jandee set aside her fork and paged through her notebook.
"Close. She gave us the corner it's on. It should be easy to find.''

"Are you up for staying an extra day?''

"Absolutely. Are you counting on the Brownlees still being
at the house on Borthwick Street?''

"I'm not counting on anything," Matt said. "I'm taking a shot
in the dark, if you want the unvarnished truth.''

He pulled out his cell phone and called Lauren's number in
Seattle. Rod Welton answered. Matt asked for a situation report,
and Welton gave it to him. Everything was normal, quiet. The
Lekanders had stayed with Lauren in the guest house, though
they'd both tried unsuccessfully to persuade her to relocate either
to their house in Hawaii or the one in Mexico. All things considered, Lauren seemed to be holding up okay.

Rod then asked how the Portland Project was going, and Matt
told him that he had almost nothing to report. Not yet, at least.

"Rod, as a juvenile probation officer, you're an officer of the court, aren't you?" Matt asked.

"That's right, same as any other probation officer."

"That means you're entitled to retrieve corrections records over the Law Enforcement Telecommunications System."

"Sure. I do it all the time."

"Do me a favor. Find out if Royal Bowman ever served time in Pelican Bay, California, or anywhere else, for that matter."

"Lauren's dad? You want me to check up on Lauren's dad?"

"Can you do it and get back to me?"

"Yeah, I guess. I'll phone it in first thing tomorrow."

"Great. Call me back as soon as you get anything."

After Matt switched off, Jandee asked what *that* had been about.

"Nothing, I hope. Let's go back to the hotel. I need to soak in a hot tub for a while."

Fifty-nine

At 11:25 A.M. on Thursday, June 19, two men walked into Shorty's Tavern in Ballard and went to the bar. One was a stocky Mediterranean-type, the other a lanky mulatto with unsettling blue eyes. Except for a couple of stringy old alcoholics who hunkered over their boilermakers at the opposite end of the bar, the place was empty. The lunchtime rush, however, would begin within a few minutes.

Cleo Castillo leaned through the cook's window and motioned to Jimmy Jaspero, the assistant manager, who was busy with the preparation of cooking oil for the deep fryers. Speaking Spanish, she told Jimmy to keep an eye on these two, because she didn't like their looks. Then she turned back to the bar, smiling, and asked the pair if they needed menus.

"We're lookin' for a dude named Matthew Burgess," the slim one said. "We were told he works here."

"Not anymore," Cleo answered. "He's been gone for—oh, two or three weeks now. I hear from him now and then, though. Can I give him a message?"

"Gone? You mean, like, he left town or somethin'?"

"Gone, like he's got himself a new job somewhere."

"And where might that be?"

"I don't know. He didn't say."

The two men looked at each other, then turned and walked out of the tavern without so much as a thank-you.

"Follow them," Cleo said to Jimmy Jaspero.

Sixty

The old gentleman's name was Clive, and he was most helpful. In fact, he seemed downright anxious to tell all he knew about the people who had lived across the street from him more than twenty-five years ago.

"They was bad people," he said. "I was damn near ready to throw a party when they finally left."

His had been the third door on North Borthwick Street that Matt Burgess and Jandee Vernon had knocked on. He was an elderly black man with bushy muttonchops that were white as snow.

"That boy of theirs, that Benny—he'd rev up his motor-sackle out here by the curb, just rev it up an' rev it up, all hours of the day and night, keep us all awake. And it was no secret they had dope over there."

Did Clive know where any of them had gone? Matt wanted to know.

"Well, that boy of theirs got hisself sent to the penitentiary down in Salem for bustin' into some fella's house over on Fremont. After he got out, he hung around the neighborhood for a while, then decided t' hell with it, and jumped off the 39th Street overpass. Landed on the grille of a big White Freightliner. They found pieces of him three miles up the Banfield Freeway, I'm told."

What about the father and mother?

"Ray took off for somewhere—I don't know where. He was

a bluesman, called hisself the Blues Ranger. Lot of people liked to hear him sing and play. Too bad he didn't content himself with singin' the blues, and forget about drugs and little girls and such."

"Little girls?"

"He liked 'em young. *Too* young, if you ask me. I saw 'em come and go from his place, girls his son would drag in for him. Hell, you wouldn't believe the rumors you'd hear about that guy. Back in the early seventies there was a string of young girls disappeared—whores, most of 'em, all from around Sandy Boulevard, and people said Ray had somethin' to do with it. The cops even came around askin' questions, but nobody ever tagged him for anything."

Matt remembered the urban myth that had spread among the junkies in Seattle's Capitol Hill years ago. Somebody was taking drugged-out runaways, raping and butchering them, always with blues music in the background. One of them escaped somehow, and lived to tell the tale. But who believed a junkie except another junkie?

"What about the mother?" Jandee asked.

"I hear she's workin' in a secondhand clothes place down in Milwaukie," Clive answered. "Her name is Nona. Nona Brownlee."

"Milwaukee, Wisconsin?" Jandee asked.

"Milwaukie, Portland. It's south of here. Get on I-5 south and take the Milwaukie exit. The place is called Same As New. Afraid I can't give directions to it. My wife would know, but she's out playin' bridge."

"We'll find it," Matt said.

With the help of their map of Portland, Matt and Jandee found Milwaukie, a suburb that sprawled eastward from the Willamette. They pulled into a service station and used the yellow pages to get the address of the Same As New, then located it on the map.

Ten minutes later they exited McLoughlin Boulevard into a crowded strip mall. The Same As New was a large, glass-fronted establishment that appeared as though it had once been a grocery store. Inside were endless rows of previously owned apparel, everything from parkas to evening dresses. A substantial crowd of shoppers, mostly women, wheeled carts up and down the aisles in search of bargains.

"I'm looking for Nona Brownlee," Matt said to a clerk. The clerk paged the assistant manager, who escorted them to the rear

of the store. Beyond a pair of swinging doors was a large room
with bright overhead lights and a battery of sewing machines.
The assistant manager led them to a shriveled woman in her late
sixties, Nona Brownlee. Nona shut down her sewing machine,
folded the secondhand dress that she'd been working on, and
offered Matt a bony hand.

"You can have twenty minutes with these people," the assistant manager told her. "Use the break room."

The break room was adjacent to the sewing room. It had soda
machines, candy machines, and a coffeepot.

"I appreciate your taking time to talk with us," Matt said.
"We'll try not to keep you long."

"Hell, keep me all day," the old woman said, lighting a cigarette.

Matt and Jandee glanced at each other. "We're here to ask
you about your husband, Ray," Matt said.

Nona inhaled a lungful of smoke and blew it out again. "If
you find that son of a bitch, tell him he owes me two hundred
and fifty dollars," she wheezed. "That's how much he stole when
he ran out on me. And that doesn't count all the money I spent
takin' care of that brat of his for five years."

What brat? Jandee asked. Did she mean Ben, their son?

"Naw, not Ben. He was good as gold. Always loved his
mama, did what I told him to do. I'm talking about the fuckin'
newborn Ray showed up with one day. He hands the kid to me
and says, 'Take care of him, make sure he stays alive.' The kid
was filthy and hungry, so weak he couldn't even cry. His mama
had wrapped him in a flimsy little doll's blanket. That was in
seventy-six, and I was forty-seven years old. You think I was up
for takin' care of a fuckin' newborn baby at the age of forty-
seven?"

Whose baby was it? Matt asked, his gut churning. He feared
he already knew the answer.

"It was Ray's kid—that's all I know. The mother could've
been any one of five or six little chippies he kept around. I don't
know what in the fuck any of them ever saw in him. He was a
mean bastard, Ray was, when he got to drinkin'. He always
slapped 'em around pretty good. Hell, he slapped *me* around, and
I stayed with him—I guess I shouldn't talk, huh?" She let out a
laugh that sounded like a boiling pot of phlegm. "Anyhoo, on
the day the kid turned five, Ray comes and gets him, takes him

away and doesn't even say thanks. If the truth was known, I'd gotten attached to the kid by that time, but what was I gonna do? You don't say no to Ray Brownlee.''

"Do you remember a girl named Lauren Bowman?" Jandee asked.

A frown pinched the old woman's brow as she pondered the name. Suddenly she raised a crooked finger. "Yeah, I remember her. A pretty one, too. Nice girl. Ray sent Ben after her, and Ben brought her in.''

"He sent Ben after her? What do you mean?"

"That's the way the son of a bitch worked. He liked young girls, but he couldn't go out and pick 'em up himself, because that would attract attention, and Ray didn't want that. So he sent Ben after 'em. Ben was a handsome brute. You should've seen him in his leather jacket, sittin' on his Harley. The girls loved him, and he'd bring 'em home. And that's when Ray pounced on 'em.'' Again she laughed her horrible laugh.

Jandee put her hand over her mouth, as if she was afraid to breathe whatever microbes Nona had coughed out. "Didn't the girls ever tell anybody? Didn't anyone ever call the police?"

"They was too scared to tell anyone. Ray pretty much kept them in line. And if you want to know the truth, some of 'em liked it. Hell, some of 'em *loved* it. There's women out there who like being roughed up and bossed around. As I recall, Lauren Bowman was one of those.''

Matt had heard enough. He took Jandee by the arm and steered her through the door, then led her outside. As he was digging for the car keys, a wave of nausea hit him, and he threw up, right there on the sidewalk. Jandee grabbed him, held his forehead.

"It's okay," she said. "It's okay.''

But Matt knew that nothing was okay.

Sixty-one

Tyler Brownlee and the "smoke" from L.A. rode the open freight elevator to the top level of the warehouse. Tyler led the two men to the steel door of the Ranger's apartment and took out the keys to the five dead bolts. The plaintive strains of an electric guitar echoed throughout the dark building—the Ranger playing the blues. Tyler thought, *Shit, the old bastard's still got the fingers.*

"Man, this place is freaky," said Shafiq, the short one, to his colleague, Cyan. "I don't mind saying I'm getting a little creeped out."

"Dawg, what's with you?" demanded Cyan. "You're supposed to be the smoke, the thing that goes bump in the night. You don't get creeped out by a few fuckin' shadows in a deserted warehouse."

Tyler laughed as he pushed the door open. Thus far, the smoke from L.A. had failed to impress him. He didn't doubt for a minute that he could grease these two right now, if the mood took him, and neither would know what hit them.

Ray Brownlee sat in his usual place, on a metal folding chair amid the clutter of amplifiers, drums, microphones, tape recorders, and MIDI equipment. He laid aside his guitar when he saw Tyler and the men from L.A.

"What's happening?" he asked.

Tyler explained that Cyan and Shafiq had spent the past thirty-six hours trying to find Matt Burgess, but without success. Finally, they had gone into the tavern at Shorty's Landing and asked about him. His boss had said that Burgess didn't live there anymore, that he'd been gone for several weeks. Where, she didn't know.

"And he's not at the Bowman-Granger estate?" the Ranger asked.

"I've been watching the place myself," Tyler said. "If he's there, he hasn't come out."

The Ranger thought for a moment, thrumming his guitar-calloused fingers against his metal chair. "Time's growing short," he said. "I'd say extreme measures are in order."

Tyler liked the sound of that. *Extreme measures* were his specialty.

Sixty-two

Jandee refilled Matt's glass with ginger ale and dropped fresh ice cubes into it. Handing it to him, she said, "Our plane doesn't leave until 7:20, so that gives you almost four hours to relax and get well."

Matt sipped the ginger ale and thanked her for babying him. Jandee had driven him back to the Heathman after he'd vomited up his breakfast in the parking lot of the Same As New. She'd shepherded him to his room, deposited him in bed, and ordered ginger ale from room service. She promised him a light lunch if he felt better later in the afternoon.

He apologized for his weak gut. While listening to Nona Brownlee's account of her husband's deeds, Matt couldn't help but visualize Lauren as Ray Brownlee's victim—beaten up, sexually abused, terrorized, and finally impregnated with Brownlee's kid. Small wonder that she'd run away to Seattle in search of Royal's loving arms. And small wonder, too, that she'd been unable to revisit the outrages she'd suffered as a young girl, unable to dredge them up again in order to disclose them to Matt.

"I guess we've done what we came to do," Jandee said, sitting on the edge of Matt's bed. "We've solved our mystery, or at least part of it. We know who we're after now."

Matt agreed. No great leap of imagination was needed to conclude that Ray Brownlee had killed Megan, Vera, and Rainy. Except . . .

"Except what?" Jandee asked.

Except that Ray Brownlee would now be in his late sixties or early seventies, judging from his wife's apparent age. How likely was it, Matt asked, that an old man could have won a hand-to-hand fight with Ian Prather, a battle-hardened underground militant?

"I hadn't thought of that," Jandee confessed.

Last but not least, how would Matt and Jandee go about finding Brownlee? Chances were slim that he was listed in the white pages.

At that moment Matt's cell phone rang. It was Rod Welton.

"I sent a query to California Corrections over LETS on Royal Bowman," he said, "and I just heard back. He's never served time in California, not at Pelican Bay or anywhere else. If you want, I can put out a query to Oregon and Washington. Maybe you just heard him wrong. Maybe he was at OSP or Walla Walla."

"That's okay, Rod. I didn't hear him wrong, I can tell you that. Let's forget about it, okay?"

"No problem. When are you coming back? I'm tired of trying to make conversation with Marc Lekander. I get the feeling he doesn't like people who aren't worth at least a hundred million."

Matt smiled and told him to expect them tonight.

"Let me guess," Jandee said after he'd switched off the phone. "That was Rod. He ran his check on Royal, and Royal never did any time at that prison in California."

Matt nodded. "Which means that Angela Quilici may have been right about him. He may in fact have deserted Lauren and her mother." Now Matt felt queasier than ever.

Sixty-three

Lauren Bowman walked out of her study and saw Rod Welton replace the telephone into its cradle.

"Who was that?" she asked.

"Matt. He says hi. He and Jandee will be back tonight."

Lauren smiled. She'd missed Matt, and Jandee, too, of course. But especially Matt. How strange, she thought, that the two of them had found each other in a world where so much energy goes into keeping the wealthy apart from everyone else—a world of gated communities, luxury boxes, business jets, and private showings. If Royal hadn't insisted that she talk to Matt . . .

The intercom rang. Manuel Esparza had answered a call at the gate, someone to see Lauren. It was Lauren's father, Royal Bowman.

"My God!" Lauren glanced at Rod, who shrugged his shoulders. She turned back to the intercom. "Let him in, Manuel."

"Yes, ma'am," Esparza said.

"Rod, can you escort him? He's not well, and . . ."

"Of course. You stay put. We'll be back in a flash."

Marc and Elise Lekander came in from the deck, saw Lauren's expression and asked what was wrong. Nothing was wrong, she told them. Royal had come out of hiding. He was here. *Now*.

"That's *wonderful*, darling," Elise said, hugging her. "You and he will have much to talk about. Perhaps Marc and I should leave you two to commiserate in private. Marc, get your things. We're going home."

"Elise, don't be silly," Lauren said. "I'm closer to you than anyone in the world. I want you to stay."

"You're sure?"

Marc spoke up. "Mother, she wants us to stay. Don't make her beg, for Christ's sake."

Moments later Rod ushered Royal Bowman into the foyer, carrying the old man's duffel for him. Lauren went to her father, wrapped her arms around him, told him how glad she was to see him. His appearance frightened her. He'd lost weight that he couldn't afford to lose. The pouches under his eyes had grown larger, darker, giving his face a cadaverous look. His skin had a yellowish cast, warning of a weakening liver.

"Sorry I stayed away so long," he said to her, giving her a final squeeze. "There were things I needed to do. I'll tell you about them sometime—maybe."

She asked him how he felt, fearing that she would hear the worst, and that's exactly what she heard. Royal could feel the cancer eating away at his insides, he said. A man couldn't feel as bad as he felt and have much time left. Such a man shouldn't spend any more time than absolutely necessary away from the people he loved.

He asked about Matt. He needed to see him. Rod explained that Matt and Jandee had gone to Portland in search of leads on the killer, but that they would be home this evening.

"Shit, I was hoping he'd be here—excuse my French," Royal said. "But look, we can't fool around any longer. We've got to get Lauren out of here. This place isn't safe."

Marc Lekander stepped forward and said that he agreed completely. At the very least, Lauren should come to stay at the Lekander estate in The Highlands, where security was tighter than the Federal Reserve's. Better yet, she should leave the city, go to Kauai or Cabo San Lucas. Marc offered to bring along Royal, Rod, and whoever else Lauren felt comfortable with.

"I don't know about going to Hawaii or Mexico," Royal said, "but we've got to get her out of *here*, and we need to do it *now*."

Rod couldn't understand this and said so. The Bowman-Granger estate was a reasonably secure place, surrounded by a high wall, guarded by electronic security. And Rod himself was no slouch with a handgun, he said, patting his shoulder holster.

"I'm telling you it's no good," Royal insisted. "I've got contacts on the street who say there's a couple of bad actors up here from L.A., and they're armed to the goddamn teeth. They plan to storm this house and take Lauren out of here. And they don't care how many people they need to kill to get it done.''

''Bad actors? What bad actors?'' Marc wanted to know.

''They're hit men,'' Royal said, his voice growling. ''They work for a South American drug cartel. They're used to fighting organized army units in the streets of Kali. How long do you think we'd last against people like that? Ten minutes, fifteen?''

Lauren shivered. She wished Matt was here—Matt with his warm arms, his cool head. Matt would know what to do. ''Where do you think we should go?'' she asked Royal.

''Somewhere nobody would ever think of looking for you,'' he answered. ''Not to any friend's house, that's for sure. We need to stay around lots of people, never give the bastards a chance to organize anything. A friend of mine owns a little house over on Bainbridge Island, which should do the trick.''

Marc asked if he was proposing that Lauren hole up in someone's little house until further notice.

''No, I'm proposing that we go there and sit tight until we can think of something better to do. We'd be safe there, because nobody in Lauren's circle of friends knows about the place, and she herself has never been there. Do you *get* it, little man?'' Marc Lekander took a step backward.

''Wait a minute,'' Rod said. ''Where did you say this information comes from?''

''I know people who know people. They hear things. That's a way of sayin' I ain't gonna tell you where I heard it. But believe me, it's bankable. We need to get out of here—*now*.''

''I believe him,'' Lauren said. ''Who's coming along?''

''The fewer, the better,'' Royal said. ''Let's make it Lauren, me, and Rod. We'll stay in touch with the rest of you by phone.''

''I'm coming along, too,'' Marc said. ''You might need another set of hands.''

''We'll be fine with Rod and his forty-five,'' Royal said. He turned to Lauren and suggested that she pack a few things, a change of clothes, whatever else would fit into a small bag.

Fifteen minutes later, Lauren said her good-byes, hoping that they wouldn't be final ones. She gave tearful hugs to Elise and Marc, begged them not to worry and promised to stay in touch. She gave Desi and Lucy long hugs, too, and kissed them on their noses. Then she slipped into her Volvo front passenger's seat. Rod drove, and Royal sat in the rear.

As the Volvo rolled toward the gate, Lauren waved to Elise and Marc, who stood in the drive with the dogs, all looking fearful and a little forlorn. The idea that this might be the last time she would see them again caused an ache in her chest.

She twisted in the seat in order to look at Royal. Again, his sickly appearance pained her. In the eleven years since her reunion with him, she'd come to depend on his down-to-earth observations about the world and the people who lived in it, as well as his advice on matters ranging from her love life to training dogs. She was losing him, she knew, and she would miss him.

They drove downtown from Magnolia and headed south on Third, through a canyon of skyscrapers. The five-o'clock rush was under way, and the traffic was brutal. They inched their way onto Occidental and joined the queue of cars lined up for the ferry terminal, which led along Alaskan Way. An hour passed before they turned into Pier 50, the Washington State Ferry Terminal. Rod nosed the Volvo into the line for the Winslow Ferry, which would take them to Bainbridge Island.

At 6:30 they drove onto the ferry, parked the Volvo. Because Lauren felt a need for fresh air, they found seats on the uppermost aft deck. Royal insisted that they remain together, even when visiting the snack bar, which was only twenty steps away. Lauren was glad that she didn't need to use the bathroom. She was also glad that she'd dressed in jeans and a sweater, for the breeze was cool, despite the sunshine.

After a long, loud blast of a horn, the ferry edged out of its slip and pointed its prow across the Sound. The superstructure throbbed with the power of the engines, and Lauren felt the tremble in her chest. As the huge vessel gathered speed, she came close to forgetting the horrors that had invaded her life in the past several weeks, the grief of lost friends, the uncertainty of the future. A clean breeze washed over her, and she almost managed to lose herself in the sights and smells of sea and sky.

Too soon the trip was over, and the ferry crawled into its slip at Winslow. Rod, Royal, and Lauren boarded the Volvo and headed north on Highway 305, which would ultimately lead to the Bainbridge Island Bridge and the picturesque town of Poulsbo.

They'd gone hardly a quarter of a mile out of Winslow when

Royal said, "Damn it, I think I just spotted somebody." He was staring at the traffic behind them.

"What do you mean, *somebody*?" Rod asked. He eyed the rearview mirror. "There are probably forty cars behind us, all of them just off the ferry."

"I mean I saw somebody I recognize, and if it's who I think it is, we're in trouble."

Lauren felt gooseflesh rise on the back of her neck. "One of the hit men?" she asked.

"Can't say for sure. Rod, take the next side road you see— preferably not somebody's driveway."

"Do you think that's a good idea? We could just keep going like we are, couldn't we? Nobody's going to hurt us in this traffic."

"Do as I say, boy. Take a left on Miller Road—we're almost there, right? You'll see a turnout on the right, where you can look across the water to Point Bolin. Pull in there and turn the car around. If anyone comes after us, we'll be able to blow right by them in the opposite direction. We'll be gone before they can turn around."

Rod did as the old man ordered, though under his breath he said, "Jesus, I don't know about this." He found the turnout, made the U-turn, and parked.

"Keep the engine running," Royal said, eyeing the road ahead.

Seconds later a large black sport utility vehicle came toward them on Miller Road. Lauren saw it and felt the blood drain from her face. Her heart pounded. She could see three figures inside the truck, all men, one of whom—the driver—had long blond hair that hung to his shoulders.

Rod spoke, his voice calm. "What's next? You want to leave them in a cloud of dust?" Lauren saw his right hand move toward his shoulder holster.

"Just sit tight," Royal said.

What happened next hardly registered in Lauren's brain, because it was too unthinkable, too absurd. It was something that made a shambles of her rationality, all her assumptions about people and trust and goodness, everything she'd ever believed about love.

Royal pulled a pistol from his duffel, held the muzzle to Rod Welton's head just above the rubber band around his ponytail, and fired. The round exited Rod's eye and shattered the windshield, spattering the instrument panel with blood and brain tissue.

Lauren later remembered that she tried to run, that one of the men from the black truck grabbed her, held her. She remembered, too, the sting of a syringe as it plunged into her neck, followed by the sudden onset of night.

Sixty-four

Matt and Jandee landed at SeaTac and retrieved Jandee's car from the long-term parking area. The drive to Jenkins Way in Magnolia took nearly two hours, thanks to traffic. Matt was exhausted by the time they passed through the gate of the Bowman-Granger estate. Anxious though he was to see Lauren, he worried about how to broach the subject of her past relationship with Ray Brownlee and the baby she'd borne. The matter had caused her great anguish, that much was clear, and Matt disliked the prospect of forcing her to live through it again. Still, he remembered what she'd said to him before he and Jandee left for Portland: *Promise me . . . you won't hate me.*

He needed to assure her that his feelings for her hadn't changed. But he also needed to tell her what he knew.

Jandee parked in the six-car garage and pointed to a green Taurus that sat in the circular drive with Matt's Jeep, Rod's old Chevy, and Elise Lekander's Rolls. "Do you recognize that car?" she asked. "I don't."

Matt stared a moment at the car, wondering why its presence seemed sinister. After all, it could belong to anyone—a household staff member, a visiting friend, *anyone.* Still, Matt wished that he had his SIG Sauer with him.

He pulled Jandee into the shadow of the garage and told her to wait at the entryway until she heard a telephone ring inside the guest house. Then she was to hit the doorbell. Matt would go into the house through the rear while those inside occupied themselves with answering the phone *and* the door. If something was amiss, he might be able to exploit the confusion and gain control of the situation. He told her not to let herself in until she'd gotten the all-clear from him.

Matt followed a crushed-granite path to the rear of the house, keeping to the shadows as much as possible. The evening was warm. The sky was full of stars, and the air full of insect music. And pollen. His eyes and nose itched furiously and several times he barely managed to stifle a sneeze.

He climbed onto the deck outside the sitting room, taking care not to make noise. After positioning himself next to the open door, he took out his cellular phone and hit the call code for Lauren Bowman's residence. He heard a telephone bleep inside, then bleep again. Then the doorbell chimed, right on cue. Desi and Lucy began to bark loudly.

Matt peeked around the doorjamb in time to see Elise Lekander pick up the phone. Someone else, presumably Marc, had gone for the door. Matt slipped into the sitting room and headed straight for the hallway, meaning to fetch his pistol from the bureau in the guest room. In the hallway, however, he confronted a man with a gun.

A Beretta nine-millimeter, from the look of it.

Matt gasped and instinctively raised his hands. The guy was about fifty, well-muscled and tall. He had a round but solid face and hair clipped to a military brush. He looked exceedingly competent.

"Mr. Burgess, I presume," he said.

"That's me," Matt said, trying to sound nonchalant.

"Why don't you sit down and have a drink? You look like you could use one. I suggest that Ms. Vernon join you."

At that moment Jandee came in from the foyer, accompanied by Marc Lekander. Jandee went to Elise, and the two women hugged each other. Then everyone moved into the sitting room.

"I'm going to holster this gun now," said the man with the military haircut, "because none of us are enemies. Not anymore, anyway. Why don't you explain what I mean, Mr. Lekander?"

With a whipped-dog look on his face, Marc introduced the gunman as Mr. Richardson Zanto, formerly of InterActs, Inc., Washington, D.C. He described InterActs' Operation Undermine, which Zanto had managed until recently, and his own role in the operation—that of informer and inside operative, a "fish," Zanto had called him. Marc had provided a steady stream of information to Zanto and his partner about the militant activities of the FAF and its allied organizations. He had even installed listening devices throughout the guest house.

"You slimy little geek," Jandee hissed at him. "You're a fucking mollusk, Marc. I knew it from the moment I set eyes on you."

"Jandee, please!" Elise said, grabbing the younger woman's hand, but Jandee jerked free of her.

"*Why?*" Jandee screamed at him. "Why did you do this, Marc? I can't believe they paid you—you're already rich beyond anything hell would have. What could possibly make you sell out Lauren, the woman you've loved since you were a pimply-faced punk?"

"They blackmailed me," Marc answered, his head hanging. "I've had—*still* have—a cocaine habit. Rick Zanto has pictures of me doing business with a dealer on a boat in Elliott Bay Marina. He promised to send the pictures to Lauren and to the boards of directors that I sit on, unless I agreed to help them."

Zanto went to the bar. "What's everyone drinking?" he asked, as if this was a casual get-together. Nobody wanted anything.

Matt asked the next obvious question. Where were Lauren and Rod? His mouth yawned in shock when Elise replied that they had gone away with Royal Bowman.

"Royal was *here*?"

Elise explained that the old man had turned up at the door unannounced. And he'd insisted that Lauren was in danger, that some hit men from Los Angeles meant to kidnap her. They'd decided to seek refuge somewhere on Bainbridge Island.

"And you let her go?"

"What were we supposed to do?" Marc asked. "Lauren herself made the decision to go with him. Besides, they promised to keep in touch by phone. When they didn't call, I decided to get in touch with Mr. Zanto here, hoping he would know what to do."

Zanto then asked what Royal Bowman looked like. Matt described the old man—scrawny, late sixties, wavy white hair, crooked nose.

Zanto was about to say something when the phone rang. He held a hand up, told Elise to answer it. He told her to act normal, that if the caller was Royal, Rod or Lauren, she should say nothing about Zanto's presence. Elise nodded and picked up the phone. Then she handed it to Matt.

"It's Royal," she said.

Matt swallowed, breathed deeply, gathered himself. "Hi, you old fart. Where the hell are you this time?"

"Don't call me an old fart—it's disrespectful. To answer your question, I've found a safe place for Lauren. She's here with me now."

"Bainbridge Island, right?"

"Well, not exactly. Something happened, and we had to change our plans."

"Put Lauren on. I want to say hi."

"Uh . . . she's asleep, Matt. I hate to wake her. Tell you what, though. Why don't you come over, and we'll drink some beers— you, me, and this Rod fella. He's a pretty good drinker for a vegan. When Lauren wakes up, you can talk to her until the cows come home."

"Sounds good. You're sure that you're safe from those people from L.A.?"

"Oh, we're safe, all right. Don't worry about that, Matt. Let me give you the address . . ."

Matt wrote down the address that Royal gave him, and visualized the neighborhood. International District, dark and dingy. Wholesalers and distributors, imports and exports, lots of warehouses. He handed the slip of paper to Zanto, whose eyes widened when he saw it.

"Okay, I'll be there in forty-five minutes," Matt said. "It'll be good to see you again, old man."

"One more thing, Matt. Come alone. There ain't a lot of room here, and I don't want to attract attention with people coming and going. I'll meet you at the main loading door on the east side of the building."

"I understand—the east side of the building. I'll be there." Matt hung up the phone. "Did you get the drift of what's going on?" he asked Zanto.

"Yeah. This address you gave me. Know where it is?"

"Approximately."

"Well, I know exactly where it is. I've been watching it for nearly two weeks. It's the home of Ray Brownlee, the father of the man who sneaked in here and assaulted Lauren."

Matt wondered if he'd heard right, then wished that he hadn't.

Sixty-five

Matt Burgess and Richardson Zanto drove to the International District in Zanto's rented Taurus. While en route, they talked tactics.

"You don't want to go in through the main entrance like the old man suggested," Zanto said. "You might get a nasty reception. Remember, he told you to come alone. Think about that."

"So, how do I get in?"

Zanto told him that he himself had been inside the warehouse, having used a key given him by Ray Brownlee's business partner, Arnie Cashmore. He hadn't gone to the top level, where Brownlee lived, but he'd explored the ground level and the basement. He'd found several locked doors, countless empty packing crates and mountains of worn-out office furniture. He'd also found a basement-entry door in the alley on the north side of the building.

"I unlocked it from the inside," Zanto said, "meaning there's now a second way to get in. I took the calculated risk of allowing some homeless skell to get in and set up housekeeping in the basement. One way or another, I intend to find out what's going on in that building."

"Tell me something," Matt said. "What's your interest in all this? You're no longer working for InterActs, as I understand it. You have no big paying client. Why are you here?"

Zanto explained that he couldn't abide the idea of someone butchering young women and getting away with it. What kind of man would close his eyes to something like that? he asked.

"Apparently the kind you used to work for," Matt replied.

Zanto cleared his throat. "Back to the matter at hand. Be advised that we're dealing with some nasty specimens here. Ray Brownlee's son, Tyler, is a genuine psychopath, from what I gather. He's big, he's strong, and he's no dummy. As for the old man . . . well, I'll let you draw your own conclusions."

"You think Royal Bowman and Ray Brownlee are the same person, don't you?"

"It's a hard notion to resist, you have to admit."

Matt agonized. He tried to deny the reality, but he couldn't. He'd confirmed that Royal had lied to him for more than two decades about having gone to prison. The fact was that Royal had abandoned his wife and toddling daughter—Lauren and her mother—in order to pursue other "love interests," as Angela Quilici had called them. But could he *really* have changed his name and continued to live in the same community with another woman? And raised another child, a boy named Ben?

And could he *really* have made a concubine of his own daughter, having used his son to lure her?

If all this was true, then Matt had counted among his best friends a monster, and had done so for more than twenty years. A monster who'd killed young women and committed incest. And dealt heroin, if Zanto was to believed. A monster who could switch faces as easily as a chameleon. Matt had worked for the man, drunk beer with him, and spent countless evenings in deep discussion with him. He'd sailed with him, traded advice with him on every subject under the sun. He'd planned to accompany him on a cruise to the South Pacific. Matt wondered how he could have been so wrong about someone.

He and Zanto parked in a dark alley more than a block from the warehouse. Zanto gave Matt a flashlight, which Matt tested and found to be in working order. They got out of the car. Zanto went to the trunk and took out a Heckler & Koch shotgun with a shortened barrel and a pistol grip. He loaded it with nine rounds of twelve-gauge buckshot, then removed his sport coat and put on a black lightweight turtleneck.

"If you're going to do this kind of work for a living, you need to look the part," he said, winking at Matt. "Got your gun?"

Matt opened his coat to show Zanto his SIG Sauer. "You'd better hope we don't meet anybody on the street," he said. "Anyone sees you carrying that howitzer, the cops will be here so fast it'll make your head spin." This was no small worry. On the block just north of this one were two popular Chinese restaurants that stayed open until two.

They set out toward the warehouse, walking quickly. Zanto talked in a low voice about how they needed to expect the worst. Matt needed to expect that someone would try to kill him tonight, he said. The old man's call to him tonight had been a lure to bloody death.

"We need to stay flexible," he went on. "We'll use the north basement door. You go in first and work your way to the stairway at the south end. There's nothing to see until you reach the corridor that leads to the stairs—except a couple of locked rooms, that is. I'll wait ten minutes, then come in behind you, which should give you enough time to reconnoiter. If you get into trouble, the bad guys won't expect me following you, and I'll be able to take them out. If anybody is left alive, you and I start asking pointed questions."

"Wrong," Matt said. "That's when I grab Lauren and get the fuck out of there. *You* can stay and ask the damn pointed questions."

"You want to get the killer, don't you?"

"Of course I want to get the killer. But my first priority is to make sure that Lauren is safe."

"We'll play it by ear," Zanto said.

It was nearly midnight by the time they reached the warehouse. Fortunately they'd encountered no passersby. They synchronized their watches in the alley on the north side of the building, then pressed their backs to the bricks and made their way to a cement stairway that led to the basement-level door that Zanto had found.

"Remember—ten minutes," Zanto whispered. Matt looked at his watch, saw that it was one minute past midnight.

Sixty-six

Lauren found herself in a battle for awareness, a battle against a tsunami of smothering black feathers. Somewhere in the distance she heard blues music . . .

> I'm a meat eater, woman—yes, I am,
> A meat eater day and night.

She forced her eyes open and saw only traces of bloodred, the pinpricks of electric light, the kind of light found on the faces of amplifiers and stereo equipment. Too, she became conscious of pain in her wrists and arms. She discovered that she was bound with leather straps to a hard plank resting at a forty-five-degree angle from the floor. And she was naked. She couldn't stop shivering.

Suddenly she wasn't alone. Someone or something had moved close to her. She could feel his body heat. Struggling against the straps, she tried to get free, but the straps held her as surely as if they'd been made of steel. The dark someone *breathed* on her, and she screamed.

> I'm a meat eater, honey.
> You've got to cook it just right . . .

Lauren wondered if this was the same creature who had managed to penetrate her own bedroom, who had forced himself on

her in the black of night. Something about his smell, or the way
he moved, the way his dirty breath licked her skin told her that
this was so.

She screamed again.

Sixty-seven

Matt heard a woman's scream. The sound cascaded down from above, caromed off cement walls and steel girders, and turned his blood to ice. He bolted forward, following the beam of his flashlight toward the south end of the building.

The basement of the warehouse was a series of open storage areas interspersed with rooms that housed the furnace, the elevator machinery, water heaters and circuit breakers. Mountains of packing crates and pallets loomed on all sides, together with junked furniture and office fixtures. Water pipes and air ducts ran in tangles overhead. Matt heard skittering in the darkness—rodents, he hoped, and not people, not some homeless soul who had tried the door in the alley and found it unlocked.

He pulled his SIG Sauer out of its holster, thumbed the safety switch. He heard the scream again, and it sounded like a plea from hell.

As he burst into the corridor that led to the stairs, he encountered a stink that gagged him. It reminded him of when he and Rags had found an undercover drug agent in the trunk of her car at SeaTac, where she'd lain for weeks after someone had blown her head off—a smell so putrid that it eats into your senses and imprints itself like a fossil in the face of a stone.

He fought his way through it to the stairwell, passing several doors. His flashlight beam knifed over heavy padlocks, and he knew somehow that the source of the smell was behind one of them, that this was where the bodies lay. In those few seconds the horrid truth coalesced in his mind, a combination of known facts and a cop's intuition—that someone with a bolt cutter could enter those rooms and find the bodies of Megan Reiner, Vera Kemmis, and Rainy Hales. And maybe others, too—the bodies of poor runaways who'd fallen under the deadly spell of heroin, mere girls lured into a trap from which they could never struggle free. Now they lay behind a padlocked door in the basement of a dark warehouse, their girlish faces rotted away, just heaps of bones.

Matt gained the ground level and edged away from the stairs, his back pressed against a wall. He saw light ahead, the yellow aura of bare bulbs. He peered around a corner, his pistol ready, and saw two armed men walk from an elevator cage toward a door that led into a large, dark open area. One was swarthy and blocky, the other black and slight. They carried MAC-10 submachine pistols.

After they disappeared through the door, Matt counted to fifty, then inched forward into the light. To his right was another door that looked as if it might open into an office. Blues music came from behind it, and he recognized the gravel voice that he'd heard on the videotapes of the murders. He tried the knob, found it unlocked. As he pushed it open, thin light spilled through from the room, another bare lightbulb, he figured. He saw a man who could only be Tyler Brownlee, based on Zanto's description—a big man with sculpted muscles and blond hair that flowed to his shoulders. He was naked, and he straddled a plank that rested at a forty-five-degree angle. A woman was strapped to it, and she, too, was naked, her hands bound above her head, her ankles bound to iron rings on the floor on either side of the plank. Music filled the air, played through an array of stereo speakers, amplifiers, and a reel-to-reel recorder.

> Hey, I'm bringin' home the best cut, baby,
> Because you know I like to eat it rare.
> I like my meat like I like my women—
> Naked, ready to eat and layin' bare.

Matt's flashlight beam found the woman's face, and he saw that it was Lauren. His rage almost choked him. Tyler Brownlee bolted upright and lifted himself away from her, his huge cock swinging wildly.

"Well, what have we here?" he shouted above the music.
"Looks like my man, Matthew Burgess. We've been looking for
you, dude."

"Shut up!" Matt screamed, leveling his SIG Sauer at Tyler's
forehead. "Get on the ground—do it *now*! Spread your hands and
feet out!"

"What're you gonna do, Matt—shoot me? Or is this some
kind of kinky sex thing?"

Matt hungered to let a round fly, but he worried about Tyler's
proximity to Lauren. Bullets did crazy things sometimes, like entering the head of somebody, then making a right turn and entering the head of somebody else who wasn't even in the line of
fire. He couldn't take the chance of hurting Lauren.

Lauren spoke, her voice tentative and weak now, as if she'd
screamed herself hoarse. "Matt, is that you? Oh, God . . ."

At that moment, the door behind Matt burst open, and one of
the men he'd seen earlier stepped through it, the short one. The
man aimed his submachine pistol at Matt and shouted something.
Matt whirled and fired at him, two rounds, three—Matt counted
them off as he'd been trained at the law enforcement academy
long ago. The first bore into the man's chest and exited his back.
The second entered his mouth and blew out the rear of his head.
He went down like a marionette whose master had cut the strings.

But then Tyler Brownlee hit Matt from behind, like a blitzing
linebacker crashing into a quarterback. Matt's forehead slammed
into the cement floor, igniting an explosion of sparks behind his
eyes. His pistol bounced out of his fist. Tyler fell on him with his
full weight, and Matt was sure that he felt a rib crack. Tyler
hoisted him up by his shirt and launched a roundhouse swing at
his face. It connected, and Matt's world went black.

Sixty-eight

Richardson Zanto heard shots—distant pops from within the warehouse, muffled by bricks and mortar. He glanced at his watch and saw that ten minutes hadn't yet passed since Matt entered the building. He had two minutes yet to go.

To hell with it, he said. He went in, his shotgun out in front of him. Having been inside the building before, he was familiar with the layout, and he reached the south stairway in less than two minutes. He climbed the stairs, and tried to ignore the stink of death around him. He'd smelled worse—in Vietnam while digging up the graves of North Vietnamese soldiers in order to view the documents they carried, letters from home, pay certificates, anything that might contribute to U.S. intelligence. That was the kind of thing soldiers did during wartime.

Combat was not an area in which Zanto's knowledge of Roman history served him. The tools and technology of warfare had changed so drastically over thousands of years as to render the Roman military experience next to useless. While the Romans seldom employed surprise against their enemies, today's warrior couldn't win without it.

Zanto had always prided himself on his ability to surprise an enemy.

He came to the turn in the corridor beyond which lay the elevator cage and the entrance to the loading bay. A quick peek around the corner showed a light-skinned black man dragging a dead body out of a room on the right. The black man looked up at just the wrong moment, saw Zanto, and went for the submachine pistol that hung on his shoulder. Zanto thrust his weapon around the edge of the wall and let fly two rounds of double-aught buckshot, the first of which knocked the man's legs out from beneath him. The man hit the floor hard, but he was a tough son of a bitch.

"Damn it, why you shootin' at me, dawg?'' he screamed.

Before Zanto could pop off another round, the man hit his trigger and launched a blizzard of nine-millimeter rounds at him, one of which nicked Zanto's left carotid artery. Zanto emptied his shotgun as he went down, more or less blowing the black man to pieces.

He sat on the floor, his blood geysering out of his neck, his vision fading quickly. For a brief moment he felt sorry for himself, facing death on the filthy floor of a warehouse, sitting in a steaming lake of his own blood. But countless others had died in worse ways, he told himself, so maybe he should be thankful. A bullet wound was far preferable to the lingering agony of cancer or Alzheimer's disease.

He thought of his daughter, his ex-wife, friends he'd known. He thought of the way he'd lived his life, and was glad about it. He'd been a soldier, a man who fought for his country. Never had he shrunk from his duty. He'd known goodness and valor.

Gravity, simplicity, piety . . .

Richardson Zanto breathed his last and slumped sideways.

Sixty-nine

Matt fought his way back to consciousness, only to find that someone had handcuffed him to a radiator pipe in the room where Lauren lay strapped to a plank. His head throbbed, and his left cheek felt huge and bulging—a broken jaw, surely. He vaguely remembered seeing Tyler Brownlee's fist coming at his face.

He chief concern, though, was Lauren. When he tried to call out to her, his swollen cheek exploded in pain, and he tasted blood in his mouth. Gradually he was able to focus on the others in the room, Tyler Brownlee—who now wore an Adidas sweat suit—and another man, smaller, older, a stooped man with a shock of white hair and a crooked nose.

It was Royal Bowman.

"Welcome back to the world of the living, Matt," Royal said, bending down to him. "For the time being, at least. You won't be staying long, I'm sorry to say."

"Royal, I don't get this," Matt said, his speech thick from the damage to his mouth and jaw. "What does it all mean? Your daughter is tied up on that piece of lumber, I'm bleeding like a stuck pig . . ."

"Don't tell me you don't get it, Matt," Royal said. "You're a smart boy, always have been. I wish that I'd had a kid like you."

Tyler spoke up. "You've got *me* for a kid. I've been everything you wanted, haven't I?"

The old man chuckled. "Yeah, Tyler. You've been everything I've wanted. Everything and more."

"And what's this shit about Lauren being your daughter?" Tyler demanded, looking wounded. "She's *not* your daughter. She's my dream, my destiny—right? That's what you've told me ever since I can remember."

Matt squinted his eyes to focus on Tyler's face. The truth hit him as he recognized the curve of the young man's jaw, his high forehead and severe cheekbones. Tyler Brownlee was related to Lauren Bowman, *closely* related. He looked enough like her to be her son.

But he was *Royal's* son, Ray Brownlee's son. And Lauren was Royal's daughter, Ray Brownlee's daughter. Which meant . . .

The truth had a filthy stink to it.

"Answer him," Lauren said. "Tell him whose daughter I am, Royal."

Royal hoisted himself to his feet. He staggered for a moment and looked very ill. The whites of his eyes had yellowed, and his skin hung on his rickety bones like old cloth. "None of that matters anymore," he said. "The only thing that matters is that I have you back, little girl. After all these years, after all the plotting and scheming, the maneuvering and the waiting, I've got you back again. You know, Lauren, I meant it when I said,

> *No matter how far you run in this big, wide world,*
> *The day's gonna come, yes it is,*
> *When you gotta pay what you owe."*

He touched her face with a calloused fingertip.

"And what is it that you think I owe?" she asked, recoiling from his touch.

"Why, everything you have and everything you are. I'm not talking about your money, kiddo, or your fancy houses, or your cars. I'm talking about *you*, your body and your mind, your *heart*. It's been seventeen years since you ran away from me, but now I have you back—not as a daughter, but as a woman. And I'll never lose you again, you can be sure of that."

"Wait a minute," Tyler said. "This is all bogus. She belongs to *me*. That's what you've told me all my life. She's my reward for doing all those things you've wanted me to do. She's the reason I learned to play the blues, right? She's the reason I sold

Mexican tar, man. Now that I have her, I don't need to do things to any other bitches, no more cutting throats and fuckin' them while they die. That's *your* program, old man, not mine.''

Royal laughed, a scratching, clawing sound, like a rat in a garbage can. "Keep telling yourself that, kid. Tell yourself you don't dig how it feels when you blow your rocks at the very moment one of those little chickee-poohs kicks off. And tell yourself that you'll stop doing it someday, that you won't *live* for it. You've seen junkies who'd cut off a finger for a fix—that's the way you'll be, next time you need to do a bitch. You'll be out on the street tryin' to snag a runaway, same as a junkie goes after dope.''

"Christ almighty, Royal," Matt said, "this can't be you talking. This isn't the man I've known for twenty years.''

Royal turned back to him, his eyes narrowed. "The man you knew was Royal Bowman, the man I've always wanted to be. Trouble is, Matt, I'm *not* Royal Bowman. He's a mask I wore so I could have some semblance of a normal life. I'm Ray Brownlee, the Blues Ranger, always have been. I like young girls, and I like to cut their throats. And I've raised two boys exactly like me, though one of 'em is no longer with us, bless his hide . . .''

"That was Ben.''

"So, you know about him. Well, it doesn't matter.''

"You're telling me," Matt said, "that you've lived a double life. In one life, you're Royal Bowman, the guy who owns Shorty's. In the other you're a sex killer and a bluesman and a heroin dealer. You expect me to believe that?''

The old man laughed again. "You don't have any choice but to believe it, Matt.''

Lauren spoke up, her voice sounding much younger, almost the voice of a high school girl. "It's true—I know it now, too. I remember when you killed my cat, Mandrake. I'd told Ben that I wasn't going to see either of you anymore, and you killed Mandrake to warn me. Do you remember that, Royal? He was just a helpless animal. He'd never hurt anyone, and you *killed* him.''

"Girl, you can't think killing that old cat was any worse than what *you* did. I mean, you gave birth to a child—a bouncing baby boy—and what did you do with him? You wrapped him in a doll's blanket and stuck him in a water-valve hole in the middle of a football field.''

"I thought he was dead!''

"Sure you did, Missy. You thought he was dead. But he wasn't, was he?" He waved a hand at Tyler, who stood open-mouthed next to the plank. "This is the kid you stuck in that hole, little girl. *Look* at him. He's our son, yours and mine!"

Matt noticed that Tyler's ears were oddly shaped, that they flopped forward along the upper edges, which was probably why the kid wore his hair long—to hide them. A genetic defect, no doubt, the effect of inbreeding. God only knew what other afflictions he'd endured, defects of the mind and brain.

Lauren wailed, a high-pitched sound that cut through the air like a siren. The truth was excruciating. "Kill me!" she screamed at the two men who stood over her. "Kill me and get it over with!"

"You see, I followed you that morning," Royal said, pushing his face close to hers. "It was a Monday, the nineteenth of June, nineteen-seventy-six. I figured you were pretty near to dropping that baby of ours, and I knew that you were a little off the deep end. I expected you to do something crazy. So I followed you, kept an eye on you. I was sitting outside your house in my car when you left just before the sun came up. I followed you to the school grounds and watched you stuff that precious little bundle into a hole in the ground. Fortunately I was able to get him before he died. It was a good thing I had a woman at home who knew how to nurse him, how to take care of him . . ."

Lauren now sobbed violently, her naked body heaving against the plank. Matt wanted desperately to go to her, to cradle her in his arms and tell her that everything would be all right, even though he himself didn't believe it. Nothing would ever again be all right, not in this world. He watched as Tyler turned away from the plank, away from Lauren and his father, his face as hard as stone.

Lauren's sobs finally subsided, and Royal directed his attention back to Matt. His expression seemed to say, *Do you understand me now? Can you appreciate how it's been for me?*

Matt swallowed, forced himself to speak in a normal, matter-of-fact tone. His and Lauren's only chance at survival, he figured, was to keep Royal talking and give Richardson Zanto time to make his move. "Tell me something," he said. "Why did you ask me to get involved with Lauren after you killed Megan? You must've known there was a risk that I would stumble onto the truth."

"I needed to know who'd put the second set of bugs in her house," Royal answered. "Tyler and I arranged for one set, but I got a little scared when our technical guys told us about the second set. A few minutes ago, while you were still unconscious, one of my young pals from L.A. killed a man in the hall outside this room. I assume he was the guy who put in the other bugs. Bullish-looking guy, early fifties, Marine Corps hair. He was with you, right?"

Matt winced. Richardson Zanto was dead, as was any hope of getting out of this mess alive. But still Matt talked. "So, you figured I would find out whoever else had bugged Lauren's place, then tell you about it, dutiful friend that I was."

"That was my plan, yeah. You see, Matt, I couldn't afford any snags in my operation. I needed to put all the pieces into place for what's going to happen later tonight. I needed to tear down Lauren's world so I could rebuild it for her, the world she was meant to have . . ."

"A world with you."

"Yeah, with *me*. I needed to tear down that little fortress she lived in, get rid of the people who made her think she was some-body valuable, somebody important."

"Her animal-rights friends, you mean?"

"Now you're getting it, Matt. I needed to show her how weak and puny they really were, and remind her that she wasn't any different—weak and puny, good for only one thing."

"So you started out by kidnapping and killing Megan Reiner."

Tyler broke his silence. "That was almost too easy, man. We'd bugged Lauren's place, right? And we had Rainy working as her cook. We knew all the details of their operation better than they did themselves. When they shut down the security system for the BioCenter, I just drove through the back gate, went into the place through the rear door and grabbed Megan. I was gone even before Lauren and her people got out."

"I'm sure you made your father very proud," Matt said. "How did you get Rainy to cooperate with you?" *Keep them talking,* Matt thought. *Talking, talking . . .*

Royal smirked, his stubbly lip curling. "She was a very *special* child," he said. "I had actually planned something *else* for her . . ." Years ago, he explained, Tyler had snatched Rainy and her girlfriend from the street on Capitol Hill and brought here, promising them dope in exchange for sex, a promise heard

many times every day in that neighborhood. The old man had
indulged himself with Rainy's friend, while Rainy watched. He
was about to let Tyler have his way with Rainy when a thought
struck him: This girl could prove useful in his cause to get Lauren
back. He needed a way to spy on Lauren, a way to get the inside
poop on her life, for Lauren had never really opened up to him
after their reunion here in Seattle. She'd always kept a large block
of her world secret from him. So he'd fashioned a new life for
Rainy Hales, molding her into the person that Lauren had
known—a vegan chef and an animal-rights activist, someone who
could wiggle her way into Lauren Bowman's world.

"I detoxed her, right here in this building," Royal went on.
"Fed her a macrobiotic diet, lots of vitamins, fruit juices. I nursed
her back to health, gave her a brand-new life. Wasn't too long—
maybe four or five months—before I was actually able to let her
start coming and going on her own. She only slipped up once,
started shootin' tar again, but we tracked her down and got her
back, put her through detox again. After that she was good as
gold, did everything we wanted. I sent her to school to learn how
to cook, and she actually became damn good at it. I gave her a
house and a car . . ."

Made her into an ally, a confederate, Matt thought. She'd
known what would happen to her if she ever tried to escape the
clutches of Ray and Tyler Brownlee—the same lethal terror that
her girlfriend had suffered.

Matt asked about the videotapes of the murders. Why had the
man he'd known as Royal Bowman subjected his daughter to the
sights and sounds of her friends' deaths?

"We made the tapes so that Lauren could fully appreciate what
was happening," Royal answered. "I needed to wake her up,
remind her who Ray Brownlee was. I needed to let her know that
she could never run away, no matter what she did. It was part of
the process of tearing down her castle. And judging from what I
see tonight, I'd say that I've succeeded, wouldn't you?"

Lauren lay on the plank with her eyes squeezed tightly shut,
whimpering.

Matt choked on his own blood. "What happens now?" he
managed to ask.

"That should be obvious," Royal said. "What happened to
Megan, Vera, and Rainy will happen to Lauren. It's got to be that

way, don't you see? It's the only way she can pay me back. It's the . . ."

"No!" Tyler shouted, whirling on his father. "This is all bogus, man, B-O-G-U-S. You're not going to kill her. She's not your daughter, and she's not my mother. She's my fuckin' destiny, you hear? She's mine."

Royal shook his head, the gesture of a weary father. "Fuck, I always knew it would come down to this." He pulled a pistol out of his frayed jacket and shot Tyler six times. Tyler whirled and gyrated as the bullets ripped into his chest and abdomen. He flailed into the amplifiers and the reel-to-reel recorder, smashing them to the floor before falling down himself. He lay on the cement in a growing sea of blood, gurgling and flinching. Within thirty seconds he was still, his skin turning gray.

"God, it's quiet in here," Royal said. He slowly took off his jacket, then fumbled with his belt. "You want to watch this, Matt, or should I kill you first?"

Matt struggled to draw a breath, the full terror of Royal's intentions gripping his heart like a claw. "No way I can talk you out of this?"

"Nah, there's no way. Sorry." Royal's trousers dropped, revealing his skinny ass, his pathetic cock. He took a knife from a drawer in a nearby table, a knife with a thin, curving blade.

"I want to watch," Matt said, struggling. A few more minutes of life was precious, even if you're forced to spend it watching the torture and murder of someone you love, he told himself. Or was it?

Royal straddled Lauren, pushing her thighs apart. She gasped but didn't resist him, didn't open her eyes. Royal brought the knife up to her neck and pressed the blade against her throat. He fumbled with his cock, trying to find where to put it.

Lauren said, "I love you, Matt."

"And I love you," Matt croaked, unable to watch now.

Suddenly Jimmy Jaspero barged into the room, wielding an aluminum baseball bat, looking for all the world like Captain Kidd's first mate. He brought the bat down on Royal's head, smashing the old man's skull, killing him instantly.

The next person through the door was Cleo Castillo, huge in her apron with *The Big Cheese* embroidered on it.

Seventy

Cleo drove Matt and Lauren back to Shorty's in her Buick, where the last of the drinking crowd had just straggled out the door. Jimmy Jaspero switched off the neons and went to work in the kitchen, cleaning up after another day's business. Cleo herded Matt and Lauren upstairs to the apartment she'd shared for decades with Royal.

"You need a long, hot bath and a good rest," she said to Lauren. "I'll get the water going."

Lauren was still too choked up to talk. She nodded her thanks and squeezed Cleo's hand. The two of them disappeared into the bathroom for twenty minutes, leaving Matt to sit by himself on the sofa. He stared through the window at the lights of the marina, the tall spars and masts of the boats, and the glittering lights of Magnolia across Salmon Bay. He tried not to think about anything, tried to keep his mind a blank.

Cleo came out of the bathroom. "That girl has had a tough time," she said. "Fortunately, she hasn't been hurt physically, but my guess is she'll have some pretty awful nightmares for a while. I hope she'll have someone nice to keep her company at night." She made known with her eyes exactly what she meant by this.

"I hope so, too," Matt said, rubbing his tender ribs.

Cleo then examined his jaw, pronounced it damaged but unbroken. "If it was broken, you wouldn't be able to talk," she assured him. "Just the same, I'm taking you to the emergency room first thing in the morning. We'll tell 'em you got whacked in the head by a mainsail boom.''

Matt thanked her and took her hand in his. "Talk to me," he said.

"What do you mean?"

"You know what I mean. Talk to me."

She told him that two bad-looking guys had come looking for him yesterday. She'd sent Jimmy Jaspero to follow them, hoping to find out who they were, what they wanted. He'd followed them to the warehouse in the International District, then telephoned back a situation report. Cleo had instructed him to stay put, to keep his eyes peeled.

"So far, so good," Matt said. "How did you know when to come charging to our rescue?"

"I didn't know for sure. Jimmy called me on his cell phone when he saw Royal, Lauren, and three other guys show up and go into the warehouse this afternoon. Two of the guys were the ones who came here looking for you. That's when I figured I'd better start asking around, find out what was up. The two shifty-looking types were smoke from L.A., I found out. I decided we needed to swing into action. We went in through a basement door in the alley—for some reason it was unlocked. If it *hadn't* have been unlocked, you'd be dead. And Lauren, too."

"Wait a minute, back up," Matt said. "You were able to find out about a couple of hit men who were looking for *me*?"

"I have ways of knowing things. I don't live in a vacuum, you know."

Matt was incredulous. "Do you mind telling me who gave you the information?"

She seemed reluctant, but he pressed her. He needed to know.

"The name probably wouldn't mean anything to you," she said.

"Try me."

"Okay, Mr. High-Pressure. Have you ever heard of anyone named Paco de Leon?"

Matt thought the name sounded familiar, but he couldn't quite place it. Did the guy have anything to do with the illegal drug business? he asked.

"He's worked for me for almost twenty-five years," she told Matt with the sweet smile that he'd grown to love. "We're the biggest sellers of Mexican-tar heroin in the Puget Sound area. They call me the Fat Woman."

Matt simply stared at her for a long time.

Epilogue

Shortly after the discovery of Rod Welton's murdered body on Bainbridge Island, Lauren Bowman received a visit from Sergeant Connie Henness and Detective Aaron Cosentino of the Seattle Police Department. They wanted to know why Welton had met his end while driving a Volvo registered to Lauren. Exhausted and enervated by her ordeal of the past few weeks, Lauren's defenses folded. She told them everything.

Everything.

The subsequent media storm lasted all summer and into the fall. Reporters besieged the estate on Jenkins Way like crusaders seeking to reduce the fortress at Antioch. Lauren Bowman's face became as well known as little JonBenet Ramsey's, her story a staple of *Hard Copy* and *Dateline*.

The King County District Attorney charged her with second-degree murder in the death of the ProGuard security man at the Northwest BioCenter, obstruction of justice, breaking and entering, burglary, theft, and criminal mischief. The DA also filed obstruction of justice charges against Matt Burgess and Alex Ragsdale, but recommended probation without jail time, inasmuch as they were instrumental in the disruption of a major heroin distribution operation. Prosecutors filed no charges against Elise Lekander, her son, or Jandee Vernon.

Neither did they file charges in the deaths of Tyler Brownlee,

Richardson Zanto, the two gunmen known as Shafiq and Cyan, or Royal Bowman, a.k.a., Ray Brownlee. Concerning the decomposing bodies of eleven young women found in a locked room in the basement of Ray Brownlee's warehouse in the International District, including those of Megan Reiner, Vera Kemmis, and Rainy Hales, authorities said only that "investigations were continuing."

Lauren pled guilty to all the charges except second-degree murder. Her attorneys persuaded the court to give her probation without jail time in consideration of her past community service and charity work. On the murder charge, however, she went to trial. The jury got the case in July of 1998, and—after thirty-nine hours of deliberation—returned a verdict of not guilty. The jurors believed Lauren's insistence that she'd done everything she could to prevent anyone from carrying deadly weapons on the Bio-Center raid.

Matt visited her a few days later at the estate on Jenkins Way. She welcomed him with genuine warmth, gave him a mug of Earl Grey tea, and invited him to sit with her in the gazebo. The day was sunny, though not overly warm. Lauren wore a bulky red sweater. Desi and Lucy slept at her feet.

"So, how's your life?" she asked.

Not bad, he replied. After quitting Shorty's, he'd found a job with a sailboat charter agency in Bellingham, a bustling little city an hour's drive north of Seattle. The pay was lousy, but the living was easy. He missed Shorty's, but he couldn't bring himself to work for someone who sold heroin—not even Cleo.

And how was Rags? Lauren wondered. Rags had gone back to school to pursue a doctorate in criminology, Matt explained. ProGuard had fired him, of course, in the wake of his conviction, but his wife's income was more than enough to sustain the family. Lauren smiled and said that she was glad.

"I'm sorry that things didn't work out for you and me," she added, averting her eyes. "I want you to know that it had nothing to do with you, Matt. It was me. With all the reporters chasing me around, the madness of the trial, working with the lawyers, I just didn't have anything left over to give anyone—not even you. I regret that."

"So do I," Matt replied. "But I understand. I really do."

"I still think you're one of the nicest people in the world."

Matt grinned. "Thanks."

They sat for a long time, sipping their tea, saying little. A seagull alighted on the rail, a bird with a strange black marking on its beak. Could it be Groucho? Matt wondered.

"I need to ask you something," he said, "and I don't mean to pull the scab off an old wound. But I've got to know. You ran away from home at the age of sixteen, came here expecting to find Royal, your dad—right?"

"That's right."

"At that time you didn't know that Royal Bowman and Ray Brownlee were the same man?"

"I had no idea. I hadn't seen Royal since I was three or four, or so I thought."

The question that bothered Matt, he said, was whether Lauren had recognized Royal Bowman as Ray Brownlee when she and he were reunited nine years after she'd run away from Portland. How could she *not* have recognized the beast who had abused her so viciously when she was a kid?

Tension registered in Lauren's face as she thought about the question, and for a moment Matt regretted having asked it. Her answer surprised him.

"Yes, I think that I *did* recognize him at first," she confessed, "but I wanted so much to believe that he was Royal, the father I'd loved and missed—not Ray. I wanted it bad enough to make it real in my mind. As time went on, I became more convinced of it, because Royal was so different from Ray, so considerate and wise. I actually loved talking with him, Matt."

"I know what you mean. So did I."

"I confided in him, asked his advice about things. I even asked him to give me away at my wedding, but he wouldn't do it. He considered himself bad for my image."

"Yes, he told me that."

"I never dreamed that he had any feelings for me other than those of a normal father for his daughter. And do you want to know something, Matt? After all that's happened, there's a part of me that misses him. Sometimes I miss him very much—not Ray Brownlee, but Royal Bowman."

Matt said nothing, only studied her face, which showed the wear and tear of the past year. God, he'd gotten used to that face, and wished he could see more of it.

"Me, too," he said. "I miss him, too." And this truth frightened him.

NOW AVAILABLE IN HARDCOVER
JOHN
SANDFORD
CERTAIN
PREY
PUTNAM

NOW AVAILABLE IN HARDCOVER

PATRICIA CORNWELL

BLACK

NOTICE

PUTNAM